BY DANIELLE L. JENSEN

THE BRIDGE KINGDOM SERIES

The Bridge Kingdom
The Traitor Queen
The Inadequate Heir
The Endless War

THE MALEDICTION NOVELS

Stolen Songbird
Hidden Huntress
Warrior Witch
The Broken Ones (Prequel)

THE DARK SHORES SERIES

Dark Shores
Dark Skies
Tarnished Empire (Prequel)
Gilded Serpent

SAGA OF THE UNFATED

A Fate Inked in Blood

A FATE
INKED IN
BLOOD

A FATE
INKED IN
BLOOD

SAGA OF THE UNFATED
BOOK 1

DANIELLE L.
JENSEN

DEL REY

NEW YORK

Published in the United States by Del Rey, an imprint of Random House,
a division of Penguin Random House LLC, New York.

DEL REY and the CIRCLE colophon are registered trademarks of
Penguin Random House LLC.

ISBN 978-0-593-59983-9

Printed in the United States of America

Book design by Sara Bereta

For Tamar—I'd be lost without you!

A FATE
INKED IN
BLOOD

CHAPTER

1

My mother taught me many skills to ensure I'd make a good wife to my husband. How to cook and clean. How to weave and sew. Where to hunt and gather. She'd have been better off teaching me the restraint needed *not* to stab said husband when he proved himself a short-witted drunkard with an acid tongue . . .

For my temper was being sorely tested today.

"What are you doing?" Vragi demanded, his breath reeking of mead as he bent over my shoulder.

"Exactly what it looks like." I ran the tip of my knife down the fish's belly, its innards spilling outward. "Cleaning the catch."

Huffing out an aggrieved breath, Vragi jerked the knife from my hand, nearly slicing open my palm. Snatching up another fish, he opened its belly and scooped out the innards into a bloody pile before stabbing the tip of my knife into the wooden block, his technique identical to my own. "You see?"

"I know how to gut a fish," I said between my teeth, every part of me desiring to gut *him*. "I've gutted thousands of fish."

"I don't like the way you do it." His lip curled. "The way you do it is wrong. People complain."

That much was true, but it wasn't complaints about fish guts.

My *dear* husband was a child of the gods, having been granted a drop of Njord's blood at his conception, which gave him powerful magic over the creatures of the sea. Except instead of using it to care for our people, he used his magic to deprive other fishermen of any catch even as he filled his own nets. Then he charged double what the fish were worth of the very people whose nets he kept empty.

Everyone knew it. But no one dared speak a word against him. He was Vragi the Savior, the man who'd delivered Selvegr from famine when the crops had failed ten years past, drawing in fish from the North Sea to fill bellies, ensuring no one went without.

A hero, everyone had called him. And maybe once that was so, but fame and greed had vanquished the generosity that had earned him the title, and now people spat at his name even as they honored him with an annual feast. That no one had put a knife in his back was mostly because he had the protection of the jarl.

But not entirely.

"We all do best to remember we might need his magic again, Freya," my mother told me when I griped. "*You* would do best to remember that he brings wealth to your home."

Wealth.

It was the reason my father had agreed—despite my vocal protests—to Vragi's proposal of marriage. Yet instead of living to see his error, my father had died on my wedding night, leaving everyone to mutter about bad omens and ill-fated matches. If it had truly been a message from the gods, they need not have bothered: I'd known from the moment Vragi had stuck his foul tongue in my mouth in front of all the guests that this marriage would be a curse.

The past year had given me daily proof.

Except it was hard to cast bitter words about him into the ears of others, for Vragi was generous to my mother, paying for all her needs while my brother earned his place in the war band of our jarl.

For my family, I will do this, I silently chanted, much as I had the night

I'd been wed. *For my family, I will endure him*. Aloud, I said, "I will do better." And because he didn't look satisfied, I added, "I will do it your way, Vragi."

"Show me." The condescension caused my teeth to clench so hard they nearly cracked, but I obliged, swiftly gutting another fish.

Vragi snorted, then spat on the ground next to me. "My mother was right—I should've married an ugly woman whose worth was in her skill. Not a pretty one whose only skill is her looks. Looks do not gut fish. Looks do not cook food. Looks do not make babies."

As far as the last went, *my* looks never would.

I spent nearly all the coin he gave me purchasing lemon juice and sponge from the traders who came to us from the South Seas, and if Vragi had ever wondered why his cock smelled of citrus after we coupled, he'd never asked. Long may his ignorance last.

"A year, woman. A whole year of marriage and servicing, and yet no son."

I bent over the board, gutting another fish to hide the angry tears threatening to fall. I'd never subject a child to this man. *Never*. "I'll make an offering." Which was no lie—at the beginning of every cycle I made a sacrifice to the goddess I was named for, begging her to keep my womb empty. Thus far, she'd been merciful.

Either that, or I'd been lucky.

As if hearing my thoughts, Vragi caught hold of my braid, jerking me to my feet. "I don't want offerings, Freya," he snarled. "I want you to try harder. I want you to do things correctly. I want you to give me what I want."

My scalp stung, only the tightness of my braid preventing him from ripping out a handful of hair, and my temper snapped. "Perhaps it is you who is doing it incorrectly, husband. That's certainly how it feels."

Silence thickened the air.

A smart woman would regret such words, but I was clearly an idiot of the first order as all I felt was a flash of wicked triumph as the barb slowly struck home. Vragi's face darkened beneath his thick beard, a vein in his temple pulsing like a purple worm. Then his knife pressed against my cheek, his breath rank as he whispered, "Maybe the key is to make you less pretty, Freya. Then you will have to learn other skills."

The steel was cold and cruel. It wiped away my triumph and replaced it with fear.

Yet . . . I couldn't concede. Couldn't allow myself to break or cry or beg, because that was what he relished: bringing me low. Instead I met his gaze and said, "Do it. Do it, Vragi, and then go to the village and see if they'll still host your feast and call you a hero when they learn you cut your wife's face to spite her beauty."

His lip curled. "They need me."

"That doesn't mean they need to honor you." And a narcissist like him needed that honor.

I watched the wheels of his mind turn; no doubt he was musing how much he could hurt me without consequence. But I refused to look away despite the cold sweat that slicked my palms. The blade pressed harder against my cheek, stinging, and I sucked in a sharp breath to control my rising panic.

He heard it.

Vragi grinned, my tiny show of weakness satisfying him. He let go of my hair, lowering his knife. "Get back to work, woman. When you're finished, bring two fish to your mother. Perhaps she'll remind you of your duties. It is her fault, and your father's"—he spat—"that you don't know them."

"Do not speak ill of my father!" I grabbed my knife, but Vragi only sneered at it.

"There is the proof," he said. "He forgot you were a daughter and taught you like your brother. Now instead of a wife, I have a grown woman who plays at being a warrior like a small child, brandishing her stick and imagining every tree her foe."

Heat burned up my chest, turning my cheeks to infernos. Because he was not wrong.

"Perhaps I've been complicit," he said. "I've allowed you too much idle time, which the gods know is the ruination of good character."

The only idle time I was allowed was the hours I slept, but I said nothing.

Vragi turned away from me, going right to the water's edge, the fjord glittering in the sunshine. Lifting his hand, he invoked Njord's name.

For a long moment, nothing happened, and I breathed a silent prayer that the god of the sea had finally recognized what a piece of shit his child was and stolen away his magic.

Wasted prayers, for a heartbeat later the water quivered. And the fish began jumping.

Only a few at first, but then dozens and dozens were hurling themselves out of the water and onto the beach until I could barely see the rocks through the teeming mass of fins and scales.

"This should keep you occupied." Vragi smirked. "Give your mother my love."

My bloody blade quivered in barely checked rage as he turned and walked away.

I stared at the fish thrashing about on the beach, desperate to return to the water. Such a waste, for there were more here than we could sell before they went to rot. And it was not the first time he'd done such a thing.

I'd once watched him beach a whale, but instead of ending the animal's life immediately, he'd allowed it to work its way back into the water, only to use his magic to draw it out again. Over and over he'd done it, all the village watching, his eyes filled with fascination as he tortured the animal for no reason beyond the fact that he could.

It had only ended when my brother pushed through the crowd and embedded an axe into the whale's brain, putting it out of its misery and allowing the rest of us to begin the process of butchering the carcass, no one celebrating what should have been a glorious day of feasting.

I refused to feel the same sort of regret again.

Pulling up my skirts, I raced to where the fish flopped, snatching up one of them and tossing it into the water. Then another and another, some of them so heavy that it took my entire strength to get them back in.

Moving along the waterline, I returned Vragi's *catch* to the sea, my stomach twisting whenever I found a fish that had succumbed, each death my own personal failure. But there were so many.

Finding a fish still alive where it had tossed itself into some brush, I picked it up and threw it over my shoulder at the water.

Instead of a splash, my ears filled with a loud curse, and I whirled to find a man standing waist-deep in the fjord, rubbing at his cheek. Which I'd clearly struck with the fish.

"Was the fish hurt?" I demanded, searching for sign of the creature, concerned I'd killed it in my attempt to save it. "Did it swim away?"

The man ceased rubbing his face and gave me an incredulous stare. "What about me?"

I stopped looking for the fish and gave him a closer look, my face instantly warming. Even with an impact-reddened cheek, he was alarmingly attractive. Tall and broad of shoulder, he appeared to be only a handful of years older than my twenty years. His black hair was shaved on the sides, the rest pulled back in a short tail behind his tattooed head. He was all high cheekbones and chiseled lines, and while most men wore beards, he bore only the scruff of a few days' absence from a razor. He wore no shirt, and water dripped off a naked torso corded with thick muscle, his sun-darkened skin marked with dozens of inky tattoos. A warrior, undoubtedly, and even without a weapon I suspected he was a significant threat.

Realizing that I hadn't responded, I crossed my arms. "What sort of fool swims in the fjord when the ice has just broken up? Are you trying to freeze to death?" To emphasize my point, I jerked my chin at the thick slab of ice floating past him.

"That is not much of an apology." He ignored the ice and moved toward the water's edge. "And it seems I'm more at risk from flying fish than freezing."

I took a wary step back, recognizing his faint accent. It was rare for Nordeland to raid this early in the spring, but not impossible, and I glanced up and down the fjord, looking for drakkar and men, but the water was empty. Moving my gaze to the far side of the fjord, I scanned the thick forest rising up the side of the mountain.

There.

Motion caught my eye, and I froze, searching for the source. But whatever it was had disappeared, likely nothing more than small game.

"I'm not a raider, if that's your concern." He stopped knee-deep in the water, his teeth bared in an amused grin. "Only a man in need of a bath."

"So you say." I cursed myself for leaving my knife on the cutting board. "You could be lying to me. Distracting me while your fellows move on my village to slaughter and pillage."

He winced. "Fine, fine. You have caught me out."

I tensed, ready to scream a warning to those within earshot, when he added, "My clansmen said to me, 'You are not such a good fighter but you are very good-looking, so your task is to swim across the fjord to flirt with the beautiful woman throwing fish. With her distracted, we will be safe to attack.'" He sighed. "It was my sole task, and already I have failed miserably."

My cheeks flushed, but growing up with an older brother meant I could give as good as I got. "Of course you failed. You have as little talent for flirting as you do for fighting."

He tilted back his head and laughed, the sound deep and rich, and despite all my intentions to remain on guard and wary, a smile worked its way onto my lips. Gods, but he was attractive—as though Baldur himself had escaped Hel's grasp in the underworld and stood before me.

"You aim as well with words as you do with fish, woman," he answered, his shoulders still shaking with mirth as he walked out of the water, soaked trousers clinging to the hard muscle of his legs and arse. "I am so wounded, I must remain on this side of the fjord forever, as my companions will never take me back."

This close, I gained an appreciation for just how large he was, head and shoulders taller than me and twice my breadth, droplets of seawater rolling down his slick skin. I should tell him to go, to leave, for I was wed and this was my husband's land, but instead I looked him up and down. "What makes you think I wish to keep you? You cannot fight. You cannot flirt. You cannot even catch fish when they are thrown right at you."

He pressed a hand to the knotted muscles of his stomach, pretending to double over as he gasped, "A mortal blow." Dropping to his knees before me, he looked up with a smirk, the sun illuminating eyes a shade of green like the first leaves of spring. "Before you finish me off, allow me to prove that I'm not entirely devoid of skills."

If anyone saw us like this, there'd be Hel to pay if they told Vragi. And perhaps I deserved it, for I was a married woman. Married to a man I loathed with every bit of my being but whom I'd never be free of, no matter how much I wished otherwise. So I said, "What skills could you possibly have that I might be interested in?"

The spark in his eyes turned to heat, and my toes curled inside my shoes as he said, "Better if I show you. I think you will not be disappointed."

My heart thundered against my ribs. This was wrong, deeply wrong, but a selfish streak within me didn't care. Wanted only to kiss this charming, attractive stranger with no care for consequences.

Except that was not who I was.

I swallowed hard, shoving away the aching, needy desire demanding I allow this to continue, instead holding out a hand, drawing him to his feet. His palms were calloused and the backs of his hands scarred in a way that belied his claim that he was no fighter. "Wherever you come from, the women must be either desperate or foolish to fall for such nonsense. Be on your way."

I struggled not to hold my breath as I waited for him to react to my rejection, for few men took it well, but he only inclined his head and said, "It seems you are neither desperate nor foolish, which some would say is my loss." He lifted my hand, not seeming to care that it stank of fish as he kissed my knuckles. "I say that it only means I must try harder, for you are a remarkable woman indeed."

The brush of his lips against my skin sent shivers coursing through my body, my mind lost in the depths of those green eyes. Letting go of my hand, he reached up to touch my face, thumb brushing across the line Vragi's knife had left on my cheek. "Where is your husband?"

"What makes you think I'm wed?" I demanded, but he only turned and walked up the slope, toward a horse I hadn't even been aware was tied to a tree.

He pulled on a shirt before glancing back at me. "Your ring. Now, where might I find him?"

Instinctively I tucked my hand, which bore a plain silver band, into the folds of my skirts. "Why do you wish to know where he is?"

"Because I'm going to kill him. I'm going to make you a free woman so that you can bed me with no concerns for propriety," he answered, tightening the girth before swinging onto the tall animal's back. "What other reason could there be?"

My stomach dropped. "You cannot!"

"I am confident that I *can*." He circled the horse around me. "You were right to say I am as talented at flirting as I am at fighting, beautiful. I will make it quick for the poor bastard's sake, and then you'll be free to pursue your every desire."

"You will not!" I gasped, despite Vragi's untimely death being one of my most frequent daydreams. "I forbid it!"

"Ah." He circled me again, the ugly roan gelding snorting loudly. "Well, in that case, I will wait for him to fall victim to a flying fish. There will be some justice in that." Giving me a smile full of all sorts of promises, he started down the beach.

"Where are you going?" I shouted, still not entirely certain whether he was teasing or serious, the real chance that he might *actually* be a raider surfacing in my head. "Are you going to kill him?"

Looking over his shoulder, he grinned. "Have you changed your mind about his continued longevity?"

Yes. I balled my hands into fists. "Of course not."

"A shame."

That was no answer, and I lifted my skirts, chasing after the horse. "Where are you going? What business have you in the village?"

"None," he called. "But Jarl Snorri does, and he'll be wondering where I wandered off to."

I slid to a stop, every part of me wanting to sink into the ground, because my brother was one of the jarl's warriors. If he learned I'd been flirting with this man . . . "You ride with the jarl?"

He winked at me. "Something like that." Then he dug his heels into his horse's sides and headed down the beach at a gallop, leaving me staring in his wake.

Unreasonably flustered, it took me until nearly midday to finish with the catch. I loaded the cart for Vragi before selecting two choice fish for my mother. By that time, the thrill of my encounter with the warrior had faded, replaced with the grim reminder that Vragi lived, I was his wife, and that I had angered him.

Wind whistled down the mountains, carrying with it the smell of melting snow, and I inhaled, glad to be away from the stink of fish and guts and my own shame, though a fair bit of all three still clung to my clothing. Pine needles crunched beneath my boots, filling my nose with their sharp scent and easing the tension in my shoulders.

It was fine. It would all be fine. This wasn't the first time I'd fought with Vragi, and it wouldn't be the last. I'd survived a year with him already and I'd survive another. And another.

But I wanted to do *more* than just survive. I wanted my days to be more than time I needed to endure. I wanted to *live* them, to relish them. To find passion and excitement in them the way I had for that fleeting moment on the beach with a stranger.

It was the wanting that made my life hard. If I could only stop *wanting,* perhaps I might find some happiness in what I had. Even as the thought rolled through my head, I cringed, because it was *exactly* something my mother would say. *Quit wanting more, Freya, and you shall be content with what you have.*

Gripping the wrapped fish under my left arm, I bent and snatched up a stick. Twisting, I cracked it against one tree and then another, moving down the pathway as though the forest around me were a horde of raiders, not caring that I was acting more like a child than a grown woman. I lifted my package of fish like a shield, knocking back imaginary attacks, my breath turning to rapid pants, sweat dampening the hair clinging to my temples.

I relished the burn in my muscles as I attacked and defended, savored every gasped breath, delighted in the sting in my palm each time my stick struck a tree. This was what I dreamed of: not of gutting fish next to the fjord to sell to the same villagers every day, but of fighting. Of joining the jarl's war band in raids against our rivals to the east and west. Of standing strong in defense of our lands against Nordelander raiders, and of earning wealth with the strength of my sword arm. Then to spend the winter with my family, feasting and drinking and laughing until raiding season came again.

My older brother, Geir, had pursued the same dream, and he was well on his way to achieving it. When I was fourteen and he was sixteen, our father had brought Geir to the allthing and Jarl Snorri had gifted Geir an arm ring, inviting him to join the raids. Now, at twenty-two, my brother was a respected warrior.

Yet when I'd voiced my desire to follow in my brother's footsteps, my words were met with laughter until my family realized I was serious; then their humor had changed to silent horror.

"You cannot, Freya," my father had finally said. "It would be only a matter of time until they discovered what you are, and then you'd never choose anything ever again."

What I was. My secret.

My curse.

"Once you have a babe, Freya, you'll give up these foolish desires to always do what your brother does," my mother had said. "You will be content."

"I am not content!" I shouted at the memory, flinging my stick into the trees. But as I did, one of the fish slipped from its wrapping to fall on the forest floor.

"Shit." Kneeling, I picked it up and did what I could to clean away the needles and dirt that clung to it, silently cursing myself for thinking the thoughts I did. For dreaming about things I couldn't have.

"I hope that wasn't intended for my belly."

I leapt to my feet, whirling to find my brother standing behind me.

"Geir!" Laughing, I closed the distance to throw my arms around his neck. "What are you doing here?"

"Rescuing my lunch, it would seem." He straightened his arms, giving me a critical once-over, and I did the same. Like me, my brother had pale skin, hair so blond as to be nearly white, and amber eyes that glowed like eclipsed suns. He'd put on more muscle since he'd gone to live in Halsar with the jarl, his frame no longer slender like mine, but thick and strong.

"You should eat more—you're scrawny," Geir said, then added, "Jarl Snorri is in the village speaking with your husband."

My skin prickled with unease, for while Vragi was often summoned to speak with our lord, the jarl had never had cause to come to him. "On what matter?"

Geir shrugged, then took one of the fish, making its gills flap with his thumbs. "Fish, I expect. What other reason is there to talk with Vragi?"

"Truer words were never spoken," I muttered, snatching the fish from his hands before starting down the path toward our family home.

"How swiftly the glow of new marriage fades." Geir fell into step next to me, his weapons clinking. The axe and seax were familiar, but the sword was new. As was the mail he wore beneath his cloak. Either plunder from raids or paid for with his cut. A flicker of envy soured my stomach. Shoving the sensation away, I cast him a sideways glare. "What glow? There was never any *glow*."

"Fair." My brother kicked a rock, sending it toppling down the path ahead of us. He'd grown a beard over the last year and it was decorated with silver rings. It made him look older than his years, and fiercer, which was likely his intent. Reaching up, I gave it a tug. "What does Ingrid think of this?"

With his good looks and charm, Geir had the pick of women, though I knew he only had eyes for my friend Ingrid, whom he'd loved since we were children. Knew that he hoped to earn enough raiding this season to build a hall and ask her father for her hand.

"She loves it. Especially the way it tickles when—"

I gave him a shove hard enough to make him stagger. "You're a pig."

Geir smirked at me. "Guilty. But you change the subject, Freya. We all know Vragi is a greedy prick, but he is your husband. With Father gone, the duty falls to me to—"

I caught his ankle with my own and jerked, grinning as my brother sprawled onto his back. Stepping on his chest with one foot, I said, "I love you, brother. But if you start lecturing me on my wifely duties, I won't like you half as well." I leaned my weight on him. "It's not been so many years since I beat you bloody that I've forgotten how."

I waited for him to laugh. For him to mock Vragi and call him a land fish. To say he was sorry that I'd been forced into this marriage against my will. To tell me I deserved better.

Instead Geir said, "We aren't children anymore." Then he grabbed my ankle and yanked.

The impact of my arse hitting the dirt rattled my spine and I nearly bit my tongue off, but Geir ignored me spitting blood as he sat upright. "Vragi has wealth and influence with Jarl Snorri. I may have been given my arm ring because of the goodwill the jarl still holds for Father, but it's because of *Vragi* that the jarl pays me to fight for him all year round. If you anger Vragi enough that he casts you aside, Snorri might not let me keep my place. And if I lose my place, how will I gain the wealth I need to marry Ingrid?"

As if I could forget.

"And if you don't care about me and Ingrid, think of Mother." Geir rested his elbows on his knees. "Vragi ensures she's cared for. Pays for men to tend the farm and feed the animals. If not of her, then think *logically* of your own position. You have a home that others covet, and the wealth to purchase endless ornaments." He reached over to flick one of the silver bands encircling my long braid. "What would you do without Vragi?"

"Fight. Raid. Earn my own wealth," I answered. "I don't need Vragi."

Geir huffed out a breath, then climbed to his feet. "Let's not quarrel. It's been months since I've seen you."

I stared at the hand he held out, part of me wanting to keep arguing. Except we both knew I'd never make a decision that would harm my family, and that made all my arguments moot. So instead, I took my brother's hand and allowed him to haul me to my feet. "Where does Jarl Snorri plan to raid this summer?"

Before Geir could answer, the sound of hooves filled our ears. A group of warriors on horseback appeared, and my stomach tightened as I recognized my husband at their head, his expression smug.

"My lord." Geir nodded at the big man who rode at Vragi's side, who must be Jarl Snorri. I'd never seen him before, having never traveled more than a few hours from Selvegr and never to his stronghold at Halsar. Tall and thick, he had dark brown hair and a beard laced with gray, his eyes lined with deep wrinkles, and his mouth set in a frown. Most would have called him attractive, but the way he stared at me made my skin crawl.

Like I was something to be possessed.

"Geir," Snorri replied, but his eyes remained fixed on me. The last thing I wanted to do was meet his gaze, so I looked beyond him at the rest of the party. Besides Vragi, there were three men dressed in mail coats. They carried seaxes, as well as axes and swords, the weapons speaking volumes of their battle fame. The lone woman with them bore no weapons beyond a short-bladed seax fastened to her belt, the bodice of her dress cut low enough to reveal a long stretch of cleavage beneath the ties of her cloak. Yet my eyes skipped past all of them to land on the one who rode at the rear of the party.

Oh gods.

Though it made sense for him to be here, shock still radiated through me at the sight of the warrior from the beach. Shock that was mirrored in his green eyes as he looked from me to Geir then back again, as the jarl spoke.

"This is the sister you always speak of, Geir?" Not waiting for my brother to respond, the jarl said to Vragi, "She's your wife, yes?"

"Yes, my lord. This is my Freya."

Not yours, I wanted to hiss. *Never yours.* But I bit my tongue, because something was going on here that turned my guts to ice, the sensation a thousand times worse because of the expression on Vragi's face.

He was grinning like a cat given a bowl full of cream. What was he so happy about? Why were Snorri and his warriors here? What did they want?

"You never mentioned to me that your sister was also a warrior, Geir," Snorri said. "Vragi tells me that she wishes to join the raids this summer, is that true?"

"No," my brother blurted out, then tried to cover the outburst with a laugh. "Freya knows only of gutting fish and keeping house. She's no warrior."

I bristled, then bit the insides of my cheeks when Snorri gave me an amused smile. "You disagree, Freya? You believe you can fight?"

"I . . ." I swallowed hard, sweat trickling down my spine because they were all staring at me. Best to give the truth, especially since my skills were known. "My father taught me to fight when I was a girl. I can handle myself."

"Your father is Erik."

"Was," I corrected. "He died a year ago."

"It was in a fight, wasn't it?"

My cheeks stung as I bit into them, unsure whether my brother had lied or if the lord had simply not cared enough to remember the details. "No, my lord. Dropped dead the night of my wedding. Herb-woman said it was his heart."

Snorri rubbed his chin. "Shame. Erik was a fierce warrior in his prime. We fought side-by-side in many shield walls. If he taught you, then what you've learned is good. And I can always use more warriors."

"She's a married woman," Geir responded before I had the chance to answer. "With respect, Freya should be focused on family, not fighting."

"Agreed," Snorri replied. "But Vragi tells me that's not the case. That Freya thinks more of fighting than of babies."

Oh gods.

Understanding of what was happening struck me at the same time it did Geir, his face blanching. Vragi wished to end our marriage and had asked the jarl to witness it. Bile burned up my throat, because as much as I wished to be rid of him, I knew the consequences. Knew it would be my family that suffered because I couldn't keep my cursed mouth shut.

"Let us see if Freya is a better warrior than she is a wife," Snorri continued. "Give her a weapon, Geir."

My brother didn't move.

The jarl's eyes hardened. "You would defy me in this?"

"I would not see my sister harmed."

Geir would protect me out of pride. I knew it, and I refused to watch it happen when all that needed to be done was for me to accept shaming. Maybe that would be enough to appease Vragi, and he'd reconsider. "Give me your sword, Geir."

My brother whirled on me, amber eyes blazing. "Freya, no!"

I held out my hand.

He stared me down, and I silently willed him to understand how this would play out. To see that the only harm I'd come to was a few bruises and a solid blow to my pride. A blow that I was willing to take for the sake of him and our mother.

Seconds passed, the tension in the clearing mounting. Then Geir reluctantly drew his weapon, handing it to me hilt-first. I closed my fingers over the leather grip, feeling the weight of it. Feeling the *rightness* of it. Behind the jarl, one of the warriors began to dismount, but Snorri shook his head at him and looked to the dark-haired warrior I'd flirted with on the beach. "Bjorn, you will test Freya's prowess."

Bjorn.

My confidence shattered at his name, understanding of *who* he was hitting me like a battering ram to the gut. He was Jarl Snorri's son and heir. Which would have been bad enough, but he was also a child of Tyr, the god having granted him a drop of blood and all the magic that came with it at his conception. My brother had told me many times of this man's prowess on the battlefield—a warrior without equal who left only the dead and dying in his wake. And *he* was who Snorri wanted me to fight?

I might have vomited, but Bjorn started laughing.

He slapped a hand against his saddle, spine bent backward as he let out loud guffaws. This went on for several moments before he wiped at his eyes, leveling a finger at Snorri. "All those who say you have no sense of humor are liars, Father."

"I made no jest." Snorri's voice was cool, and beneath his beard, his jaw worked back and forth with obvious annoyance.

Or at least, obvious to me. Bjorn only barked out a laugh. "You want *me* to fight this . . . girl? To fight a fishmonger's wife who has barely the strength to lift the weapon in her hand?"

It was a struggle not to scowl, for while the weapon was heavy, it was no heavier than a bucket of fish and I carried those all day.

"Yes, Bjorn. That's exactly what I wish you to do." Snorri tilted his head. "Unless you wish to give me cause to doubt your loyalty by refusing?"

Father and son stared each other down, the tension palpable enough that the other warriors shifted in their saddles. This was a test, that much was evident, and it was my misfortune to be caught in the middle of it.

It was Bjorn who conceded, breaking off the stalemate with a shrug. "As you like."

He slid off his horse, then strode toward me with predatory grace, flirtatious smile long gone. I was swiftly reminded of how much larger than me he was, and all of it muscle. But that wasn't what filled me with fear. No, the fear that lit my veins and made me want to run, made me want to cower, came when his mouth formed the name *Tyr* and an axe made of fire appeared in his hand.

I could feel the heat of it, the weapon burning far hotter than natural flame, the flickers of red and orange and blue so bright they stung my eyes. The flame of a god. The flame of war.

"What do you wish to achieve?" he asked Snorri. "You want proof she can't fight? Here—"

He swung at me.

I stumbled back with a yelp, tripping on a root and falling on my arse, losing my weapon.

"There's your proof. Send her back to her husband and the fish."

"That is not the proof I seek," Snorri answered, and my stomach flipped with the fear that this would cost me far more than pride.

I climbed to my feet to discover that the other warriors had my brother by the arms, holding him back. Vragi sniggered from beyond.

"To first blood, then?" Bjorn demanded. There was anger in his voice, the flames of his axe flaring with the emotion. He didn't want this fight, but that didn't mean he wouldn't do it to prove his loyalty. To do otherwise meant dire consequences, which I doubted he would be willing to suffer for a woman he didn't know.

"No." Snorri dismounted and handed the reins of his horse to another warrior before crossing his arms. "To the death."

My stomach dropped, the world around me suddenly too bright. *To the death?*

"This is madness," Bjorn snarled. "You'd have me kill this woman? Why? Because that waste of flesh"—he gestured at Vragi—"wants a new wife?"

"Vragi is a child of Njord. He is a man of value, and he's proven his loyalty."

I was no longer certain if this was about me. Or if it was about Bjorn. Or if it was about something else entirely. The only thing I knew for certain was that fear strangled me, refusing to give me a voice.

"And I haven't?" Bjorn lifted his flaming axe, and the jarl had the wits to take a wary step backward. "I've done everything you ever asked of me."

"Then what is one more thing?" Snorri tilted his head. "You will do this, or you will give back your arm band and go into exile, no longer my son in name or spirit. And lest you think your sacrifice will spare the woman, know that it will not. I'll merely have someone else fight in your stead."

The muscles in Bjorn's jaw stood out in stark relief and his green eyes were narrow with fury, but he gave a tight nod. "Fine."

"Freya!" my brother shouted. "Run!"

I couldn't unfreeze from where I stood. Couldn't think of what I might do to extract both me and Geir from this situation with our lives. The only path I saw was to fight.

And to win.

"What if I kill him?"

I half expected Snorri to laugh, but he only lifted one shoulder. "If you kill Bjorn, Freya, I'll pull that arm band from his corpse and put it on you. You may have his place in my drakkar when we sail on summer raids, and his share of the wealth that comes with it."

I lifted my chin, hating that there was part of me that felt the allure of such a prize. "And a divorce from Vragi."

That drew a soft chuckle from Snorri's lips, and he glanced at Vragi. "You agree to the end of this marriage?"

My husband sneered. "Gladly."

The chances of me defeating a famed warrior such as Bjorn were slim. Made far slimmer still by him being gifted by Tyr. But fights were unpredictable, and I was not without skill. "Fine."

Snorri nodded, then looked to the beautiful woman watching from her horse. "We will have a song of this, Steinunn. One way or another."

"As you say, my lord," the woman answered, curiosity growing in her eyes as she met my stare. Whatever was going on here, she clearly knew no more than I did. Rolling my shoulders to ease the tension in them, I said to one of the still-mounted warriors, "Might I have use of your shield?"

He shrugged, then reached to unhook it from his saddle. "This will not save you," he said. "But anyone willing to fight Bjorn has earned their place in Valhalla."

His words bolstered my strength as I took the shield, gripping the handle behind the thick steel boss, but I showed none of my confidence as I circled Bjorn. The heat from his axe drew sweat on my brow, but he seemed untouched by it. Must be untouched by it, given he held naked fire with his bare hand.

"Sorry for this, Freya," he said. "May Odin himself greet you with a full cup."

"I'm sure he will." I smiled sweetly. "Because you'll warn him to be ready for me when you arrive. Which will be sooner than you think."

A grin split his face, and for a heartbeat I once again saw the man who'd flirted with me on the beach. If I somehow managed to kill him, I would not relish it, but that didn't mean I'd hesitate with a killing blow. Bjorn glanced over his shoulder at Vragi. "You're a fool to—"

I struck.

My sword sliced toward his stomach, but some sixth sense must have warned him, because Bjorn twisted away at the last moment, the tip of my blade catching only the fabric of his shirt. Pacing in a circle, he eyed me. "This wasn't how I thought it would go."

"Fate cares little for your opinion on how things should go." Blood roared in my veins, my eyes skipping to the flaming axe, though I knew that wasn't what I should be watching. Knew it was the eyes and the body, not the weapon, that led. "All that is and all that will be is already woven by the Norns."

I cut at him again, our weapons colliding and his strength sending me staggering.

"If you are going to proselytize, best to be correct about it." He blocked another swipe of my blade but did not offer any attack of his own. "My fate is my own to weave."

Because he had god's blood in his veins. I knew that. Knew it well, because Vragi often bragged of that power despite it being one impossible to prove. "Then it will be a fate decided by your father, for it seems you do what he tells you to."

Anger flared in Bjorn's gaze and I attacked again, blade swinging hard at his ribs. He danced out of the way, far faster than I'd have guessed for a man his size. He gave a halfhearted swipe at my sword and as the two weapons collided, I flinched. Flames flickered over my blade, and I wrenched it away, blocking another slash of his axe with my shield.

The blade embedded in the wood below the boss and I dug in my heels as he wrenched it free, the force nearly pulling the shield from my hand. But worse, the smell of smoldering wood filled my nose, smoke rising where the shield had ignited.

Yet I didn't dare drop it.

Fear raged through me, my body soaked with sweat and everything seeming too bright. I needed to attack now, before fire forced me to drop my shield. Before my strength failed me.

I threw myself forward in a series of attacks, panic rising as he deflected them one after another, his face expressionless as he stayed on the defense.

Why bother attacking, given the fire burning my shield would do the work for him?

"Show your worth, Bjorn," Snorri snarled. "Show her what it really means to fight!"

My breath came in rapid pants as I swung again and again, knowing that my only chance was to win. To kill him, as much as I didn't want to. "Why are you doing this?" I demanded of Snorri between gasps. "What do you have to gain from my death?"

"I gain nothing from your death," he answered. "So fight!"

None of this made sense.

Bjorn alone seemed to agree. "There's no sport to this contest. It's nothing more than this weasel-cocked fishmonger wanting bigger men to punish his wife for his own failings beneath the furs."

"I plowed her nightly," Vragi shouted. "It's her fault!"

"Perhaps you plowed the wrong field!" Bjorn laughed and jumped out of the way of my swing, knocking his axe against my shield as though batting a fly.

My temper flared bright, less for the crass implication and more for the fact he wasn't even giving me the honor of trying. "Lemon juice made quick work of any seed his prick had to sow."

Probably not wise to give up my secret, but given that my death seemed imminent, it was worth seeing the look of stunned outrage on Vragi's face. Bjorn howled with laughter, staggering backward and clutching at his stomach, though he was quick to block my attack when I tried to stab him.

"Gods, Vragi," he laughed. "The world is truly better off without your progeny if you don't question why your woman tastes of lemons."

Tastes? I froze, staring at Bjorn, who gave me a slow smile.

"Seems he was most definitely doing it wrong."

"Bjorn, shut the fuck up!" Snorri paced in a circle around us. "Kill her now or I'm going to cut out your tongue to silence you!"

The humor fell away from Bjorn's eyes. "I wish fate had been kinder to you, Freya."

Without warning, he attacked.

Gone were the halfhearted swats and effortless parries, and in their place were heavy blows that sent me staggering.

I'd thought I knew how to fight. What it would be like to be in a real battle. Nothing could have prepared me for the understanding that no matter how hard I swung, how quick I parried, the end was coming for me.

My shield burned, smoke and heat stinging my eyes, but I didn't dare drop it. Bjorn attacked again. I moved to defend, but his axe caught hold of my blade and ripped it from my grip, sending it spinning into the forest.

This was it.

This was the moment.

Yet Bjorn hesitated, stepping back instead of moving in for the kill. A killer, yes. But not a murderer.

"Get it over with," Snorri shouted. "You've dragged this out long enough. Kill her!"

I was afraid. So painfully afraid that though I sucked in breath after desperate breath, it felt like nothing reached my lungs. Like I was being strangled by my own terror. Yet I managed to heft the burning shield, ready to fight to the end. Ready to die with honor. Ready to earn my place in Valhalla.

The burning axe blurred toward me, striking my shield. A split formed in the wood even as I stumbled backward, barely keeping my feet. My arm ached with the force of the impact, and a sob tore from my lips.

He swung again.

I saw it as though time had slowed. Knew the force of the blow would shatter the shield and sever my arm. Knew that I'd smell my own burned flesh. My own scorched blood.

My courage wavered, then failed me.

"Hlin," I gasped out the name forbidden to me all my life. "Protect me!"

A clap of thunder shattered my ears as Bjorn's flaming axe struck my shield, which was no longer formed of wood but of silver light. The impact sent him soaring through the air, his body slamming into a tree a dozen paces from me with enough force that the trunk split.

Bjorn fell to the ground in a heap, stunned, his axe landing in a pile of pine needles and swiftly setting them ablaze.

Yet no one did anything to smother the flames. No one moved. No one so much as spoke.

Slowly, Bjorn pushed himself upright, shaking his head to clear it even as his eyes fixed on me. His voice shook as he said, "She's the shield maiden."

A shiver ran through me, and I vanquished my magic. But it was too late. They'd all seen.

They all *knew.*

"You see, my lord," Vragi said, his voice loud and grating. "It is as I said: Freya is a child of the goddess Hlin and has been hiding her magic."

Though it mattered little, the first thought that rose in my head was: How did he know?

Vragi chuckled, seeing the question in my eyes. "All those times you sneaked away, I thought you were lying with another man. So I followed you. Caught you out sure enough, even if it had nothing to do with another cock."

My stomach hollowed. How had I been so blastedly stupid? Why hadn't I taken more care?

"Steinunn," Snorri said. "This will be the song of a generation, and it will be composed by your magic."

The woman didn't answer, only stared at me with such intensity I had to look away.

Bjorn smothered the fire his axe had caused, though the weapon still blazed in his hand as he drew closer. "I take it you don't actually want me to kill her."

Snorri snorted. "I'm not sure you could if you tried. It was foretold that her name would be born in the fire of a god. Her fate was never to die at your hand."

"She's unfated," Bjorn retorted. "No one could predict whether I'd kill her, not even the gods."

A huff of amusement exited Snorri. "You think I don't know my own son? I knew you'd withhold a killing blow long enough for terror to force her hand."

Snorri had played us off one another.

The hollowness in my chest began to fill with the smoldering heat of anger. That heat turned to inferno as Snorri pulled a purse from inside his coat, tossing it to Vragi. "As compensation for your lost bride price. And for your loyalty."

"You traitorous fucking prick!" I snarled. "Is there no end to your greed?"

Vragi pulled a gold necklace out of the purse, admiring it as he said, "It's not greed, Freya. I'm only honoring the gods by setting you to your true purpose. You really should be thanking me."

"Thanking you?"

"Yes." He grinned. "You will soon be second wife to the jarl, which means you'll be living in his great hall with endless baubles and riches. And he'll take you to fight in the raids, which is what you wanted."

Second wife. I looked to Snorri with horror, and though I saw annoyance in his eyes, he gave a nod of confirmation. "Nearly two decades ago, a seer spoke a prophecy to me of a shield maiden who'd been birthed the night of a red moon. She told me that this woman's name would be born in the fire of the gods, and she would unite the people of Skaland beneath the rule of the one who controlled her fate."

"Fate is woven by the Norns." My tongue felt thick and I swallowed hard. "*They* control it."

"All is fated *except* the lives of the children of the gods," Snorri corrected. "Your path is unknown and as you walk it, you rearrange the threads of all those around you."

A dull whining noise filled my ears, the sun turning impossibly bright. I was no one, and Hlin . . . she was the most minor of gods, barely thought of and never mentioned. Certainly not powerful enough to unite the clans beneath one man.

"You are to be a king-maker, Freya," Snorri said, moving to grip me by the arms. "And as your husband, the one who decides your fate, I *will* be that king."

This was why my father had demanded I keep my magic a secret, why he had been so convinced that I'd be used against my will if I revealed my magic. He'd been one of Snorri's warriors, which meant he would have heard of the prophecy. Would have known Snorri's intent, and hadn't wanted that life for me. I didn't want that life for me. "No!"

"It's not your choice," he answered. "With your father dead, it's Geir's decision."

The warriors restraining my brother dragged him forward, and he spat blood in the dirt before the jarl. "If Freya says no, it is no. I'll not dishonor my sister by forcing her into another marriage she does not wish."

"I think you should reconsider." Snorri stepped over the spittle, moving to stand before my brother. "I demand loyalty from my warriors, most especially those who sail on my drakkar. This is not loyalty, boy."

Geir clenched his teeth, and I watched his dreams go up in smoke.

My heart broke as Geir touched the iron ring on his arm, but then Vragi said loudly, "I heard Ingrid's father is looking to make a good match for her." He hefted the purse he'd been paid to betray me. "I think this would make a fair bride price."

Geir's face blanched even as my stomach plummeted, because we both knew Ingrid's father would accept the gold no matter how Ingrid protested. I couldn't let that happen. Couldn't allow both my brother's and my best friend's lives to be ruined for the sake of my own. Especially when it had been my recklessness that had put us in this situation in the first place. "Fine." My voice sounded strangled and strange. "I'll marry you. On one condition. My brother keeps his ring and his place."

Snorri scratched thoughtfully at his beard, then nodded. "Agreed." His eyes flicked to Geir, who gave a tight nod, looking anywhere but at me. "Agreed."

Snorri addressed the group. "You all bear witness? Freya has agreed to be my bride. Does anyone contest my right to take her?"

Everyone muttered their agreement. Everyone, that is, except Bjorn. His axe still blazed in his hand, his gaze fixed intently on me as he lifted his weapon, seeming on the verge of taking action. And for reasons I couldn't quite articulate, instinct drove me to take a step back, my heart giving a rapid *thump thump*.

But he only lowered the weapon again, giving a slight shake of his head.

"Then it is done." Snorri motioned for his warriors to pull Geir to his feet. "You will keep your ring and place, Geir, but we must address the matter of your loyalty. You knew I sought a daughter of Hlin but said nothing to me of your sister, despite knowing the goddess's blood runs in her veins. For that, you must be punished." He hefted the axe he held.

"No!" The shout tore from my lips, shrill with panic. "You gave your word!"

I moved to step between them, but Bjorn was faster. He caught me around the waist, hauling me backward so my shoulder blades pressed against his chest. "He won't kill him," he said in my ear, breath hot. "Once it is done, it will be *done*. Don't get in the way."

"Let me go!" I struggled and fought, trying to slam my heels down on his boots, but he only lifted me off my feet like a child. "Geir!"

My brother stood straight-backed with his chin up. Accepting his fate.

Snorri swung.

The flat of the blade struck my brother in the shin, the sound of cracking bone echoing through the trees. I screamed.

Geir did not.

My brother's face turned deathly white, but he emitted not a sound as he dropped to the ground, his hands clenched into fists.

Snorri fastened his axe back at his waist. "You will rejoin me when you can walk, understood?"

"Yes, my lord," Geir gasped out.

I clawed at Bjorn's arms, trying to get to my brother. Needing to help him. But Bjorn would not let me go.

Snorri met my gaze, eyes boring into mine. "You are a sought-after woman, shield maiden. With Steinunn's songs, word of you will swiftly spread and everyone will seek to possess you. Many may seek to strike at those you care about to harm you." He paused. "*My* men will watch over your family to ensure nothing . . . *unfortunate* should befall them."

His words stole the breath from my chest, my stomach plummeting. It was no promise to protect my family—it was a threat to ensure my compliance. Given what he'd just done to Geir, there was no doubt in my mind that this man was capable of far worse if he was crossed, so I gave a tight nod of understanding.

No one moved. No one spoke, the only sound my brother's ragged breaths of pain.

"I'll be off, then," Vragi announced, breaking the silence. Going to his horse, he swiftly mounted. "Wouldn't want Geir to beat me to a meeting with Ingrid's father." His laugh was cruel.

My fury burned hot, and I screamed, "Don't you dare! You leave her be!"

"Ingrid will make a fine wife," Vragi answered with a chuckle.

To my right, Geir was crawling after Vragi. Was begging for someone to lend him a horse. My brother, *begging*. "You have what you want," he cried. "You are rid of Freya, paid with gold, you do not need Ingrid!"

I would not stand for this.

Slamming my head back, I caught Bjorn hard in the chin and he dropped me. The second my feet hit the ground, I closed my fingers over the fiery handle of his axe, ripping it from his hand. Agony lanced up my arm as the flames licked over my skin, burning my flesh, and I screamed as I raised it over my head, fire kissing my cheek.

And then I threw the weapon.

It flipped end-over-end as it arced through the air, sparks trailing in its wake.

Embedding with a meaty *thunk* in the back of Vragi's skull.

CHAPTER

3

I stared at the burning axe in the back of my husband's head. Watched as he slowly crumpled and slid off the side of the horse to land with a thud on the ground. Only then did the axe vanish, leaving behind blotches of brightness across my vision.

"You fool!" Snorri shouted.

Bjorn stared at me, eyes full of shock and horror. "What were you thinking?"

"He deserved it," I whispered. Vragi's hair was burning, the smell acrid. "He's a greedy, traitorous bastard the world is better off without."

Not *is*. Was.

"How could you let that happen, Bjorn?" Snorri snarled, lunging at his son before drawing up short. "How could you let her disarm you?"

"I didn't think she'd do it." Bjorn gave a rapid shake of his head. "No one has ever tried it. No one is mad enough to touch Tyr's fire!"

It occurred to me then that they weren't angry I'd murdered Vragi. They were angry that—

The pain struck.

Agony like nothing I'd ever experienced lanced up my arm and I looked down to see my wrist and the back of my hand red and blistered, only my palm and fingers seeming exempt from the pain. I started to turn my hand over, but Bjorn's fingers locked on my elbow. "You don't want to look." He caught my chin with his other hand, forcing me to meet his gaze. "Looking will make it worse."

His eyes were such a lovely shade of green, the lashes around them dark, and though the pain grew with each throbbing pulse, the thought that filled my head was that it wasn't fair for a man to have such long lashes. "Is it bad?"

"Yes."

"Oh."

I swayed on my feet as he said to Snorri, "If you wish your shield maiden to keep her hand, we must return to Halsar so Liv can help her."

Snorri cursed, then a frown split his brow. "It was foretold her name would be born in fire. I'd believed that meant Tyr's fire was forcing her to reveal her gift, but that would have been an act of fear. Whereas this . . ." He paused, eyes growing bright with zealotry, "*this* is an act of bravery that will give Steinunn a song to be sung by skalds for generations. This is an act the gods will reward."

If this was the gods' idea of a reward, I prayed I'd never feel the pain of punishment.

Snorri wasn't through. "Lest the rest of you see the favor the gods show her as license for apathy, know that if she loses her hand, I'll cut the fingers off every one of you myself!"

"An answer for everything," Bjorn muttered under his breath before shouting, "Get the salve from my saddlebags." His hand still gripped my chin, holding my face high so that I couldn't look down.

"I'm sorry," I said to him, a tremor running through me.

"You should be." He held my gaze, and I swore it was the only thing keeping me from screaming. "All the women in Halsar will curse your name if I lose half my fingers."

I blinked, then comprehended what he meant. My teeth bared in a snarl over him making light of my pain. "Or perhaps they'll praise me for sparing them your grasping hands."

He grinned, his teeth bright white against his sun-browned skin. "You only think that because you haven't heard of my reputation. After a day or two in Halsar you will know the truth of things."

All I wanted was to scream and scream and scream, but I forced myself to say, "The truth women tell other women is not the same truth they tell men."

His smile grew. "There can be only one truth. All else is falsity."

I managed to choke out, "Exactly."

He laughed, but his hold on my face and arm tightened. A second later, I understood why as someone's hands touched my burns, the pain turning the world bright white, only Bjorn's grip keeping me upright as I howled and sobbed.

"Easy, Freya." His voice was low and soft. "The salve will take away the pain."

I drew in a ragged breath.

"Bjorn," someone muttered, "this is—"

"I know," he interrupted. "We need to hurry."

The urgency fueled my fear, but I needed to see. Needed to know how bad it was. "Let me look."

His jaw tightened. "Freya . . ."

I pulled my chin from his grip and looked down. The skin of my wrist and hand was covered with a thick red paste, but not my palm. Because my palm . . .

The skin was *gone*.

I stared at the blackened mess of ash, gagged, then twisted and vomited, the world swimming.

"I warned you." Bjorn wrapped a cloth around my burns, then stooped down, his arms going behind my knees and shoulders.

"I can walk," I protested, though that might have been a lie.

Was definitely a lie.

"I'm sure you can." He lifted me as though I weighed no more than a child, settling me against his chest. "But this will give you a better story for Steinunn to sing about. You always want a good story to go with your scars."

"Freya!"

Geir was trying to crawl toward me, tears streaming down his face. "Why did you do it?" he wept. "Your hand is ruined!"

"It's not ruined, you idiot," Bjorn snapped. "And your mewling is not helpful."

Geir's eyes darkened. "It's *your* fault, Firehand. It was your axe that did this to her."

Through my dizziness and fear, my anger rose. "I did it to myself," I said between my teeth. "I don't regret it. Vragi would have ruined Ingrid's life. And yours."

"I'm your brother—I'm the one who is supposed to protect *you*."

His words only fueled my anger. "If you think that's the way of it, then you really haven't been paying attention."

"Get him on a horse and send him back to his mother," Snorri snapped at his men. "And Geir, I don't want to see your face until you learn to hold your tongue."

The pain in my hand was easing, whatever concoction Bjorn smeared on it numbing me from elbow to fingertip. Yet instead of feeling better, I felt cold as ice, shivers taking over as Bjorn carried me to his horse. He lifted me onto the animal's shoulders, then swiftly swung into the saddle, pulling me against him. My arse was pressed against his pelvis and his arm was wrapped around my middle, the proximity reminding me of my exchange with him on the beach. "I can ride alone."

"Not enough horses."

"Then behind," I whispered. "I can ride behind you."

He snorted, heeling the horse into a trot. "I just watched you put an axe in a man's skull. You think I'm fool enough to put you at my back?"

"I don't have a weapon." The motion of the horse as it sped into a swift canter drove me against him with each stride. "I think you're safe."

Bjorn's chest shook as he laughed. "I respectfully disagree, shield maiden. You've proven yourself opportunistic."

In the face of the pain, I'd almost forgotten that the secret I'd hidden all my life was now revealed. There'd been moments I'd dreamed of screaming it to the world, of owning my heritage despite my father's warnings. But now that it was known, I had to face the nightmare that would be my reality. "Don't call me that."

"You're right," he said. "It's not original—I shall think of something better. Perhaps Freya Onehand. Or Freya Axethief. Or Freya Scorched-Palm."

Selvegr appeared in the distance, but it was blurry, the buildings merging into one another in a grotesque smear. "I don't like you."

"Good. You shouldn't." His arm tightened around my waist as he urged the horse into a gallop. "The salve will make you tired. Might make you fall asleep. Don't fight that mercy, Freya."

"I won't fall asleep." I couldn't. I wouldn't. Yet with every stride, drowsiness drew me down and down, away from the fear and the pain. The last thing I remembered before darkness claimed me was Bjorn's voice in my ear. "I won't let you fall."

CHAPTER

4

I woke to fog and pain and the sensation of being lowered. Panic rose in my chest, and I struggled to get away from the hands gripping me even as the world spun. "Let me go," I mumbled, lashing out blindly as my heels struck the ground. "Let me go!"

"Easy, Freya," a deep voice said from behind me. A voice I recognized, though when I turned to look at him, his face was a blur. "Bjorn?" His name stuck in my throat, my mouth dry as sand and my tongue thick.

"The salve is wearing off," he said by way of answer. "You'll see clearly soon enough, though you might wish otherwise when the pain returns." He lifted his head. "Send someone to fetch Liv. Tell her it's a burn." He hesitated. "Tyr's fire."

"You heard him," a woman's voice shouted. "Go! Be swift about it." Then in a tone as cold as frost, she added, "Why did you hurt her, you cursed fool? What good is a shield maiden with only one hand?"

"She only needs one to hold a shield." Bjorn's tone was light, but his fingers tightened where they gripped my waist.

I turned to see who'd speak so to the son of the jarl, my vision focusing enough to reveal a woman perhaps two dozen years my senior. Her long reddish-brown hair hung in loose curls that framed a lovely face, though my eyes went to the heavy gold earrings that glinted in the sun. Not just gold, but jewels, and I gaped at them in fascination.

"Is she dense as well as maimed?" the woman demanded, and my eyes snapped to hers. They were the palest of blues, with a thin rim of black around them. The color reminded me of frozen waterfalls in the dead of winter.

"A matter under debate," Bjorn answered. "Freya, this is Ylva, Jarl Snorri's wife and lady of Halsar."

Didn't that make her his mother?

"My lady." I tried to incline my head in respect, but the motion sent a wave of dizziness over me, and if not for Bjorn's support, I'd have staggered into her.

Ylva made a noise of disgust. "Where is my husband?"

"He rides slow, you know that. Where can I put Freya?"

Bjorn had been right about the pain. I could see clearly now, but each pulse of my blood seemed to ratchet the agony to a higher level. My skin was icy cold where it wasn't burning, and I started to shiver anew. "I don't feel well."

"She looks like she's dying," Ylva said. "Where is Snorri?"

"On my heels, I'm sure."

Nausea rolled up inside me, and I pulled from Bjorn's grip to vomit, though all that came up was bile. The force of it drove me to my knees and would've seen my hand planted into the mud if Bjorn hadn't grabbed my elbow, holding it high.

"Lovely." Ylva huffed out a breath. "Bring her inside. Assuming she lives, this will be her home now."

Home.

As Bjorn lifted me, careful not to touch my hand, my eyes went to the building we stood before. A great hall. Though shaped the same as any other home, this structure was twice the height of any I'd ever seen, the planks forming the walls carved with runes and knotwork, and the twin doors large enough to allow five men to enter abreast. As we stepped into the dim interior, my eyes skipped over a raised platform where two large chairs sat. Before them were tables flanking a stone hearth at least a dozen feet long. From the ceiling high above dangled interwoven racks of antlers decorated with silver, and a second level overlooked the common area.

They took me past the tables to the rear of the space, which was separated from the room by thick hangings suspended from the level above. There were several cots there, and Bjorn steered me toward one of them.

With no small amount of relief, I lay down, the furs beneath me thick and soft, as were those Bjorn drew over me, though they did nothing to drive away the chill. I shivered and shook, most of the water from the cup he held to my mouth pouring down my chin rather than my throat. His hand curled around the base of my head, lifting it and holding me steady. I swallowed the water greedily, then slumped back. "Hurts."

"I know."

I bit the insides of my cheeks to keep my tears in check, not wanting to show any more weakness. "How could you know? It doesn't burn you." My tone was more bitter than I intended.

"Tyr's fire doesn't, but ordinary fire does." He turned, pulling up his shirt to reveal hard muscle, tattooed skin, and, across one shoulder blade, a twist of faded white scar unmarked by the black ink of his tattoos. "Set a cabin afire the first time I called the flame as a child. A burning beam fell on me. It's not a pain you forget."

It wasn't.

This was the sort of pain that lived in memory.

I watched as he settled on a stool next to the bed. He bent to examine my hand—which I was studiously *not* looking at—and I took the opportunity to run my eyes over his high cheekbones and strong jaw, his nose slightly crooked where I suspected it had once been broken. Stubble almost hid a dimple in his chin, and at this angle, I could see the edges of a crimson tattoo on the back of his neck, which would be the mark of his bloodline. His hair was a pure sort of black I'd rarely seen, the sunlight coming in from the opening in the roof turning strands of it blue rather than brown.

A piece had come loose from the tie at the back of his head, and it chose that moment to come untucked from behind his ear, falling across his cheek. Instinctively I lifted my right hand to brush it away, but the motion sent a stab of agony up my arm.

My *right* hand.

The hand I used for everything, and I might lose it. Fear of *that* more than the pain itself sent a hot tear trickling down my cheek, and I squeezed my eyes shut. When I opened them, it was to find Bjorn regarding me intently, his expression unreadable. "Was it worth it?" he asked.

The memory of my brother crawling after Vragi, desperate to stop him, filled my mind's eye. If I hadn't acted, Vragi would have taken Ingrid just for spite, destroyed her, then cast her aside. Or more likely, once he was able to walk, Geir would have killed Vragi and then been executed for murder by Snorri. Now, at least, they'd have a chance. *If it cost me my hand, so be it.* "Yes."

Bjorn made a low humming sound, then nodded. "Thought you might say that."

Silence stretched between us, and in it, the pain worsened. Desperate to knock it back, I said, "You let me go. Why?"

"What makes you say that? You've got a hard skull—my chin still aches." He'd returned to his examination of my injuries. "You got away from me."

"Liar," I whispered, agony making me bold. If there was ever a chance to ask hard questions, now was the time.

Bjorn went entirely still, then turned his head, sunlight causing his green eyes to glow. "Vragi was a piece of shit who betrayed his own wife for wealth. Didn't seem right to deny you your vengeance, though I thought you'd attack him with your fists, not . . ." He trailed off, making a face. "I underestimated how intensely you hated him."

I *had* hated him, but searching for the emotion now, I found nothing. Felt nothing, despite having murdered my own husband in cold blood. The absence of reaction, good or bad, within me was unnerving and I swallowed hard.

The scrape of shoes on the wooden floor caught our attention. Bjorn stood as a small, fair-skinned woman with a halo of crimson curls appeared, Ylva at her heels. "Liv."

"Why is it that if there is trouble, you are always at the center of it, Bjorn?"

"*Always* is an exaggeration." He grinned at her, all good looks, white teeth, and sparkling eyes—a look I imagined got him out of a fair bit of said trouble, but the small woman only snorted. "Go flirt with someone who's interested, you wool-brained creature. I've neither time nor interest in your nonsense."

I huffed out a laugh, and the woman turned her soft brown eyes on me and smiled. "If you can laugh, then you're not in the grave just yet." She set her satchel next to the bed, then sat on the stool Bjorn had vacated, gently removing the cloth covering my hand.

"She grabbed my axe in a fit of murderous rage." Bjorn leaned against the wall, then winked at me. "I would not anger her if I were you. Or if you do, don't turn your back on her."

"And yet you'll probably not take your own advice." Liv made a soft sound, then shook her head and my heart sank even as my fear bloomed bright. She asked, "What's your name?"

"Never mind her name, will she keep the hand?" Ylva pushed around Bjorn to bend over the bed, making a face at my wound. "She is the shield maiden we've been searching for. She will make Snorri king of Skaland, but only if she isn't rendered useless by her own foolish choices."

Liv stiffened, glancing to Bjorn for confirmation, but I barely noticed the exchange. *Useless.* My eyes burned and I blinked rapidly, every dream I'd ever had going up in smoke. "My name is Freya, Erik's daughter."

"Pray to Hlin, Freya. For it is in the hands of the gods as to whether you will recover." Liv looked to Ylva. "Make an offering to Eir. A goat should suffice, but you must do it yourself."

Ylva's lip curled, but she said nothing, only nodded and left, shouting at the servants beyond.

"That should keep her busy for a time." Liv dug into her satchel, extracting a small jar of honey as well as a handful of what looked like moss, setting them on a table. "But first let us look to your pain."

She put a yellow substance into a clay pot, then held a candle to it until it ignited. Leaning toward my face, she met my eyes. "Breathe deep," she said, then blew the smoke toward me. I dutifully inhaled, then choked and coughed, sucking in more smoke as I did. Almost instantly, my muscles ceased their shivering and I slumped back against the furs.

"Better?" Liv asked.

I could still feel the burns, but they no longer made me want to scream. "Yes," I murmured, sinking into a strange sense of euphoria. As though I were in my body . . . but not. "Is it your magic that I am feeling?" I knew little of the magic of the children of Eir, for they were rare and usually served jarls.

"No." Liv smiled. "Just a flower with many uses."

"Don't get used to it, Freya Charhand. That flower has been the ruin of many," Bjorn said, and my gaze drifted to his face, uncaring that I was unabashedly staring at him.

"It's unnatural for someone to have such a beautiful face."

One of his eyebrows rose. "I cannot tell if that was meant as a compliment or an insult."

"I'm not sure," I breathed, feeling an inexplicable desire to touch him to see if he was real or if I was imagining him. "When I saw you coming out of the water, I thought for a moment that Baldur had escaped Helheim, for you couldn't possibly be human."

"I think your bit of smoke has done its duty, Liv," Bjorn said. "Best get on with things, right?"

"Are you blushing, Bjorn?" The healer gave a sly smile. "I hadn't thought it possible . . ."

"It's hot in here."

"It's not," I corrected him, admiring the slight flush of his cheeks. "It's cold. But you always feel warm, like there is a fire burning inside of you. A fire I'd like to—"

Bjorn lifted my arm, and I broke off, staring with fascination at the red skin marked with blisters, feeling none of the nausea I had earlier at the sight of my charred and blackened palm. Liv picked the worst of it off with tiny silver tweezers, revealing parts of my hand that should not feel the touch of air. Then she smeared honey across my injuries before plucking up the moss and pressing it into the sticky mess on my palm. "Eir," she whispered, "cast your eyes down upon this woman. If she is worthy, allow me to help her."

Nothing happened.

Even through the haze of the narcotic, I felt a twinge of fear. Had I been judged unworthy? It would make sense, for had I not hidden my own gift rather than using it, as Hlin intended? Had I not murdered in cold blood the one who'd revealed my secret? Perhaps this was a sign I was not blessed but cursed. A sign the gods had turned their backs on me.

Bjorn's grip on my elbow tightened almost painfully, and I slowly shifted my gaze to find him staring at my palm, his jaw tight and his eyes filled with . . . *panic*? "Don't be petty, Eir," he said between his teeth. "You know who deserves the punishment, and it is not her."

"Bjorn . . ." Liv's voice was warning. "Don't challenge the gods else they might—"

The moss began to grow.

At first, I thought I was seeing things. Yet within heartbeats, the dense green plant covered my palm, circling its way around the back of my hand and swiftly covering my fingers and wrist, not ceasing until all my burns were concealed. "Gods," I breathed, staring at my moss-covered limb as Bjorn carefully lowered it to rest on my stomach. "I've never seen anything like it."

Liv was watching Bjorn, her brow still furrowed, and I was not certain whether she was addressing me or him when she said, "Eir has allowed me to heal you, but what form that takes is up to her. When the moss withers, what we find beneath may be flesh as pure as a newborn babe's or the gnarled limb of an ancient crone."

"I understand." A lie, because while Snorri said I was favored, I did not feel so. "Thank you."

Liv inclined her head. "I serve Eir. Now you must rest, Freya. Let yourself sleep so that your body heals."

Indeed, I felt the weight of the smoke I'd imbibed dragging me deeper, as though I were sinking into a warm lake, sunlight filling my eyes. I smiled, allowing my lids to shut as I drifted . . .

"She'll stay under for hours," I vaguely heard Liv say. Then, in little more than a whisper, she added, "Is it true? She's the shield maiden?"

Bjorn made a noise of confirmation. "I struck her shield with my axe and her magic threw me a dozen paces across the clearing and into a tree. On which note, my arse is going to be black and blue for days. You wouldn't mind—"

"Incentive to keep your trousers on for once," Liv retorted. "Her arrival means war, and you know it."

"War is inevitable."

Liv didn't answer, and feet thudded against the wooden floor as someone strode away. Curiosity pushed back some of the fog, and I peeled open my eyelids. Liv was gone and Bjorn stood next to my cot, his gaze fixed on my hand. "Why is she so angry?" I asked.

Bjorn jerked as though he'd been caught doing something he should not have been. After a heartbeat of silence, he finally said, "Liv dislikes violence—she's seen too much of what is left in its wake—and your appearance means more will come."

A shiver passed over me. "Because of the seer's prophecy? She thinks I'll cause a war?"

He was silent for a long moment, then said, "The seer saw a future where you unite all the people of Skaland beneath one king. In our world, power is most often achieved with violence." He hesitated, then added, "And Hlin is a goddess of war." He drew the furs higher up my chest, cocooning me in warmth. "But she also protects."

Frustration wormed its way through the haze. "What does that mean?"

"You are unfated, Freya. Nothing the seer foretold is set in stone."

Without another word, he walked out of sight.

CHAPTER

5

A beam of light stabbed me in the eyes, and I silently cursed Vragi for leaving the door open when he went outside to piss. Groaning, I rolled away from the light, then froze as my cheek brushed over fur of unfamiliar texture.

Memory slammed into me: Vragi's laughter as he betrayed me, Geir crawling on the ground, my hand consumed by the fire of a god, and pain . . . pain like nothing I'd experienced before.

Pain that was now . . . *gone.*

I sat up, the furs covering me falling away. My clothes were my own, marked with blood and bits of ash, stinking of sweat and fish, but that was the least of my concerns as I stared down at my hand.

It was still wrapped with moss, but the plant was now dry and dead. I tentatively touched the moss with my left hand, equal parts desperate and terrified to see what lay beneath.

"I told you the gods favored you," a voice said, and I straightened to find Jarl Snorri standing next to the hangings separating the space from the rest of the hall. "They wished for you to be revealed by fire, not to be consumed by it."

I wasn't convinced that was true, given my circumstances, but I kept my mouth shut as he crossed over to the bed. Without asking, he pulled the moss free, bits of dead plant and ash falling onto the dark furs. My breath caught as I saw what lay beneath.

"Make a fist," he ordered.

I dutifully did so, muscles and tendons obeying with minimal protest.

"Ugly," he said. "But strong enough to grip a weapon, and the seer said nothing of you uniting Skaland with your looks."

I tried and failed not to flinch, hunting for gratitude that I hadn't lost use of my hand and finding it lacking. For I saw what Snorri saw. Scars. The skin was twisted and stretched, in some places pink and in others completely white. Turning it over revealed that Liv's magic had replaced the skin that the fire had melted away, but it was thick and almost devoid of sensation. My eyes burned with tears, and I blinked rapidly, not wanting Snorri to see that his comment had stung. Not wanting *anyone* to know how vain I truly was.

Snorri retreated from the room and returned with a shield painted bright yellow and red. "Get up." He held out the heavy wooden circle. "Prove that you can call Hlin's magic when your life isn't on the line."

The floor was cold beneath my bare feet as I slid off the bed and accepted the shield, the muscles of my left arm straining to support it. "And if I can't?"

Snorri eyed me silently. "Failure always has a price, Freya. But it isn't always paid by the one who fails."

A prickle of fear skittered down my back. With Geir injured, my family was at the mercy of Snorri's men.

Swallowing hard, I hefted the shield and squared my shoulders. *Please,* I silently prayed. *Please don't abandon me now, Goddess.* Then I parted my lips and invoked her name, "Hlin."

A familiar silver glow streaked out of the fingertips of my left hand, covering the shield and rendering it nearly weightless. It illuminated the room, casting shadows off Snorri's smiling face. Tentatively, he reached out to touch the shield, then trailed his fingers over the smooth surface of the magic.

I wished it would fling him back as it had Bjorn. Wished it would launch him with such violence as to shatter his body. But it did not.

"You'll be a force to be reckoned with on the battlefield," he breathed. "Steinunn has already begun her composition, and with her song, word of our strength will spread like wildfire. Soon all will swear oaths to me."

"How?" I demanded. "How does my ability to protect *myself* in battle make such a huge difference?"

His eyes flared bright. "Because the seer told me it was so, which means the gods have seen it."

Had seen me being used like a tool—and that sat poorly with me. "How can you be certain the seer meant you?"

His face darkened and I instantly regretted running my mouth; I was always saying the first things that came to my mind despite having suffered consequences for doing so time and again.

"Because the seer spoke the prophecy to Snorri, not anyone else, you idiot girl." Ylva stepped around a hanging, coming toward us. "Disregard her ignorance, my love. She's the daughter of a farmer. The wife of a fishmonger. This is probably the first time she's been more than a few miles from the hovel her mother birthed her in."

Every one of those things was true, but I still bristled at the implication that they made me ignorant or stupid. My parents had taught me the history of our people and the stories of the gods, but more than that, they'd taught me what I needed to survive. I opened my mouth to demand if she could claim as much, but before I could, Ylva said, "Once you are wed, Snorri will control your fate, because he will control *you*. Which is why the wedding will be today."

Today? Gods . . . I swallowed my dismay even as I watched Snorri's jaw tighten. "We should wait for Frigg's Day so as to ensure the union is blessed," he said.

Ylva huffed out a loud breath. "And risk someone else stealing her? You *must* claim her, husband. All of Skaland must know that the shield maiden is *yours*."

As though I were a cow. Or a pig. Or worse, a brood mare, though given he had Bjorn for an heir, I doubted children were what he sought from me. Even if they were, there were ways other than lemons to prevent such things. But my skin still crawled at the thought of being bedded by this man.

Grit your teeth and bear it, I silently ordered myself. *It's not as though you're some maid who has never been bedded. You endured Vragi. You can endure Snorri as well.*

I had to, because my family depended on it.

Snorri exhaled a long breath, his gaze fixed on his wife. "This union is a slap to your face, my love. I wish there was another way, but the gods demand this of us."

The declaration was unexpected, at least for me. I lowered my head, embarrassed to be caught in the midst of this conversation, for I sensed that Snorri's sentiment was genuine.

Through my eyelashes, I watched Ylva's face soften, and my discomfort grew as she drew toward her husband, kissing him passionately. My cheeks burned and I moved my gaze to the floor, fighting the desire to edge past them and escape this moment.

"You do this as much for me as for yourself." Ylva's voice was velvet soft. "It is only a matter of time until Harald crosses the strait, and we have not the strength to fight him. Skaland must be united, and it is the will of the gods that they will be united beneath your rule. It is a sacrifice to share your hand with another, but one I will gladly accept to protect our people from our enemies."

My stomach twisted with unexpected guilt, because I'd not considered that either of them had a higher purpose.

"You are the greatest blessing the gods have bestowed upon me, Ylva," Snorri murmured, and my cheeks heated as they embraced, their roaming hands suggesting that if not for my presence, they'd be ridding themselves of their clothing. That they might anyway, my presence be damned. So I dropped the shield.

The second it left my grip, the magic disappeared, and it landed with a loud clatter against the floor, the pair jerking apart.

"Apologies," I murmured. "I seem not to have fully recovered my strength."

Snorri snorted, not fooled by the lie. Yet he stepped back from Ylva even as he said to her, "Prepare for the feast, my love. And prepare Freya to be my bride."

The servants descended like a horde of raiders, stripping me of my clothing and pushing me into a bath so hot, it nearly scalded my skin. Though I was hardly used to being bathed by others, that wasn't what consumed my thoughts as I was scrubbed with soap and polished with sand until my skin was nearly raw. It was that in the space of a day, my entire life had been turned upside down, the gods giving and taking in equal measure.

Seers did not lie.

They had the blood of Odin himself, and they spoke with the knowledge of the gods, though their prophecy was rarely clear until the events they foretold came to pass. So if the seer spoke these words directly to Snorri, they were the truth, in some fashion. It was possible that Snorri was lying, but . . . my gut told me his fervor was genuine.

Because it explained *why* my father had ordered me to keep my magic secret.

Children of the gods were created when one of the gods gifted a child a drop of their divine blood upon conception. In some instances, the gods were active participants in the sex, but it was not necessary—they need only be present for the act of creation. Which meant that while some parents might suspect the third party of their tryst had gifted them a child with divine blood, some were entirely oblivious until the day the child's magic appeared. The latter had been the case for me.

The truth had been revealed when I was seven and had shouted Hlin's name while fighting with Geir. It was a game all children played despite it earning smacks from any adult in earshot for disrespecting the gods: Shout the name of one known to grant their blood and see if magic manifested. Geir and I had invoked Tyr and Thor and Freyja and countless other of the gods, but not once had I thought of Hlin. It had only been because the fight had gotten out of hand, my brother's stick falling heavy on my tiny shield, that I'd grown desperate, calling the goddess's name. The magic that came to my aid hadn't thrown Geir the way it had Bjorn, but it had sent him sprawling.

And my father had witnessed it all.

Never in my life had I seen such a look of panic on his face as I did in that moment; the wideness of his eyes and the slackness of his open mouth were emblazoned on my memory. As was the way he had shaken me so hard my teeth rattled, his breath hot in my face as he shouted, "You never say her name again! Do you hear me? You never say her name!" Then he'd rounded on Geir, gripping my brother by the arms so hard it had left bruises. "You never tell anyone what happened this day! Your sister's life depends on it!"

His reaction made more of an impact on me than the magic itself, and for a long time, fear of seeing my father angered had kept the goddess's name from my lips and questions off my tongue. But time tempered my fear and fueled my curiosity. Children of the gods were rare, Vragi the only one I'd seen with my own eyes, but stories of deeds done by those with magic filled the air at every gathering. Those with god's blood were fabled and honored, and I wanted to join their ranks. Wanted to fight in battles and have my victories sung about by skalds, but every time I gained the nerve to press my father about *why* my magic was to be hidden, he'd react with fury. Realizing that he'd give me no answers, it wasn't long until I was sneaking out and experimenting, most often with Geir along with me.

Of course we got caught.

My father's wrath had been a thing to behold, a terrible twist of anger and fear that no child wishes to see in their parent's eyes as he'd again forbidden me to use my magic.

"Why must I hide it when no one else does?" I'd demanded. "In every story about children of the gods, the gift of blood and magic is treated as an honor, but you act as though I've been cursed. Tell me why!"

"Because you are Hlin's child, Freya. The only one alive," he said. "And you were born under the blood moon. If anyone discovers this truth, you will be used. Used and fought over by men with power until you are dead. Do you understand?" He'd shouted the last in my face. "If anyone learns, your life will never be your own!"

He'd refused further explanation of why Hlin's blood made me uniquely coveted among the children of the gods, yet I'd taken him at his word with the blind faith of a child who trusted her father above all others. Yet, also like a child, I hadn't *fucking listened*.

My eyes stung because my father had known of the seer's prophecy. He'd once been one of Snorri's trusted warriors, so he'd either witnessed the foretelling or been told about it, which was why he'd known what Snorri would do if my heritage were ever discovered. If only I'd listened . . .

I'd still be married to Vragi. Would be facing a lifetime of drudgery and cruelty beneath my husband's hand.

The Norns give.

And the Norns take.

"Does it hurt?"

I jumped at the servant's question, my thoughts vanquished. She'd been buffing the nails on my left hand and was now trimming what remained of the nails on my right hand. "Not like it did. Now it just aches like an injury years old."

My words must have eased her mind, for her grip firmed on my hand, her brow furrowed as she cut away the blackened nail. "Is it true you wielded the Firehand's axe to murder your own husband?"

Wielded was a strong word. "Yes."

I waited for the admission to trigger something in me. Relief. Guilt. Anything. Yet as before, I felt nothing.

"I'm sure he deserved it." The servant frowned, then asked, "But didn't you know that the axe would burn you?"

Had I known?

Logically, I suppose that I had, but that hadn't been my concern. It had been whether I'd be able to wrest it from Bjorn's grip. It had been whether my aim would be true. "I needed a weapon, and it was the only one available."

All the women paused to stare at me, but the one bent over my nails only giggled. "Worked out in your favor, I suppose. I'd suffer a scald to sit on Bjorn's lap for a few hours."

Anger swelled in my chest at the stupidity of her comment. At the idea that I'd willingly endured the most traumatic moment of my life for the chance to sit in a man's lap. "It melted the skin off my palm. Turned my flesh to ash." Spotting several flecks of said ash sitting on the edge of the tub, I bent my head and blew them in her face. "If you're willing to do so much to rub your arse against a man's cock, you're desperate indeed."

I waited for the jab to land, wanting the petty satisfaction of seeing her embarrassment, but the woman's dark eyes only met mine with a smile. "Or he's that good in bed."

All the other women laughed, and despite knowing the comment was foolish, it was me who flushed. Me who fell silent as they drew me from the bath and set to combing out the long lengths of my hair, trimming the ends so that bits of white gold covered the floor.

I gritted my teeth as the servant woman began to braid, my hair drawn so tight that my head ached. Taking a deep breath, I tried to turn my mind back to more pressing issues. But instead it lingered on Bjorn.

More heat rose to my cheeks as I remembered the things I'd said to him with Liv present, comparing him to the god of beauty like a girl who hadn't had her first bleed, despite being a grown woman who'd endured a year of marriage. Visions of my behavior replayed through my mind, my horror growing with each passing moment. Bad enough that we'd had our flirtation on the beach. At least then we'd had no notion of each other's identity, but then I'd gone on to all but declare my lust for him in front of Liv, fully aware that I was intended to wed his father. It was no wonder he'd been mortified. While it was tempting to blame Liv's narcotics for my behavior, all they'd done was loosen my tongue of the truth.

When I closed my eyes, the vision of him coming out of the water filled my mind's eye, all tattooed skin and muscle, not a spare ounce of flesh on him. Every bit a warrior, and that face . . . Mortals shouldn't be allowed such beauty for it made fools of everyone else, his silver tongue making it all the worse because even if he'd been ugly as a pig's arse, Bjorn was bloody charming. Yes, he'd very nearly killed me when we'd been forced to fight, but given that I'd been equally willing to put a sword through his heart, it seemed petty to hold it against him.

Stop it, Freya, I chided myself. *Think about something else. Think of worms or night soil, or better yet, the fact you're apparently destined to unite Skaland as his father's wife. Think of anything but Bjorn.*

I might as well have told myself to flap my arms and fly for all the good my admonitions did. Bjorn's face, his body, and the ghostly echoes of his touch tormented my thoughts as the servants finished my braids and painted my eyes with kohl, the fantasies only vanquished when they brought me the dress I was to wear. Finer than anything I'd ever seen, the dress was thin white wool, the shoes butter-soft leather, and the jewelry . . . Not in all my life had I dreamed of wearing such wealth, my throat and wrists wrapped with silver and gold, one of the women pushing needles through my earlobes so that I might wear the heavy earrings.

Then Ylva appeared carrying a bridal crown.

It was made of twisted wires of gold and silver strung with pieces of polished amber the same color as my eyes. Ylva herself fastened it to my braids with endless tiny pins. She turned me to face a round piece of polished metal so that I might see my appearance, the servants all smiling and laughing, pleased with their efforts.

"Finally," Ylva breathed. "Finally, you look like a child of the gods."

I stared at my reflection, feeling as though I stared into the eyes of a stranger.

Ylva placed a mantle of gleaming white fur over my shoulders, my braids almost indistinguishable in color as she smoothed them over the expensive pelt. "Snorri will be pleased." Then she snapped her fingers. "Gloves. She must be perfection."

All eyes immediately moved to my right hand, and I fought the urge to hide my scarred fingers in the pocket of my dress, not sure what was worse, disgust or pity—only that I hated both. So I voiced no argument when one of them handed me a pair of white wool gloves, feeling no sensation in my right palm as I pulled them on.

Numb.

The crack Geir's leg had made when Snorri had broken it filled my head and I flinched, because I knew so much worse could be done.

I needed to be numb. To do what needed to be done, to say the things that needed to be said, and to *be* what these people wanted me to be, because those I loved most depended on my compliance.

And I refused to fail them, no matter how much it cost me.

CHAPTER

6

It was snowing.

That was the first thing that struck me as I stepped out of the great hall. Snow in springtime was far from rare, but I couldn't help but feel that the gray sky and flat light were fitting for the day. Fat flakes of white spiraled down, the narrow paths leading between homes thick with mud and slush, forcing me to hold my skirts up lest I arrive at the ceremony looking like I'd been wallowing with the pigs.

The people of Halsar came out of their homes to watch me pass, the expressions of those who met my gaze cold despite the fact all would be feasted tonight by their lord. "Your people do not seem to favor this marriage," I said softly to Ylva, who walked at my left, her mouth drawn in an unsmiling line.

"Because they do not know the power you bring," she said. "They see only an insult to their beloved lady of Halsar."

I'd have rolled my eyes at her ego except that while the people scowled at me, they smiled at Ylva, touching her as she passed and offering her praise for her strength. I wanted to snarl at them that it was their jarl who had made this choice, therefore it was their jarl who deserved their ire, but it would be a waste of breath. They wanted to blame me.

"Freya!" A familiar voice reached me, and I turned my head to find Ingrid standing between two buildings, a sword clutched in her hands. Her brown hair was sodden, her freckled face pink from the cold as she stepped toward me. For a heartbeat, I was certain that she'd come to tell me not to do it. To tell me that she and Geir would accept the permanent loss of his place in Snorri's war band if it meant sparing me this union. To tell me—

The thought vanished as a pair of warriors drew their weapons and leapt between Ingrid and me.

"Stop," I shouted, trying to intervene, but another warrior caught hold of my arm. "She's my friend!"

"You cannot know that for certain," Ylva snapped. "Now that your identity is known, friends may become enemies to achieve their own ends."

I was tempted to snap back that she needed to be more selective in her friendships, but one of the men had Ingrid by the arm, the other right up in her face. Twisting, I kicked the man holding me in the knee, ignoring his shouts as I stormed toward my friend, mud splattering the skirt I'd tried so hard to keep clean. "Let her go! Now!"

The men made no move to unhand Ingrid. I wasn't certain if it was because they didn't recognize my authority or if they believed that Ingrid, who was timid as a mouse and could barely wield a cooking knife without cutting herself, was truly a threat.

"Let the woman go."

I tensed at Bjorn's voice, for I'd not realized he'd been part of the procession. Though I was glad he was when the warrior holding Ingrid immediately complied with his order.

"It is not your place to involve yourself, Bjorn," Ylva snapped. "Already Freya has been injured while in your *care*."

Leaning against a wall, Bjorn disregarded the comment and said, "If Freya says this woman is a friend, then you should believe her, Ylva. Or do you not trust the woman you're about to share your husband with?"

Ylva's face purpled. "She's naive. She—"

"Is a widowed woman, not a child, so you should not treat her as one." Bjorn lifted one shoulder. "Though . . . she *is* about to wed a man old enough to be her father, so perhaps it is fair."

"Bjorn, you need—"

Ignoring Ylva, he turned to Ingrid. "What's your name?"

"Ingrid." My friend looked ready to piss herself from fear, and I hated that. Hated that she'd come all this way to speak to me, only to be treated in such a manner.

"The Ingrid that Geir is so desperate to wed that he threw his own sister to the wolves?" Bjorn snorted in disgust. "You could do better than that spineless piece of weasel shit."

It was my turn to snarl, "Bjorn, don't be an arse!" but he paid me no more mind than he had Ylva as he said, "You aren't here to harm Freya, are you, Ingrid?"

A tear ran down my friend's face and she snuffled out a "No. I'd never hurt Freya."

"I didn't think so." Hooking his thumbs in his belt, Bjorn looked to me. "Say what needs saying, Freya, but be quick about it."

Giving him a withering glare for his comment about my brother, I elbowed my way past the warriors, drawing Ingrid enough away to give a semblance of privacy. "What are you doing here?" I asked, trying to ignore the lingering hope that Ingrid came bearing salvation.

"I came to thank you." She wiped the tears from her face. "Geir told me everything. What you've agreed to and why. What you did. That you did it to spare us. From the bottom of my heart, thank you, Freya."

My stomach gave a slight twist of discomfort as my foolish hope turned to ash and I looked away from her. Nothing she could have said would have dissuaded me from this course of action. Yet it still stung that she hadn't offered any protest. Still hurt that she wasn't willing to suffer a blow to her future to spare mine. The fact that I wouldn't have accepted didn't matter; what would have mattered was that she cared enough about me to offer.

She cares, I silently chided myself. *She's just afraid.* "Is Geir all right?"

Ingrid gave a tight nod. "He would've come if he could, only the pain is bad. But your mother says it was a clean break and will heal well with time and rest." She tentatively held out the sword. "Geir sent this. It was your father's."

My chin quivered as a rush of emotion raced through me, for this was the weapon that Geir would have gifted Ingrid when they were wed, and she was giving it to me to wield. Not the sacrifice I'd foolishly hoped for, but it still meant all the world to me that they'd wanted me to have it. Unsheathing it, I smiled to see that it had been polished and sharpened. "Thank you."

Ingrid whispered, "I'm sure the jarl will be honored to wield it."

My smile immediately fell away. Not a gift for me, but a gift for Snorri.

When I'd wed Vragi, I'd given him my grandfather's sword, polished to a high shine, whereas the one he'd given me was a rusted blade pilfered from the grave of a distant cousin, so poorly made that the hilt broke off in the middle of the ceremony.

Logically I knew that my family needed to provide a blade for me to gift Snorri, but did it have to be this one? This was the last piece of my father that existed. It was precious to me, which both Ingrid and Geir knew, yet they were giving it to Snorri to earn his favor. The urge to tell her to take it back filled my core. Instead I shoved it into its sheath.

"Freya," Ylva said loudly. "You may speak to her afterward. The jarl should not be waiting on you."

The desire to twist around and scream at Ylva to shut her mouth nearly overwhelmed me, but I managed to keep my anger in check, instead leaning close to Ingrid. "Don't stay. It isn't safe. Get home and warn everyone to stay away unless the jarl summons them, understood? Out of sight, out of mind."

The snowflakes melting on her face mixed with her tears, but Ingrid nodded. "Congratulations, Freya. I know you didn't ask for this match, but I think you will find more happiness in it than you would have with Vragi. You will get to be a warrior, like you always dreamed. And you'll be able to use your magic."

I blinked, something about the way she said the last, without shock or hesitation, triggering a realization. "You knew."

Ingrid bit her lip, then nodded. "Geir told me some years ago. I think . . . I think keeping the secret weighed upon him." Her expression grew earnest. "But I didn't tell anyone, Freya. I swear it."

Weighed upon *him*? My chest hollowed and I looked at the mud between us. For most of my life, I'd hidden my magic, *my heritage,* which meant keeping it from everyone I'd ever known. Never once had I told, because I'd understood intrinsically that it wouldn't just be me who would be hurt if my secret got out, it would be my family. "It doesn't much matter now."

Ingrid hugged me tightly, my one hand trapped between us, the hilt of the sword digging into my breastbone painfully. "This is a gift from the gods, Freya. You must look at it as such."

I didn't trust myself to say anything, so instead I only nodded and turned back to those waiting. Ylva scowled at me, but Bjorn's gaze was on Ingrid, who was splashing away through the mud. "I take it back," he said. "She does not deserve better than your brother."

"What do you know?" I muttered, not bothering to hike up my skirts again, for the hems were already stained gray and dripping.

"Very little," he said. "But I'm neither deaf nor blind, so I saw how she spun your sacrifice into a gift from the gods so that she need not feel guilt over it. You are well rid of her."

He wasn't entirely wrong, but Bjorn's words only made the hollowness in my core grow.

Alone, that was how I felt. As though I faced a great army, and all those I'd been so certain would be at my back had vanished. My eyes stung and I blinked rapidly to keep tears from forming, but a few still escaped, mixing with the melting snow running down my face as I walked toward the beach.

I'd not gone more than a handful of steps when Bjorn's hand closed on my arm. "Ingrid's cowardice does not diminish the honor of what you did."

Swallowing, I met his emerald gaze as I said, "I regret nothing," then pulled from his grip and carried on.

A crowd had gathered, Snorri standing apart with an ancient woman who I supposed was the matriarch who'd conduct the ceremony. My eyes drifted from them to the long stretch of dock, next to which sat several drakkar, the flags on their masts fluttering in the wind. They were huge, capable of holding at least a hundred warriors, and I allowed myself to imagine what it would be like to stand in one, the drummer beating a thundering rhythm as the oarsmen drove the drakkar into battle. What it would be like to leap into the water, shield up against a rain of arrows, racing onto a beach where the sword in my hand would clash against that of my enemies as armies collided. My fingers clenched on the hilt of my father's weapon, my heart driving away the sluggish weight of grief in my veins and filling them with fire. For Ingrid had not been wrong that there was much to this new path I faced that sang to my soul.

And that, at least, was something to live for.

The ceremony was brief and lifeless, both Snorri and I saying what needed to be said, then exchanging blades, the one he gave to me newly forged and unsharpened, rendering it as devoid of sentiment as it was of edge. If he noticed or cared that the sword I gave him was my father's, he didn't show it. Yet the moment the ceremony was over, it was as though a bolt of Thor's lightning struck, filling Snorri with an urgent energy as he turned me to face the crowd.

"Twenty years ago," he shouted, "the seer spoke a prophecy of a shield maiden, a child of Hlin, born under the blood moon and destined to unite the people of Skaland beneath the rule of the one who controlled her fate. A prophecy that said her name would be born in the fire of the gods. For twenty years, I have searched for this maiden, hunted for the woman who'd unite our people against our common enemy, King Harald of Nordeland."

The crowd shifted restlessly, several calling out curses at the king who ruled across the Northern Strait.

"Many of you have asked why I would wed this woman when I have a wife such as Ylva," he continued. "Let me assure you, it is not for love or lust, but for you, my people! For this woman is the shield maiden, the child of Hlin, her name revealed in the fire of Tyr!"

He took the shield one of his warriors held out and offered it to me. My skin burned hot despite my dress being soaked with melted snow, and taking it in my grip, I whispered, "Hlin."

Magic flared to life inside of me, rushing through my hand in a hot flood to cover the shield with silver light, glowing like a beacon. The crowd gasped and stepped back, their eyes wide at the sight of magic they'd only heard of in stories. Magic they didn't understand, which explained their apprehension.

"She will bring us battle fame!" Snorri roared. "She will bring us wealth! She will bring us power! She will bring us victory and vengeance against the bastards of Nordeland! For with her in our shield wall, we will be favored by the gods themselves!"

The people of Halsar roared along with him, hands in the air, the wariness in their eyes replaced with delight at the promises of their lord. Promises he'd made but which I was supposed to deliver, though the gods only knew how.

My gaze skipped over the people who not an hour ago seemed ready to spit at my feet and who now screamed my name, then it landed on Bjorn. He'd stood with Ylva during the ceremony but had since moved to the rear of the crowd, his arms crossed and expression tight. As our eyes locked, the corner of his mouth quirked up in a half smile that appeared as forced as the one currently gracing my face, though I didn't understand the source of his displeasure.

"She was born in fire," Snorri shouted. "Now let her be marked by the blood of the god who made her."

Before I could react, Ylva stepped behind me and tore the dress down the back. Gasping, I clutched the fabric to my breasts even as she said, "Kneel."

"What are you doing?" I hissed, equal parts horrified and afraid.

"You have hidden your powers for too long," she said. "Past time that you were marked so that all might know your lineage."

The blood tattoo.

I should've known it was coming. Vragi's tattoo had been on his thigh, a fish with crimson scales rendered in such detail it had looked real. A living tattoo gifted by ritual after his magic appeared. I should've been marked well over a decade ago, but that would have revealed what my father had been desperate to keep hidden.

Slowly, I lowered myself to my knees in the cold sand.

"Bare your flesh so you might receive Hlin's mark," Ylva demanded, and though I was loath to expose myself before a crowd, I pulled the dress down to my waist and removed my gloves, keeping one arm across my breasts. Forcing my eyes up from the sand revealed that no one was leering at me, every face solemn as they watched. I could feel Bjorn's scrutiny but instead of meeting his gaze, I looked back to the sand, my heart a riot in my chest.

A drum began a slow beat, and Ylva walked in a circle around me, drawing runes in the sand. My heart thundered faster at the revelation that Ylva was a volva—a witch capable of using runic magic. Which made her far more powerful than I'd believed.

She chanted as she moved, calling out to the gods to witness this moment. As she finished the circle, the runes flared and the drum ceased, the hairs on my arms standing on end. A knife appeared in Ylva's hand, and I tensed, for while she might need me, this woman held no warmth for me in her heart. "Hlin," Ylva cried out, voice carrying on the wind as it swirled around us, creating a cyclone of snow. "I beseech you! If this child is worthy, claim her as your own, else still her heart so that she might wield your power no more!"

My heart skipped. I'd never seen this ritual performed. Vragi had undergone it as a young child long before I was born, so I didn't know the words. Didn't know that the ritual could end in death, for none of the stories ever spoke of a god rejecting their child. But everyone else was nodding, so it must be the truth.

A thrill of fear turned my already chilled skin to ice as she approached, knife glinting in the muted light. "Bare yourself, girl," she said in a low voice. "Or find yourself judged unworthy."

What if I *was* unworthy?

I'd hidden my magic, my heritage, all my life, which had to have angered the goddess who'd gifted her blood to me. I'd treated it as though I were ashamed.

But I wasn't.

Taking a deep breath, I dropped my arm and lifted my face at the same time.

Though prudence demanded that I look elsewhere, my eyes locked with Bjorn's. The snow billowed and swirled between us, and I clung to the strength in his gaze as the tip of Ylva's knife pressed into the divot at the center of my collarbone.

She sliced downward, leaving a trail of fire from my throat to between my breasts, but I didn't flinch. Didn't break Bjorn's stare as hot droplets of blood rolled down my skin. Didn't so much as breathe as I waited to be judged.

And waited.

And waited.

My chin quivered, panic seeping into my veins, because if I was found unworthy, all of Snorri's plans would be destroyed. What were the chances that he wouldn't punish me in every way he possibly could, seeing me as the one to blame?

Then a crackle of energy surged across my skin.

The first warning that all was not as it should be was Ylva's startled gasp. It tore my gaze from Bjorn's in time to watch her stumble backward across the circle of runes, her eyes fixed on my chest. I looked down, terror consuming me as my blood spidered outward from the wound, infinitely greater in volume than the shallow slice should have provided. "Oh gods," I breathed. "What is happening?"

"You left her!" Bjorn shouted. "You left her in there alone!"

His words barely registered as the wound gaped, invisible fingers digging into my flesh and stretching it wide. A shrill scream tore from my lips. Rivulets of blood snaked across my chest and down my arms, invisible hands wrenching me left and then right.

"Freya!"

I howled in response, fighting to get away from the god's grip, knowing that I'd been judged unworthy and that Hlin herself was going to rip me apart. My knees left the ground, the goddess lifting me into the air like a doll, blood gushing in torrents from the wound that now reached down to the bone, the white of my sternum visible. What felt like claws dug into muscle and bone, pulling and pulling.

"Ylva, break the circle!"

The lady of Halsar only gaped in horror, for it was too late.

My rib cage sprung wide, revealing my pulsing heart. *Thump thump. Thump thump.*

I screamed and screamed, and then with a sudden whoosh, I dropped to the ground. Gasping, I dug my fingers into the sand, certain I had only a few heartbeats of life left in me.

"Freya?" Hands gripped my arms.

I looked up into Bjorn's panicked eyes even as I heard Ylva screech, "You cursed fool! Do you have any idea of what you might have unleashed?"

Bjorn ignored her, eyes raking over my body. "Are you all right?"

How could he ask that? How could he ask if I was all right when my chest had been ripped open. How . . .

The thought vanished as I looked down at my naked body, my chest whole but for a thin white scar, not a drop of crimson marring my white skin.

Not possible.

"I . . ." My mouth was as dry as sand. "She . . . she—"

"Is she marked?" Snorri was abruptly at my side, lifting my braids and pawing at me, searching. "Did Hlin claim her?"

He grew silent as Bjorn held up my left hand. On the back of it, painted in crimson, was a shield. The detail was unlike anything a mortal artist could have rendered, and with each thud of my heart, the blood forming it pulsed.

"She has been claimed!" Snorri roared. Catching hold of my wrist, he dragged me out of Bjorn's grasp and to my feet, holding my tattoo up for all to see while I desperately pulled my bodice into place with my free hand. "Hlin has claimed her daughter and we have our shield maiden!"

The crowd, deathly silent until that moment, shouted their approval.

"Let us feast!" Snorri bellowed, finally letting go of me so that I could pull on the sleeves of my dress. "To the great hall!"

As one, the people surged to the hall, ever eager to be fed. Snorri motioned for me to follow them, but Ylva's cold fingers latched on my right wrist, turning my palm skyward. "Look."

Unease twisted in my stomach at the sight. It was as though my palm had been tattooed prior to my burns, whatever image that had once been depicted twisted and stretched into an unrecognizable mess.

"A second tattoo," Snorri murmured. "I've never heard of such a thing."

"Nor I," Ylva said, and both looked to Bjorn, who shook his head, his gaze fixed on my palm.

"I can't tell what it depicts." Snorri bent closer and I curbed the urge to withdraw my hand, disliking the scrutiny.

"Likely because Hlin didn't have time to finish it before Bjorn went barging in and destroyed my circle," Ylva snapped.

"Because you abandoned her in there!" Bjorn glared at Ylva. "You're the volva. You're supposed to stay in the circle, but you left her in there to be torn apart."

Snorri stilled. "What precisely did you see, Bjorn? Ylva? For all I saw was Freya on her knees."

I was tired of being talked over as though I wasn't even here. "He saw me torn in half."

Bjorn gave a tight nod. "Was as if she were a prize being warred over, and both sides would rather see her destroyed than concede to the other."

"A portent." Snorri exhaled a long breath. "The circle allowed Hlin to grant us a vision. A warning of what is to come and what will occur if we don't take care: Freya will be destroyed."

Fear wormed its way down my spine.

"But that's not all." Snorri tapped his chin thoughtfully. "She also gave us an answer as to how we might avoid such a fate for Freya. Recall the story of the Binding of Fenrir, in which Tyr sacrifices his arm so that the gods might be protected from the wolf." He gestured to my scarred hand. "It is clear that you, my son, must sacrifice to protect that which will save us all."

Bjorn blinked, then gave a sharp shake of his head. "You're grasping, Father. Seeing connections that don't exist to explain that which cannot be explained."

"The gods gifted us their stories so that we might understand our own lives." Snorri gripped Bjorn's shoulders. "The gods brought you back to me so that I might find Freya. And it seems the gods desire you to be the one to keep her life safe so that I might achieve all that has been foreseen. It is your destiny."

A shiver ran over me as the wind swirled, snowflakes melting on my outstretched palm as I waited to see how Bjorn would respond. Only to have my stomach sink as he spat, "No. I'll have no part of this." He twisted on his heels and stormed away.

Silence stretched.

"He'll come to see reason," Snorri finally said. "The gods demand it. Now let us feast."

I said nothing as I followed him and Ylva to the great hall, but in my mind was a truth that Snorri had forgotten: Bjorn was unfated, which meant that no matter what the Norns planned for him, his destiny was his own to weave.

CHAPTER

7

After the servants swiftly repaired my dress, I was seated at the
table on the dais to Snorri's left, Ylva at his right. The clansmen and women filled the spaces of the many long benches,
the tables loaded with trenchers of food and pitchers of mead. The
hall itself was decorated with garlands, and through the smell of
woodsmoke and cooking was the sharp scent of pine. The villagers
came one after another to offer us their well-wishes, but for all they
spoke kind words, the sideways looks they gave me were of mistrust
and uncertainty.

It was hard to blame them.

I'd walked into their lives, burned and bloody, usurped their beloved
lady's husband, and then caused a ritual to turn into utter chaos. All
because twenty years ago, some seer had spoken words to their lord that
I had the power to unite the fractured clans of Skaland and make Snorri
their king.

It felt like something out of a skald's story, except I'd been raised to
honor the gods and look for the signs they left us, so no part of me
believed that the seer's words were untrue. But that didn't mean I didn't
have questions.

Exactly how was I intended to unite the people? What had the seer seen me doing that would accomplish such a feat?

Yes, I was a child of a god, possessed of magic, but Hlin was a *minor* god. Bjorn had the blood of Tyr in his veins, one of the most powerful gods. A god of war and a leader, but also a bringer of justice. It made sense for someone like Bjorn to do the deeds the seer had foretold, but instead his only role in the foretelling had been to provide the fire that would reveal my name.

Which . . . *had* happened.

It made me wonder if Snorri's theory was true. Did the gods see Bjorn's fate entwined with mine? Was he crucial to the seer's foretelling coming to pass?

I lifted my right hand to bite at my fingernails, only to remember that I once again wore the gloves Ylva had given me. Though now I wasn't certain whether her desire was to cover my scars or to cover the mangled tattoo on my right palm lest it stir up more conflict than it already had.

Conflict that had driven Bjorn away and kept him away all through the feast, for he clearly wanted no part of the future his father envisioned for him.

And given my own circumstances, I could understand that.

Nibbling on a piece of chicken, I again scanned the crowd for him, but my thoughts were interrupted by a soft voice.

"Freya?"

Standing before the dais was the beautiful woman who'd been with Snorri when I'd fought Bjorn. As pale of skin as I was myself, she wore a crimson gown of delicate wool that again revealed her ample cleavage, the fabric clinging to the full curves of her hips. Her light brown hair was loose tonight, falling in ringlets to her waist, the only weapon she wore a small seax fastened to her belt. Again, I was struck with a strange sense of distance from her. As though while she stood before me, seeing and hearing and smelling the festivities, she stood apart.

"We've not been properly introduced. My name is Steinunn," the woman said. "I am Jarl Snorri's skald."

Only then did I notice the crimson tattoo of a harp on the side of her neck, the strings pulsing with each beat of her heart. Not just any skald, but a child of the gods as sure as I was myself, though her blood came from Bragi. I'd never witnessed a performance myself, but I'd been told that a skald's song would grant visions that transported listeners into the story. I'd heard that they only served jarls and kings who could afford to keep them in fine form, which explained Steinunn's rich attire, but I'd never heard Geir speak of her. "Have you served Snorri a long time?"

Steinunn shook her head. "No. I came to join him when I heard of the seer's foretelling that he would become king. To chronicle such a tale in a song will bring me great honor and fame, and I . . ." She trailed off, hesitating before shaking her head. "There was no reason to remain where I was."

There was a story in that hesitation, but before I could press, the skald swiftly said, "The jarl wishes me to speak to you so that I might hear your story of your inking. I am composing a ballad to spread *your* fame."

Glancing sideways, I saw Snorri and Ylva embroiled in a conversation with two men, neither paying me an ounce of attention. "You weren't there?"

"I was," the skald answered. "I saw what everyone else saw. Yet I know that was not all that transpired. If you tell me your story, I will sing it and all who hear will know the truth of the moment."

My own screams echoed in my head along with the remembered agony of being torn apart, my beating heart exposed. Shivering, I shook my head. "It was a mercy no one saw."

"Ylva saw something, which makes sense as it was her ritual. Yet Bjorn also saw." Steinunn tilted her head. "It will make a better story if I might sing of what fate he was so desperate to spare you from."

"Then ask him." I was being rude, but this felt like being accosted by a village gossip who you knew would share everything you said with anyone who would listen.

Steinunn gave me a rueful smile. "I'd as soon get water from a stone as stories from Bjorn."

I opened my mouth to tell her to expect the same from me, but the doors to the great hall chose that moment to swing inward, Bjorn appearing in a swirl of wind and snow. Many shouted his name in greeting, and he laughed, accepting a drink before sitting across the table from some of Snorri's other warriors.

"Perhaps later," I said to Steinunn, though I barely noticed her nodding and retreating into the feast as a pretty redhead sat next to Bjorn. She said something to him, her lips pressed against his ear, and whatever it was made him laugh, the deep sound reaching me even over the din. Encouraged, the redhead slipped an arm around his neck, her other hand toying with the front of his shirt.

A flicker of annoyance made my toes curl, and I took several mouthfuls of mead to drown it. But the sensation refused to be banished. After what had occurred during the ritual, why did he think it was acceptable to carry on like nothing had happened? Like he hadn't watched me ripped in two and then risked releasing calamity by breaking the circle of runic magic to help me?

Like his destiny wasn't entwined with mine?

Chewing on the insides of my cheeks, I tried to look everywhere but at them, but my eyes kept jumping back to Bjorn and the redhead, sourness filling my stomach. The sourness of jealousy, which I had no right to feel. Yet it was too easy to remember when I'd been the recipient of his flirtation and, irrational as it was, I hated that our moment was obviously a regular occurrence for him.

Men who look like him constantly have women flirting with them, I told myself. *Bjorn likely puts as much thought into flirtation as he does to breathing, both are so common to him.*

Rational thought after rational thought marched through my head, but they did as much good as spitting into the wind as my temper flared hotter with each passing second. I took another large mouthful of my drink, alcohol buzzing loudly in my veins and drowning good sense.

He obviously thought he could forget about everything that had happened. That he could go on with his life exactly as he wanted while I was stuck married to Snorri, my every breath under scrutiny and control, and my family's well-being held over my head if I so much as considered a wrong move. Yet Bjorn could just say *no* and never suffer an ounce of consequence for doing so.

"I don't think so," I muttered. Though I knew it was the drink talking, I rose from my chair and circled the table, making my way down into the chaos. People moved to make space for me, giving me nods of wary respect, and someone pressed a full cup into my hand. I took a long swallow to drown what remained of my sagacity, if I possessed any at all, then squeezed between the two warriors sitting across from Bjorn. "I need a word, Bjorn. In private."

He pulled his attention from the redhead long enough to say, "Save your words for tomorrow. Preferably later in the day because I don't plan to get much sleep tonight."

The redhead giggled and I scowled, heat rising to my face. My first instinct was to leave. Well, not my first . . . my first was to toss the contents of my cup in his face and *then* leave. "I wish to discuss Snorri's theory. Either you speak to me alone or you speak to me in front of everyone. Your choice."

Eyebrows rose on all within earshot, several chuckling as though I were nothing more than a silly girl who'd had too much to drink and would regret it tomorrow. I refused to acknowledge that they might be right.

"There is nothing to discuss." Bjorn smirked at the redhead, and I curbed the urge to bounce my cup off the side of his head. "You'll learn soon enough, but my father is remarkably adept at twisting stories and myths so that they support his way of thinking. If a bird shits on his head, he'll find a story to spin to make it seem a message from Odin himself. But sometimes, Freya, it's just shit."

As he said the last, he turned away from the redhead. His gaze latched on my balled-up fists. "Why are you wearing gloves in this heat?"

"Because of what lies beneath," I snapped, feeling the attention of those around us. From their frowns, several appeared not to take kindly to Bjorn's words about his father, though I doubted he cared. "You saw the scars. The tattoos. The gods clearly believe I needed a reminder that actions have consequences but that doesn't mean I need to stare at the consequences all night."

Bjorn's eyes lifted from my hands to meet my stare. "I thought you had no regrets."

"I don't." And I didn't.

He rested his elbows on the table. "Then why are you hiding your hand?"

I blinked, struggling for words because my hand wasn't what I'd come here to talk about. "Because it's ugly. That's why. No one wants to look at it, least of all me!"

Bjorn leaned across the table, mouth next to my ear. "Nothing about you is ugly, Freya, least of all the scars you earned defending your honor and family," he said. "And those tattoos are a sign you have the blood of a goddess in your veins. You should wear them with pride, not hide them as though they were a brand of shame."

"This isn't what I came to talk about." My pulse was roaring. "How I look is *not* of any importance."

Bjorn drained his cup, setting it on the table with a thud. "Then take them off. Take them off and we'll discuss whatever it is you wish to discuss."

I swallowed hard, feeling Ylva's eyes burning into me. "You're drunk."

"So are you." He leaned across the table again. "Take them off, Freya, or I'll start to wonder if you have regrets. And if you have regrets, I might start to feel differently about you."

I twitched, the admission that he thought much of anything of me somehow startling. "I care little about what you, or anyone else, think of me."

"Prove it."

His voice was full of challenge, and the challenge called to my soul. Made me want to rise to it. I was no coward, and even if proving so meant doing something stupid, I fully intended to do it. "Fine."

Jerking off the gloves, I tossed them into the fire, the white wool turning to ash. Then I turned and rested my elbows on the table, fingers interlocked, and stared him down. Never mind that my heart was galloping. "Satisfied?"

His expression changed, but not to disgust. Instead, devilish delight made his eyes sparkle, the slow smile that formed on his lips making my heart skitter. "Not yet."

In a flash of motion, he leapt on top of the table, reaching down for me.

"What are you doing?" I demanded, but Bjorn didn't grace me with an answer, only closed his hands over my wrists and lifted me as though I weighed no more than a child.

"Lift your cups," he roared. "Drink in honor of Freya the shield maiden, child of Hlin and lady of Halsar! Skol!"

He pulled my right hand into the air as everyone in the hall roared "*Skol,*" hammering their fists on tables and their feet on the floor. Then they lifted their cups and drank. Someone pushed a cup into my hand as my gaze met Ylva's. The true lady of Halsar was not cheering. Yet though her eyes were cold as frost, she lifted her cup to her lips and drank.

As did I. I swallowed mouthful after mouthful of mead, some escaping to pour down my chin, then slammed my cup down on the table next to my feet. Only then did I realize that Bjorn still gripped my wrist, for he drew me back up and said, "What was it that you wanted to ask me?"

I hesitated, and he tilted his head. "No one can hear you over the noise."

That was definitely true, for men and women still toasted, cups clacking together and mead spilling everywhere. But that didn't mean they weren't watching. My tongue felt thick; nonetheless I forced myself to ask, "Do you believe what your father said is true? About you? And me? That you're destined to keep me safe."

All the laughter faded from Bjorn's eyes and my heart sank. "No, Freya. Believe what you will. But please don't believe that."

"Freya."

I jerked, turning to find Snorri looking up at me, Ylva standing a few paces back.

"It's time." His voice was grave, and that, more than his words, made me understand *exactly* what he meant. The marriage needed to be consummated to be legitimate, and all here would bear witness with their ears. I bit the insides of my cheeks, not certain whether it made me feel better or worse that Snorri didn't look particularly happy with what was about to occur.

You can do this, I told myself. *You will do it.*

Giving him a tight nod, I moved to get off the table but Bjorn's grip on my wrist held me back. I turned to look up at him, his expression intense although I wasn't certain what emotions lay behind his eyes. "Not all scars we earn are skin-deep, Freya Born-in-Fire." He loosened his grip, my hand sliding through his. Though my scarred palm was numb, I swore I felt his fingers trail across it, and the sensation caused me to shiver. "There is no less honor in them."

"Born-in-Fire," I repeated, unsure of how I felt about the moniker, only that hearing it made my skin prickle and my heart race.

Snorri's hand closed around my left wrist. He tugged me off the table and led me through the hall, Ylva following, all the revelers cheering and toasting us as we passed. I stared at the door to the chambers that must be those he shared with Ylva, my feet like lead and every instinct telling me to pull away. To run.

But I would not run. I was Freya Born-in-Fire, and I would do whatever it took to protect my family. So instead I squared my shoulders.

And followed him in.

CHAPTER

8

The room was larger than the whole of my childhood home. The walls were decorated with hangings and the floors with furs, and a hearth glowed with a banked fire to ward away the chill. But it was the bed, large enough to fit an entire family, that immediately drew my eyes.

You're no maid, I chided myself. *It isn't going to hurt.*

Words that meant little, for it was not the fear of pain that made my skin crawl, but revulsion at having to sleep with a man for whom I held no affection. No desire. All while his wife looked on.

Born-in-Fire.

"Disrobe."

Clenching my teeth, I started to unfasten my dress, but froze as Ylva blurted out, "I can't do this."

Turning, I found the lady of Halsar doubled over, hands pressed to her face. "I thought I was strong enough to see this through," she whispered. "But to have you bed another woman? It's too much to endure again. It will break me."

Snorri's expression softened and he knelt before his wife. "My love, you know you possess my heart. This"—he gave a backward gesture to me—"is a political arrangement. My heart and body care nothing for this woman, but the gods wish for her to be under my control, so it must be done."

Ylva burst into tears, and guilt bit at my insides. All this time, I'd thought her nothing more than a bitch bent on making my life miserable because she enjoyed it. Not once had I considered how it must feel to watch your beloved husband take another wife.

Snorri pulled her into his arms. "There is no choice, Ylva. You know this. Unless the marriage is consummated, it will not be legitimate. Our enemies will learn of this and fight between one another to steal her away, just as in the vision Hlin granted. Freya will be destroyed and Skaland will remain fractured and weak."

I held my breath, because as much as I did *not* want to have sex with this man, the agony of being ripped in two was all too vivid. All paths led to pain, but at least the former was one I knew I could endure.

Ylva lifted her head. Though her fair skin was blotchy and her eyes red, her voice was steady as she said, "What if there was another way? One that did not require you to share her bed?"

"No matter what we do, the gods will know this marriage is not legitimate." Snorri gave a sharp shake of his head. "They will not favor me if I don't bend to their will."

"But is *this* truly their will?" Ylva wiped at her eyes. "The foretelling said nothing of marriage, nothing of consummation, only of control. The gods surely wish for you to wield her like a weapon, not beget a child upon her to leash her heart."

Sickness washed over me. Had that been their plan? To tie me to them with a child?

"What alternative do you suggest?"

Ylva's jaw tightened, and she looked to the floor. "We could use the runes."

Witchcraft. Sorcery. Every instinct told me to run, even as logic whispered that I wouldn't get far.

"I could bind her to you." Ylva's voice grew stronger, likely bolstered by the fact Snorri had yet to dismiss her plan. "By oath."

I swallowed hard, my eyes skipping back and forth between the pair. No matter what, I was trapped in this situation. The only uncertainty that remained was which tie would bind me: my body or my word. And I knew which I'd prefer. Knew that I'd do anything, swear anything, to keep a child from being caught up in this nightmare. "I'll swear an oath."

Their heads swiveled, eyes latching on me with such intensity that it was hard not to cringe. But I had to persevere. "It must be on the condition that Snorri swears never to touch me."

If he was offended, Snorri didn't show it, only rubbed his bearded chin and then turned to his wife. "If anyone were to learn of this magic, your life would be in danger, my love. For the only way to break the spell is your death."

"Then we continue the deceit that I am your wife," I said. "The gods enjoy cleverness, so they will look upon the deception as a brilliant strategy worthy of a king."

The moment the words exited my lips, Snorri's eyes brightened, reference to his promised destiny washing away what uncertainty he had for Ylva's plan.

Outside the room, the revelers were shouting and laughing, lewd comments floating through the walls, most of them suggestions for Snorri, and tension mounted.

"The people will want proof of consummation to believe it," he said.

Don't be a pawn, a voice whispered in my head. *Find ways to take control!* "Fake it," I said. "It isn't as though they expect the evidence of a maid, so Ylva will provide as much proof as I would. None would dare call their jarl a liar."

Ylva's eyes flared. Crossing the room, she caught hold of my arms, her fingernails digging deep into my skin as she pushed me against a wall, her mouth close to my ear as she said, "I don't trust you."

The feeling was mutual, but I was flush on the tiny bit of power I'd gained.

"The best alliances," I said softly, "are those in which each party holds something against the other. Let us be the best of allies, Ylva."

"If you *ever* betray us," she whispered, "I won't just kill you. I'll make you watch while everyone you care about is carved apart, piece by piece, and when you are reduced to a broken thing, I'll bury you alive."

I believed her. Believed this woman would do *exactly* what she threatened, and for that reason I would not cross her. But that didn't mean I needed to be cowed by her. Not blinking, I said, "Understood."

"Cast the spell, Ylva," Snorri said. "Let us cement the control that will deliver me my destiny."

I watched in silence as Ylva retrieved a silver plate, setting it on a table. Removing a knife from her belt, she made a shallow cut on Snorri's palm, allowing the blood to pool in the center of the plate. Then she motioned to me. "Give me your hand."

"Don't cut the tattoos," Snorri warned. Ylva scowled but drew her blade across the back of my arm.

I winced but said nothing as she held the wound over the plate, my blood dripping down to mix with Snorri's.

With her finger, Ylva swirled the blood together and then used it to paint runes around the edge of the plate. "Freya," she said. "Repeat after me. I vow to serve no man not of this blood."

If I said these words, I'd be bound for the rest of my life. Or at least the rest of Ylva's. But the alternative was so much worse. "I vow to serve no man not of this blood."

"I vow allegiance to him who is of this blood. I vow to protect, at all cost, him who is of this blood. I vow to speak no word of this bargain except to him who is of this blood."

I repeated the words.

"Now you, my love."

Snorri was silent for a long moment, then he said, "Before the eyes of the gods, I vow loyalty of my body and heart to my one true wife."

Ylva's eyes jerked up and there was no mistaking the swell of emotion in them. "You honor me." Then she drew a final rune on the plate and everything, including the pool of blood, flared bright before disappearing into smoke. "It is done."

I felt no different, and I wasn't certain if that was a good or a bad thing, for part of me wished to feel the weight of what we'd done.

Ylva moved to retrieve a dark cloak, which she draped over my shoulders before pulling up the hood. "I'll not have you watching."

I shrugged, allowing her to push me toward the rear wall. Beneath the rug was a trap door, and as Ylva opened it, night air rushed into the room. "Stay in the hole," she said. "Do not wander."

I could easily have turned my back and covered my ears, but offered no argument, only dropped into the opening. Almost immediately, I heard the sounds of kissing, and though I was no prude, I had no desire to hear more.

Removing the pieces of wood concealing the escape tunnel, I climbed outside. It was a dark night, the moon and the stars obscured by heavy clouds that smelled of more snow, and I leaned against the great hall as I tightened my cloak against the chill.

Laughs and shouts echoed through Halsar, and I kept to the shadows as several men staggered into the village, arms clasped around shoulders as they sang. From inside, drummers had struck up and there'd be dancing and merriment until dawn. On any other day, I'd be in the thick of it, laughing and singing and drinking until I was sick. But all I wanted to do now was cling to the cold shadows, my heart devoid of cheer.

Born-in-Fire.

I frowned, reexamining my poor humor. On the surface, it felt as though I'd made many concessions, but was that truly the case? Though we'd only just met, I'd spent my life sworn to Snorri as the jarl of these lands. The only thing that had changed was that now magic bound me to the oaths I'd inherited from my father. There was little point in dwelling, for the deal was done. Better to dedicate my mind to understanding how I was expected to achieve the results the gods foresaw for me.

How better to learn that than from the individual who had seen my future.

Lifting my head, I scanned the darkness. What were the chances that Snorri didn't keep the individual who'd spoken his precious prophecy close? I hadn't seen Odin's mark, which I knew was a raven, on anyone at the feast, but that didn't mean the seer wasn't somewhere in the village. And this might be my only chance to speak with them without someone looming over my shoulder.

Praying that Snorri would take his time with Ylva, I stepped away from the hall. I kept my head low as I strode down the narrow path between buildings. Mud squished beneath my shoes, my nose filling with the smell of dung and fish and woodsmoke, the homes quiet, for nearly everyone was at the great hall celebrating. From time to time, I passed men standing next to small fires, ostensibly on watch duty, but none paid me any mind.

The faint breeze sent wooden wind chimes swaying, the soft clicks welcome after the noise in the hall, and I walked past building after building, searching for the symbols that would mark one as a seer's abode. I found nothing, eventually reaching the docks stretching out into the black fjord. Walking to the end of them, I paused to take several deep breaths.

I'd never spoken to a seer before. They were either in the service of a jarl or too expensive for any but the most desperate and wealthy to consult, and my mother always said knowing the future was a curse because, good or bad, you couldn't change it.

Except that *I* could. The one drop of blood Hlin had gifted me gave me the power to change my fate.

Though how I'd know whether I was succeeding in changing it was a mystery to me.

Without a clear picture of the future, every action that I took might be already woven by the Norns.

Thinking about it made my head hurt. All I wanted was to stand on the docks with the cold air filling my lungs until my mind cleared. Except Snorri and Ylva might have already noticed my absence, and I'd probably pushed them far enough tonight.

One more moment, I told myself. *A dozen more breaths.*

Then my skin prickled.

Cursing myself for wandering off without even a knife, I spun on my heel, my heart leaping into a gallop at the sight of a shadowy figure a few paces behind me. My lips parted, a scream for help rising, and then I recognized the height and breadth. "Bjorn? What are you doing here?"

"I might ask you the same thing." His voice was strange and clipped, and unease filled my chest as I grappled for a lie.

"Ylva was upset. Snorri wished time to make things up to her."

Bjorn gave a soft snort. "Twice in one night. Didn't think the old bastard had it in him."

"What are you doing out here?" I repeated the question, mostly because I wasn't certain whether I should be worried that he caught me wandering alone.

"Wasn't in the mood to celebrate."

He took a step forward and I instinctively took a step back, my heel finding the edge of the dock. "Neither am I." Hesitating, I added, "This wasn't where I expected to find myself. Nor the path I'd have chosen, but unfated as everyone says that I am, I still find myself trapped."

Bjorn went still. "You could run."

Could I? Could I race away into the night and find myself a simple life that didn't violate the oaths I'd made? Maybe, but my family would pay the price. "I can't."

He huffed out a breath, frustration seeming to ripple out from him. "How did I know you'd say that?"

My unease suddenly turned to trepidation, though I wasn't entirely certain why. "What difference does it make to you?"

"Every difference." His hands balled into fists, but then he abruptly went still. "Do you hear that?"

I inhaled and exhaled, listening, then a rhythmic sound filled my ears. It came from the water and grew louder with every passing second.

Oars. The sound was oars moving in their locks, blades splashing into the water.

Not a single set, but many.

Bjorn stepped up next to me, both of us peering out at the water. My skin turning to ice as I spotted the shadow of not one vessel, but the shadows of *many*.

Raiders.

"Fuck," Bjorn snarled, then caught hold of my arm, both of us racing down the dock. There wouldn't be much time, and I prayed that the warriors enjoying my wedding festivities were armed and sober enough to swing a weapon.

I *knew* raids. Had lived through them. Had lost friends and family to them. They were vicious and bloody, and the victors rarely spared *anyone* they caught.

And Halsar was far from prepared for an attack.

Mud splattered my skirts as we crossed the beach. We had minutes, if that, before the drakkar hit shore, and then the enemy would sweep through the streets, killing as they went. And they shouldn't even be here. "There is still ice on the water. How are the Nordelanders raiding so early?"

"Whoever it is isn't here to raid—they're here for you!"

For me? "Why?" I demanded between gasped breaths. "How could anyone even know I'm here?"

"Because the foretelling is no secret," he answered. "And every jarl across Skaland has been watching and waiting for the day Snorri found you so that they can put you in your grave."

The sweat pouring down my skin seemed to freeze to ice. "Why do they want me dead?"

A stupid question, because I knew.

Bjorn looked down at me, his eyes shadowed. "Very few relish the idea of being ruled."

Dragging me behind the great hall, Bjorn slid to a stop next to the entrance to the escape tunnel. "Get inside. Warn my father." Then he broke into a sprint toward the front entrance.

I crawled on my hands and knees in the mud, and then slammed my hands against the trap door. "Snorri! Ylva! Raiders!"

The trap door swung open, revealing a bare-chested Snorri. "Raiders," I gasped out again. "Many ships. They'll have landed by now." Remembering that I wasn't supposed to have ventured out, I added, "I heard the warning shouts!"

"Raiders?" Ylva demanded. "Not possible! There is too much ice on the strait for Nordeland to come."

"Well, then it's another jarl," I snapped. "If you don't believe me—"

Shouts of alarm filtered in from the main hall, one name being repeated over and over again.

"Gnut!" Snorri roared the name, his eyes blazing in fury. Reaching down, he hauled me into the room.

Gnut Olafson was jarl of the territories to the east of us, familiar to me only because his stronghold was one fjord over from my village and we often needed to pay his warriors to leave us be. Close as Gnut's territories were, he still must have had a spy within Halsar with magical abilities to have learned of my identity so soon. The means mattered little, though; he was here now. All because of me. Because of what I would supposedly do. And he was here to kill me. "I need a weapon."

Snorri leveled a finger at me. "You need to stay here with those who can't fight, where you can be kept safe."

"But I *can* fight!" For the first time in my life, I finally had the chance to defend my people against raiders without hiding my magic and it was being taken from me.

"For twenty years I hunted you." Snorri gripped my arms hard enough that I'd have bruises tomorrow. "I refuse to lose my promised destiny within hours of possessing you."

Possessing. The word made my muscles tighten as though my body itself rejected such a notion, but I said nothing as I watched him pull on a shirt and then a vest of mail before belting on a sword. "Keep her here," he ordered Ylva, then strode out into the chaos of the great hall.

I paced back and forth as Ylva pulled a dress over her naked body, which was a combination of long lines and rich curves that helped explain Snorri's devotion to her, though in my opinion even perfect breasts couldn't compensate for her personality. "Don't be frightened, Freya," she said. "Snorri will defeat him, and Gnut's people will see the smoke from the pyres of their dead warriors when they wake in the morning. It will be an omen that the foretelling is coming to fruition, and respect for Snorri will grow."

I wasn't afraid. I was furious. People would die tonight defending me, and instead of battling alongside them, I was hiding with the helpless. "Our people will die, too. Don't you care about them?"

"Of course I care," she snapped. "I wish for our people to be strong—strong enough that no one dares to attack us, and the only way for that to happen is for Skaland to be united. You will make that happen."

"How?" I was in her face, though I didn't remember moving. "I am the child of a minor god, my magic useful only in protecting myself in combat. What is it that you believe I can do that will cause all of Skaland to follow Snorri?"

"Only the gods know, but whatever you do, our skald will see. And she will sing the songs of your exploits across all of Skaland until every man and woman swears an oath to Snorri."

"All she will sing, then, is that I hid from danger in the great hall like a child." I turned and walked out of the room.

The hall was empty of warriors, with only women, children, and the elderly sitting silently where before they had danced, the garlands hanging from pillars and rafters drooping, the remains of the feast congealing on the platters. It smelled of mead and vomit and fear, and it took all my restraint not to force my way out the doors, because this was *not* where I belonged.

I needed a weapon. I needed to defend these people. I needed to *fight*.

Spotting the sword Snorri had gifted me at the wedding ceremony where it leaned against my chair, I reached for it before remembering the dull blade. Then my eyes latched on my father's sword. Snorri's sword, now, but I didn't care as I picked it up, examining the keen edge.

Sharp enough to cut. Sharp enough to kill.

Tossing aside my cloak, I strode toward the doors, but Ylva's voice stopped me in my tracks. "On your life, you do not allow her to leave."

The two men she'd been speaking to shifted in front of the doors, their arms crossed, weapons in hand. Seasoned fighters from the look of them, but if I took up one of the many shields decorating the hall and called my magic, there was a chance I could get past them.

Except what if I hurt them in the process?

Injuring warriors, and potentially myself, when there was a battle raging outside and dozens of innocents inside needing protection, was a stupid plan.

A better plan would be to find another way out.

"Fine." I lowered my sword, but as though sensing my thoughts, Ylva said, "The room is locked, Freya. Sit down, pour yourself a drink, and stay out of trouble."

Gods, but I was beginning to loathe this woman. Gritting my teeth, I took a seat at a table near the edge of the room, sword rested across my thighs.

Screams and shouts filtered through the walls. Clansmen and women who hadn't been at the feast and who were fleeing Gnut's warriors, and part of me started to worry that I didn't need to leave to find the fight.

Because it would find me.

Drumming my fingers on the table, I considered my options. Either fight the men barring my path or try to get through the locked doors to Snorri's quarters, then out through the escape tunnel. Neither guaranteed success.

The screams outside clawed at my insides. Every muscle in my body tensed, needing to move. Children wept in their mothers' arms, all of them knowing what would come if the hall was breached. All of them knowing it would be our bodies that burned, the smoke rising like that which escaped through the—

Opening above.

I flicked my gaze to the hole in the roof of the great hall, not even visible in the shadows, though I knew it was there. Big enough for me to fit through if only I could climb into the rafters without anyone noticing.

Except what could I do from the rooftop?

The answer lay in a bow and quiver someone had left behind, likely in favor of a shield and blade. Getting to my feet, I strode to the table the weapons leaned against, slinging them over my shoulder before heading to a ladder leading to the upper level.

"What are you doing?" Ylva snapped.

"If they get in," I answered, "I'll kill as many as I can."

The lady of Halsar eyed me warily, wisely concerned that I might put an arrow in her back, but there was little she could say with everyone else looking on.

I climbed up to the narrow space filled with cots and personal belongings. I leaned against the railing, waiting for Ylva to stop checking that I wasn't trying to escape. Which didn't take long.

Fists pounded against the doors, the people outside screaming to be let in. I half expected Ylva to deny them, but she gave the warriors at the doors a tight nod and they lifted the beam, a tide of bloodied and terrified people flowing inside.

This was my chance.

Eyeing the beams and rafters while I tucked my skirts into my belt, I took one final look to ensure no one was watching, then climbed. I'd spent my youth chasing after my brother, which meant climbing many trees, and I put the skills to good use as I heaved myself up, doing my best to remain silent. This high, the smoke was chokingly thick and a cough slipped from my throat.

"She's in the rafters!"

Shit.

Not bothering to look down, I reached for the opening and hauled myself onto the roof of the great hall. Blinking and coughing, I crawled down the broad center beam, my tears finally clearing away in the thinning smoke so that I could see.

Part of me wished I'd remained blinded.

All through Halsar, homes burned, and in the streets, battle raged. Small groups of warriors fought against one another, men and women falling on both sides. It was too dark to make out faces, but there was one whose identity there was no mistaking.

Bjorn fought alone against a group of warriors, his axe a glowing blur as it arced through the air, a shield in his other hand. I watched in stunned silence as he sent a warrior's weapon spinning away, then reversed his momentum, axe cutting deep into the man's neck. Stepping over the body, he blocked a blow from another warrior with his shield, then swung his axe. The man caught the blow with his own axe, the weapons locking. The haft of the man's weapon caught flame, but before he could retreat, Bjorn slammed his shield into the man's face. He dropped with a scream, trying to crawl away while clutching his ruined face, but Bjorn's axe sliced into his chest, the fiery blade cutting through metal and flesh with ease even as he lifted his other arm to block another attack.

His shield shattered.

Rather than falling back, Bjorn threw a broken piece at the attacker's face, then swung, his axe cutting through the man's sword like a hot knife through butter. The warrior twisted and broke into a run. He only made it a few paces before Bjorn threw his axe, the weapon embedding in the warrior's back. As the man fell, the flaming axe disappeared, only to reappear in Bjorn's hand, already swinging at the next opponent.

I realized then why Snorri had accused him of holding back when he'd fought against me, because this . . . this was not the warrior I'd battled. This seemed as though Tyr himself had stepped onto the mortal plane.

The skin on the back of my neck prickled and I turned.

Shadows approached the great hall from the south, moving silently and without torchlight, but there was no mistaking the way the moon glinted off metal. The attack from the water had only been a distraction while the bulk of Gnut's men came at Halsar from behind. Their goal, the great hall itself.

No. Not the great hall.

Me.

I was their goal, and they'd kill everyone in their path in order to achieve it.

Anger chased away my fear, and I knelt next to the opening in the roof to shout, "Ylva, another force approaches from the south! Send someone to warn Snorri!"

Not waiting for a response, I scuttled down the length of the great hall to the north end. "Bjorn!" I screamed, trying to get his attention. "They are attacking from the rear! Bjorn!"

But he couldn't hear me over the din, his attention wholly fixed on the danger before him. As was the attention of everyone else, none of Snorri's warriors aware of the threat approaching from the rear.

Below, one of Ylva's guards sprinted toward the battle. But before he'd gone a dozen paces, he dropped, an arrow sticking out of his leg. He crawled on hands and knees, and another arrow shot from the dark, scarcely missing him.

Extracting an arrow from my quiver, I searched the darkness for the archer and caught sight of a shadow. My arm quivered as I drew the bowstring, for the weapon was designed for someone much taller and stronger. Then I loosed the arrow.

It shot through the night, and the shadow I'd aimed at screamed.

But my efforts were in vain.

Another warrior raced out of the shadows between buildings. He lifted his axe high, and before I could nock another arrow, he sliced off the crawling man's head. I gasped as blood splattered, the man's corpse slumping to the muddy earth.

The warrior who'd killed him went still, then looked up, his eyes fixing on me.

Instinctively I crouched, but he only grinned and pointed at me. Blood dripped from his axe as he took up a torch, walking toward the great hall. If he set it ablaze, everyone inside would either burn or be forced out the doors to face the rapidly approaching wall of warriors coming from the rear.

It would be slaughter.

Pulling out another arrow, I ground my teeth and drew the bowstring, cursing my weakness as my arm shuddered. The arrow flew, striking the ground at the warrior's feet, and though I couldn't hear him, his shoulders shook with laughter.

I tried again and missed, a shriek of frustration tearing from my lips because I couldn't keep the bow steady enough to aim.

I drew another arrow, but the warrior stepped out of my line of sight, hidden by the edge of the roof. "Shit," I snarled, praying to all the gods that the wood would be too damp to burn even as I heard his mockery from below. "Turn over the shield maiden," he crooned. "Hand her to me and I promise we'll let you live."

A lie if I'd ever heard one, so I didn't bother responding.

Could I jump down and kill him? I moved to the midpoint of the building to eye the distance, my heart beating manically in my chest and my palms slick with sweat.

It was too far. With my luck, I'd break an ankle and that arsehole would cut off my head while I was writhing in pain. Besides, killing him wouldn't solve the problem, for as I looked south, it was to see that the rest of Gnut's forces now stood before the great hall, their shields raised high. "Give us the shield maiden," one shouted. "Give her to us and we'll go in peace."

More lies.

They'd slit my throat and then set the great hall on fire just for spite, killing everyone they could before Snorri and his warriors arrived to drive them back. Given the silence from within the great hall, those inside knew the same. Ylva was likely biding her time, praying her husband would arrive to save her.

And me.

Yet as Gnut's warriors stepped closer to the great hall, torches in hand, I knew rescue wouldn't come soon enough. At least, not from where Ylva expected it.

Crawling to the north end of the roof, I stared through the haze of smoke to the fjord where the enemy's ships rested against the beach. Then I moved my gaze to the building nearest the great hall. A long jump, but not nearly as long as the drop to the ground below.

I could do it. And then it would only be a matter of climbing down to warn Bjorn and the others.

Standing, I hooked the bow around my shoulders and carefully backed up several paces. I was an easy target for any archer, so I didn't hesitate. My shoes thudded against the wood as I sprinted down the beam, but the sound seemed distant as I stared at the gap between the buildings, my fear demanding that I stop. Begging that I not take this risk.

Born-in-Fire.

I jumped.

Cold wind whistled past my ears as I flew through the air, the roof of the building rushing to meet me. My feet struck first, jarring my spine, then I toppled forward to land on my hands and knees, thatch flying everywhere.

I crouched in place for a heartbeat, gasping for breath.

Then the roof collapsed beneath me.

CHAPTER

10

A shriek tore from my lips as I fell, cutting off as I landed on my back, the wind knocked out of me.

My desperate gasps for breath were deafening, my body aching from the impact and my ears full of the panicked squeal of the pigs whose pen I'd landed in. They raced around me, their hooves clipping my arms and legs, but it wasn't the pig shit that made my skin crawl. It was the certainty that I was running out of time.

Drawing my sword, I scrambled to my feet even as my eyes latched onto a shadowy figure coming through the open door.

"Have you lost your bloody mind?" Bjorn hissed, stepping into the light filtering through the hole in the roof. "What were you doing on the roof?"

Ignoring both questions, I stepped over a pig, cringing as one of my braids slapped me in the face, the hair covered in shit. I was lucky Bjorn had already given me a moniker because this was prime fodder for his humor. "There's another force at the south end of the great hall. The attack from the water was a diversion."

Bjorn swore. "We had guards stationed in the woods watching. That none brought warning means someone told Gnut where they were hidden and they've been killed."

I swallowed hard. "They're demanding Ylva hand me over or they'll put fire to the hall."

"They'll do that regardless." Bjorn reached into the pigsty and hauled me out. "You were right to escape. When my father discovers you gone, he'll believe you dead or that Gnut took you, which he can't take out on your family. Head south and don't stop until you're out of Skaland, and then never come back."

"What are you talking about?" I demanded. "I didn't jump to escape, you arse. I jumped because the great hall is full of people who need help. We need to find Snorri and bring him to the hall's defense."

"I'll warn him," he answered. "You run. Gnut is the first jarl to come for you, but he won't be the last. Far more dangerous men than him will soon turn their eyes on you."

A chill ran through me, but I shook my head. "I'm not abandoning my people to save my own skin."

I tried to pull away, but his grip was implacable as he said, "There is no saving the hall, Freya. My father is caught between two forces and half of his men are drunk. If it comes to it, he'll take you and abandon Halsar."

There were children in there, but I suspected that was not enough of a motivator. "Ylva's in there. They'll kill her."

"Ylva crawled out of the great hall. She ran, likely in search of Snorri. It's only a matter of time until they come looking for you and your chance at freedom will be lost. No matter what Ylva says, he'll sacrifice everyone in that hall for the sake of keeping warriors alive until they've sobered up, because he values their lives more than those hiding inside."

I believed that. Knew that Snorri's obsession with becoming king would drive him to sacrifice everything. But that didn't mean that I'd do the same. "What about you, Bjorn? Whose lives do you value?"

Silence.

I didn't know if that meant he agreed with his father or not, so I said, "I'm not standing by while innocents die in a fight over me. If you try to stop me, I'll stab you in the stomach."

Bjorn snorted. "How do you propose to save them? To run past them, shield blazing bright, and hope the whole lot of Gnut's army chases after you?"

"Hardly." I lifted my sword. "I'm going to light his ships on fire and lure him down to the beach."

It was the best plan I could think of.

A fleet of drakkar would cost a fortune in time and gold to replace. When they saw the fire, Gnut's men would abandon the fight to save the vessels so they wouldn't lose their ability to retreat. At least, that's what I hoped.

"The ships will be under guard. Gnut's no fool—he'll protect his line of retreat."

My hands balled into fists. "Then help me."

Tension thickened between us, and I could hardly breathe. Not because I thought Bjorn would try to stop me but because I wanted him to help me. Wanted him to be the sort of man who'd do what it took to save all those in the hall. The breath I was holding came out in a gust as Bjorn finally said, "Lead the way, Born-in-Fire."

We moved through the darkness and flame of Halsar, stepping over bodies and avoiding skirmishes, the smell of smoke thick on the air. More than once I heard, "She can't have gotten far," and knew they were talking of me. Bjorn had been right that Snorri's focus was not on protecting his people but on finding me. I kept glancing backward, expecting to see great gouts of fire rising behind us. Expecting to hear screams as people either burned or fled, only to be cut down by the blades of Gnut's warriors. Expecting the lancing pain of knowing that I'd failed to help them at all.

"That they haven't fired the hall may mean they want you alive," Bjorn said softly. "Perhaps Gnut fancies himself a future king."

His words did *nothing* to ease my nerves.

We reached the edge of the town, Bjorn pulling me low, our shoulders pressed together as we eyed the beach and ships. I could feel the heat of him through the sleeve of my dress, almost as though fire burned inside of him as surely as it did the axe for which he was famed. He smelled of fresh-spilled blood and sweat, but also of leather and pine. Given the circumstances, I shouldn't have cared, but part of me cringed that I currently reeked of pig.

"We'll have to go in from behind," Bjorn murmured. "There are too many watching the ships to overpower without them sounding an alarm. Can you swim?"

"Yes." I unfastened my heavy dress, slipping it off my shoulders and dropping it in a heap, only to turn my head and find Bjorn watching me.

"This idea of yours improves with every passing moment," he said, a hint of laughter in his voice. "Thank you for convincing me to come with you. The first story I'll tell as I walk through the gates of Valhalla, which may happen sooner than I'd anticipated, is of the shield maiden who stripped near naked to charge into battle."

"I can't swim in a heavy dress," I snapped. "And I'm sure those in Valhalla will swiftly discover that your presence is much more tolerable when you keep your mouth shut."

He pulled off his blood-soaked shirt and tossed it aside. I scowled at him. "Why did you do that?"

"It's a very heavy shirt," he answered. "It might weigh me down. These too." Bjorn started to unfasten his belt, but I swatted at his hand, choice words rising to my lips until I saw a slice along his ribs, his side streaked with blood. "You're hurt."

"It's nothing." He reached down to pick up a stick about as thick as my wrist. "Leave the sword. You won't be able to swim with it. Take this instead."

I took the stick, shivering as wind blew over us, the thin shift I wore doing nothing to guard me from the chill. Bjorn moved to block the breeze, then murmured, "I'll light it once we're out of sight."

Keeping far away from the pooled torchlight of those guarding the drakkar, we crept down to the water. I flinched, the cold piercing my bones as I waded out, the depth eventually forcing me to swim. My breathing came in ragged little gasps, instinct demanding that I retreat, that I find somewhere warm, but a backward glance at the great hall in the distance gave me courage to press forward.

It was almost impossible to see, so I followed the faint sounds Bjorn made as he swam ahead, able to move more quickly, given he wasn't hindered by a stick. He circled around, then came at the drakkar from behind. Shivers wracked my body, my limbs growing stiffer with each passing second. Real concern that I might drown washed over me, and it was a relief when my feet struck ground. It was shallow enough to stand, though the swells of the fjord came up to my chin.

"I'll lift you into the drakkar," he whispered. "Light the sails and then get back in the water. We only want to draw them out of Halsar, not sink the fleet and force them to stand their ground. I'll get the other ship."

I gave a tight nod and then his hands closed over my hips. Despite the freezing water, his palms were hot through the soaked fabric of my shift, his hands big enough to span my hips, his thumbs pressing into the curve of my arse. The sensation sent a jolt of heat through me that was intensified when I felt his breath against my neck, my spine, and the backs of my thighs as he slowly lifted me to avoid any splash.

Catching hold of the side with my free hand, I checked to ensure no one was looking before hooking an ankle over and hauling myself in. Lowering the stick over the side, I waited.

"Tyr, grant me your flame," Bjorn whispered, and I cringed as his axe burned to life, the glow so bright it seemed impossible no one would notice. But the eyes of the warriors guarding the drakkar remained fixed on Halsar. Seconds later, the crackle of flames reached my ears. I lifted the burning stick and pulled it out of view within the drakkar, keeping low as I crawled toward the lowered sails. One eye on the guards, I held the flames to the folds of fabric, grinning as they caught.

Get back in the water. Bjorn's instructions repeated in my ears, but my eyes went to the drakkar next to the one I knelt in. What if Gnut's warriors refused to abandon the fight for a drakkar or two? What if they needed more incentive?

With mead still fueling my impulses, I jumped to the next drakkar as fire crawled up the mast behind me. Whether it was the crackle of flame or the sound of my feet hitting wood, I wasn't sure, but the warriors turned, their eyes widening in horror. "Fire!" one of them shouted, and I dived toward the sail, shoving the burning stick deep into the folds.

"Stop her!"

My pulse roared as feet thundered down the dock, and I lunged toward the edge of the drakkar and the relative safety of the water.

Only for my legs to jerk out from under me.

Cursing, I twisted to find my ankle tangled in a rope. And the warriors were nearly upon me.

Terror turned my skin to ice, my heart fighting its way up my throat as I fumbled with the rope, trying to jerk my foot free. But the loop only tightened.

"Come on," I pleaded, clawing at it with my scarred right hand, then switching to my left. "Come on!"

My nails scratched my skin as I got my fingers under the rope and pulled, managing to loosen the loop enough to get my foot free. Crawling to the edge, I tried to hurl myself over—

Only to be struck in the back with what felt like a battering ram.

I toppled and landed headfirst in the water, the weight of the warrior who'd struck me driving me down and down until I hit the rocky sea floor.

Panic pulsed through me and I twisted, clawing and scratching, doing everything I could to get out from under him. He only caught hold of my wrists, pressing them against the rocks hard enough to bruise.

I slammed my knees into his stomach and was rewarded with a rush of bubbles, but his hold didn't falter, his feet churning to hold us both down. Again, I tried to kick him, but I couldn't get leverage. Couldn't hit him hard enough to make him let me go.

Pressure grew inside my chest. My body jerked this way and that but I couldn't get free. And I needed to *breathe*.

Hlin, I begged, *help me!*

Magic surged inside me, waiting for me to use it, but my wrists were pinned. Which meant my magic was *useless*. I was useless.

And I needed to breathe. *Gods,* I needed to breathe!

Light flared overhead. A cloud of warmth washed over my face. The hands holding me down went limp.

I kicked my legs, trying to get to the surface for precious air, but I collided with the dead man.

Which way was up?

Which way was air?

My vision dimmed as my chest spasmed, my mouth opening to suck in air that was not there and—

Hands closed around my arms, hauling me upward. My head broke the surface right as I sucked in what had nearly been the last breath I'd ever take.

"I told you to get back in the water, not light the whole cursed fleet on fire!"

I was in no position to argue, only to gulp breaths as Bjorn pulled me away from shore. Away from the brilliant glow of fire and the desperate shouts of Gnut's warriors, who were tossing water on the flames.

"It's working," Bjorn said, the stubble of his chin brushing against my cheek. "They're retreating to save the ships. Look."

He was right. Warriors spilled out of Halsar, weapons sheathed in favor of buckets, the dozens of men working in frenzied unison to salvage the three ships we'd set ablaze.

Slowly, the flames faded to embers, but as the men stood with buckets in hand, a drumbeat filled the air.

From the darkness of the streets, Snorri and his warriors appeared. No longer scattered and disorganized and drunk, the men and women moved with shields locked in a wall that would be no easy task to breach. As one, they made their way to the beach before stopping. And waiting.

A massive man wearing a helmet started down the dock. He pulled his axe from his belt and my breath caught.

The battle wasn't over.

Despite all the death and destruction, they were going to keep fighting.

I'm not worth it, I wanted to scream. *I'm not worth all of this death!*

Except instead of attacking, the big man shouted, "Keep your shield maiden, Snorri. But know that every man here will die before calling you lord."

"Your deaths are already woven." The certainty in the statement made me shiver, and Bjorn's grip on me tightened for a heartbeat before relaxing as we watched the enemy turn their backs on Halsar.

It was over.

We'd won.

"Your first victory, Born-in-Fire," Bjorn murmured.

Fighting back a grin, I started to swim to the beach, only for my muscles to seize up from the cold. I floundered, but Bjorn's arm wrapped around me. "I've got you."

Though every muscle in my body screamed, I managed to say, "And here I thought your only value was your good looks."

"You keep telling me I'm good-looking," he answered as he pulled me back toward the beach. "If you aren't careful, I'm going to start to think your intentions toward me are less than honorable."

"Don't worry," I mumbled as he hauled me onto the beach, rocks digging into my back as I looked up at him. "Your looks aren't good enough to compensate for your tongue."

In the faint light, I saw him smirk. "Don't underestimate my tongue, Freya. Especially in the dark."

Despite being near frozen to death, my cheeks burned hot. "You have no shame."

"I am merely being honest, Born-in-Fire."

The cold had clearly turned my wits to ice because I was left grasping for a retort. Annoyed that he'd gotten the last word, I tried to stand. Only for my legs to buckle.

Bjorn caught me before my knees hit the rocks, pulling me onto his lap.

"I'm freezing."

"You're fine." Bjorn belied his words by pulling me against his warm chest. "Besides, you needed a bath. You reeked of pig shit."

"Bjorn," I muttered into his throat, "fuck you."

He laughed, and I felt it where my breasts were pressed against his chest, only the thin fabric of my shift separating my skin from his. He was so cursedly warm, and I snuggled closer, wanting to drain the heat from him into my numb flesh.

Bjorn's hand curved against the small of my back, and I found myself deeply aware of each flex of his fingers, for they sent spikes of sensation deep into my core. There was comfort in his touch, a safety that I'd never felt with a man before, and my sluggish mind slowly turned over why that might be, given I hardly knew him, before landing on the reason.

It was because there was no demand in his touch.

No sense that he intended to take anything from me or to use me the way so many others had. A touch entirely without agenda beyond chasing away the cold. Tension seeped from my body, and I relaxed against him, focusing on the steady beat of his heart. Slowly, my shivers eased, my pulse no longer a frantic beast running out of control. The numbness retreated from my limbs, sensation returning to my fingers, and I felt the hard muscle of his back beneath my grip.

I had no right to do so for many reasons, but, of their own accord, my fingers trailed over the burn scar running over his shoulder blade. Bjorn shivered and drew in a deep breath, the movement causing his stubbled cheek to brush the sensitive skin of mine. An ache formed between my thighs, and I became excruciatingly aware that my bottom, clad only in soaked linen undergarments, was pressed against him in a most intimate way.

My imagination drifted, painting an alternate world where it had been Bjorn I was wed to today. Where it was Bjorn's bedchamber I'd walked into. Where it was Bjorn who'd satisfy the lust in me that I'd always kept buried.

You hardly know him, I chided myself, but my body clearly thought it knew him well enough, for liquid heat formed between my legs. I shifted so that I could look at him, my eyes fixing on his full mouth. It was nearly always smirking, but not now. Instead, his lips were parted, his breathing as rapid as my own.

"Freya . . ."

I shivered at the sound of my name on his lips, his voice deep and rasping. But then, beyond, I heard the shouts of men and women, my name repeated over and over. They were searching for me, and if *anyone* found us like this, especially after what I'd negotiated with Ylva . . .

Gods, but I was an idiot.

Pushing away from him, I climbed to my feet, hoping he didn't notice that my legs could barely hold me upright. "They're looking for me."

Bjorn didn't answer, only rose with enviable grace, water dripping down his muscular torso to mix with blood that still oozed from the wound along his ribs. Without another word, he strode down the beach to where the warriors searched. I followed him, but slowly, allowing the distance between us to grow. It was a distance I needed to maintain, because clearly being close to Bjorn caused me to lose my head. I couldn't afford that, and neither could my family.

My skin grew colder as Bjorn drew away from me until he was nothing more than a dark shadow in the distance. If only the same could be said of the ember of *want* that burned in my heart.

P art of me had feared that Snorri would be furious that I'd dis-
       obeyed him. Instead, he was elated that it had been me who'd set
       fire to the ships, seeing it as proof of the veracity of the seer's
foretelling. That Bjorn had been as much behind the fires as I went in
one of Snorri's ears and out the other, and I was half tempted to tell
him that I'd be a corpse floating on the fjord if not for his son.

But Ylva's eyes dissected me with every word, so I bit my tongue,
knowing that if she suspected anything lay between me and Bjorn she'd
make both of us pay, one way or another. Better to say nothing, which
was easy, given that it was no moment for celebration. Victorious or
not, buildings in Halsar still burned, dozens of corpses cooled on the
ground, and many more screamed and cried from injuries.

At least a dozen men were brought to the great hall with injuries
so catastrophic, it seemed a miracle they were still breathing, and if
not for Liv's magic, they'd have gone to Valhalla before dawn lit the
sky.

But not even the healer could do anything for the dead.

Eighteen lives lost, I'd heard the servants whisper as I did what I
could to help those not mortally injured, cleansing wounds and wrap-

ping them tight with bandages. Most of them were warriors, but not all. A fact I had to face as I joined the procession down to the beach the following morning. Four pyres sat unlit, and as I set my eyes on the faces of the deceased, my chest tightened so painfully I could hardly breathe. Gnut's men hadn't just slaughtered those who'd opposed them, they'd slaughtered those they'd found sleeping in their beds. The very old. And the very young.

Logically, I knew the death toll would've been much higher if I hadn't given the early warning, yet it still felt like a failure. Hlin had granted me magic so that I might provide protection, and while my actions had helped end the battle, it had been too late for many. And I hated that. Hated that these people had died because men like Gnut and Snorri valued my life—or death—more than anything else.

Standing next to Ylva and Snorri, I toyed with the hilt of my father's sword, which I had kept. Snorri had said nothing about its absence, nor even seemed to notice that I had a weapon belted to my waist at all. Together, we watched an ancient woman conduct the rituals, the pyres piled with offerings, those watching either weeping or stone-faced. It wasn't long until the flames burned high, dark smoke rising into the clear sky and the scent of charring hair and flesh filling my nose. Snorri had ensured that all knew I'd lit the ships on fire, downplaying Bjorn's involvement, but I didn't fail to notice that many still cast dark gazes full of blame my way.

Discomfited, I looked away and my gaze locked on a hooded figure walking slowly down the waterline, obscured by haze. At first I thought it was only the smoke from the pyres. But as I watched, I realized the smoke was coming from the individual. Not just smoke, but bits of ember and ash, as though the individual were aflame.

"Ylva." I caught hold of her arm. "Look at that person. They're . . ."

My words trailed away, for the individual was gone.

"Who?" Ylva demanded, following my gaze, which led to the empty beach.

"There was a hooded figure walking," I said. "They . . . they looked as though they were burning, but I don't know where they went."

Ylva made a noise of annoyance. "Silence your tongue, girl. These people died for you—show them some respect."

My anger flared, because while Gnut might have come to kill me, I wasn't alone at fault. As guilty as I felt for the deaths and injuries, it still frustrated me that it was not their jarl the people held accountable, for he had failed to protect them despite knowing the threat. Yet none of that seemed to matter, for more and more people cast dark glares in my direction, their bodies tense with anger.

Only for every single one of them to abruptly turn back to the pyres as a wave of heat warmed the back of my neck.

Bjorn stood behind me and to my right, his axe ablaze in one hand, the flat of the blade resting against his bare forearm as though it were made of no more than steel. It was the first time I'd seen him since he'd told Snorri that I was responsible for the drakkar fires, and though I had more pressing concerns, my foolish mind instantly went to the moment on the beach when he'd held me against the cold. A good reminder of why I needed to stay as far away from him as I could.

"Where were you, Bjorn?" Snorri muttered. "You were supposed to light the pyres. You dishonor the dead in your absence."

"I slept late." Though there was nothing in his expression or tone to suggest he spoke anything other than the truth, I sensed he was lying. *Why?*

Snorri's frown deepened but before he could respond, I said, "There would be thrice their number if not for Bjorn's actions. The dead know that. As should the living."

Snorri gave a soft snort, turning back to the pyres, the smoke now rising in a tower that seemed to touch the clouds above. "Tonight we feast to honor the dead," he roared. "Tomorrow, we make plans for our revenge against Jarl Gnut!"

The people of Halsar howled their approval, warriors lifting their weapons into the air, but as I turned to follow Ylva and Snorri back to the great hall, I still felt the prickle of ill will directed at my back.

"I would speak to you, Freya," Snorri said as we approached the building. "And you as well, Bjorn."

My heart skittered with the sudden terror that someone had seen me and Bjorn on the beach or, worse, into my lustful heart, but Bjorn appeared unconcerned. Nodding, he extinguished his axe and strode through the doors into the great hall.

The injured were still being tended, and we walked past the rows of quiet forms and behind the large chairs on the dais before Snorri paused. "We must discuss your actions last night, Freya."

I held my breath even as Ylva, who'd been silent, snarled, "What must be discussed is her punishment. She defied your orders. Have her beaten for her actions lest she defy you again. She's supposed to be under your control, but last night demonstrated that she needs a tighter leash."

I opened my mouth to retort, but Bjorn beat me to it. "If anyone is to be beaten for failing my father's orders, it's you, Ylva."

Wouldn't that be an interesting turn of events, I thought even as Ylva glared at Bjorn, her eyes bright with anger. "As always, you speak out of turn."

"I speak the truth," Bjorn said with a laugh. "My father did not order Freya to remain in the great hall, he ordered *you* to keep her here. Which you failed to do. Not because she overwhelmed your every attempt to heed your husband's commands, but, by all accounts, because you failed to notice your shield maiden climbing into the rafters. You should be punished lest your attention wander again."

"Bjorn . . ." Snorri's voice dripped with warning, and indeed, I wanted to kick him in the shins, because all he was accomplishing was making tensions between me and Ylva worse.

"I speak only the truth that has been repeated by all who were here last night," Bjorn said. "You should be rewarding Freya for following her instincts, else Halsar, and most of its people, would be ash. And

Ylva, you should be on your knees thanking her for twisting the threads of fate, else you'd be the cause of all that death."

If I hadn't been dripping sweat from the anxiety currently twisting my stomach into ropes, I'd have laughed as Ylva's eyes widened with outrage.

Snorri rubbed at his temples. "You've made your point, Bjorn. As it is, I've no intention of beating anyone. Hlin warned us and we failed to take appropriate precaution. I don't intend to make the mistake of ignoring what else she revealed."

Bjorn's face blanched as understanding took hold. "I told you I wouldn't—"

"Your fate is entwined with Freya's," Snorri interrupted. "You are destined to use your strength and skills to protect her. But more than that, you must use them to teach her."

"I—"

"Freya has proven the gods favor her," Snorri said. "Yet the people grieve, blaming her for last night's raid. Some might go so far as to seek vengeance upon her, which you must protect her against. You must also help turn her into a warrior they see as worth following."

"I know nothing of teaching someone how to fight," Bjorn snapped. "This is—"

"These are the reasons I asked you here, Bjorn," Snorri continued. "Not to enjoy the sound of your voice, but because I would have *you* make her ready. I would have *you,* my son and heir, make a warrior of our shield maiden. I would have *you* teach her to fight in a shield wall. And"—he looked between the two of us—"because Hlin foresaw that it would be you who will keep her safe, *you* will remain at her side, day and night, until she has fulfilled her destiny."

Bjorn's green eyes darkened, his hands balled into fists. "This is not *my* destiny."

The last vestiges of Snorri's patience evaporated. "You are my son. You will abide or you will *leave.* Am I understood?"

For a heartbeat, I thought Bjorn would walk out, and a shocking stab of pain lanced through me. But he only clenched his teeth, the "Fine" that exited between them more growl than word. "Might I have one more night of freedom before you bind me to her?"

"One night," Snorri snapped. "But at dawn, you will join Freya and never leave her side."

I closed my eyes, silently cursing the gods for giving me what I wanted even as they took it away.

CHAPTER

12

S cowling, I stared at the sun, which, given it was late morning, was
high in the sky. Bjorn was supposed to have been at the great hall
an hour after dawn. My morning had been wasted sitting around
waiting, and I was thoroughly pissed off.

"Bjorn isn't much for mornings," Liv said, coming up from behind
me. "The only reason one typically sees him at dawn is because he's yet
to go to bed."

That didn't surprise me at all.

Liv, however, *had* been at the great hall at dawn, checking on the
progress of the injured. Despite the gravity of their wounds, several
had already departed, fully recovered, while others still suffered.
Some, I knew, had never woken up, the goddess Eir having declined
to save them. *How does she decide?* I quietly wondered, rubbing at the
fingerprint-shaped bruises on my arms from Snorri shaking me. *How
does the goddess choose who lives and who dies?* But instead of asking Liv
the question, I posed another. "You know him well?"

The healer shrugged. "As well as anyone, I suppose. I was raised on
a farm north of Halsar, but I didn't come to serve Snorri until after my
gift manifested, which was after Bjorn was taken to Nordeland."

I blinked. "Nordeland?"

One of Liv's eyebrows rose, then she shook her head. "I forget how things are in a small village, not knowing any of the events going on more than an hour's ride in any direction." She sighed. "There are days I'd give anything to go back to a life of blissful ignorance."

From someone else, namely Ylva, the words would have felt like an insult, but not from Liv. She was merely telling it as it was, not casting judgment. "I'd prefer not to be ignorant in this."

She gave a slight nod. "King Harald of Nordeland heard of the foretelling and, knowing a united Skaland would pose a danger to him, came to Halsar to kidnap Bjorn. He intended to hold him hostage so that Snorri would never move against Nordeland. Bjorn's mother was killed during the kidnapping. Burned alive, they say."

I pressed my fingers to my mouth, horrified.

"Snorri attempted to free Bjorn many times. But it was not until three years ago that he succeeded, and it was at great cost in ships and men. Yet well worth it, for Harald lost his hostage and Snorri regained the son whose magic had the power to reveal the shield maiden. Though there are some who wish he'd never returned."

"Ylva?" The lady of Halsar's name rose easily to my lips.

Liv sighed. "Yes. Snorri was handfasted to Ylva when Bjorn was conceived with Saga during a moment of indiscretion. Though Ylva now has a son by him, as firstborn, Bjorn remained his heir. Status which he couldn't claim as Harald's prisoner."

I twitched, remembering the night of the wedding, how Ylva had said she couldn't stand Snorri being with another woman again. The first instance must have been Bjorn's mother, and it had cost Ylva greatly.

"Ylva's son is alive, then?" I asked. "If he is, why haven't I met him?"

Liv nodded. "Leif is fifteen. He's on a hunting expedition with his cousins, though I expect he'll return soon enough. Snorri needs warriors more than Halsar needs meat."

This revelation explained the animosity between Bjorn and Ylva. "When Bjorn returned, he regained his status as heir?"

"Yes." Liv sat next to me on the bench, fixing her skirts. "But Leif has spent his whole life in Halsar and is Ylva's son, so there are many who'd prefer him to be Snorri's heir."

"But it's Bjorn's birthright," I said, not certain why I felt so defensive.

Liv smirked. "I see the flirt has won you over, though perhaps seeing the other side of his personality will cure you of that."

She jerked her chin toward the front of the hall, and I turned in time to watch Bjorn trip over the entranceway, nearly sprawling to the floor before catching his balance. Liv laughed, but my eyes only burned, because nothing about this was funny. Quite the opposite.

"You're late," I snapped at the same time as Liv said, "I hope you feel half as bad as you look, Bjorn."

He ignored me and grinned at her. "Not yet, but soon enough."

His meaning registered and a rush of anger surged through me. "Are you still drunk?"

"Not as drunk as I was." He turned his grin on me, but the straw stuck in his hair ruined the effect. That and the fact that I was angry enough to kick him in the balls. "Don't give me that look, Freya," he added. "I was only doing my best to enjoy my final hours of liberty before my father chains me to your side."

I balled my hands into fists, hating the hollowness forming in my stomach. "Your *liberty* ended several hours ago."

His gaze flattened. "And it already feels like eternity."

I rolled my eyes to hide the hitch in my breath, because his behavior stung. More than anyone in Halsar, I'd felt connected to him. He'd shown me kindness and respect and had defended me against Ylva. But it seemed all of that didn't matter as much as I'd thought. At least, not to him. "Get over it."

"As pleasant as this conversation is"—Liv rose to her feet—"I've better things to do than watch you two bicker."

Bjorn parroted her words as she walked away, which I was tempted to point out only *proved* them, but then he rounded on me. "Well? Are you ready?"

Don't let him get to you, I screeched at myself. *Don't you dare give him the satisfaction.* So through my teeth, I said, "Where do you wish to conduct my training?"

"Given you're likely to fall on your arse many times, we'll go somewhere less muddy," he said. "The docks will do if you can manage not to fall in the water."

Don't let him—

Fuck him. I wasn't going to take this behavior quietly. "I'm not the one struggling to stand steady on a flat floor."

He huffed out an amused breath. "We shall see who makes it to the end of the lesson without getting wet." Then he winked.

A fiery hot blush raced up my chest to my face. "Don't flatter yourself. I'm not some simpering maid whose thighs turn slick just because an idiot man winks at her."

One of the servants walking by heard my words and gaped. Bjorn gave her an apologetic smile. "I was talking about the fjord, Freya." Then he shook his head. "Such a filthy mind you have. I think I'll be most corrupted by our time together."

The servant looked back and forth between us, then hurried off. If I hadn't so recently discovered what it felt like for flesh to burn, I would have sworn my entire body was aflame.

"Let's go," Bjorn said, "before you fill my virtuous mind with any more talk of slick thighs and hard nipples."

"I said nothing about nipples, you drunk idiot," I hissed, picking up the two shields I'd secured and scampering after him.

Bjorn threw up his hands. "You see, Freya? Already you are influencing me, and I've only been in your company a matter of minutes. What sordid things will my tongue come up with after an hour with you? A day? A year? You will be the ruin of my virtue."

"The only thing that you need worry about is me cutting out your tongue if you don't shut up," I snapped, then stomped ahead of him down to the water, not caring that mud splattered my new trousers or that my shirt was already damp with nervous sweat.

"From most people that would be an empty threat," he answered, "but you're a woman who keeps her word, so I will guard my tongue."

I didn't think that meant he'd any intention of keeping silent.

The dock would normally be busy with fishermen and merchants coming and going, but today it was silent as a grave, the people of Halsar instead engaged with rebuilding the homes that had been lost to fires set by Gnut's men.

My feet made echoing thumps as I stomped to the far end, the fjord a glittering steel blue. Though the spring air was cool and the tips of the surrounding mountains were still covered with snow, the overhead sun was warm enough that I didn't regret leaving my cloak at the great hall. In fact, it was warm enough to—

I turned around in time to see Bjorn dropping his shirt onto the dock, hard muscles and tattooed skin all in clear view. Setting the shields at my feet, I crossed my arms. "Worried about falling in?" I refused to say the word *wet*.

"No." He hooked his thumbs over his belt, his trousers drifting low enough to reveal the sharp V of muscle that disappeared into them. The injury he'd taken last night was gone, presumably healed with Liv's magic. Realizing I was staring at the tantalizing stretch of bare skin, I jerked my eyes to his face while gesturing at his discarded shirt.

He only shrugged. "I rarely wear a shirt when I fight."

This time my eye roll was entirely unfeigned. "Is that part of your strategy, then? To distract the enemy with your rippling muscles so you might kill them while they gape at your splendor?"

"It is madness how well it works," he agreed. "You'd think that when I run toward them, screaming battle cries and vows for blood, it would be the burning axe they commented on, but no. It's always, 'Look at that Bjorn's ripping muscles. If I survive this battle, I vow to drink less mead so that my belly looks like his.'"

I scowled, annoyed that he was getting the better of me. Again. "Why, then?"

"Because fabric burns." He smirked. "So I either take it off before or risk having to rip it off in the middle of a fight."

"Leather doesn't burn," I said flatly, knowing precisely what the warriors wore when they fought. "Neither does steel. So either you are vain or you are very stupid."

Bjorn spread his arms wide. "Why not both?"

"Why not indeed," I grumbled, bending to pick up a shield, gripping it tight. "Snorri has ordered you to teach me to fight in a shield wall. You may begin to do so now."

"Yes, *my lady* of Halsar." He cast his green eyes skyward. "In the shield wall, you must hold a shield."

"Really?" I said. "That part I didn't know."

"You must hold a shield for a *long time*." He bent low, his nose less than a handspan from my already-quivering arm, then met my gaze with raised eyebrows. "I suspect you can't hold it for more than five minutes."

He turned on his heel and retreated back up the dock a few paces before flopping down on his arse. Then he rolled up his shirt, using it as a cushion as he lay on his back and closed his eyes, seemingly intent on sunning himself while I stood here quivering and sweating.

Arrogant prick!

"Arm up, Freya," he called, though there was no way he could see me. "You're protecting your heart, not your knees."

Arsehole! I lifted the shield higher, grinding my teeth as my arm protested the strain. But I'd do it. For however long I had to, I'd stand here. This might not be how I'd envisioned being trained as a warrior, but that didn't mean I'd quit.

I can do this, I silently chanted. *I can do this.*

Minutes passed, and with each one I prayed that Bjorn would say it had been long enough. That I'd proven myself.

But he said nothing. I wasn't sure if he was even awake. On the beach, more and more people had gathered, watching and chuckling as though this were all a big joke. Even the children joined in, several of them holding up shields with shaking arms, mocking my attempts.

My temper snapped.

"Get up!" I barked. "You are here to teach, not to take a nap in the sun. I wish to do something else."

Bjorn cracked one eye. "You think that is how it goes in battle? That you get tired and announce to your enemy, 'I am tired. Let us do something else instead. Let us roast a chicken and drink a cup until my arm steadies.'" He sat upright. "If your strength fails you in battle, Freya, you'll die."

"I'm aware," I said between my teeth. "But I wish you to test my strength a different way."

"Fine." He rose to his feet, then retrieved the other shield. "Ready?"

Before I had a chance to respond, he slammed it into mine. The impact sent me staggering, and I nearly fell off the end of the dock. Gasping, I stumbled back to the center, barely managing to get my shield up before he struck. Again I staggered, nearly going over the edge. "Why are you so angry about having to do this?"

Because there was no denying that he *was* angry.

Behind the swagger and jokes and indifference was rage, and I didn't understand why. Didn't understand why teaching me to fight and watching my back was such a horrible thing.

"Because it's bullshit." He smashed his shield into mine with enough force that my heels slid over the edge of the dock, only luck keeping me from falling. "My fate is not tied to yours—that's just Snorri spinning words to get what he wants. It's not my destiny to protect you."

The latter made sense, in a way, but the former . . . "What if he's right? Other than Ylva, you were the only one who saw the vision of me being torn apart. That has to mean something."

"Probably because I have god's blood."

"So do Steinunn and Liv," I countered. "Steinunn says that she saw nothing."

His expression darkened, though I wasn't certain if it was the mention of the skald or the fact I'd disproved his argument. "This is not my fate."

He slammed his shield into mine and my arm shuddered, nearly buckling. One more blow like that and I was going to take the edge of my shield in my chin, but I refused to give in. Refused to call it quits.

"My fate"—he paused in his attack, although I wasn't certain if it was to give me a rest or because he was more interested in airing his grievances than fighting—"is to win battles, not spend day and night defending another man's wife."

"I see." My tone frigid, I added, "A woman is only worth your time if you might end up in her bed, is that the truth of it?"

"And if it is?"

Even if it was the truth, his behavior was unfair, because it was Snorri who'd forced him into this role, not me. Yet I was the one Bjorn was taking his displeasure out on. And I wasn't going to take it.

Bjorn came at me again, and as I braced, I murmured, "Hlin, give me strength."

Power surged through me, magic enveloping my shield. I watched Bjorn's eyes widen, but it was too late for him to stop his blow.

His shield struck my magic, and the impact launched him backward with such force that he flew through the air, landing in the fjord with a splash.

Vanquishing my magic, I moved to the end of the dock and watched him come spluttering to the surface, his shield floating nearby. "It seems you are the one who is wet, Bjorn."

He glared at me and then swam toward the dock with powerful strokes, shield abandoned in the water. "Magic will only take you so far," he snarled. "Snorri wants you to become a warrior, not a glowing beacon in the shield wall that everyone will try to kill."

"Fuck Snorri," I shouted at him. "And fuck you, too."

He reached for the edge of the dock to pull himself up, but I wasn't through. So I stomped on his fingers, earning a yelp of pain.

"You think I want to be a figurehead?" I demanded. "You think I asked to be named in a seer's prophecy? I was going about my life when you rode into it and tore it to shreds."

"Because life with Vragi was such a fine thing? You hated him."

Bjorn started to reach up for the dock again, then hesitated as I lifted my foot.

"Perhaps you ought to consider Vragi's fate before you test me any further."

"Threats will not force me to be satisfied with spending life as your shadow."

"I don't give a shit if you're satisfied!" I shouted, even though it was a lie. It *would* bother me knowing that he resented being around me. "Because no one gives a shit if I'm satisfied! I didn't agree to Snorri's ultimatum for myself, I did it to protect my family, which is clearly something *you* don't understand. Because we *are* family now."

An emotion I couldn't quite read flickered through his eyes, and Bjorn looked away. Immediately, I regretted my words. He'd spent much of his life separated from his family, kept as a prisoner. If he didn't understand, it was because he'd never had a chance to.

Swallowing hard, I forced myself to finish. "If you continue to try to make things worse than they are, I will return the favor tenfold. So perhaps you might do us both the favor of saving your ire for the individual who has forced us to such close proximity."

Bjorn said nothing, only treaded water, his shield slowly drifting past us toward shore.

"You may get out of the water now," I said, extremely aware that we were being watched. "And then you may apologize."

"I'm too afraid to get out." He continued swimming in place. "You have thrown me in the water, possibly broken my fingers, and threatened to murder me. At least in the fjord I don't need to fear you pursuing me."

Though I knew damn well Bjorn had no fear of me, a hint of unease filled my chest that I'd gone too far. My mother always said that I had the temper of a caged mink, prone to saying the worst sorts of things, only to regret them later. "I'm not going to murder you."

"Just batter my feelings until I wish I were dead?"

"I'm not—" I scowled as a smile grew on his face and I crossed my aching arms. "I won't do anything to you that you don't deserve. Now get out and apologize and we may carry on."

He eyed me for a moment, then swam closer and took hold of the dock. Only to snatch his hand back with a hiss of pain.

Concern flooded me. Had I truly broken his fingers? Should I go fetch Liv?

"Help me up," he muttered, reaching with his other hand.

Without thinking I grasped it, realizing his deception a heartbeat before he pulled. A shriek tore from my lips as I fell headfirst into the fjord, the shock of cold worse than I remembered.

Righting myself, I spat out a mouthful of seawater and glared at him. "This is not a good start."

He inclined his head. "I am sorry for being an arse and not showing you the respect you deserve, Freya Born-in-Fire."

"And you needed to get me wet to tell me that?" I was bloody freezing, and from the beach I could hear the laughter of the onlookers who'd watched me go arse-up into the fjord.

"I needed to be a little bit *more* sorry before I could get an apology from my mouth," he said. "But now it is said, and we may move on."

"Don't be so certain," I grumbled, watching as he swam under the dock, then reached up to hook his fingers through the boards. Every muscle in his body stood out in stark relief as he hung from the dock, water running in rivulets through the dips and valleys of taut skin.

He eyed me for a long moment, green eyes thoughtful, then asked, "Has Snorri told you anything of his plans for you? Said anything about how he believes you will make him king?"

"No," I answered around chattering teeth. "He's barely spoken to me at all."

"Marriage at its finest." Bjorn chuckled, but before I could ball up my fist to punch him in his stomach, he added, "No one knows. I asked around last night and spent a small fortune in mead, but no one knows anything."

My cheeks heated as I realized that he'd not, as I'd thought, spent the entirety of his night getting drunk and having sex with random women. He'd spent at least some of it trying to discover the answer to the question I was desperate to answer myself. "If he were to confide in anyone, I should think it would be you."

He looked away, scanning the fjord, though there was nothing to be seen but water. "We are not as close as you might think."

I had no business prying, but I still asked, "Because of the years you spent in Nordeland?"

Bjorn's eyes shot back to me. "What do you know of that?"

"Nothing other than that you were taken prisoner as a child and that Snorri rescued you." I had a million questions I wished to ask, but I settled on the one that had bothered me the most. "Why didn't you escape?"

It was understandable why he hadn't tried to escape as a child, but much less so as a grown man, because as a child of Tyr, Bjorn was *always* armed. And even untrained, a boy with an axe made of a god's fire could do a great deal of damage.

Silence.

I cringed internally. *When will you learn to shut your mouth, Freya?*

He cleared his throat. "I swore blood oaths as a child not to try to escape. Harald has many powerful individuals in his service, including those adept with rune magic."

"Being rescued didn't violate your oath?" I asked, curious given that I'd recently sworn my own.

"Clearly not."

"I heard that Snorri lost many men and drakkar rescuing you," I said, unsure why I kept pressing the topic. "He must care for you very much to have kept trying."

"He knew he needed the fire of a god to find you," Bjorn answered. "His rescue attempts didn't begin until I'd been in Nordeland for two years, which was when he learned my magic had manifested."

Oh.

It hadn't been sentiment that had driven Snorri to rescue his son, but the selfish need to claim the destiny he dreamed of. It was no wonder they weren't close. Needing to change the subject before I dug up any more wounds, I said, "What about the seer who spoke the foretelling. Why not ask them for information about what I'm supposed to do?"

"Because *she* is dead."

His voice was sharp, and understanding slowly dawned on me as I put the pieces together. Swallowing hard, I said, "The seer was your mother?"

Bjorn gave a tight nod.

A million questions reared in my head, but it was more than apparent that Bjorn wanted nothing to do with this conversation. Still, I hazarded one. "Were you there when she spoke the foretelling?"

"I was too young to remember."

Of course, that made sense. "Did she ever say anything else about me? Ever say why the gods believed I'd be able to achieve such a fate?"

He hesitated, then said, "Her gift was her downfall. I don't enjoy talking about it."

Gods, I needed to cut out my own tongue because one day I'd build my own barrow with it. But before I could start in on apologies, footfalls thudded down the dock overhead. A heartbeat later, Snorri's voice filtered down. "Get out of the water. Your brother has returned with news."

My curiosity grew with each passing second as we walked, dripping, back to the great hall. Neither Snorri nor Bjorn said anything, both their jaws set and expressions unreadable, and it made me wonder about Bjorn's relationship with his younger half-brother.

I got my answer the moment we walked into the hall. A boy a few summers shy of manhood raced across the floor to collide with Bjorn, clearly delighted to see his elder brother as they pounded each other on the back. Beyond, Ylva stood by the fire with her arms crossed and mouth drawn into a thin line as she watched the exchange.

"Is it true you killed a full score of Gnut's warriors?" Leif demanded. "Then set fire to his ships?"

Bjorn shook his head. "I merely provided the flame. Was Freya who set them ablaze."

At my name, Leif turned from his brother, looking me up and down. I gave him the same courtesy. He was only slightly taller than I was, and quite slight, his hair golden blond where his brother's was dark, and his eyes blue rather than green. They had the same high cheekbones and square jaw, though Leif's chin had several years to go before it would manage a beard worth growing. He would age into a fine-looking man, I suspected, though he lacked Bjorn's almost otherworldly beauty. It made me wonder what Bjorn's mother had looked like, for it must be her who'd given him such different coloring. "You are the shield maiden, then?" he asked, and without waiting for a response added, "I suppose I must congratulate you on your marriage to my father."

Absolutely nothing in his tone suggested congratulations, which was perhaps fair, given that Ylva was his mother, but I gave him a slight nod. "Thank you."

He scowled, then turned his back on me in favor of his brother. "We captured a spy."

Bjorn shifted on his feet, eyes narrowing. "Whose spy?"

An older warrior, a man with brown skin and silver-streaked dark hair twisted into a knot behind his head, stepped forward. "We don't know. No one recognizes her and she's refused to speak."

"You should have put fire to her feet, Ragnar." Ylva moved to rest a hand on Leif's shoulder. "She'd have sung for you then."

The older warrior tugged on his beard, which was long enough that the silver rings on it brushed against the chest of his mail vest. "Thought better to bring her to the jarl, my lady."

"Perhaps she is not a spy," Bjorn interjected. "Perhaps she doesn't speak our language."

Ragnar snorted. "She understands well enough. And she tried to escape. Twice."

"Compelling enough evidence for you, Bjorn?" Ylva's voice was saccharine and Leif cast a sideways frown at her. "It was a fair question, Mother."

She snorted. "He merely balks at the thought of torturing a woman."

"Whereas you seem to relish the thought," Bjorn retorted.

Leif threw up his skinny arms, face visibly annoyed. "You two fight like cornered cats. Father, how you stand them constantly carrying on like this is beyond my understanding. You should put an end to it for all our sakes."

"Would require gagging them both, day and night. Or cutting out their tongues." Snorri waved a hand at them. "Both of you be silent, for once. Ragnar, bring the prisoner in and we will see what she has to say for herself."

I found the dynamic fascinating. The conflict between Bjorn and Ylva was obviously something Leif and Snorri were well aware of, though Leif seemed more troubled by it, which suggested he played peacemaker more often than not. Where would I fit into this mix of personalities? Would I make things better? Or worse?

Worse, I thought, not missing the sidelong look Leif gave me as Ragnar left the great hall. The old warrior returned moments later with a woman, a sack obscuring her face and her wrists bound. She wore a nondescript brown dress, the front stained with blood and the hem soaked with mud. Light brown hair that was streaked with gray hung in clumps down her back.

Snorri reached up and pulled the sack from the woman's head, revealing an aged woman with colorless eyes. She blinked once at me—

And then her head toppled from her neck.

The smell of burnt hair and flesh filling my nose as her body slumped to the ground, blood seeping from the nearly cauterized stump.

I jerked backward even as Ylva shrieked, covering Leif's eyes with one hand, though he shoved her away with annoyance, eyes skipping between the corpse and his brother.

"Explain yourself," Snorri roared at Bjorn, who had already vanquished his axe, his arms crossed and his face fixed.

"Her name is Ragnhild. She's sworn to Harald, and"—he reached down to tear open the back of her dress, revealing the crimson tattoo of an eye—"she's a child of Hoenir."

I pressed a hand to my mouth, staring at the head resting near my feet. Hoenir's children were able to speak into the minds of those who bore their tokens, showing them visions. And Ragnhild had seen me.

"Didn't you check her for marks?" Snorri demanded of Leif, whose cheeks colored as he said, "I wasn't about to undress an old woman."

"Your morals get in the way of good sense!" Snorri lifted a hand as though he might strike his younger son, but instead spat on the floor.

"With luck, I killed her before she sent him any visions," Bjorn said. "Else your most dangerous enemy knows your shield maiden has been found."

"What she saw matters little!" Ylva snapped. "Harald would have learned about Freya soon enough, yet for the sake of keeping him in the dark a week or two longer, you sacrificed the opportunity for us to learn something about him. We could have made Ragnhild talk!"

"Unlikely, given that she has no tongue and Harald has her only token."

I swallowed hard. "What is her token?"

His green eyes met mine. "He wears her dried tongue on a cord around his neck at all times. He is the only person she could speak to."

It was a struggle on many levels to keep from vomiting. "Did he cut it out?"

Bjorn shook his head. "Her former master did. Harald took it from around his neck when he killed him." His eyes moved to Ylva. "Harald will learn of her, yes. But delaying the information gives us time to prepare. Time to make alliances so that you might defend against his attack, which will come. He has no desire to see Skaland united beneath your rule, especially given he knows you plan to bring war to Nordeland."

"For twenty years, I've waited for Freya." Snorri rubbed at his temple. "And now that I have her, I find myself in a race against time, faced with doom should I take one wrong step."

I struggled not to snort in disgust. For my entire life, he'd had time to prepare for this moment, whereas until a matter of days ago, I'd been entirely unaware that powerful men across two nations were plotting their moves for the day I made my name known. Snorri had no excuse not to be prepared.

Dropping his hand from his temple, Snorri looked at Bjorn. "When is the soonest he could come?"

Bjorn cleared his throat. "A matter of weeks."

"With the losses we took against Gnut, we wouldn't stand a chance in resisting Harald," Ragnar said, even as Leif blurted out, "Are you sure this woman is worth it, Father? Perhaps it's better to kill her and be done with it. She seems more likely to get us all killed than to see you to power."

Next to me, Bjorn's axe flared to life before disappearing again, and Leif frowned at him. "I merely pose the question of Father, for as jarl, it is his decision."

"There is no decision to be made," Ylva snapped. "Freya will make your father king of Skaland if only we hold true to the course, and as his son, you stand to benefit most."

Leif cast his eyes skyward. "*Bjorn* stands to benefit most, Mother. But I will be proud to fight at his side whether he becomes jarl or king, it makes no difference. I ask though, how much will our family stand to lose by keeping this woman alive? How much will Halsar lose? For me, I say it is not worth it."

Though the boy spoke of killing me, I found myself in approval of Leif's reasoning, for he seemed to value lives above power and reputation and ambition. Wise beyond his years and having clearly been raised to understand what should be important to a jarl.

"The gods would punish us for spitting in the face of the gift they've given," Snorri answered. "Even if they did not, if we were to kill Freya, it would be seen by our enemies as weakness. They'd see me backing away from an opportunity for greatness out of cowardice and fear, and all our enemies would come for us. We stay the course."

Leif frowned, the expression turning to a scowl as Ylva nodded approvingly, but before the boy could say anything, Bjorn asked, "What is the course? How do you plan to gain the alliances you need in the short time you might have before the raids come?"

A practical question.

"By gathering all the jarls of Skaland together and convincing them that united, we stand at better odds." Snorri smiled. "Which gives us more proof that the gods favor us, for the jarls already travel to meet in one place. Ready your things, for we ride to pay homage to the gods at Fjalltindr."

Fjalltindr was the sacred temple on the very top of the mountain
known as Hammar. Every nine years there was a gathering that
drew people from near and far to pay tribute to the gods and
offer their sacrifices. I'd never been before, my parents having always
claimed that it was not a place for children, and this would be the first
time it took place since I'd come of age.

The great hall was in a flurry of activity, two dozen horses and a
number of pack animals already saddled and loaded when I emerged in
dry clothes and a thick cloak. Ylva was directing the process, the lady
of Halsar no longer attired in a costly dress, but in warrior's clothes,
including a mail shirt, a long seax hanging from her belt. I had no
doubt that she knew how to use it.

Particularly when her opponent's back was turned.

"You will remain with the warriors I'm leaving behind to protect
Halsar," Snorri said to Leif. "You will be lord in my absence. Send word
across my territories calling for those who can fight and tell them to
prepare."

"Prepare to be attacked?" Leif crossed his arms, expression displeased. "There will be anger, Father."

"Remind them that we are favored by the gods," Snorri answered as he mounted his horse. "If they care not for that, then remind them that those who fight for me will be rewarded." Turning away from his son, he said to me, "We lost horses in the fire, so we are short. You will ride with Bjorn."

There wasn't much I could say to that as Snorri reached down to lift Ylva, who settled comfortably behind him. Steinunn also shared a mount, though with a young thrall woman, the skald watching my every move, though no emotion showed on her face. Sighing, I walked over to Bjorn's big roan gelding, noting that he was also wearing mail. "What happened to riding shirtless into battle?" I grumbled, my aching arms protesting as he pulled me up behind him, knowing it would be my arse suffering in a few hours. The horse likely wouldn't be impressed, either.

"*You're* riding behind me, Born-in-Fire," he said, heeling the horse into a walk. "And it is very nearly guaranteed that I'll say something to anger you on the journey. It's a long ride and I've no talent for silence."

"Well, that is certainly the truth." I barely managed to curb a yelp as he urged the horse into a canter that nearly sent me toppling off the back. I clung to Bjorn's waist as he followed Snorri out of Halsar, but as we left the town, a hooded figure on a rocky outcropping caught my attention.

It was the same figure I'd seen during the funeral of the victims of the raid, smoke and ash drifting away on a wind despite the air being still.

"Bjorn!" I pointed. "Do you see that person?"

He turned his head, and through the mail and all the padding he wore beneath it, I felt him tense. "Where? I see no one."

A chill of fear ran down my spine, because if Bjorn couldn't see the figure, I was either losing my mind or this was a specter revealing itself only to me. "Stop the horse."

Bjorn drew up his mount, the rest of our party following suit even as Snorri demanded, "Why are you stopping?"

I pointed again at the specter, which remained with its head lowered, embers and ash falling around it. "Do any of you see that hooded figure? The embers? The smoke?"

Confusion radiated across our party as everyone looked to where I pointed, shaking their heads. *Nothing.* Yet the horses seemed aware, all of them snorting and stomping, their ears pinned flat.

"A specter," Snorri breathed. "Perhaps even one of the gods having stepped onto the mortal plane. Speak to him, Freya."

My palms turned clammy because that was the last thing I wanted to do. "Try to get closer."

Bjorn urged his mount toward the outcropping until the horse finally dug in its heels, refusing to go closer. "What do you want?" I shouted at the specter.

"So polite, Born-in-Fire," Bjorn murmured, but I ignored him as the specter's head tracked toward me, face still hidden by the hood. Then it lifted its hand and spoke, voice rough and pained.

"She, the unfated, she the child of Hlin, she who was born in fire must give sacrifice to the gods on the mount at the first night of the full moon else her thread will be cut short, the future that was foreseen unwoven."

The words settled into my head, understanding of what they meant twisting my guts with nausea.

"Did it answer?" Bjorn asked, and I gave a tight nod. "Yes." Louder, I asked, "Why? Why must I do this?"

"She must earn her fate," the specter answered, then exploded into embers and smoke.

The horse reared, and I cursed, clinging to Bjorn's waist to keep from falling while he settled the animal.

"How did the specter answer?" Snorri demanded, riding his snorting mount in circles around us. "Did it identify itself?"

"It said that I must earn my fate," I answered, righting myself behind Bjorn. "That I must give sacrifice to the gods on the mount on the first night of the full moon, or my thread will be cut short."

"A test!" Snorri's eyes brightened. "Surely the specter was one of the gods, for they delight in such things."

A test that, if I failed, would see me dead. Needless to say, I did not share in Snorri's enthusiasm.

"The gods will not grant you greatness for nothing," he said. "You must prove yourself to them."

It was not lost on me that I'd once dreamed of greatness, and now, presented with it, it felt like the last thing I wanted.

Besides, I was unfated. How could the specter, the gods, or *anyone* truly predict what my future held? How could they know for certain that if I didn't go to Fjalltindr, I'd die? Maybe I could alter my destiny and escape this. Maybe I could wait for a moment when backs were turned and run. I could retrieve my family, and together we could flee out of Snorri's reach. I could weave a new fate for myself. The race of thoughts made me abruptly regret not taking Bjorn up on his offer to help me escape.

As though hearing my thoughts, Snorri added, "If you destroy the fate foreseen for me, Freya, you had best hope that you are dead. For my wrath will burn like wildfire, and it will turn on everything you love."

Hate boiled in my chest because the gods weren't the threat I feared. It was the bastard standing before me.

"We've wasted enough time! We ride to Fjalltindr," he ordered, spinning his horse and setting off at a gallop.

Instead of following, Bjorn twisted in the saddle, wrapping one arm around my waist, and pulling me in front of him. As I struggled to right my legs around the horse's shoulders, he said, "I don't think the specter was threatening you, Freya. I think it was warning you that there will be those along the way who will try to kill you."

"As if I didn't already know that."

"The mountaintop is sacred ground." Bjorn's hand pressed against my ribs to hold me steady. "No weapons are allowed, as all deaths must be in sacrifice to the gods, which means some level of safety within Fjalltindr's borders."

I didn't take much comfort in that. "How long will it take us to reach the mountain?"

"Tomorrow we'll reach the village at the base of the mountain, where we'll leave the horses," he said. "Then another half day's climb."

A night out in the open. I swallowed hard. "I think we should ride faster."

By the time dusk fell, the horses were laboring hard and my body ached from bouncing up and down for hours on Bjorn's lap. Judging from his groans as he slowly dismounted his horse, falling on his back in the dirt and shouting at the sky that he'd lost the ability to sire children, he'd not fared much better.

Yet it was the first time since we'd left Halsar that anyone laughed, so I welcomed the release of tension even if it was at my expense. The warriors jostled and elbowed one another as they tended the mounts, the thralls Snorri had brought moving to prepare dinner while their mistress perched on a rock, clearly above doing anything at all.

I hesitated, not certain where I belonged, then moved to join the thralls. For while I didn't know how to prepare the defense of a camp, I did know how to make a fire and dress game.

Carefully stacking a pile of kindling, I stuffed moss under the sticks. My scarred hand was painfully stiff, likely from my *training* with Bjorn, and I struggled to grip my knife to strike the flint.

"There's an easier way." Bjorn crouched next to me, axe appearing in his hand. The crimson fire flickered and danced as he shoved it into my carefully assembled stack of wood, knocking everything askew before disappearing into the darkness.

I eyed the weapon, this the first opportunity I'd had to really scrutinize the axe up close. It gave off tremendous heat, though the sweat that beaded on my brow was more from nerves than the temperature, as I remembered how it had felt when it seared my palm. How in the heartbeat I'd held it, the crimson fire had enveloped my hand as though it intended to consume me. As though Tyr himself wanted to punish me for wielding a weapon never meant for my hands.

Yet my curiosity was greater than my fear, and I bent closer, squinting against the glow. Beneath the flickers of fire, the axe itself appeared to be made from translucent glass with patterns etched along the blade and haft.

Realizing the thralls were watching, I pushed kindling on top of the axe. The wood swiftly ignited, the oranges and golds and blues of natural flame mixing with the blood-red god-fire as I added larger pieces.

"Will you describe to me the specter's appearance?" Steinunn knelt next to me, her cloak slipping dangerously close to Bjorn's axe. I reached to move the fabric even as I said, "Hooded. Embers and smoke poured from it as though it were aflame beneath its cloak."

"How did seeing it make you feel? What were your thoughts?"

My jaw tightened, the invasiveness of her queries again rubbing me the wrong way. As though sensing my irritation, the skald swiftly said, "It is how my magic works, Freya. I chronicle the stories of our people as ballads, but for them to possess heart and emotion, they must be told from the perspective of those they are about, not my own observations. I seek only to do justice to your growing fame."

"It feels strange to share with someone I barely know."

A rare flicker of emotion appeared in the skald's eyes, then she looked away. "I'm not used to speaking about myself. Most desire for me to sing of their exploits, so conversation is about them, not me."

My irritation fled in favor of sympathy, and for the first time since we'd met, I truly focused on the skald as I considered the cost of her gift. What it would feel like if everyone you spoke to cared only about telling you their stories on the chance of expanding their fame in a ballad, and nothing about the woman who wrote the songs. Steinunn was used as a tool, just as I was. "I would like to know more about you."

Steinunn stiffened, then wiped her palms on her skirt. "There is little to tell. I was born in a small fishing village on the coast. When I turned fourteen, our jarl took me into service, though it was short-lived, for another jarl soon learned of my gift and paid him in gold to bring me into his service. So it was for many years, jarls buying my service from one another."

Like a thrall. "You had no choice where you went?"

Steinunn lifted a shoulder in a shrug. "For the most part, I was well compensated and cared for, and in recent years, my . . . liberty has grown." Her jaw clenched as she said the last, but then she gave me a smile, the moment of discomfort gone as swiftly as it had appeared.

I opened my mouth to ask whether she had or wanted a family, then closed it again. If she had a family, they weren't in Halsar, and she might not appreciate me raising the topic. "So you wish to know how I felt? That is how your magic works?"

Steinunn nodded.

Keeping my eyes on Bjorn's axe, I bit the insides of my cheeks. Admitting that I had been afraid seemed counter to the story Snorri wished to spread about me, but if I said otherwise, the woman would likely know it was a lie.

"Perhaps if I show you," the skald said, and opening her full lips, she began to sing. Softly, so that only I would hear, her beautiful voice filled my ears, telling the tale of the raid against Halsar. Yet it was not the words that drew a gasp from my lips, it was visions of darkness and flame that filled my eyes, blocking out the world around me, fear forming like a vise around my chest.

"Save your caterwauling for those who didn't live through that battle, Steinunn."

Bjorn's voice cut through the song and the skald fell silent, the vision immediately fading away.

"I'm following your father's orders," she snapped, the first sign of anger I'd ever seen from her. "It is Snorri who wishes Freya's fame to grow."

"I felt afraid," I blurted out, not wishing to be at the center of a confrontation between these two, who clearly were *not* friends. "But I also wanted answers."

I held my breath, praying that would be sufficient.

"Thank you, Freya." Steinunn rose to her feet, not saying a word to Bjorn as she pushed past him.

"You shouldn't be so rude," I said to him as he knelt near the fire. "She's got no more choice in what she does than I do."

Bjorn grunted, though whether it was in agreement or denial, I wasn't sure. "I once allowed her to pick my thoughts, not realizing what her magic could do. Days later, she sang to all of Halsar and I realized that her power would allow all who heard her song to . . . *become* me in that moment. To see what I saw. To feel what I felt. To cast their judgment upon me for something I'd never have shared with them, if given the choice. It was . . . *intrusive.*"

It struck me as strange that a man such as him would resent anything that brought him notoriety. He was above all else a raider, and to warriors like Bjorn, nothing mattered more than battle fame. Except I'd once dreamed of such things, and those opening verses of the raid on Halsar had not brought me pride and elation, but rather fear. Perhaps, however improbably, Bjorn felt the same. But still . . . "That doesn't mean you need to be rude to her."

"You might reconsider your stance after a few more months of her prying into every detail of your actions," he answered. "It's the only way I can get her to leave me be."

Chewing the insides of my cheeks, I debated whether this was something I wished to argue about and decided on changing the subject. Gesturing at his axe, I asked, "Does it have to be an axe? Or could you make it any weapon?"

Bjorn huffed a breath at the subject change but said, "It has always been an axe. For others with Tyr's blood, a sword or knife."

"And it looks the same every time you summon it?"

His axe abruptly disappeared, as though he liked my scrutiny of it as little as he did Steinunn's intrusions into his thoughts. "More or less." Circling the fire, he sat cross-legged next to me. "Is Hlin's shield always the same?"

I frowned, considering the question. "It takes the shape of the shield I'm holding."

"Does it need to be a proper shield? Or could your magic turn anything into a shield?" He reached over and picked up a pot, brandishing it. "Such magic would keep anyone from crossing you in the kitchen. Are you a good cook, by the way?"

"Don't be an arse—of course I'm a good cook." Wrenching the pot from his grip, I turned it over in my hand, then lifted it. "Hlin, protect me."

Power flooded my veins, the warmth of it driving away the chill in the air. It flowed from my hand to cover the pot, its glow doing more than the fire to illuminate the darkness. Vaguely, I was aware that everyone had stopped to stare at me, but my attention was all for Bjorn, who was eyeing the pot thoughtfully.

Extracting a knife from his belt, he slammed the tip into my pot. The weapon bounced off with enough force that it went spinning out of his grip and into the dirt, but rather than retrieving the blade, he motioned for me to rise. Nerves prickled my skin, but I obliged him, my nerves turning to fear as his axe appeared in his hand.

"Bjorn . . ." Snorri said, stepping forward. "I don't think this—"

"Do you trust that I won't miss?" Bjorn said to me, acting as though his father hadn't even spoken.

I swallowed. "Bjorn, I'm wielding a cooking pot."

"You're wielding Hlin's power," he corrected. "So perhaps the better question is whether you trust the goddess? Or whether you trust yourself?"

Did I? Hlin's magic had held against Tyr's once before, but Bjorn had been unprepared. What if this time his axe sliced through my magic?

The memory of the pain I'd felt when the axe had burned me filled my head, feeling so real I looked down at my hand to ensure it wasn't aflame. My breathing accelerated, my pulse a dull roar in my ears as the arm holding the pot trembled.

"Bjorn," Snorri snarled, "if you hurt her, I'll cut out your gods-cursed heart!"

Bjorn did not so much as blink, only asked softly, "Well, Freya?"

Terror and nausea rolled in my guts, every instinct telling me to back down. To say that I couldn't do it. That I needed a proper shield and time to test just how powerful Hlin's magic was. But a defiant, albeit potentially idiotic, part of my heart forced two words up through my strangled throat and across my dry tongue. "Do it."

Bjorn threw the axe.

I clenched my teeth, fighting the instinct to dive sideways, instead holding my pot steady, a scream filling my ears. Crimson flame flipped end-over-end toward me, the screaming—which I realized was my own—abruptly drowned out by a concussive blast that shattered the air like thunder.

The axe ricocheted off my pot, smashing through tree branches and up into the sky before winking out.

Ylva gasped loudly, but Bjorn only laughed, his eyes bright as he reached out to touch the glowing pot.

"Careful!" I tensed, afraid that the magic would shatter his hand. But with utter fearlessness, he pressed his palm against the magic.

Instead of repelling his touch, my magic allowed Bjorn's hand to sink into it like water. I felt the moment he touched the pot itself, a gentle pressure, whereas with the impact of his axe, I'd felt nothing. The sensation moved up my arm and down into my core, as though he touched not magic and metal, but my bare skin, and I shivered.

"You get what you give," he murmured, then lifted his eyes from the magic to meet mine. "Or perhaps more accurately, *you* give what you get."

The rest of the world fell away as I considered his words, it feeling for all the world like he was the first person to ever understand me.

Except . . . that wasn't quite it.

My family understood me. My friends understood me. But there were parts of me that they wanted to change, whereas Bjorn seemed to accept the way I was. Seemed to encourage the parts of my character that everyone else in my life had tried to quash. A quiver ran through me, a powerful mix of emotions filling my chest in a way that made it hard to breathe.

Then Snorri spoke, shattering the moment. "Her magic is more powerful than yours? The shield maiden is stronger than you?"

My jaw tightened at the use of my title rather than my name, a reminder that to Snorri, I was a thing, not a person.

If Bjorn's ego was bruised by the comment, he didn't show it, only shrugged. "That certainly seems to be the case."

I waited for him to caveat the statement. To argue that in battle, I wouldn't stand a chance against him. But he didn't. Didn't tear me down in order to make himself look strong, as so many men did.

"Yet more proof the gods favor her." Snorri smiled. "That they favor me."

I couldn't stop myself from demanding, "Why? How is the strength of my magic proof the gods favor you as the future king of Skaland?"

"Shut your disrespectful mouth, girl!" Ylva shoved past Bjorn, and I lowered my pot lest I accidentally send her flying across the camp. "A tool is only as good as the hand that wields it, and it was *Snorri* who received the foretelling. You are nothing without him."

My jaw tightened, but before I could retort, Snorri said, "Be at ease, my love. She has not your experience and wisdom to have faith in the gods."

"It is true," Bjorn said. "I'd estimate two decades' less experience. Or is it three, Ylva?"

Snorri struck.

One moment Bjorn was laughing, and the next he was on his knees, bleeding from his mouth.

"You are my son, Bjorn, and I love you." Snorri's voice was rimmed with frost. "But do not see my affection as weakness. Dishonor Ylva, and you dishonor me. Now apologize."

Bjorn's jaw worked back and forth, his eyes narrow and full of anger as he stood.

No, it was more than that.

He *hated* Ylva. Hated her more than could reasonably be justified by what I'd seen and heard. He opened his mouth and I tensed, sensing the words about to come out would be anything but an apology. But Bjorn only took a deep inhale, then let the breath out slowly.

Ylva crossed her arms, eyes narrowed. "I was grateful my husband was able to rescue you from our enemies, Bjorn, but every day, you test that gratitude."

"Don't lie to me, Ylva," he retorted. "I know it angers you that I took Leif's place as heir. But at least have the decency to own it rather than hiding behind false sentiment."

"Fine!" she snarled. "I do not wish for you to inherit. You were gone too long and are more of a Nordelander than a Skalander. The people deserve to be ruled by one of their own. By a legitimate son!"

I clapped a hand to my mouth, shocked at her words, but Bjorn did not so much as blink.

"Enough!" Snorri shouted. "You will both cease in this pointless quarrel."

Bjorn didn't seem to have even heard his father, only lowered his head to Ylva's level and said, "I heard you once said the same thing to my mother."

I took a step back, for though I stood in the midst of this argument, I'd ceased to be part of it. All around, warriors and servants were doing their best to look anywhere but at the disagreement before them.

Ylva blanched at the accusation, but it was Snorri who roared, "Who told you this lie? Ylva was a friend to your mother, and you know it."

"It doesn't matter." Bjorn twisted away. "It is history. It is done. Forget I said anything."

Then he strode away into the darkness.

Snorri started in the direction Bjorn had gone, but Ylva caught his arm. "He won't listen while he's angry," she said. "And the more you deny it, the more he'll believe it's true."

"It was Harald," Snorri seethed. "That's his way. To whisper poison and lies into ears, twisting loyalties."

"Likely so," Ylva answered. "Which begs the question of what else he whispered in Bjorn's ears during those long years your son was in his care."

I ground my teeth. Even in this moment, Ylva was manipulating circumstances to her advantage. But at least Snorri seemed to see it. "Your relationship with Bjorn would be better if you weren't always trying to find ways to discredit him. And to what end? To make Leif look good? I already know my son is a fine boy and will make a fine warrior, but he is not my firstborn. Is not the one Tyr chose to honor with a drop of blood."

I took a step back, intending to seek out Bjorn, but immediately regretted moving when Ylva looked at me with a scowl, as though all this were my doing. Reaching into the pouch on her belt, she extracted a jar and tossed it at me. "Liv said you are to use this every night. It will ease the pain and stiffness so that you might remain of value. Now go find something useful to keep yourself busy."

Shoving the salve pot in my pocket, I walked back to the fire where the thralls were working together to prepare a meal. Ylva had brought several of them, all about my age, and likely captured in raids of neighboring territories. Theirs was a hard life, and a short one, unless Ylva chose to make them free women at some point. "How might I help?"

One of them opened her mouth, probably to tell me that it was not necessary, so I swiftly said, "Ylva wishes for me to be useful." The young woman gave her mistress a sideways glance, then handed me a spoon. "Stir from time to time."

I dutifully obeyed, though my eyes kept drifting to the perimeter of the camp, waiting for Bjorn to reappear. What had he meant in his comment about his mother? Had Ylva somehow been involved in what had happened to her?

A million questions with no answers. Dipping the spoon into the stew, I tasted it and struggled not to make a face, for it was bland. Reaching for the tiny sacks of spice the women had left out, I added in salt and a few others, tasting it again and finding it more to my liking. "It's ready."

The women doled out bowls to everyone, and I sat apart while I ate my meal and stewed over my circumstances. When I was finished, I set my bowl aside and opened the salve Ylva had given me. The contents were waxy and pungent, but though the smell was not unpleasant, I sealed it.

"You actually need to use it for it to help."

I twitched at Bjorn's voice, having not heard him come out of the shadowed woods. He sat across the fire from me, picking up a stick and poking pensively at the embers before adding more wood. Then he looked up. "Well? Aren't you going to put it on?"

My fingers were painfully stiff and would probably be worse come the morning, but for reasons I couldn't explain, I set aside the jar.

And was rewarded with a noise of exasperation from Bjorn, who rose and circled the fire. "Give me the salve."

Deeply aware that all eyes were on us, I handed over the little pot, wincing as he extracted a large glob, the frugalness in me protesting the excess.

"Clearly you aren't aware of the chests of silver my father has buried in various locations about his territory," he said. "Trust me, he cares more about you being able to use your hand than paying for pots of salve."

Frugality was ingrained in my character, but in this, he had a point. Extending my arm, I waited for him to deposit the glob of salve on my palm. Instead, Bjorn took hold of my hand and smeared the salve over the twisted tattoo on my right palm. I tensed, self-conscious about him touching the scars despite his claims that they were marks of honor. Yet if the texture of my skin bothered him, Bjorn didn't show it, his brow furrowed in concentration as his strong fingers dug into the stiff tendons, the heat of his flesh doing more to warm my skin than the fire.

Not that I relaxed.

Relaxing was impossible, for the intimacy of this act was not lost on me. I was another man's wife. Not just any man's, but his father's.

Yet I didn't pull away.

The shadows from the firelight danced over Bjorn's hands, tendons standing out against suntanned skin marked with tiny white scars, many of which looked as though they'd been burns. My eyes traveled up his muscled forearms, examining all the tattoos, the black faded enough that he must have had them for many years. I wondered if they had meaning to him or if they were nothing more than decorations that struck his fancy, but I refrained from asking the question.

I didn't want to disrupt the moment. Didn't want to do anything that would cause him to remove his hands from mine. Not because the pain was easing beneath his care, but because the diminishing stiffness in my fingers was being replaced with a growing tension in my core.

You are a cursed fool, Freya. An idiot who deserves to be slapped upside the head for lusting over that which you cannot have.

Not only did my body ignore my admonitions, but the ache also deepened, and with it, my imagination flared to life. Flickers of images danced across my thoughts of Bjorn *without* the shirt he currently wore. Without the trousers. Without any garments between us, his hands on my body and his lips on mine.

Stop it, I pleaded to my imagination, but the Freya who owned those thoughts only smirked and gave me *more.*

My imagination was a curse.

It had always been a curse, giving me the false belief that what it conjured might become reality, which always led to disappointment. As displeased as I'd been about my father's choice to wed me to Vragi, I'd still dreamed of the pleasures I'd experience on my wedding night, my imagination fueled by the stories told to me by other women. The reality had proven a bitter tonic, for Vragi had only demanded I disrobe, then bent me over the bed and serviced me like a horse, finishing in moments and leaving nothing but a cold and hollow void in his wake.

"Deep thoughts for the late hour," Bjorn said softly, and I jerked my eyes up to meet his gaze, feeling caught out despite my memories of Vragi having vanquished the lust burning in my body.

Though now I burned with embarrassment.

"I wasn't thinking of anything." I pulled my hand from his grip and hid it in the fold of my cloak. "Thank you for your assistance. The pain is much reduced."

Bjorn shrugged. "It's nothing."

If only that were the case.

"Apologies," he added after a moment. "For before. You were trying to make sense of the role my father sees for you, and I turned the conversation to my own grievances, which robbed you of the opportunity."

I lifted one shoulder, for some reason unable to meet his gaze. "He had no intention of telling me anything."

"I think it's because he doesn't know." Picking up the stick, Bjorn poked at the fire, voice low as he added, "He knows of warring and raiding and twisting stories of the gods to serve his purposes. But as to how you might inspire Skaland to swear oaths to him as king? I think he's as in the dark as you or me."

I bit my bottom lip, the night air somehow colder than it had been a moment ago.

"You should get some rest," he said, rising to his feet. "We'll break camp before dawn and ride hard tomorrow."

Spreading out my furs, I lay down and pulled a thick pelt on top of me, my eyes on the glowing embers. In the absence of our conversation, the camp was quiet, the only sounds the crackle and pop of smoldering wood, the wind in the pine boughs above, and the faint snoring of one of the warriors.

Which meant it was impossible to miss the meaty *crunch* that filled the air.

Sitting upright, I gaped in horror as one of the warriors on guard toppled into the circle of firelight, an axe embedded in his skull. Before I could scream a warning, warriors appeared among the trees, faces marked with warpaint and weapons glinting in the light, their battle cries filling my chest with the purest form of terror.

"Kill the shield maiden!" one of them shrieked. "Kill all the women!"

One of the thralls darted ahead of them, screaming as she tried to get away. Before she made it two steps, a man sliced at her back. She fell, dead before she hit the ground, and the warrior's eyes fixed on me.

My instincts took over.

Leaping to my feet, I drew my sword before bending to pick up a shield, emotion making my arm strong. It was *me* they wanted dead. So it would be *me* they had to kill. "Hlin," I screamed, "give me your strength!"

Magic filled me, then spilled out of my hand to encase the shield, illuminating the night with brilliant silver light. All eyes turned on me, and then with a roar, the attackers surged. Not just a few men and women, but dozens spilling out from the trees, their eyes full of murder.

And I stood alone.

Or so I thought.

A shield appeared next to mine, and I turned to find Bjorn next to me, his axe burning bright. His face was splattered with blood, but he grinned. "Arm up, Born-in-Fire." Then, louder, he shouted, "Shield wall!"

Other warriors hurried into position, Snorri among them. Shields locked into place, forming a circle within which Ylva, Steinunn, and the thralls crouched. Though I could smell their terror, mine was gone. In its place, a wild, furious defiance fueled my strength. And my magic.

The glow spilled outward, covering Bjorn's shield first and then the others, spreading like a tide until the shield wall glowed with starlight.

Yet the enemy didn't hesitate.

Whether it was because they didn't know what Hlin's power could do or that they were too caught up in battle rage to care, the enemy raced toward us as a wall of shield, axe, and blade. The collision was deafening, my magic hurling them back with such force that they collided with their fellows, knocking them from their feet. Screams and the snap of breaking bones filled the night, then Snorri shouted, "Attack!"

For a heartbeat, I wavered, then a voice whispered in my head, *They attacked you. Attacked your people. They deserve this fate.* I allowed the rage behind that voice to take control.

Hacking and stabbing at the enemy as my pulse roared, I killed and maimed those who'd come to do the same to me. Blood splattered my face and I tasted copper on my tongue, but I didn't care. They'd brought this fight to me, but I'd be the one who finished it.

And then it was over.

Gasping for breath, I turned in a circle, searching for someone to fight. Someone to kill. But all the enemy was on the ground, either dead or soon to be so, the light from my shield illuminating the gore-soaked scene.

Men and women reduced to carcasses. To parts. The rage that had fueled me fled, replaced with sick horror over the scene before me. A scene that I'd helped create. My fingers turned to ice, bile burning in my throat because each breath I sucked in smelled of blood and opened bowel. *They deserved it!* I desperately reminded myself. *They'd have done the same to you, given the chance!*

"Are you hurt?"

I lifted my head to find Bjorn before me, eyes narrowed with concern.

"It smells," I blurted out. "I didn't realize it would stink this bad."

It was a stupid thing to say. A stupid thing to think, but Bjorn only gave a grim nod. "A sweet-smelling victory is a myth, Born-in-Fire."

Yet one I'd believed in.

I swallowed hard, feeling painfully naive, but before I was forced to acknowledge so to him, a commotion caught our attention.

Snorri was bent over a warrior, the dying man's guts spilling out of a charred hole in his chain mail, suggesting Bjorn had been the one to strike the blow.

"It's been a long time since we crossed blades, Jarl Torvin," Snorri said, wiping gore from his brow. "It would've been better if you'd kept it that way."

Torvin spat a mouthful of blood. "Your time will come soon enough," he gasped out. "You possess the king-maker but have not the strength to keep her. Everyone is coming for her, to kill her or take her, and you'll be a corpse alongside me soon enough."

Snorri laughed. "How can I fear death when the gods themselves have foreseen my greatness?"

"They foresaw greatness," Torvin whispered. "But is it yours? Or is it for the taking?"

Snorri's face darkened and, rotating his axe head up, he shoved the haft into Torvin's mouth, smiling as the man choked and gagged, clutching at his throat before finally going still.

No one spoke as Snorri straightened. "Ready the horses. We ride through the night to Fjalltindr."

Bjorn cleared his throat. "They cut the lines and scattered the horses. It will take some time to track them down."

"We don't have time," Ylva said. "You heard him—every jarl in Skaland is coming for her."

"We've lost a third of our men," Bjorn said. "We should return to Halsar."

Blood dribbled down Snorri's face, and I found myself staring at what looked like bits of skull caught in his beard. "No," he said. "The specter said that if Freya isn't able to give sacrifice on the first night of the full moon her thread will be cut short. And if she's dead, I will not achieve my destiny."

How many will die in the quest to get me to that moment? The question rippled through my thoughts, and I gripped my sword hilt. All this death for a chance at power.

"If what Torvin said is true, then more will be waiting to ambush us on the path up the mountain," Bjorn said. "It's narrow and we'll be at a great disadvantage against those holding higher ground."

Silence hung over the survivors of the battle, and though my fate sat at the center of this, I held my tongue.

Because I did not know which way forward was best.

If I didn't make it to Fjalltindr, it meant I was dead, so turning back wasn't an option. But that didn't mean I'd survive pressing forward. Perhaps not even the gods knew for certain.

"There's another path," Snorri said, finally breaking the silence.

"You and Freya will go that route while the rest of us provide diversion."

Bjorn stared at him. "You don't honestly mean . . . ?"

"No one will think to guard that route."

"Because only a lunatic would attempt that climb," Bjorn exploded, sending a flood of unease through me. If it was dangerous enough to dissuade *Bjorn,* it must truly be madness to consider it.

I opened my mouth to demand an explanation, but before I could speak, Snorri said, "The gods have set Freya to this test, and Hlin herself has set you to guard her back."

"No." Bjorn was pale. "I'd rather fight my way through every clan in Skaland than go that route."

"Which route?" I demanded. "What is this path you speak of?"

Snorri didn't so much as look my way, but Bjorn's gaze met mine. "It's called the Path to Helheim. It's a set of stairs and tunnels that runs inside the sheer side of the mountain."

The idea of tunnels set my pulse to thrumming, as I had no liking for being underground, but I didn't think Bjorn would blanch at the idea of confined spaces. "What is so dangerous about it?"

Bjorn's tone was flat as he said, "It's full of draug."

The undead.

My skin crawled as memories of the stories I'd heard as a child filled my mind, corpses that couldn't be killed with mortal weapons.

"Allegedly," Snorri said. "There is no proof."

"Hard for there to be any proof when any fool who attempts the climb is consumed," Bjorn snapped. "The area around the entrance is littered with bones. Not even animals will venture close."

"There is no choice." Snorri's hands fisted. "Freya must be there for the full moon. The specter told her that she must earn her fate, which means she must pass every test the gods set for her."

"The specter spoke in riddles," Bjorn retorted. "You might unwittingly be sending Freya to her death."

"Is it Freya's death you fear"—Snorri's face was hard as granite—"or your own, Bjorn?"

No one spoke. No one even seemed to breathe.

"Are you my son or are you a coward, because you cannot be both," Snorri said softly. "Choose."

It was no choice, I knew that. Either Bjorn walked toward death and kept his honor, or he lived and was branded a coward, which meant he'd be exiled and ostracized by all he crossed paths with.

Stepping forward, I said, "I won't condemn anyone to die just to spare myself death. I especially won't condemn anyone to spend eternity as a draug." Because that was the fate that awaited anyone who was killed by one.

Bjorn opened his mouth to speak, but Ylva interrupted him. "If you fail to make it by the full moon, Freya, you will cease to be of value. As will your family. Am I clear?"

I pressed my hands flat against my thighs because the alternative was to strike her. Hard. And I didn't think I'd be able to stop with one blow. Didn't think I'd be able to stop until her face was pulp beneath my fists. "The gods see *all,* Ylva. There will be a reckoning for this."

"Foretellings are the words of the gods. Of Odin himself," she answered. "They'd not have set us on this path if they did not intend to reward us for doing whatever it took to reach the end."

I was tempted to point out that neither she nor Snorri were the ones who had to face the draug, but instead I said, "Then I'll go alone."

"No!" All three of them spoke at once, and all, I thought, for different reasons. Ylva, because she hoped the draug would kill Bjorn and clear the way for Leif. Snorri, because he feared losing his destiny. And Bjorn . . . I wasn't entirely sure what his reasons were, only that his *no* had been more vehement than the others.

"It makes sense," I said.

"It does not make sense." Bjorn crossed his arms. "You don't know the way. Going at all is insanity, but going by yourself is blind stupidity."

"Agreed," Snorri said. "Hlin wishes for him to see you through to fulfill your destiny, which means he must be with you through each test."

Part of me thought that I should argue. Another part of me wondered if Snorri was right. "Fine."

Holding his fingers to his lips, Bjorn whistled, and a heartbeat later, his ugly roan horse emerged from the trees, walking toward its master. "Pack only what you need. And what you're willing to carry." His gaze met mine. "Leave behind anything you don't want lost to this world."

My gaze instinctively went to the sword I still held, sticky with the blood of the men whose lives it had taken. It was the last thing I had of my father's, and if I died, it should go to Geir, not be left to rust in a cave.

A dark voice whispered inside my head, *Why? Because he valued it so greatly?*

My jaw tightened, for the voice spoke true. Wiping the blade clean on the body of one of the fallen, I sheathed it at my side before turning to Snorri. "I want my own horse."

Conversation was impossible as Bjorn led me through the forested paths, my attention all for guiding my horse, a small bay mare that Snorri had chosen for her even temper, for I was not the most experienced rider.

We did not ride alone.

Steinunn galloped at my horse's heels, along with one of Snorri's men. The jarl had insisted the skald come with us to witness our trial and the warrior to take the horses back to the main group, retreat apparently not an option. Given what the skald had told me about how her magic functioned, I didn't see why her presence was necessary, but Snorri refused to hear my argument that the woman remain with the main group.

The air grew colder as we climbed, patches of snow clinging to the shadows of the pine trees, the horses' hooves crunching in the bed of needles and filling my nose with their scent. Ahead, Hammar loomed.

The mountain was indeed hammer shaped, the north, east, and west sides near-vertical cliffs, though Bjorn said the south side possessed a gentler slope. As we approached the north-facing cliff, Bjorn slowed his pace, reining his mount around something on the ground. I tugged on the reins of my own horse, and my heart skittered as I saw what he'd been avoiding.

Bones.

Once I saw the first bleached lengths, I saw them everywhere. Flesh-less bones of all sizes and sorts.

And not just from animals.

Sweat broke out on my spine as my horse passed a human skull sitting on a rock, a gaping hole in the side of it. To its left, the rest of the skeleton was tangled in some brush, the breeze causing the bones to shift and move as though life yet remained.

"Wolves?" Steinunn suggested from behind, and Bjorn only cast a disparaging snort at the skald over his shoulder before pressing forward.

Wind blew through the forest, the branches of the trees creaking and groaning. Another sound joined the mix, a strange hollow clacking that made my skin crawl. "What is that?"

Bjorn lifted a hand, and I followed the line of sight to the source. Bones had been hung as wind chimes from the trees, femurs and ribs rattling against one another to create terrible music.

"Steinunn's wolfpack enjoys decorating, it seems," Bjorn said, resting a hand on his horse's shoulder as the animal shied away from the awful creation.

My own mare snorted loudly, her ears pinning against her head before she ground to a stop. I thumped my heels against her sides, trying to drive her forward, but she refused. Not that I could blame her, for wafting toward us was a haze of steam that carried with it the smell of rot.

Steinunn's horse reared and tried to turn, eyes showing their whites as it ignored her attempts to press farther. Snorri's warrior was having worse luck. Even Bjorn's mount was resisting now, head lowered and snorting at the wisps of steam.

"If only my father showed as much sense as you," he muttered to his horse, dismounting and leading the animal back to tether it to a tree. "We'll leave the horses here and go the rest of the way on foot."

"I'll take the horses now," the warrior announced, his jaw tight as he stared at the bones.

"No." Bjorn patted his horse's neck. "Freya needs to see the path before she makes the choice to climb. Wait an hour, then take the horses and rejoin my father's party, if you can reach the southern path in time."

Other than the wind and the bone chimes, there was no sound as we moved down the rocky path, and my eyes went to the cliff rising toward the clouds, too sheer for anyone but the best of climbers to scale.

I was not the best of climbers.

Not that I was afraid of heights, but I did have a healthy appreciation of what it would mean to fall such a distance, my imagination readily supplying the image of my skull shattering like a melon on the ground.

We broke out of the trees, all three of us stopping to stare at the opening at the base of the cliff. It was large enough that I'd barely need to stoop to enter, but beyond was total blackness broken only by the great gouts of steam that blasted forth every few moments.

"Just a wolf den, right, Steinunn?" Bjorn crouched on his heels, his eyes roving over the scene.

Setting my shield on the ground, I glanced to my right at the other woman, noting that her face was as white as a sheet. "It is a path to Helheim," she whispered, then rounded on Bjorn. "I will tell Snorri so myself, Bjorn. Will vouch for you that it was madness to enter."

Bjorn met my gaze. "It is your choice, Freya. I won't make you go in there."

I swallowed hard, the stench of rot making my stomach twist and threaten to spill itself. My body felt like ice, yet sweat pooled at the base of my spine and under my breasts, my heart pounding like a drum beneath my ribs. There was no easy way up the mountain. The southern slope was guarded with men who'd see me dead, and this path by draug who'd do the same. Yet if the specter was to be believed, turning back would be equally deadly.

There was no good choice. At least, not for me.

"What will Snorri do to you if I don't attempt the climb?" I asked Bjorn. "Will he accept that you respected my wishes? Or will *you* be punished for not forcing me to go in there?"

"Don't make this decision about me," he answered. "I'll go where you go, and if that's to find a mead hall where we get very drunk while waiting for the knife to fall, so be it."

Chewing on my thumbnail, I stared at the dark opening, knowing that I'd rather die fighting than as a coward. "I suppose we should start climbing."

Bjorn didn't question my decision. Didn't ask if I was sure. Only said to Steinunn, "You're not coming with us. Make your way back to the horses."

Steinunn was not so easily cowed. "The jarl ordered me to stay with you."

"To spy on my every move?"

The skald twitched, and I winced knowing that it wouldn't improve Bjorn's opinion of her. But rather than denying it, Steinunn said, "To witness your trials so that I might tell Freya's story. So that they might know the truth about what she is."

I frowned, but before I could speak, Bjorn said, "The dead do not sing, and death will be your fate should you walk this path."

His outlook on our prospects of survival made me want to change my mind, except the specter's words could not be denied. There was no turning back. Not for me. But Steinunn's fate didn't have to remain entwined with mine. "If I live, I'll tell you everything that happened," I said to her. "I'll answer all your questions, I swear it." My eyes flicked to Bjorn. "You as well."

He snorted. "I'll cut out my own tongue before I tell Snorri's little spy a word."

Irritation at his stubbornness chased away some of my fear, but we didn't have time to stand here arguing. "Is my word enough, Steinunn?"

The other woman was silent for a long moment, then said, "I look forward to hearing your story, Freya Born-in-Fire."

"Then it is settled," Bjorn said. "If you hurry, you'll be able to reach my father's warrior and the horses before they leave. Else you have a long walk ahead of you."

Steinunn crossed her arms, meeting his stare. "You cross Snorri at every turn, Bjorn. There will come a day that you pay the price for that."

"But not today." Bjorn gestured to me. "Lead the way."

Knowing my nerves would fail me if I delayed another second, I started toward the opening in the cliff wall, Bjorn following at my heels. Each rush of steam looked like breath on a cold day from a great sentient beast that consumed the wary and unwary alike. "What do we do for light?"

In answer, Bjorn's fiery axe appeared in his hand, and together, we stepped inside.

CHAPTER

16

I'd thought the tunnel would immediately rise in some form of
staircase inside the cliff, but what greeted us instead was a passage
that carved deeper into the mountain. Gouts of steam hissed from
cracks in the floor, forcing us to time each step lest we be scalded.
Bjorn's axe cast a pool of light that reached only a half dozen feet, the
darkness seeming to consume the brilliance of the god-fire.

"Do you really think she's spying for Snorri?"

"Of course she is," Bjorn answered. "She's the perfect spy, for everyone answers her questions in the hope of a mention in one of her songs.
Even if they didn't, she's always lurking in the corners, watching and
listening. You'd do well to mind your words around her."

On that, he might have a point, but . . . "I feel bad for her."

"Why? She's given everything."

"There's something sad about her. I . . ." I shook my head, unable to
give justification to the feeling. Besides, Steinunn, and whether or not
she was spying for Snorri, was hardly my foremost concern. "How did
the draug come to be here?" I cast a backward glance toward the entrance, only to find the sunlight already gone, the tunnel having bent
without my noticing. "Who were they?"

"It is forbidden to carry a weapon through the temple borders or to take a life not in sacrifice to the gods," Bjorn answered. "As the story goes, a jarl coveted the wealth of Fjalltindr and sought to take it. He and his trusted warriors came for the ritual, and in the celebration that followed, they stole much of the gold and silver that had been left as offerings and fled with it down this path. One by one, they were struck down by divine force, made to bear the burden of their master's curse and guard the tunnels until the end of days. Most believe that the treasure they stole still remains within the caverns, and many have attempted to steal it for themselves. None have ever returned, and it is said that any who touch the treasure of Fjalltindr are cursed to become draug themselves. So if you see anything valuable on the steps, best leave it alone."

"Noted," I muttered, stepping over a dead rabbit, its skin torn by what looked like claws. "What about your axe? Can you still call it within the temple's borders?"

"I wouldn't even attempt to do so." Bjorn stopped at the base of a staircase leading up, each step only half a handspan deep, the rock slimy with moisture. At his feet, the hindquarters of a deer sat rotting. "It's a weapon."

"What about my shield?"

He glanced over his shoulder at me. "You willing to risk finding out?"

Given what had happened to the jarl and his men, that was a definite *no*.

The steps rose up and up, and it wasn't long until my calves screamed from the effort of keeping my balance on the slippery rock. I suspected it was worse for Bjorn, for he was tall enough to have to hunch over, but he never paused.

And with every step, the mountain pressed in.

There was no way to know how deep inside we were, or even how far off the ground we'd traveled, and the walls of the tunnel seemed to narrow even as the air grew hotter and more fetid. Strange sounds filled the cavern, and more than once I swore I heard the sound of feet. The whisper of strange voices. I sucked in breath after rapid breath, my heart beating chaotically in my chest as the walls moved ever closer.

It's just your imagination, I told myself. *There's plenty of space.*

Bjorn chose that moment to grumble, "This is the first time in my life I've wished I were smaller," before turning sideways to squeeze between stone walls, moisture sizzling as it struck his axe. Then he stopped, turning his head to look back at me. "You all right, Born-in-Fire?"

I was quivering, but I forced a nod. "Fine. Why?"

"You look like you might vomit." His brow furrowed. "Or faint."

"I'm not going to fucking faint, Bjorn," I snapped, then regretted it as my voice echoed through the tunnels. We both froze, listening, but other than the endless hiss of steam venting, there was no sound but our breathing. "I swear I've heard footsteps," I whispered. "Voices. Do you hear them?"

He was quiet, then said, "The imagination plays tricks."

Cold crept up my fingertips because he hadn't denied hearing things. "I don't think we're alone in here."

"Doesn't mean there are draug," Bjorn said softly. "It could be that the bones and chimes are tricks set out by the gothar to dissuade those who wish to harm or thieve. Could be that it's all myth and legend."

"Maybe," I whispered, remembering all the dead things I'd stepped over on the endless stairs. Creatures that had not died easily. "Either way, I don't care to linger."

Bjorn gave a tight nod of agreement, then continued his sideways progress through the tight space, the mail he wore scraping against the rock.

And then he stumbled.

Something metallic shot past my feet, and I managed a backward glance in time to see a golden cup crusted with jewels go bouncing down the steps and out of sight.

Clank.

Clank.

Clank.

The sound of the metal striking against stone as it went down and down and down echoed louder than any shout. Worse, it felt like it went on forever, my stomach twisted into knots by the time it finally silenced.

I held my breath, waiting for some sign that we'd been heard. For some sign that something other than us walked the tunnels of these mountains.

"It would seem that—" Bjorn cut off as the air *stirred.*

Hot mist swirled around my face as though the mountain had taken a deep breath. As though the mountain had . . . *awakened.*

"Fuck," Bjorn whispered.

I squeezed through the tight spot to where he stood. Only to have my jaw drop. The stairs beneath his feet glimmered with coins and cups of silver and gold, rubies and emeralds winking in the axe's light.

The stolen treasure, and if that part of the story was true, then—

A scream pierced the darkness. Then another and another.

Great shuddering shrieks coming from every direction and none. Voices beyond number, their howls full of grief and pain and *rage.* Drums not of this world took the place of screams, the rapid rhythm punctuated by sounds of footfalls. Not boots or shoes or even the slap of bare feet, but the scratch of . . . of *bones* against stone.

And they were coming closer.

"Run!" I gasped, but Bjorn had already locked his hand around my wrist, dragging me upward.

Terror chased away my exhaustion and I took the steps three at a time, shield bouncing against my back. The stairs ended, and Bjorn cut right down a narrow tunnel, dragging me with him.

Then he slid to a stop.

I collided with him, his chain mail digging into my forehead as my skull bounced off his shoulder. Stunned, I looked past him.

Part of me wished I hadn't.

Four skeletal figures raced toward us, their forms illuminated by a strange green light. Scraps of leather and armor hung from their bony forms, chilling war cries echoing out of their gaping jaws, teeth blackened and foul. But the weapons in their hands gleamed brilliant bright, as though even in death the draug cared for them.

Twisting, I looked back the way we'd come, but the same green light illuminated the stairs, drums and footfalls growing louder by the second.

We were trapped.

"Freya," Bjorn said, unhooking his shield from his shoulder, "get ready to fight."

Ripping my own shield off my back, I drew my sword and then invoked Hlin's name. Magic flared over my shield as draug exploded from the stairwell. My back to Bjorn's, I widened my stance and braced, fetid steam filling my mouth with every rapid breath I took.

Empty eye sockets fixed on me, more of their awful screams shattering the air as they surged forward, weapons raised.

"*Born-in-Fire*," I whispered, then screamed my own battle cry.

A draug threw itself at me, and for a heartbeat I thought my magic would fail. That the draug would slam through my shield, fingers clawing and teeth gnashing. But the silver glow was the power of a goddess, and it was as though it took hold of the draug and flung it with the strength of Hlin herself.

The draug sailed through the air, smashing into those behind it. Righting themselves, the creatures crouched on all fours, hissing like beasts. Except instead of attacking again, the draug bent their heads together, and my hopes that they were mindless entities disappeared like smoke. Cursed and skeletal as they were, some of the warriors they'd once been remained.

Sweat slicked my palms as one of them leapt, clinging to the ceiling, its neck bending backward unnaturally so that it could watch me as it prowled closer. Another clung to the wall, finger bones slipping into cracks in the stone, knife clenched between its teeth. But it was the largest, which strode with heavy scraping strides, that led their attack.

My breath came in too-quick pants, and it took all my willpower not to retreat. Not that there was anywhere to go. Behind me, Bjorn grunted with effort as he battled screeching draug, but I dared not look. Not when he was trusting me to guard his back.

The draug moved closer. My shield was nowhere near wide enough to block the width of the tunnel, and my attention skipped from the one on the ceiling to the one on the wall to the one striding upright, its jaw cracking open in a parody of a grin.

Step. The bones of his feet scraped on the stone. *Step.*

It tensed, preparing to attack.

But it was the one on the ceiling that moved.

I shifted my shield, clenching my teeth as he rebounded off it, barely managing to move my arm in time to knock back the one that sprang from its perch on the wall.

And not nearly fast enough for the third.

His sword slashed past the right edge of my shield. I jerked my own blade up to parry and the impact of his weapon against mine sent me staggering. He swung again, and my arm shuddered as I knocked it away.

Beyond, the other draug were back on their feet, and more had exited from the stairwell, the stink of rot wafting ahead of them.

The big draug tried again to slice at me. This time, I blocked the blow with my shield. My magic sent the weapon flying out of his hand, and I took advantage, thrusting my sword toward his heart.

Only for the weapon to pass right through the creature as though it were no more than air.

The shock cast me off balance, and I staggered.

Right into the draug's grasp.

Its skeletal fingers closed around my throat, mouth stretching wide to reveal blackened teeth as it pulled me toward it. Pain lanced down my neck, my lungs desperately trying to draw in breath, and beyond, the other draug moved to take advantage.

I tried to cut at the creature with my sword, but the draug only let out a breathy laugh, stink rolling over me.

No weapon forged by mortal hands can harm them. Bjorn's warning filled my ears, but I couldn't move my shield to strike without giving the other draug space to pass. If I did, they'd stab Bjorn in the back, and I refused to allow that to happen while my heart still beat.

Which might not be much longer.

My chest convulsed with the need to breathe, and mindless desperation drove me to try to stab the draug over and over, but the tip of my sword only slammed into the tunnel wall.

So I let go of my blade.

The weapon clattered to the ground as I balled my hand into a fist and swung. My knuckles split as they collided with the creature's skull, but though it recoiled, it didn't let go.

My lungs were agony and my vision was blurring, but I bared my teeth and swung again. And again. My knuckles bruised but the pain was secondary to the need for *air* as tears slicked my face. Then the draug caught hold of my wrist, bony fingers digging into tendon and flesh, and . . .

Flame flashed overhead, and Bjorn's axe cleaved through the creature's skull. For a terrifying heartbeat, its grip on my throat remained strong.

Then it exploded into ash.

I sucked in a breath, the world swimming, but I managed to keep my shield up, protecting Bjorn's left as he carved into the draug, leaving explosions of ash in his wake. The creatures shrieked in fury and fear, one trying to flee, but Bjorn threw his axe, the fiery blade turning it to dust. Bjorn spun, the axe reappearing in his hand as he searched for another opponent.

But we once again stood alone in the tunnel.

"I'm sorry." My voice was raspy and barely audible as I reached down to pick up my sword and sheathe it, my battered hand barely managing the task as pain lanced up my wrist and arm. Yet for all the pain, what I felt most was shame. "My weapon passed right through it and—"

"I saw what you did." He caught hold of my waist and pulled me close, the light from our magic revealing a deep cut on his brow that spilled blood down his face. On the ground farther up the tunnel, his shield rested in pieces. "Don't you *ever* put yourself in danger for me again."

My pounding heart flipped at the intensity of his voice, the warmth from his hand spreading where it pressed against my back. The adrenaline racing through my veins, now deprived of a threat, turned to another purpose and I found myself leaning closer. "Why? Because your father will kill you if I so much as stub my toe?"

Bjorn's fingers tightened, sending a jolt like lightning into my core. "No," he answered. "Because I don't deserve it."

"Why would you say that?" I demanded. "Because I assure you, some foretelling doesn't make my life worth more than yours."

"There are many who'd argue that is *precisely* what it means."

"Well, I'm not one of them." I stared into his eyes, which reflected the glow of his axe. His rapid breath was hot against my face, his fingers still gripping me tightly, my mail-clad breasts grazing his chest. "And before you start arguing, allow me to remind you that I don't give a shit about what you think when what you think is complete shit."

Bjorn huffed out a laugh. "If the gods decide you are not a king-maker, Born-in-Fire, you should become a skald. People would come from all around to hear the poetry of your words. Steinunn would be out of a job."

My cheeks flushed. "Kiss my arse, Bjorn."

A smirk worked its way onto his face. "Perhaps later. I doubt that was the last we've seen of the draug, and while meeting my end with my lips pressed against your backside might not be the worst death, I don't think it will earn me a place in Valhalla."

My skin was blazing, but I managed to get out, "I'm sure you wouldn't be the first arse-licker to enter Valhalla."

"It's licking now, is it?" His shoulders shook with mirth, and I cursed myself because I never seemed to get the better of him. "Such a filthy mind, Freya. Does your mother know the things you say?"

I was not going to win this round, but I vowed that once we were out of these cursed tunnels, there'd be a reckoning. "We should go."

Bjorn looked like he might say more, but then shrugged and started up the tunnel, leaving me to follow at his heels. Though the screams and drums no longer deafened the air, I knew the whispers and faint tread of feet were not my imagination.

We were being watched. And when the draug came again, they'd be prepared.

Neither of us spoke as we carried on our climb up the mountain, and for me, much of that was driven by exhaustion. Each step was an act of will, my legs like lead, the shield once again strapped to my back having tripled in weight since we started our climb. My bruised throat ached and my battered knuckles throbbed.

But none of it compared to the gnawing sense that we were being trailed, our enemy waiting for the right moment to ambush us. Judging from the tension radiating from Bjorn, he felt the same, meaning it wasn't my imagination.

Climbing over a crumbled stretch of stairs, Bjorn reached back to help me over. The left side of his face was a mask of blood, the wound on his brow still seeping. "You should let me bandage that cut," I said. "You're leaving a trail of blood."

"I'm fine." Our hands interlocked, his large enough to conceal mine entirely, holding tight until I was over the broken rocks. "And the cowardly vermin know we're here regardless of what I do or don't do."

The air swirled, and I shot Bjorn a glare as he lifted me over another broken stretch. "Perhaps provoking them isn't the best course."

"Why not?" He started down the tunnel, still gripping my hand. "Thieving bastards plan to attack anyway." Louder, he added, "Why not do it like men instead of lying in wait, you cowardly pricks!"

"Bjorn!" I hissed, hot air gusting around me. "Shut. Up."

"They're planning an ambush," he muttered. "Might as well pick our ground."

While there was logic to the thought, I was also of the opinion that we could at least *try* to quietly get to the top without another fight.

Whereas Bjorn was obviously itching for one.

Spotting a pile of treasure, he kicked the lot of it, sending it scattering over the tunnel floor. "Come out and fight like your balls didn't rot off decades ago!"

The mountain exhaled, and then in the distance, the drumming renewed. Loud thundering beats that made my head throb. "You have maggots for brains," I snarled. "Stupid, idiotic fool of a man!"

Bjorn unhooked my shield from my back and handed it to me. "It hurts my feelings when you call me names, Freya. Besides, you should have more faith—I've got a plan."

"That doesn't mean it's a good plan." My voice was shrill, my fear latching onto the scrape of skeletal feet racing in our direction. There were more than before. Far more.

"It is perfection. Trust me." He pushed me toward the opening we'd just climbed through. "Keep that blocked."

Spitting every curse I knew, I invoked Hlin and then pressed the shield to the opening. There was space above and below it. More than enough for hands to reach through. Hands with weapons in them. I muttered, "It's amazing you've lived this long," turning my head so as to look at Bjorn while berating him, only to have my tongue freeze and my skin turn to ice.

For coming down the tunnel toward us was a sickly green glow. The stink of decay rolled ahead on an icy breeze, filling the small chamber and making me gag, and I had to clench my teeth to keep from vomiting on the floor. The first of the draug appeared carrying rotting shields, which they interlaced in a wall to face Bjorn, more filing in behind to fill the space at their backs. The glow stretched down the tunnel behind them, dozens upon dozens.

How could there be so many?

Then I remembered . . . it wasn't only the jarl's men who'd stolen the gods' offerings at Fjalltindr who were cursed to this place; it was all who'd come into these tunnels since, intending to take the treasure but instead succumbing to the draug.

A reminder that if Bjorn and I died, we wouldn't join the gods but be condemned to haunt this place for eternity.

There was no time to dwell on such a fate, for beyond my shield, something scratched. Then a hand reached through the gap between stone and shield. Not long dead; flesh still clung to the draug's bones as the arm bent upward, trying to lock onto my wrist. I swatted at it, my stomach roiling as bits of flesh caught on my fingers.

"Bitch-child of Hlin," the draug hissed, apparently still possessed of its tongue. "Your flesh will fill my belly soon enough."

In answer, I caught hold of its forearm and twisted until the elbow dislocated, relishing its cry of pain despite knowing the draug might well have the last word.

Behind me, Bjorn's voice echoed through the chamber. "I see my reputation has reached even the bowels of this shithole."

"You are no one to us, child of Tyr," one of the draug rasped out, a black and rotten tongue flapping in its mouth. It tried to ease past Bjorn, keeping to the sides of the chamber, its eyes fixed on me. But Bjorn stretched out his arm, blazing axe blocking the creature's path.

"If I am no one," he said, "then why have so many of you gathered to fight me? I am but one man who stands alone."

If I hadn't been busy wrestling with a rotten arm, I'd have pointed out to him that he did not stand alone. But the first draug was clawing my shoes while another tried to stab me with a blade shoved over the top of my shield.

"It seems to me that you are either liars or that you are," Bjorn paused, and I could imagine the smirk on his face, "cowards."

The draug snarled at the insult, several of them releasing chilling battle cries, but none surged to attack.

Because they were afraid.

No weapon of this world could end the terrible existence that they clung to, but the axe that burned in Bjorn's hand was not of this world. It was the fire of a god and thus capable of turning them to ash. If I were condemned to this fate, I would welcome an end, yet they flinched as the axe disappeared from Bjorn's right hand, only to materialize in his left, blocking another creature attempting to reach me.

"Most cowardly of all is your leader," Bjorn continued, his voice dripping with mockery. "He condemned you to this fate and yet has failed to show himself. Where is your jarl? Does he cower behind the lines, afraid to face the fire of the gods who cursed you to this place?"

I didn't understand what Bjorn could gain from taunting them besides a last bit of satisfaction before he died, for there was no hope of us killing so many. And given that once dead, we'd likely join their ranks, I couldn't help but think there'd be consequences for provoking them.

My thoughts on the shortsightedness of Bjorn's plan vanished as the fetid air swirled, the shield wall parting to reveal an enormous hulking creature.

Skeletal as the rest, it wore a full coat of mail that rattled as it moved, its skull concealed by a helmet, and several weapons belted at its waist. In a voice like howling wind, it demanded, "Who are you to call me coward, Bjorn Firehand?"

"So you *have* heard of me." Bjorn rocked on his heels, clearly amused, though how he wasn't pissing himself from fear was beyond me.

"I have heard many tales in the intervening hours since you stepped into my domain," the creature hissed. "And told many of my own."

"I've only heard the one about you being a common thief, but by all means, if there is more to tell, I am happy to listen."

The draug jarl opened its jaw and let out a scream of wrath, the noise like knives to my eardrums.

Bjorn didn't so much as flinch, only waited for the echoes to silence. "It explains why none recall your name, Jarl. You have no battle fame."

"I shall win great fame and honor for your death, Firehand," the creature hissed. "A song sung by skalds for generations to come."

"Seems unlikely, given none shall hear of it."

How he could be so brazen, I did not know, for my chest felt bound and my tongue dry as sand.

"It will be sung," the draug repeated, teeth baring in a grin.

Bjorn shrugged. "Then I suppose we ought to make it a song worth hearing. I challenge you to single combat. I win, you let us pass. I lose, well . . . I'll have to spend an eternity listening to songs of your prowess."

My breath caught. Perhaps his plan wasn't as idiotic as I'd first believed.

The draug tilted its skull, seeming to consider Bjorn's proposal, though there wasn't a warrior present, living or dead, who didn't know what he'd have to say. To decline would only prove Bjorn's accusation that he was a coward. He'd lose the respect of all those who followed him, and if his cares were the same in death as they were in life, the loss of reputation *would* matter to him.

"So be it." The jarl's answer blew over me, strands of hair whipping around my face. Yet I swore he smiled as he added, "As long as it be on the terms of the living. Which means, Bjorn Firehand, you must fight using a mortal weapon."

My stomach dropped. Was that true?

I had my answer when Bjorn went deathly still. "You cannot be killed by steel."

The jarl's laugh was echoed by his followers. "That is true, Bjorn Firehand. So now your choice is whether to die with honor. Or without. Either way, you will join my ranks."

"That's not fair," I shouted, unable to contain my voice. "The cursed dead do not deserve terms set for mortals."

The jarl laughed again. "Perhaps so, child of Hlin, but Bjorn Firehand issued the challenge." His teeth clacked together, flakes of black falling from them. "Now we shall see what his reputation is worth to him."

I opened my mouth to argue, but Bjorn cut me off. "I agree." He turned on his heel, striding toward me. "I need your shield, Freya. Theirs are all half rotten."

"No," I said. "We fight. There's a chance we can get through them."

Bjorn shook his head. "I'll not die a coward."

"Who cares?" The words tore from my throat. "They are the cursed dead—what does it matter what they think?"

"It doesn't." His voice was clipped. "Do what you need to do to survive, Born-in-Fire. You aren't bound by my word."

He set his flaming axe on the ground near me, then reached for my shield. My magic disappeared the moment the wood was out of my grip. "Trust Hlin's power, Freya."

I ground my teeth. What good was my magic with no shield in my hand?

"Leave the woman be during the fight," the jarl ordered his followers, and the other draug retreated, their bony feet scratching the ground. "After he's dead, do what you will to her, but the Firehand is mine."

Horror soured my stomach as I pressed my back to the wall, helplessness twisting my guts into ropes as Bjorn squared off against the jarl. One of the other draug approached. It looked to have once been a woman, rags of a dress hanging from its skeletal frame. It handed Bjorn an axe, then it caught hold of both combatants' wrists and lifted them high. From all around, the draug screamed in delight, and I dropped my sword to press my hands against my ears, the sound agony. But I saw the creature's fleshless jaw move as it spoke. "Begin."

Preternaturally fast, the jarl swung his weapon.

Bjorn was ready.

His borrowed weapon was up in a flash, the axe catching the jarl's sword even as he wrenched it sideways. A less experienced fighter would have lost his blade, but the jarl moved with Bjorn, extracting his sword and swinging again.

Bjorn caught the blow with my shield, grunting from the strength of the impact and staggering back. The jarl grinned, revealing his blackened teeth, then struck again. Bjorn parried, but the jarl's sword cleaved the haft of his borrowed axe and sent the blade flying.

Bjorn cursed, barely managing to block another blow with the shield. Then another and another, the wood cracking and splintering under the onslaught.

Lifting my sword, I shouted, "Bjorn, take mine!" and held it out, hilt first.

He reacted instantly, blocking a blow, and then twisting away. He snatched my weapon from my grip, rotating in time to block another blow.

It went on, Bjorn defending but never going on the offensive because there was no point. My sword would pass right through the draug's body without doing any harm. The jarl could not be killed except with the power of a god, which Bjorn was stubbornly resisting despite his axe being right there.

All for fucking honor.

My breath came in painful little gasps as I envisioned him dying, yet another to fall because of me and everything I supposedly represented. Tears flowed down my cheeks, because instead of going to Valhalla as he deserved, Bjorn would rise as one of the draug. And I'd have to leave him here. Would have to figure out a way to fight past these creatures so that I might survive, for dying seemed the greatest insult I could possibly give to Bjorn's sacrifice.

Which meant I needed to find a way to get out.

Bjorn's shield shattered under one of the jarl's blows, broken pieces flying everywhere. My eyes skipped over the chunks of wood, all too small to be the slightest bit effective. Nothing within reach was large enough to use, which meant I'd need to try to wrest a shield from one of the draug.

"*Fuck,*" I breathed, seeing that Bjorn's strength was fading and I'd found no solution. He'd said to trust Hlin, but what did that mean?

Bjorn stumbled beneath a heavy blow, the reopened cut on his brow splattering the ground with blood, droplets sizzling as they struck his axe where it still rested near my feet.

The axe.

I stared at the weapon, understanding of what I needed to do sending beads of sweat running down my back.

Could I do it again? Could I pick it up? And if I did, what would I be able to do, given my hand would be incinerated in a matter of moments? What had Bjorn believed I could accomplish?

Think, Freya, I silently screamed.

What had been his original plan? What had he hoped to achieve by drawing them here and challenging the jarl, because I didn't believe for a heartbeat that these vermin would honor the terms agreed to by their vanquished leader.

Unless they had to?

Made to bear the burden of their master's curse. Bjorn's voice filled my head, and I abruptly understood what I needed to do.

Pick it up, I ordered myself. *End this.*

Sweat rolled down my cheeks to mix with my tears, my fear of the pain battling with my fear of watching Bjorn die. Of dying myself.

Do it.

My heart throbbed with terror as I edged closer to the axe. Already the heat of it made me sick, my head spinning.

A sharp hiss of pain caught my attention, my eyes jerking back to the fight to see Bjorn stumble, a gash just above his elbow spilling crimson across the ground. The jarl pushed the advantage, swinging hard.

Steel clashed against steel, my sword flipping out of Bjorn's hands, the jarl's mouth gaping wide as he laughed.

There was no more time.

I reached for the axe, clenching my teeth against the pain that would come. Just before I took hold of the weapon, Bjorn's words filled my ears: *Trust Hlin's power.*

"Hlin," I gasped out. "Protect me."

Magic surged into my body right as Bjorn fell, landing hard on his back. Tears of terror dripped into my mouth, but I forced myself to focus. Not to push the magic outward, but to draw it over my fingers. My palm. My wrist, until it all glowed with the goddess's light.

Please let this work. I closed my hand over the handle of the axe, and braced for the burn.

But the smell of charring flesh did *not* fill my nose.

Rising to my feet, I hefted the weapon as the draug pressed a bony foot down on Bjorn's chest.

"You are defeated," the jarl whispered, not seeming to notice that I held the axe as he said to his followers, "You may have the woman after he's dead, but only I will feast on the flesh of the Firehand."

The jarl lifted his weapon, and Bjorn grinned. "I forfeit the challenge."

The draug hesitated, seemingly surprised, and in that heartbeat, I let the axe fly.

It flipped end-over-end, embedding with a *thunk* in the jarl's chest. Slowly, he looked down, vacant eye sockets latching onto the burning weapon.

My heart skipped with the fear that I'd erred. That Tyr disapproved of my actions and would deny me his power.

The jarl took one step toward me, reaching—

Only to explode into ash, weapons and armor dropping into a pile on the ground.

And not just him.

All around us, the draug sworn to the jarl turned to ash, the curse binding them to this place broken with the death of their lord. I gaped in amazement as weapons and bits of armor clattered to the tunnel floor, ash billowing up in choking clouds.

If only that were the end of it.

Those who'd come into these tunnels to search for the lost treasure and died for their efforts remained, for it was not the jarl's greed that had cursed them, but their own.

Teeth clacking, they filtered into the chamber, warily eyeing the burning axe that Bjorn held once again. Fear warring with an endless unsatiable hunger for living flesh.

Bjorn retrieved my sword for me, and with my newfound knowledge of my gift I covered it with magic as we stood back-to-back. "There are fewer of them," he muttered. "Unlike the jarl's men, these are not trained warriors."

Yet they had numbers.

My grip tightened on my sword, fury rising hot and fast inside me, drowning my fear. Fury that these shells of men would be the end of us despite all we'd done. Despite how hard we'd fought. Snorri and the others said that I was favored by the gods, but was this how they showed their favor? The draug were bound here by the will of the gods and the will of the gods alone, which meant it was the gods' will that we face them.

"I curse you," I hissed, not certain if I meant the draug or the gods or both. "I curse you to Helheim, you shades of men. May Hel rule you until the end of days, for you do not deserve the honor of Valhalla!"

The air in the tunnel abruptly turned to ice, and beneath my feet the ground quivered with such violence that I'd have fallen if Bjorn hadn't caught my arm.

The draug shrieked and tried to flee, but before any went more than a step, what looked like blackened tree roots reached up through the tunnel floor. They wrapped around each of the draug, the creatures screaming as they tried to claw their way free.

I recoiled against Bjorn, shock stealing my breath when, as one, the roots descended and disappeared.

Leaving only scattered bone and scraps of clothing in their wake.

They were gone. All the draug were gone.

"Good to see the gods finally being helpful to our cause," Bjorn said, but his voice was stilted, devoid of its usual humor.

I swallowed because the alternative was to vomit. "I suppose we needed to pass their test."

"Not we," Bjorn said. "*You.* Though you took your time doing it."

"I believe the words you are looking for are *thank you for saving my arse, Freya.*"

The quip stole the last of my bravado. My legs buckled and I fell on my bottom, resting my forehead against my knees to stop the spinning.

Bjorn sat next to me, holding out a waterskin, from which I took a long drink. "It was *my* idea."

"Your idea?" I tried to glare at him, which was hard, given that I was on the verge of fainting. Or puking. Or both. "How could you have possibly known that would work?"

"I couldn't." All the humor vanished from Bjorn's face as he clasped my forearms. "But I knew that you'd do what needed to be done."

"Your confidence is misplaced." I remembered how I'd hesitated. How afraid I'd been.

Bjorn tilted his head, his expression considering. "I have a great many doubts," he finally said. "But the courage of Freya Born-in-Fire is not one of them."

My chest tightened even as a flood of warmth filled my body, because no one had ever given me such a compliment, about something that mattered so much. It meant even more coming from him. I searched for the words to tell him so, but instead found myself arguing. "I'm not courageous. I was terrified to pick it up. Terrified that it would burn through my magic. It was shameful that it took me so long to overcome my cowardice."

Bjorn let out a laugh that sounded oddly strangled. "If we are having a moment of honesty, in those last few seconds before you killed the jarl, I had some concerns I might shit myself out of pure terror."

I snorted out a laugh, knowing full well that he was trying to make me feel better. "Bjorn, the only thing you shit is bluster and foolery."

"It was a valid fear." He reached down to pull me to my feet, drawing me up the tunnel and away from the remains of the draug. "If you'd made it out alive, it would only have been a matter of time until your tongue was loosened by wine and you told everyone what truly happened. Then not only would I be cursed for eternity to these tunnels as a draug, I'd forever be known to mortals as Bjorn Shitshimself."

My shoulders shook, I was laughing so hard. "I would never tell."

"Women always talk." He led me up a section of stairs, my legs wobbling with each step. "Especially to one another. There is no secret sacred enough to your kind to silence your tongue when you gather. Especially when there is wine."

I smiled even though I barely had the strength to keep moving. "You speak as though from experience. Tell me, what grave secret of yours was aired by a woman? What did she know that you were so desperate to keep from mocking ears?"

"I have no secrets." He winked as he looked down at me, arm moving from my shoulders to around my waist, supporting me. "Only *large* truths that I hope women will not share lest they bring envy into the hearts of their fellow women, which, in turn, will bring their men to my doorstep in a jealous rage spurred by a sense of inadequacy."

"Ah." My cheeks flushed, because I suspected what he alluded to *was* the truth. Bjorn was a large man, so it only made sense that he had a large—"So your demands for discretion are entirely altruistic?"

"I'm glad you understand my self-sacrifice in the name of the greater good."

I snorted. "I'd sooner believe you're hung like Thor himself than that you'd sacrifice a drop of piss to protect the vanity of other men."

Bjorn lifted me over some rubble. "This is why I like you, Freya. You've got a brain between your ears and a saucy tongue to voice the thoughts within it."

Heat flooded me. "Trying to distract me with compliments? You're losing your edge, Bjorn. Next you'll tell me that I'm pretty and I'll lose all respect for your wit."

"It is hard to keep one's wits when faced with a woman as beautiful as the sight of shore to a man who has been lost at sea."

My heart skipped, then sped. Because that was an entirely different sort of compliment, meaningful in an entirely different kind of way. I'd spent so much time thinking about how I felt about him, but this was the first time I truly considered how he felt about me. "Bjorn—"

My legs chose that moment to give out from exhaustion, and only his grip on my waist kept me from crashing to the ground.

"My feet hurt," he declared, lowering me so that my back rested against the tunnel wall. Setting his axe on the ground, he sat next to me. "And I'm hungry. Fighting makes me hungry."

"I'm sorry," I muttered. "I don't know why I'm so tired."

Bjorn dug around his pack, extracting some dried meat, which he handed to me. "Because you've barely slept in days. Because you just climbed halfway up a mountain. Because you just battled an army of draug. Because—"

"You made your point." Biting off a piece of the meat, I chewed, my eyes blindly staring at the crimson flames of his axe. I *was* exhausted, but my mind kept skipping from thought to thought, too overwhelmed to focus but unable to relax.

A scuff of noise followed by the sound of scattering pebbles caught my attention and I tensed, staring back the way we came. Bjorn went still as well, but then he shook his head. "The draug are vanquished, Freya. They are a threat no longer."

I knew that. Had seen it with my own eyes, but I still stared into the blackness for a long time until my heart settled, my breathing slowing enough for me to take a bite of the meat I held.

We ate and drank in silence, the only sound the draft of wind through the tunnels and the crackle of Bjorn's axe, which had turned the stone it rested upon black. With the distance we'd climbed, long gone were the gusts of fetid steam, and the cold seeped into my bones, the draft coming from above frigid. Shivering, I held my hands out to the heat of the flame, my right knuckles seeping blood from punching the draug. My fingers ached with stiffness, my skin painfully tight, a constant reminder of the moment my life had changed.

"Where is Liv's salve?" Bjorn asked. "You're to use it every day."

The thought of digging it out felt exhausting. "I don't need it."

"You do."

"I don't know where it is." Glancing up at him, I added, "You're the one who is injured." No lie, given that half of his face was covered in dried blood, his sleeve was soaked in crimson, and I was sure he was sporting many bruises from his battle with the draug jarl.

"You're right," he answered. "Not only am I in a great deal of pain, but this cut"—he tapped his face—"was also from a rusty draug blade and is likely going to fester, thus ruining my good looks. And I know how you value them, Born-in-Fire, because you've told me twice."

It was impossible not to roll my eyes. "I told you to let me tend to it. You said you were fine."

"I changed my mind."

Sighing, I twisted onto my knees, my chilled muscles protesting the motion as I lifted up enough to look at the injury. Just below the hairline, the cut was about as long as my little finger, and was likely down to the bone. It should've been stitched but I didn't have the tools. Digging into my bag, I retrieved a clean rag, which I dampened with water, and then cleaned away all the blood.

It was hard to focus with his breath brushing my throat and his skin hot beneath my cold hands. "This was from a blade?"

"A *rusty* blade."

Frowning, I shook my head. "When we reach Fjalltindr, someone will have herbs to better clean this. Cloves, perhaps," I added, having seen some in the spices carried by Snorri's thralls.

"There are cloves in Liv's salve."

"True," I muttered, reaching into my bag, my hand closing over the little pot before I froze. "You arse."

"Always with the insults." Bjorn slid his hand down my arm and into my bag, where my hand clutched the pot of salve, his fingers wrapping over mine. The sensation sent sparks dancing over my skin, and my stomach did flips as he drew our hands out of the bag.

Unfolding my fingers, he extracted the pot from my grip and opened it with his thumb. "Lucky for me that you didn't lose it. Or"—he dug out a glob and smeared it across his cut—"lucky for you, as now my face is saved."

"You are so vain." Flopping on my bottom with my back against the wall, I crossed my arms. "It's not right for a man to think so highly of his own appearance."

"You're the one who said you thought Baldur had finally been freed by Hel when you first saw me," he replied, prying my arm away from my side and depositing a glob of salve on my scarred palm. "And also the one who thought I blinded my enemies with beauty by charging them shirtless. And—"

"I hate you."

"If only that were true," he murmured, his strong fingers digging into the stiff tendons of my hand, driving away the cold and the pain and replacing them with something else entirely. A longing to feel them touching other parts of me.

A longing to touch him.

I said nothing, only watched him work on my hand long after the salve was rubbed into my scarred skin. Then he turned it over, tracing the twisted lines of the second tattoo Hlin had given me. Needing to break the silence, I asked, "I wonder what it was meant to look like?"

"Maybe this *is* what it was meant to look like," he countered, taking my other hand and examining the crimson shield tattooed across the back, the lines pulsing with each beat of my heart. "The gods foresaw that you'd take my axe. That you'd be burned. What they saw was why they said your name would be born in fire."

"Unless I acted differently than they foresaw," I said. "Unless I altered the fate the Norns planned for me. Maybe that's why this tattoo is twisted, because from that moment, the path they saw for me ceased to exist."

"Only the gods can answer that." Bjorn hesitated, still holding my hands. "Or a seer."

"Know one?" I asked, then immediately regretted it when he dropped my hands. "I'm sorry."

"Don't be. What happened to my mother was not your fault."

And clearly not anything he wished to talk about. I wracked my brain for a way to change the subject that wouldn't feel awkward, finally blurting out, "What does your tattoo depict?"

Bjorn huffed out an amused breath. "Which one?"

"The one Tyr gave you, obviously."

"That one's hardly hidden." He gave me a sideways glance, the corner of his mouth turned up once again. "I thought you meant the one on my arse."

My chin quivered with the effort it took not to laugh. "I already know what that one depicts."

"Do you now." Both his eyebrows rose. "Have you been spying on me when I bathe, Born-in-Fire?"

"Difficult, given that you *don't*." Keeping my expression steady, I added, "And I don't need to see it to know that it depicts the poor decisions that you make when you are drunk, whereas I imagine Tyr put more care into his selection when he inked you in blood."

Tipping his head back, Bjorn laughed, the rich sound filling the tunnel with echoes. "You are a goddess among women," he finally said, wiping tears from his eyes. "Look for yourself, then."

He turned his back to me and lowered his head to expose his neck. His height kept me from getting a good look, so I rose back onto my knees, holding his hair to one side and leaning close. "More light."

"Demanding," he murmured, but picked up his axe, holding it high to illuminate his skin.

Not unexpectedly, the tattoo was shaped like an axe, the blade etched in incredible detail, though the rune representing Tyr was what drew my eye. Like my own tattoo, the crimson inkwork pulsed with the beat of his heart, and, beneath my scrutiny, it seemed to throb faster. "Nervous?"

"My neck is exposed to *you*, Born-in-Fire," he answered. "I'm fucking terrified."

Smiling, I traced my left index finger over the thin red lines. He shivered beneath my touch, and his reaction stoked the embers of desire in me that felt impossible to extinguish. Swallowing the dryness in my throat, I said, "You're the one holding the weapon."

"And yet I feel entirely at your mercy," he said under his breath, lowering his axe back to the ground. Bjorn turned to face me, and on my knees as I was, we were at eye level. Breathing the same air, though the tension between us was so thick I felt light-headed.

"Satisfied?" he asked, green eyes rendered black by the shadows.

I wasn't. Not even a little bit, but the things it would take to sate me were so *very* forbidden. "It's good work."

Bjorn inclined his head without breaking our gaze, and I suddenly found I couldn't breathe at all. We were alone in these tunnels, which meant there was nothing to stop us but ourselves, and I felt my will to do so waning.

I wanted him.

Wanted his lips on mine. Wanted to feel his hands on my body. Wanted to touch the hard muscles and taut skin beneath his clothing and mail until I knew every inch of him.

He's your husband's son, a voice screamed in my head. *Nothing good could come of this!*

Husband in name only, I screamed back at the voice. *A sham of a marriage!*

That doesn't mean you aren't bound! That doesn't mean you won't pay if you get caught!

The thought rattled sense into me, and I looked away. Lowered myself down so that my back was pressed against the wall, my eyes again fixed on his axe. As my desire faded, so did the adrenaline that had come with it, and exhaustion pressed down. Cold leached into my legs, into my back, and I shivered.

"Come here." Bjorn's voice was low and rough, and I didn't resist as he pulled me against him, the heat of his body driving away the chill. I rested my head against his chest, so painfully tired but unable to close my eyes. Unable to relax because the misery in my heart refused to let me.

"What's it like in Nordeland?" Perhaps no better a topic than his murdered mother, but I needed to fill the silence with something heavy. With something that would pull me down and down until I finally fell asleep.

Bjorn cleared his throat. "Colder. Harder. It makes Skaland seem like soft living by comparison."

That was hard to imagine, though I didn't doubt that he was telling the truth. "What are the people like?"

"The same. Yet entirely different." He hesitated, then added, "It's hard to explain, but if you were to go there, I think you'd understand."

Nordeland was Skaland's greatest enemy, the most vicious of raiders, and I struggled to reconcile that truth with his words, for all I saw were monsters who slaughtered families and burned villages, stealing everything of value. "They treated you well?"

"Yes. Very well."

His voice was tight, but I pressed anyway. "Snorri wishes to make war against them. Will that be difficult for you? To fight those who raised you?"

Bjorn didn't answer, but I kept quiet, waiting, and eventually he said, "No matter how I feel about the people, vengeance must be had against the one who hurt my mother. I've sworn an oath to take everything from him, and anyone who stands in the way is nothing more than a casualty of war."

A shiver ran over me, and I started to turn to look up at him, but his grip tightened. Holding me in place, he murmured, "Go to sleep, Born-in-Fire. In a few hours, we'll finish the climb to the summit and see just what the gods have in store for you."

CHAPTER

17

"Freya, wake up."

I groaned and pried my eyelids open, my body protesting movement as I straightened. "How long was I asleep?"

"Only a couple of hours," Bjorn answered, climbing to his feet. "But we can't stay any longer. It's already midday and you need to be at the temple for the full moon."

"How can you tell the hour?" I winced as he pulled me to my feet, everything hurting.

"Instinct."

He rubbed at his eyes, and I noticed the shadows beneath them. "Didn't you sleep?"

"My axe disappears if I fall asleep," he said, "and you were cold."

I should've felt guilty, but instead a rush of warmth filled my core at the kindness. "Thank you."

Bjorn shrugged. "Be glad you weren't born in Nordeland. You wouldn't survive your first winter with how you deal with the cold."

I couldn't really argue with that, choosing instead to sling my pack over my shoulders. "Let's climb."

Neither of us spoke as we continued our way up the mountain, which unfortunately gave me time to dwell on the conversation we'd had before I'd fallen asleep. On the tension between us.

I knew I wasn't imagining it. Knew that there was an attraction between us that wasn't one-sided. What I didn't know was what I should do about it. Satisfying the lust was a stupid risk. Not only because of the consequences of being caught, but because I didn't think it was an itch that would disappear upon scratching, rather one that would intensify with each pass of my nails over my skin. Or his skin, to be more precise. Having him would only make me want him more, and adulterers always got caught.

Adulterer.

The word made me cringe but at the same time made me want to spit in anger, because it wasn't accurate. Snorri and I weren't truly wed, so how I felt for Bjorn wasn't a betrayal of a marital commitment. But it *was* most definitely in violation of the blood oath I'd sworn.

I frowned, for though I'd not forgotten the oath I'd made the night of my wedding, I'd been more concerned with the consequences that would be visited upon my family if I violated it than the implications of the magic. Would the spell Ylva had cast keep me from violating my word like some sort of magical chains? Or would I somehow be harmed if I broke my oath? I didn't know, and *asking* such a question of Ylva would only draw her attention to the very thing I was desperate to hide.

It doesn't matter, I reminded myself. *You're not going to do it.*

Bjorn chose that moment to look back at me. "You're quiet."

"Nothing to say." I winced at the lost opportunity as he shrugged and faced forward again.

It will be easier once we are out of these tunnels, because we won't be alone together, so there will be no temptation. Even as the thought passed through my head, I knew I was only lying to myself. It would be there, and with Snorri insisting that Bjorn had been divinely mandated to guard my every step, we'd constantly be together, which meant we'd be constantly tempted.

Deal with it, I told myself sternly. *You're not an animal to be ruled by lust. Quit thinking these thoughts and they'll go away.*

Only a fool would be thinking about sex anyway. There were far, *far* more pressing concerns, such as what would happen when I reached the summit for this ritual. Far more pressing questions, such as why *I,* of all of the gods' children, was to play such an important role and how I'd accomplish all that had been foreseen of me. *That* was what I should be thinking about.

Yet my mind shied away from those questions because all of it felt out of my control. What good was dwelling on something I didn't understand and couldn't influence? It would only drive me to madness, especially in this moment when there was no way to discover the answers to any of those questions.

Hiding from it won't make it go away.

I ignored the thought and glanced up at Bjorn, who led the way. My chest tightened as I drank in his broad shoulders and tapered waist, his sleeves pushed up to just beneath the sleeves of his mail shirt to bare the thick muscles of his forearms. He held his axe slightly away from him to keep from igniting his trousers, and I admired the focus it must take to keep his magic constantly burning. The effort it took must be exhausting.

It was this admiration that concerned me, because the things I was feeling . . . they weren't just physical. I liked him. Liked how he was both terrifyingly ruthless and heartbreakingly kind. Liked how he made me laugh and how his wit kept me on my toes. Liked the way I felt not just safe in his presence, but strong. I *wanted* to be close to him, and I was terrified of how my feelings might grow if I kept feeding that want.

Talk to him.

Gods help me, but that was the logical thing to do. Bjorn stood to lose as much as I did in betraying his father if we succumbed to the tension between us. Perhaps if we discussed the issue and came to a unified stance that we'd not pursue any of this, we'd save ourselves a great deal of heartache.

Say something, I urged myself. *Now is the time.*

My lips parted, but rather than anything useful coming forth, I only gaped like a fish with my tongue frozen. What if I was wrong? What if this attraction was entirely one-sided and the admission of my feelings horrified him? In my mind's eye, I imagined saying, *Bjorn, I know I'm married to your father, but we need to address how we both want to strip naked and have sex,* and a look of panic and disgust filling his eyes as embarrassment slowly buried me with barrow stones.

Better that than the alternative, a voice whispered. *Quit being such a coward and broach the issue.*

Gathering my courage, I said, "Bjorn—"

But he was pointing up the steps to where the faint glow of sunlight illuminated the walls. "It appears we've reached the top."

For the first time in what felt like an eternity, I inhaled clean mountain air. We'd made it to Fjalltindr.

Which meant the moment to speak, and the moment to *act,* was over.

A crushing wave of relief washed over me, and pushing past Bjorn, I all but sprinted up the last set of stairs and stepped out onto a mountaintop.

All around was cloud and mist, and I waited for my eyes to adjust lest I accidentally fall off the edge of the cliff I'd just fought so hard to climb. As I blinked away stinging tears, trees came into view, as well as ground covered with a light dusting of snow.

Standing on that ground was a man who gaped at me, eyes wide and mouth hanging open.

"How . . . ?" he said, reaching out to touch me as though to ascertain whether I were real. "How . . . ?"

"The draug are vanquished," Bjorn announced, stepping up next to me and causing the man to jerk back. "For which you may give your thanks to Freya Born-in-Fire, child of Hlin and lady of Halsar."

I bit the insides of my cheeks, wishing with all my heart that I might shirk that last title.

The man, who, judging from his robes, was a gothi of the temple, stared at us both with an open mouth before finally spluttering, "She vanquished the draug?"

"That is what I said, yes." Bjorn leaned an elbow on the stone structure that sheltered the stairs we'd exited. "The temple's wealth remains within the pathways to be collected, though I'd be mindful of sticky fingers lest the tunnel's vacancy be a short-lived affair."

The gothi blinked, then gave his head a shake. "This is an act of the gods, truly."

Bjorn opened his mouth, but I stepped on his foot, not interested in reliving a highly embellished version of events so soon. Besides, I'd come here for a purpose, and I was keen to see it through. "Might we carry on to the temple?"

"Of course, child of Hlin." The gothi inclined his head. "You may only enter through the main gates after submitting to the will of the gods." He gestured to a narrow path running along the clifftop that appeared to see little traffic. "Follow the track until you reach the bridge, where one of my fellows will be waiting to accept your submission."

If there was only one way into the temple, what were the chances it wasn't being guarded by the many jarls who wished to see me dead?

Bjorn was clearly thinking the same thing, because he said, "We've had a difficult journey and done Fjalltindr a great service, so perhaps you might make an exception and allow us to enter here." He gestured toward the trees, and through them I could pick out structures, as well as people moving around them. "Who is to know?"

The gothi's chest puffed out and he lifted his chin. "I'm afraid that's not possible. Even for you."

I winced, because after days of little sleep, now was not the time to test Bjorn's good humor. My concerns were verified as Bjorn's jaw tightened in annoyance.

"And who is to stop me? You? I welcome you to try." Shaking his head, Bjorn started toward the trees. "Let's go, Freya. I can smell food cooking from here."

He made it a half dozen steps and then staggered back as though he'd struck some sort of invisible barrier. Rubbing his forehead and cursing with annoyance, Bjorn reached out and his hand came to a stop midair, like it was pressed against perfectly clear glass. I caught the gothi smirking, though he wisely smoothed his expression before Bjorn turned around, his voice solemn as he repeated, "You must pass through the gates."

Bjorn's eyes were narrow with frustration, and I felt the same way. We'd climbed through darkness and violence and death, only to be stymied by tradition. "Do you know who I am?" he snapped.

The gothi gave him a condescending smile, which I thought rather brave even if Bjorn deserved it. I myself was struggling not to roll my eyes despite knowing that Bjorn was acting out of desperation, not vanity. "I'm afraid you did not give your name when you introduced your lady. But regardless of your battle fame, you must pass through the gates. It is the will of the gods."

Bjorn's jaw worked back and forth, then he gave the gothi a smile of his own that had the man taking an alarmed step back. "Fine. Freya, let's go."

After we'd gone a distance, Bjorn muttering increasingly colorful curses under his breath, I said, "What are we going to do?"

"We're going to have a look to see if the gates are under guard. Perhaps the gods' favor will continue, and we'll walk in uncontested."

Given that this was supposed to be a test, I thought that unlikely but didn't bother saying so.

We followed the narrow trail around the mountaintop, cloud and mist obscuring the view, though I could feel the breathlessness of altitude. It made me wonder if the placement of the temple was to get us as close to the sky, and the gods, as possible, but when I looked up, it was to find only more cloud. My stomach growled as the smells of cooking food washed over us, those already inside the confines of Fjalltindr's borders laughing and playing music with seemingly no care in the world. Except there was no way to reach them, for both Bjorn and I tested the invisible barrier every dozen feet and never found a break. He even had me stand on his shoulders to reach as high as I could, but the barrier reached into the clouds. When two massive stone pillars finally came into view, I was starved and cranky and ready to toss anyone who got in my way off the cliff.

Catching hold of my hand, Bjorn pulled me behind some brush, both of us peering through the leafless branches. This was my first glimpse of the path up the southern slope. From what I could see, it was a difficult climb up a steep and dangerous trail, the final paces requiring travelers to cross a narrow span of rock that stretched over a chasm to reach the open ground before the gates.

Before said gates loitered eight warriors. More stood on the far side of the chasm, where there were signs that a camp had been created, which suggested more permanence than just waiting to be admitted to the temple grounds.

"Do you know who they are?" I whispered.

Bjorn gave a tight nod, pointing to a big warrior with a bushy red beard and shaved head. "That is Jarl Sten."

Jarl Sten was built like a bull and carried an axe I'd probably struggle to lift. "I don't suppose he's on good terms with your father?"

Bjorn cast me a sideways glance, suggesting that to have hoped for such was idiocy.

"Fine," I muttered, casting a glance skyward. The sun was drifting downward, which meant we had only a matter of an hour or two until the moon appeared. "We kill them and then cross through the gates and get on with what we came here to do."

Bjorn's eyebrows rose. "Perhaps as well as possessing the blood of a god, you are also descended from the Valkyries of old."

"Why do you say that?"

"You're starting to see violence as the best solution."

That wasn't even close to the truth. I saw violence as the answer because the alternative was to see violence enacted upon me. "How is it not the solution here?"

"Because," he answered, "my understanding is that to get through the gates into Fjalltindr, you must get on your knees and honor each of the gods by name."

I stared at him, realizing with a start that having lived most of his life in Nordeland, Bjorn had never been to the temple before, either. "Which gods?"

"All of them." When I blanched, he laughed softly. "Not all battles are won with steel, Born-in-Fire—some are won by guile."

"What do you propose?" I asked, simultaneously worried and curious, because Bjorn's grin was wide, his green eyes gleaming bright. And I knew what *that* meant.

"I propose that we go see how the gothar are doing in gathering their gold."

CHAPTER

18

Not an hour later, Bjorn and I once again approached the gates, though this time we were dressed in the hooded robes of gothar, the deep cowls serving the double purpose of warmth and deception.

It had *not* been difficult to get the clothing, for as Bjorn had antici- pated, the gothi and one of his fellows had immediately ventured into the tunnels in search of the stolen wealth. After extinguishing their lantern, Bjorn had then informed them he'd leave them alone in the dark unless they gave up their clothing, which had them stripping faster than men on their wedding nights.

Bjorn left them in the dark anyway, loosely trussed so that they could get free and find their way out.

Eventually.

I'd felt guilty walking away with the echoes of weeping pleas filling my ears, and had muttered, "Leaving them down there in the dark was cruel."

"It was not cruel. The bastards planned to pocket some of the wealth before anyone else knew of it, which might well have seen them turned to draug by the gods they claim to serve. We saved both men from themselves. Now walk faster, we're running short on time."

Bjorn led me down the path at a trot until we were nearly in sight of the gates, then slowed to a sedate stride.

I mimicked him, keeping my head lowered as we approached the waiting warriors.

Never suspecting that their target might be coming from this direction, none of them paid us any attention. Neither did they make room for us to pass, forcing Bjorn and me to weave among them. My heart thundered, my stomach twisting into knots, and I feared one of them would notice my rapid breathing. Would know that it was Bjorn and me, not a pair of hapless gothar.

But they only grumbled about the cold, half of them seeming to believe this was a fool's errand and the other half seeming to believe I'd come striding across the bridge, shield ablaze. Not a one suspecting that I stood right next to them, which meant that in a few paces, we'd reached the gates.

An elderly gothi with tufts of white hair on his head waited, and I dropped to my knees in front of him, Bjorn following suit. The old man blinked at us in confusion, and I lifted my face to meet his gaze, saying softly, "The draug are vanquished."

His eyes, clouded with cataracts, widened, then skipped to the warriors standing only a few feet behind me. I tensed, watching as he pieced together my identity, praying to every god that he'd not sell me out to those who'd see me dead. Instead, the old gothi smiled, then intoned, "Do you submit to Odin, Thor, Frigg, Freyr, and"—he winked—"Freyja?"

"Yes," I croaked, curbing the urge to look behind me, the sensation of having my enemies at my back while I was defenseless on my knees infinitely worse than meeting them head-on.

"To Tyr, Hlin, Njord, and Loki?"

"Yes," Bjorn answered, even as I willed the old man to speak faster. There were dozens and dozens of gods left, and each passing second risked discovery.

I barely heard the names of the gods, only mumbled my assent with each pause, every part of me certain that the warriors behind us would hear the hammering of my heart. Would smell the sweat of nerves and fear rising to my skin, or notice that Bjorn's scarred hands, visible where they pressed against the ground, were *not* the hands of the gothi. Or worse, would question why gothar of the temple were on their knees performing a submission to the gods at all.

It wasn't until shouts filled the air that I realized my fears were misplaced.

I twitched, lifting my face to look through the gates. Beyond, two men stripped to their undergarments strode toward us. As I stared, horror filling my guts, one of them pointed. "It was them! They vanquished the draug, then accosted us so they might sneak into Fjalltindr!"

Those people lingering just inside the gates heard, whispers of interest racing like wildfire among them, several turning to see who the men were pointing at.

"I should have killed them." Bjorn sighed. "This is Tyr punishing me for abandoning my better instincts."

If I weren't about to drown in a flood of panic, I'd have smacked him, but the warriors behind us were stirring at the commotion, which meant that we had a matter of seconds. A crowd was gathering inside the gates, the pair of gothar pointing at me as they repeated their story.

The old man rattled off the names of the gods faster now, Bjorn and I muttering our assent, and my brain scrambled to remember how many were left. *Too many* was the number I came up with a heartbeat before a hand closed on my hood and ripped it backward.

"It's her!" a male voice snarled.

Bjorn was already on his feet, robes cast off and axe burning in his hand. "Is this a fight you truly wish to pick?" he asked the warriors. "Are you so certain a child of a minor god is worth your lives?"

I wasn't worth it. None of this made sense. Yet everyone seemed ready to slaughter one another over me anyway.

"Girl," the old man hissed, drawing my attention back to him. "Do you submit?"

I had no notion which gods he'd just named, and I prayed those in question wouldn't feel disrespected as I blurted out, "Yes, I submit!"

"We've heard of the seer's prophecy, Firehand," one of the warriors retorted. "And no one wishes to swear oaths to Jarl Snorri."

I didn't blame them, but I doubted saying so would help my cause.

The old gothi was glaring at me, which meant I'd missed another set of names in my distraction. "Yes!" I snapped, lifting my hands to check if the barrier had lifted, but it remained implacable. "Faster!"

"You know how seers are," Bjorn answered. "They speak in riddles, nothing of what they say of the future clear until the moment to do anything about it has passed."

"Except when it comes to the children of the gods," the warrior retorted. "The shield maiden's fate is uncertain. As is yours, Firehand."

Bjorn laughed. "Then how this fight ends may be a surprise to you and the gods alike. Although I think not."

A scream filled my ears, and I twisted in time to watch a warrior clutching a charred hole in his chest topple backward off the cliff, Bjorn's axe already clashing with the weapon of the next. His axe locked with the sword, and Bjorn punched the warrior in the face before slicing the man's leg from his body, the shrieks deafening. Men falling one after another to Bjorn's skill. Except Jarl Sten was already halfway across the bridge with more men. Twenty against one.

Hands closed on my shoulders, and I jerked around to see the old man was clutching my stolen robes. "If you wish to live, you must focus," he snapped. "Do you submit to Sigyn and Snotra?"

Why were there so many gods? Why were there so many names? "Yes!"

More shrieks, the stink of burning flesh turning the air acrid. My skin crawled with the need to turn and face the danger, but the old man was shouting more names.

"Yes!" I waited for him to ramble off more gods, but the old man only said, "That's it, girl! Drop your weapons and step through!"

Not a fucking chance.

Twisting, I pulled my sword, "Bjorn—"

Bjorn's hand struck me in the chest. I toppled through the barrier, the magic wrenching the sword from my hand as I landed on my arse next to the gathered gothar. Bjorn kicked my weapon out of reach, shouting at the gothi, "Restrain her!"

"You idiot!" I screamed as hands closed on my arms, hauling me backward. "You cursed fool of a man!"

If Bjorn heard, he didn't react.

Sten and the rest of his men were across the bridge, converging on Bjorn with their shields locked in a wall, spears protruding through the gaps. "Yield, Firehand," the jarl shouted. "Yield and we will let you live."

"Why would I yield when I'm winning?" Bjorn nudged a dying man with his boot. "You and yours should yield. Retreat from this place with your lives, if not your honor."

"Not with the shield maiden still alive," Sten snarled. "Without her, Snorri is nothing. Without her, the future Saga foresaw is no more."

Bjorn laughed. "You have not the power to change her fate." Then he threw his axe into one of the shields, bits of burning wood flying into the air as the man who held it staggered into those behind him.

"Attack," Sten roared. Men pushed forward, Bjorn's axe still embedded in the man's shield, the wood nearly engulfed.

Bjorn bent to retrieve my fallen sword as one of the men stabbed at him over his shield rim, the spear tip slicing at his face. Bjorn only sidestepped it and thrust my sword through the same gap, the man screaming as the blade punctured his chest.

Bjorn's axe appeared in his hand again as he dodged yet another stabbing spear, and he reached out to hook a woman's shield, jerking her forward. She stumbled and swung her own axe at Bjorn's head, but he ducked even as he chopped at her side, fiery axe slicing into her torso, rings from her chain mail exploding outward as she screamed.

Blood sprayed as he stepped over her corpse to press into the gap she'd left in the shield wall, men and women falling as he carved into them before retreating, his face splattered with crimson.

"Hold the wall," Sten shouted, taking the woman's place, and the shields locked again. There was no mistaking the fear in the eyes of

Sten's warriors, but they held their line. One threw his spear at Bjorn, and I gasped, but Bjorn knocked the weapon from the air with his axe. Yet more followed the man's lead, throwing their spears one after another.

I screamed, struggling against the half dozen gothar keeping me from going to Bjorn's aid as he fell, his back slamming against the barrier.

"No!" I screamed, certain that he'd been mortally wounded. Certain that I was going to lose him.

But instead of collapsing dead, Bjorn pulled a fallen shield in front of him.

A heartbeat later, two of the attacking warriors screamed and fell, arrows in their backs.

What was happening?

Dropping low, I peered past Bjorn and through the legs of the mass of men. Beyond, a group of warriors gathered on the far side of the bridge, bows in hand.

Snorri was at their head.

"Loose!" he roared, and a rain of arrows fell upon Sten and his men. And they had nowhere to go.

Several tried to pass through the gate, only to rebound off the barrier, arrows finding their backs. Others, seeing there was no escape, threw themselves at Bjorn, desperate to use him to block the barrage.

Bjorn slashed at one with his axe. The man howled as he clutched a charred wound on his arm, but the others grabbed at Bjorn's shield and dragged it away from him. More arrows fell, one slicing so close to his arm that I gasped as it bounced off the barrier.

Wrenching free of the gothar, I threw myself forward but someone grabbed my legs. I fell against Bjorn, and knowing I'd get no further, I reached around him. The heat of his axe singed the fabric of my sleeve as I closed my fingers over his, digging in my nails lest I lose my grip. "Hlin," I hissed. "Protect me."

Protect *him*.

Magic flowed from my hands, covering Bjorn in a silvery glow right as a warrior swung at him with a sword. I screamed a warning, but Bjorn calmly lifted one arm.

The sword rebounded off my magic with enough force that it spun over the warrior's head and into the chasm. Arrows fell all around us, yet while I braced for the inevitable bite of pain if one struck true, Bjorn didn't so much as flinch. All around us warriors fell, filling my ears with shrieks of pain and wet gasps as they breathed their last.

And then there was silence.

I drew in ragged breath after ragged breath. My nails dug into Bjorn's hand, my other arm was wrapped around his waist, and my face was pressed into his thigh. The group of gothar had ceased trying to haul me back through the barrier. My legs stung where their fingers had dug in, my skin likely to be covered with bruises tomorrow. If I lived that long.

"It's over," Bjorn said softly. "They're dead."

I believed him, but I couldn't let go of my magic. Couldn't lower my defenses with blood roaring hot in my veins, fueled by anger and fear. Couldn't let go of him when I'd come so close to losing him entirely.

"Freya, my father's coming."

His father. My *husband*.

Snorri had been our salvation, yet I'd almost have rather faced another clan trying to kill me than face him.

"Freya." Snorri's deep voice cut the silence. "Lower your shield."

A flash of bitterness filled me, but I complied and released my magic, then my grip on Bjorn's hand. There were five crimson crescents on his skin from where my nails had scored his flesh, and a droplet of blood trickled from one of them to splash to the ground. A shiver ran through me, but I sat back on my haunches and lifted my face to meet Snorri's gaze.

Ylva stood at his elbow, the rest of the warriors of his party beyond.

"You defeated the draug and passed the test." Snorri's mouth broke into a wide smile. "I knew you would. The gods have plans for you."

I wasn't sure why, but his words sent a flush of anger through me. He'd risked my life and Bjorn's based on blind faith in riddles whispered by a specter, and yet stood here as though all had gone according to his well-mapped plan.

"So I keep hearing." My voice was raspy, which was just as well because it concealed the frigidness of my tone. "You appear to have made it up the mountain unscathed."

Snorri shrugged. "Involved a bit of trickery, but the gods reward the clever and the sacrifices made were worth us reaching you in time."

I looked over the warriors again, all the faces I'd expected to be there present, none appearing worse for wear. "What losses?"

Snorri didn't so much as blink. "The thralls. We passed them off as you. Three times it worked, those who'd been sent to ambush us chasing after a blond woman dressed as a warrior who'd *escaped* us."

Dead. All three women were *dead.*

My stomach heaved. Twisting away, I vomited its few contents onto the dirt, because *sacrifices* implied they had the choice. Implied they'd *wanted* to die, when the reality was that Snorri had probably threatened them with a worse death if they'd refused.

Cruel, heartless prick. I remained on my hands and knees, spitting foulness on the ground, because if I turned back around, it would be to kill him.

Or at least, I'd try.

And when I inevitably failed, because far better warriors than me were close at hand, my family would be punished in some way.

Bite your tongue, Freya, I ordered myself. *The dead are beyond your help but you've yet the power to curse the living.*

"I think it not wise to linger here, given that more will come," Bjorn said. Turning to the old gothi, he added, "Shall we pick up where I left off?"

The old man was gaping at the carnage, but at Bjorn's words he blinked, then nodded. "Yes. Yes, of course, child of Tyr."

Bjorn dropped to his knees to finish the rite, and as he did, Snorri's warriors moved to strip the dead of valuables before dragging the bodies to one side, where, I presumed, they'd eventually be burned. Enemy or not, they were Skalanders and would be honored in death.

"We'll await you at the Hall of the Gods." Bjorn cast the words over his shoulder at his father as he stepped through the barrier. Grasping my shoulders, he steered me through the masses of onlookers, all of whom gave us a wide berth, whispers of "they vanquished the draug" repeating over and over.

"Shouldn't we wait?" I muttered as we moved into the sea of tents and cookfires, dozens upon dozens of men, women, and a few children moving about them. There had to be hundreds here from places near and far.

"Given you appeared ready to murder my father with your bare hands, I thought distance a prudent choice. Will give you a chance to calm down." He squeezed my shoulders, then let go, the heat left behind from his hands fading too quickly. "I'm hungry. And thirsty—fighting always makes me crave strong drink."

As if hearing his words, a man sitting next to a fire shouted, "Bjorn!" then filled a cup from the jug at his feet. He handed it to Bjorn after they pounded each other vigorously on the back, promising to find each other later, before carrying on.

"Distance isn't going to calm me down," I informed him as he drained his cup. Another man at another fire laughed and refilled it, only for the process to be repeated at the next fire. Bjorn was apparently well known, and well liked, even outside of his father's territories.

"There is nothing to be done," he answered. "Seeking vengeance for those women will cost you more than you're willing to pay. You know this; that is why you didn't shove Snorri off the cliff. Here, drink, it's going to my head too quickly and I don't like to get drunk alone."

I took a few swallows from the cup he gave me before handing it back. Mead made my tongue work faster and my head slower, and my high temper wouldn't help. "Snorri should be wary lest he push me too far. There is a limit."

"Is there?" Bjorn's gaze met mine and I stared into his green eyes, finding curiosity rather than condemnation as he added, "My father holds your family hostage, and you've proven time and again that there is nothing you won't do to protect them, no sacrifice you won't make. Even though, if I might add, they don't deserve it. Which means he can do whatever he wants, and you will abide."

"That's not true!" My protest felt weak in my own ears, the verity of his words piling onto my shoulders like leaden weights, dragging me down. "What would you have me do? What would you do?"

He shrugged. "For me to be in such a situation would require there being someone among the living who might be used as leverage against me."

A pang struck me in the stomach that there *wasn't* anyone he cared so much for, but I shoved away the sensation. "If there is nothing in your life worth dying for, then what is there worth living for?"

"Reputation. Battle fame."

Bjorn's response should have disgusted me in its selfishness, but . . . there was a hollowness beneath the flippancy that made me wonder if some part of him wished it were otherwise. "Well, you have that," I said and drained the cup in my hand.

In silence, we approached the entrance to an enormous hall, the carved wooden doors flung wide. Stepping inside, I paused to allow my eyes to adjust to the dimness, and when they did, focused on the enormous wooden likenesses of the gods set about the hall.

I started to walk toward them, but Bjorn froze.

My skin prickled and my attention shot to that which I hadn't noticed—the man standing in our path, a broad woman with her blond hair in war braids standing slightly behind him.

The man, who was perhaps of an age with Snorri, smiled, his lips curling up to reveal white teeth. "It has been a long time, Bjorn."

Bjorn was quiet for a heartbeat, and a sideways glance showed me that he was rigid with tension when he finally said, "It has, King Harald."

King Harald.

My heart skittered in my chest. This was the king of Nordeland. This was the man who'd kept Bjorn hostage all those long years. Which meant this was the man who'd killed Bjorn's mother.

"I'm surprised to see you here." Bjorn's light tone belied the tension radiating from him. "It's a long journey from Nordeland to Fjalltindr. And a dangerous one."

"I felt the urge to prove my devotion to the gods," Harald answered. "I don't want Thor to look upon me with disfavor when I take to the seas this summer."

The tall woman with him gave a soft snort of amusement, and the mead in my stomach soured. *Taking to the seas* in the summer meant *raiding,* and Skaland was Nordeland's nearest target.

Though Bjorn had to know that, he said, "Planning a journey? The seashore is most relaxing in the warmer months."

The king gave a small smile, then shrugged, the motion made elegant by his long, lean frame. Indeed, if not for my instinctual distaste for him, I'd have thought him more than passingly attractive with his high cheekbones and golden-brown hair, which hung in loose waves to his shoulders, his short beard secured by a gold clip. "We shall see what the Norns have in store for us. Already there have been surprising developments."

His eyes, which were the palest of grays, latched onto mine, and I knew he meant *me*. I was the surprising development. Despite Bjorn killing his spy, King Harald knew who I was and what I represented. A fact that was confirmed as he said, "You are the shield maiden, yes? What is your name?"

There seemed little point in denying my identity. "Freya, Erik's daughter."

"I'm surprised you remain alive," he said. "Many seek your death, for they do not wish to see Skaland with a king, and even less to swear allegiance to Snorri. Though I see they have all failed to kill you as they swore to do."

Bjorn shifted restlessly next to me, and I wondered if he was considering the same thing as I was: whether Harald counted himself among those who wished my death. Weapons might not be allowed within Fjalltindr but that wouldn't stop his men from ambushing us outside the borders.

"A bit of foresight would have told those who sought Freya's death that there was another path to be taken," Bjorn answered. "One worth the risks, given the gods have spoken of a future that has not yet come to pass."

The twisted phrasing felt strange in my ears, but the king responded before I could give it more thought.

"It's true, then, the whispers racing through Fjalltindr? She vanquished the draug from the tunnels?" Harald didn't wait for an answer, only tilted his head and asked, "How? They cannot be slain with a mortal weapon and Hlin's shield only protects."

"It seems she is favored by more than just Hlin."

Given Tyr had once been content to burn half the skin off my hand, *that* was definitely not the case. But if convincing those set on killing me that I was favored by all the gods would dissuade them from putting seaxes in my heart, I'd be more than happy to scream the lie day and night. My honor had its limits.

One of the king's eyebrows rose. "Interesting."

The thud of many feet on steps filtered up from behind us, and I half turned to find Snorri and Ylva approaching, warriors behind them.

"Jarl Snorri. Or is it King Snorri now?" King Harald smiled widely, though it held little warmth. "It has been an age. I was only just catching up with Bjorn. We miss his presence and would give a great deal to have him back in Nordeland."

A chill raced across my skin.

"Harald." Snorri stepped next to Bjorn's elbow, not addressing the king's comment as he said, "I see you've met my new wife."

Harald's eyes darkened and I realized that Snorri *had* answered the king's threat. If the foretelling came to pass and Skaland united under one king, not only would we be able to repel Nordeland's raids, we would have the strength to raid Nordeland itself.

"Yes. *Freyaaaa,*" the king answered, showing no sign of being cowed as he drew out my name. "As beautiful as she is formidable. May she bear you many children, as well as a crown, my old friend."

Snorri crossed his arms, jaw tight.

"I'd say that it must be pleasing to have found the shield maiden of your prophecy, yet the rumor is that she has cost you far more than she's earned," the king said. "Halsar attacked, men lost to Gnut, more lost along the way to Fjalltindr. I'd be concerned that I'd misinterpreted Saga's words."

"We are here to give our offering to the gods," Snorri interrupted. "Not for idle chatter with our enemies."

"*Enemies* is such a strong word. Especially given we were once friends and allies."

"Once," Snorri snarled. "Then you murdered my seer and stole my son from me. Kept him as your thrall!"

A flash of emotion passed across the king's face but his smile swiftly returned. "As a *hostage,* whom I raised as though he were my own son in honor of our friendship," the king corrected. "And what choice did I have? Though I was innocent, you blamed me for Saga's death to all who'd listen, using it to create support among your people for raiding my shores. If I'd not kept Bjorn at my side, those raids would have come to fruition. You'd have slaughtered my people, and it would've been *war.*"

"It *will* be war." Snorri stepped nose-to-nose with the king. "You can no longer use my son to defend yourself, Harald. Soon he will stand across from you on the field of battle with the shield maiden at his side, and Nordeland will bleed as Skaland has all these long years you denied it a king. Before the gods"—he gestured violently at the statues—"I swear it will be so!"

I bit the insides of my cheeks. Not only did Snorri wish to become king of our people, but he also intended to wield Skaland like a weapon against the man whom he seemed to blame for delaying his destiny.

My pulse raced as visions of sailing across the strait to make war against Nordeland filled my eyes, and I wasn't sure how I felt about it. Part of me reveled in the idea of striking back against the man who'd kept Bjorn from his family to achieve his own ends.

But another part of me remembered how Bjorn had spoken of the kindness of the Nordelanders to him while he was a prisoner.

I glanced sideways at Bjorn, whose eyes were fixed on the ground rather than on the arguing men. *Do something,* I willed him. *Say something.*

But he barely seemed to be aware of the argument before him.

My anger flared to life because I hated seeing him behave this way, so entirely not himself. Being in the presence of the man who'd kept him prisoner should have him raging, but instead he was utterly still, eyes lowered. My anger found its way to my tongue. "Any man who uses a child to hide from battle is a coward who will never see Valhalla. It will be Hel who takes you in death, King."

No sooner had the words been spoken than the ground beneath our feet quivered. Everyone in the hall started in alarm, except for Snorri, who laughed. "You see?" he said. "The gods are watching her and show their favor."

"Indeed," Harald replied. "She is even more formidable than I'd anticipated." Stepping sideways out of our path, he added, "I will not stand between you and the gods, old friend."

Snorri snorted, then caught hold of my arm and hauled me forward, everyone else following at our heels, including Bjorn. Yet once we'd all passed, Harald called out, "Bjorn. What befell Ragnhild?"

At mention of the spy, Bjorn stopped in his tracks and turned back. "She's dead, although I suspect you know that."

Harald inclined his head in agreement. "Who killed her?"

Silence.

"What difference does it make?" Snorri demanded, stepping between Bjorn and Harald. "She spied on me and suffered the consequences."

"No difference." Harald lifted one shoulder, his gaze meeting mine. "Though yours was the last face she saw, Freya, and she died because of it. Come, Tora."

Without another word, the king of Nordeland and the tall woman left the hall, leaving us alone with the statues of the gods.

"Harald is not our current concern," Ylva said, shoving Snorri in the opposite direction. "Nor an immediate threat."

"The woman with him is Tora, child of Thor," he answered. "And he'll have Skade with him as well, both of them deadly."

I had no notion of who this Skade might be, but a child of Thor could call lightning, and that was terrifying enough.

If Ylva felt the same, she didn't show it, only said, "Neither can use their magic within Fjalltindr, so they are an obstacle for a later hour. We must do what we came for. All your vows of war will mean nothing if Freya does not make her sacrifice and the gods turn on her for her failure."

Snorri resisted, his eyes fixed on the door Harald had exited, but then he growled and extracted a handful of silver coins from his pocket, which he pressed into my hands. "Ask the gods for their favor."

Ask them yourself was what I wanted to say, but instead I nodded and stepped toward the statues.

The hall had no floor, only raw bedrock through which a stream flowed, its branches creating islands on which statues sat. Piles of offerings rested at each god's feet, and I stepped across the water to set a silver coin beneath Njord's likeness.

Njord, I ask your forgiveness for . . . I hesitated, memories washing over me. Not memories of the way Vragi had treated me, but rather memories of how he'd used the magic Njord's blood had gifted him. Remembered the whale he beached over and over again for sport. Remembered all the fish that had not filled bellies but rotted on beaches for his carelessness. *He dishonored your gift.*

I set another coin at the feet of the goddess I'd been named for, immediately thinking of my brother. *Freyja, please grant Geir and Ingrid love and happiness. And many babies,* I added, knowing that this was Ingrid's wish.

With Bjorn, Snorri, and Ylva at my heels, I went from god to god, giving my offering and asking for the gods to favor those I loved. Those I knew to be in need. Those I knew to be deserving.

When I reached Loki, it was me I thought of. Loki was the trickster, his children gifted with his ability to transform themselves into the shapes of others to achieve their ends. Deceivers asked for his favor.

And with all the lies I was telling, I was a deceiver of the first order.

Loki, please . . . I trailed off, unwilling to ask him to grant me a liar's tongue to better keep my deceptions alive, because while that was the role I had to play, it was not who I was in my heart. So instead I asked for nothing, only set a coin at his feet.

As I turned to the last god, the Allfather Odin, I heard Snorri say, "I can keep silent no more, Bjorn."

No one had spoken while I'd given my offerings, so I slowed my step, curious about what Snorri might say while he thought me distracted.

"Why did you just stand there? Harald denied Skaland its king by keeping you his prisoner, and while I voiced the promise of vengeance, you cowered like a beaten dog."

Anger flamed to life in my chest, but I bit my lip and kept silent.

"It was either do nothing or commit murder on the grounds of Fjalltindr," Bjorn answered. "Be glad I checked my violence, Father."

Snorri snorted, seemingly unconvinced. "Act like the weapon you are. Put fear into the hearts of our enemies. Be worthy of Tyr's fire."

Snap back, I willed Bjorn. *Put him in his place.* But he only said, "Yes, Father."

Scowling, I stepped over the pooled water to place a coin at Odin's feet. "Odin," I whispered. *Allfather, if it is your will, please see Bjorn released from the burden of his past so that he might fight those who deserve his vengeance. Accept this offering on his behalf.*

A shiver passed over me, my skin prickling. But the sensation quickly passed, leaving me suddenly drained. I'd barely slept in days, climbed mountains infested with monsters, and fought battles with words and weapons. All I wanted was to curl up on a flat surface somewhere and not move until dawn tomorrow.

Except judging from the rhythmic drumming outside, sleep was not an option.

"The ritual is beginning," Ylva said. "We must go prepare, and quickly."

Surrounded by Snorri's warriors, we went to a small hall that appeared to have been granted to Snorri for his use. We paused outside, Ylva using a stick of charcoal to draw runes on the door, the markings flaring bright and then seeming to sink into the wood when she was finished. "While we call this hall home, no one with ill intent to any of our party may enter," she murmured. "Though it will not stop them from burning it down around our heads."

"I'll post guards," Snorri said, then motioned for me to go inside.

The hall was simply furnished with many cots, and a fire burned in the hearth, but otherwise, it was empty.

"Where is Steinunn?" Snorri asked of Bjorn, genuine concern in his voice. "Did she fall?"

"It was too dangerous for her to come," Bjorn answered. "I sent her back with your warrior. Told her to try to catch up to you."

Snorri's face darkened. "We saw no sign of her. She was supposed to travel with you for a reason, Bjorn."

The gleam in Bjorn's eye told me he was thinking of making this situation worse, so I said, "She resisted, only agreeing to part ways with us after I gave my word that I'd tell her all she wished to know. And it's well she didn't make the climb, for she'd have surely fallen to the draug in the battle." He seemed unappeased, so I added, "Steinunn herself told me her magic is more powerful when her song tells a story from the eyes of those who endure the trials, so it is best that it will be my story she sings without the influence of seeing the events herself."

I held my breath as Snorri silently considered my words, then he nodded and said, "You will tell her all at the soonest opportunity. As it is, I wished her here to sing the ballad of your birth in fire and your marking for all clans to hear, and now that must wait."

"I'll tell her everything," I lied, because there were most definitely moments in the tunnels that the world did *not* need to know.

Snorri gave me a curt nod, turning once again to Bjorn, and Ylva shoved me behind a curtain. "Clothes off. With all my thralls dead to ensure you lived, you'll have to bathe yourself. Do it swiftly."

You killed them, not me, I wanted to say. Instead I remained silent, pulling off my chain-mail shirt and then the garments underneath, cringing at the stink of metal, sweat, and blood that clung to me. Boots and trousers joined the pile on the floor, and I hoped I'd have time to wash them before having to don them again, because the smell would only worsen.

A bucket of steaming water arrived, and I struggled to unravel my braids with one hand. My right had stiffened horribly, the tightness of my scars made worse by the bruising I'd gained punching the draug.

"Cursed, useless girl." Ylva abandoned her own washing to help me. "Head in the bucket."

She swiftly washed my hair before leaving me to scrub the filth from my body with a rag. From the bags, she extracted a simple dress, which she helped me into before dressing herself.

"What will happen tonight?" I asked, finally in the position to get answers to the questions I'd been avoiding thinking about. An enormous price had been paid to get me here for the ritual, yet I still had no notion of what would occur.

"All those who have traveled to Fjalltindr will make sacrifices to the gods," Ylva said. "As will you."

"That's it?" Not that I was complaining. If killing a chicken was all that I had to do, I'd gladly do it.

"There is a celebration afterwards, but you will come back here where we can ensure your safety. The runes on the hall will protect you." She went to the wall where a dozen masks hung on hooks and selected one fashioned to look like a raven, a long cape of black feathers hanging from it. She fit it on my head, and when I looked up, it was to see the sharp beak protruding above my forehead. With ash, she shadowed the skin around my eyes as though I were going to war. Fastening a mask with deer antlers on her own head, she said, "We sent a messenger back to Halsar after you separated from us. Even now, Ragnar will be coming with all haste with the rest of our fighting men to ensure we get back down this mountain alive."

"They'll be leaving Halsar undefended?"

"Yes." Her gaze was frosty. "I hope you appreciate what is being done to keep you safe."

All of *that* so that I could kill a chicken in front of a crowd of people.

As though hearing my thoughts, Ylva gripped my shoulders, staring unblinkingly at me from behind her mask. "You are a child of the gods, girl. You are one of the Unfated, which means everything you do has the power to alter your destiny, and the destinies of those around you, for good and ill."

Not for the first time, I hated that fact. Longed to be fully mortal so that everything I'd ever do was already woven. For it felt like I was running down an unmapped path where I might easily lose my way, dragging myself and all those I cared for to our doom.

Ylva looked me up and down, her lips pinched tight. "We have no more time, so this will have to do."

When we stepped out from behind the curtain, it was to find Snorri and Bjorn waiting unmasked and in silence, the tension between them high. Both had removed their mail, and Bjorn had scrubbed the blood from his face, revealing shadows beneath his green eyes. Exhausted, yet he moved unerringly to my elbow, his father giving him a nod of approval before stepping outside, where the warriors waited.

Snorri and Ylva led the group through the trees, hundreds of people moving in the same direction. Many men and women wore elaborate masks like my own, often accompanied by decorated hides or cloaks of feathers, which made it seem like a herd of beasts approaching the ritual.

Bjorn walked at my left, his eyes roving over any who drew near. A woman walked against the flow, her face concealed by a mask of raven feathers that blended into her dark hair. Bjorn tensed as she drew close and my own heart skittered, seeing threats at every turn. But she only murmured, "What path do you follow?"

I blinked, opening my mouth to answer her, but Bjorn caught my arm and drew me forward. "Seems like many have already indulged in mushroom tea."

Frowning, I cast a backward glance at the woman, but she'd already disappeared into the trees, so I turned my eyes to where torches glowed, illuminating a gathering of hundreds of people standing before a large flat rock. Drummers pounded the same rhythm they had before, low and ominous, and through the tree foliage a full moon glowed overhead.

As though they'd been waiting for our arrival, the drums increased their intensity, and the gothar appeared carrying bowls of liquid, offering mouthfuls to every individual they passed. One approached our group, but the warriors all shook their heads, declining the offering.

"You will drink," Ylva said to me under her breath as both Snorri and Bjorn declined. "The tea will bring you closer to the gods."

The last thing I wanted to do was drink the contents of the bowl. Even from here, I could smell the earthy musk of mushrooms, and I'd not lived such a sheltered life as to be unaware of what would happen if I drank.

The gothi smiled and lifted the bowl to my lips. I pretended to drink, but Ylva wasn't fooled. "You think they can't see?" she hissed. "You think they don't know?"

I highly doubted the gods gave a shit whether I consumed mushroom tea or not, but I wouldn't put it past Ylva to hold me down and force the entire bowl down my throat, so I took a tiny mouthful. Ylva declined to drink, and Bjorn gave a soft laugh at my scowl. "May the tea show you sweet visions, Born-in-Fire."

Fuck.

I had no interest in seeing things, but short of sticking my fingers down my throat and vomiting in front of everyone, there wasn't much to be done.

Peering between the heads of those taller than me, I watched a man lift a goat onto the altar, the creature showing little awareness, and therefore little concern, about its impending death. The drums grew louder, the man's words to the gods drowned out by the noise. A blade made of white bone caught the moonlight and blood sprayed, the animal slumping as its lifeblood flowed into carved channels and dripped into waiting basins. A gothi dipped his hand in it, using it to mark the faces of those who'd offered the sacrifice. Blood dripped down foreheads and cheeks, and I swore I heard the droplets hit the ground despite distance making that impossible.

A shiver ran over me, the air charged in a way I'd never felt before. As if deeds done and words spoken in this place meant *more* than they did anywhere else. As though we truly were closer to the gods.

Discomfited, I stopped watching, focusing instead on the bald head of a man a few paces before me.

But the sensation didn't lessen.

The air grew thick, smelling of thunder and rain. My skin crawled as the feeling intensified, and I broke my gaze from the bald head to glance at my companions. All were watching the altar, but as my eyes skipped over Bjorn, he rubbed his bare forearms, the dusting of dark hair on them lifting as though he were cold.

Bjorn never got cold.

What was going on?

Those around us who'd consumed the tea gaped at the sacrifice on the altar with strange, unblinking stares. I focused inward to see if my tiny mouthful of tea had taken effect.

Would I know? Would I be able to tell if what I was seeing was real or hallucination?

Glancing back to the ritual revealed that several more sacrifices had been made during my distraction. All around me, men and women bore streaks of blood the gothar had smeared across their faces. The coppery smell filled my nose.

Bump, bump.

My heart rate escalated, matching the rhythm of the drums, the world around me pulsing.

Bump, bump.

"It is time," Ylva whispered into my ear. "Do not fail."

One of Snorri's warriors walked up to the altar. Except it wasn't a chicken he held in his hand, but rather a rope attached to a bull, and I swallowed hard, feeling a hand press against my back. The crowd ahead of me parted, the people swaying in rhythm to the drums as I approached.

Or were they standing still?

Each time I looked at the crowd, I saw something different. Wasn't sure whether what I saw was real or whether the tea was making me see things.

Each step grew harder, my breath coming in rapid pants as it had when I was racing up the mountain, but I drew no closer to the altar. I broke into a run, then stumbled, suddenly on top of the rock, reaching a hand out to the bull to touch its warm hide.

It shivered, turning its large head to stare at me, eyes like black pits.

A gothi pressed the knife into my hand.

I stared at the bone blade, the blood covering it swirling and moving like the tides of the sea, the smell choking me.

"I'll hold him steady."

Bjorn's voice filled my ears. He had one hand on the lead, the other bracing one of the creature's horns. The bull was old, his muzzle gray. He shifted uneasily, though whether it was from the smell of blood, the crowd, or some sixth sense that his end was near, I couldn't say.

"Do you know how?"

Bjorn sounded distant, as though he stood a dozen feet away from me, not at my elbow.

"Yes."

The gothi began shouting to the gods, offering the sacrifice, but it was hard to hear him as the wind rose. It caught and pulled at my clothes and the raven's feathers I wore, the branches of the surrounding forest rustling against one another, the trees themselves creaking and groaning from the onslaught.

The gothi went silent, and Bjorn said, "Now, Freya."

I tightened my grip on the knife. Above, lightning flashed, branches of light shattering the night before everything turned dark. The people turned their faces skyward in time to watch a mass of black birds descend, flying in chaotic circles even as the forest came alive with the sounds of creatures calling, their voices a cacophony of noise. The bull shifted restlessly and bellowed.

"Freya," Bjorn hissed, "if he decides to bolt, I won't be able to stop him."

I couldn't move. Couldn't tear my eyes from the circling birds. Omens. Signs the gods watched, and I found myself uncertain whether this was an offering they wanted. But the specter had said that if I did not do this, my life would be forfeit.

Lightning arced across the sky. Once, twice, three times, the thunder deafening yet not loud enough to drown out the beat of the drums. The bull twisted, pulling against Bjorn's grip even as the birds descended, wings brushing my face as they circled, the bull's eyes rolling as it started to panic.

"Freya!"

If I failed, my family's lives would be forfeit.

"Accept this offering," I breathed, then pulled the knife across the bull's jugular.

It lunged, dragging Bjorn with it, and then dropped to its knees, blood raining down to fill the channels, draining into a basin held by a gothi.

Everything went silent, even the drums, the ravens vanishing like smoke.

I quivered, watching as the bull slumped, its side going still with death.

No one spoke. No one moved. No one seemed to even breathe.

The gothi reacted first, lifting the basin and dipping his fingers into the crimson contents. But it was the basin, not his hand, that I focused on, the blood swirling as though a maelstrom had settled into its depths.

Thud.

Thud.

Thud.

Each droplet of blood that fell from the gothi's hands resounded in my ears like rocks being dropped from far above. I jerked with each impact, the noise deafening.

The gothi reached for me, and it took every ounce of will I possessed not to recoil as he dragged his fingers across my face, the blood hot against my icy flesh.

A pulse of air struck me the moment his fingers left my skin, and my stomach dropped as though I were falling from a great height. Surrounding the crowd was a circle of hooded figures, each holding a torch that burned with silver fire.

I couldn't move. Could barely breathe. "Bjorn," I whispered, "I'm seeing things that aren't there."

"No." His breath caught. "They are here."

The gods were here.

Not one of them, but . . . but *all* of them. My eyes skipped from figure to figure, not certain if I was shocked or terrified or both. The air swirled, carrying with it a voice, neither male nor female, that whispered, "Freya Born-in-Fire, child of two bloods, we *see* you."

Then the figures disappeared.

I stood rigid, unable to move even if I'd wanted to, because the gods . . . the gods had been here. And they'd come because of *me.*

What remained to be seen was whether that was for good or ill, as I still had little notion of what future they saw for me. Why they cared for the child of the most minor of their ranks.

Why me?

As though I possessed no more intelligence than the dead bull at my feet, I gaped at the crowd, wondering how many realized that this had been no tea-induced delusion. Too many, I decided, seeing eyes that stared at me with clarity. Snorri, Ylva, and their warriors, yes. But also King Harald, whose gaze was thoughtful as he stood with his slender arms crossed at the rear of the crowd, Tora still at his elbow.

My knees were weak, demanding that I sit, but thankfully Bjorn had enough wit to own the situation. Grabbing my bloody hand, which still gripped the bone knife, he lifted it high. "The gods are watching," he roared. "Do not disappoint them in your revels!"

The crowd answered with a roar of approval, men and women dispersing into the trees to where bonfires burned and jugs of mead awaited.

"Are you all right?" Bjorn asked, his hands squeezing mine.

"I . . . I . . ." Twisting out of his grip, I barely made it to the edge of the altar before dropping to my knees to vomit. Bjorn pulled the raven mask off me, then held back my hair as I heaved for the second time today, the muscles in my stomach aching from the abuse.

Spitting, I turned to look at him. "Why? Why are they watching me?"

Before he could speak, Snorri and Ylva were upon us.

"There can be no denying the foretelling now," Snorri said. "We must get Freya back to the hall until reinforcements arrive, for she is prize enough that some might tempt the peace of Fjalltindr."

Easing to my feet, I didn't resist as Snorri led me past the dozens of bonfires, those surrounding them laughing and dancing as they ate and drank. We made our way to the hall Ylva had warded, warriors taking up posts around it as I was brought inside.

The moment I was through the doors, I broke away from Snorri. "I need to sleep."

What I needed was to think, to ask questions, to understand what had happened. But days with little rest had more than caught up with me and I knew none of those things would happen without a few hours of unconsciousness. Thankfully no one argued, Snorri, Ylva, and Bjorn speaking in terse voices as I went to the curtained area where I'd dressed and used the basin of water to scrub the blood from my face.

Not bothering to take off the dress, I collapsed on a cot, using the last vestiges of my energy to pull the furs over my body.

Freya Born-in-Fire, child of two bloods, we see you.

The unearthly voices repeated in my head, and I shivered, rolling so that I was looking at the curtain. Through it, I could make out the shadows of the three.

"Now is the time to form alliances," Snorri said. "Now, with the appearance of the gods and their validation of the prophecy fresh in their minds."

Had the gods validated the seer's foretelling? All they'd said was that they were watching, which could mean anything.

"A matter of hours ago, these same men were trying to take Freya or kill her, and you think this is enough for them to accept your rule?" Bjorn snorted in disgust. "If anything, they will only try harder."

"Which is why I must convince them of the imminent threat Harald presents to us all," Snorri answered. "Alone, no clan can stand against him, but united? He will think twice about raiding our shores again. Especially once we turn to raiding his territories."

"That is your intent, then?" Bjorn asked. "To move immediately against Harald with Freya in the center of your shield wall?"

Silence, then Snorri said, "Such a proposition should enthuse you, my son. Harald didn't raise you out of the kindness of his heart. He *hid* you from us so as to deny me my destiny as king. To deny Skaland the strength it needed to stand against his raiders. You should be screaming for vengeance."

"I do wish revenge," Bjorn snapped back, the venom in his voice suggesting that he wished that revenge very much indeed. "But until quite recently, Freya's days were spent gutting fish and keeping house. Yet you think magic and prophecy enough for her to lead your warriors into battle despite her knowing nothing of war. It seems an ideal way to get everyone killed."

I winced, but given Bjorn was correct, taking insult seemed foolish.

"For once, Bjorn speaks reason." Ylva's voice startled me, as I'd half forgotten she was there. "You speak of warring against Harald when we've yet to form a single alliance with another jarl. Let us look to the first step before the second, lest we stumble."

"Which is precisely what I proposed to do, yet instead I stand here listening to you two prattle!" Snorri made an aggrieved noise. "You remain here with Freya while I pursue conversation that will achieve our ends."

"Take our warriors with you," Ylva said. "You need a show of strength when you meet with the other jarls."

"They need to remain to protect Freya."

"The wards will prevent anyone from attempting to come in."

Snorri shook his head. "It's too risky."

"You need the jarls to believe you have the strength to deliver on what you have promised," Ylva said. "Besides, Bjorn will be here with her."

Snorri hesitated, then said, "Fine. Stay within the wards."

His boots thudded against the wooden floor, and the curtain moved on the draft of air as he opened the door and departed.

"I need to sleep." Bjorn's tone was cool. "Wake me only if absolutely necessary."

"I've never needed you for anything before, Bjorn." Ylva's voice was equally frosty. "And I think that unlikely to change over the next few hours."

I heard the creak of Bjorn settling onto a cot and the room grew silent. As was typical of men, his breathing deepened with sleep while my mind continued to turn over events, refusing to calm enough for me to drift off.

Every time I closed my eyes, visions of the gods appearing filled my mind's eye, that strange collective voice like thunder, *Freya Born-in-Fire, child of two bloods, we see you.* What had they meant? *Child of two bloods* was clear enough, for I had both mortal and divine blood in my veins, but so did every other child of the gods. What exactly did they *see* in me that was worth all of them stepping onto the mortal plane at once? What was it about me that was so special? How did they foresee me uniting a nation of clans that raided and warred against one another year in and year out? Clans that did not *want* to be united.

Because Bjorn was right that I was no warrior of legend whose battle fame would awe and inspire warriors to follow me. Nor was I a gifted orator whose words had the power to convince even the most stubborn naysayers.

Why me? Why not Bjorn or someone like him?

And . . . and why did the gods care if Skaland was united at all? For as long as memory, we'd been divided, as were all the other nations who worshipped our gods, save Nordeland. What did the gods stand to gain in that changing? Why had they chosen me to do it?

And why, of all men, did they want Snorri to be king?

Someone stirred, and I recognized the soft tread of Ylva's feet as she moved about the hall. Then the curtain blew inward.

I tensed at the draft, certain that my disloyal thoughts had summoned my *husband* back, but when the air stilled, no one spoke.

Curious, I reached down and pulled up the edge of the curtain, taking in the darkened hall. Bjorn was stretched out on a cot, but otherwise the space was empty.

Ylva was gone.

She's just stepped out to take a piss, I told myself. *Go to sleep while you can, you idiot.*

Rolling onto my back, I closed my eyes, focusing on the sound of Bjorn's breathing. Except doing so caused me to think about *him.* Rolling onto my side again, I lifted the curtain, my breath hitching. He'd moved onto his stomach and, ever overheated, had kicked off the sleeping furs, which meant his naked back was revealed.

Go to sleep, Freya. Except tearing my gaze from the hard lines of his thick muscles required a stronger woman than I'd ever be. I followed the designs of his tattoos, remembering how he'd shivered when I'd touched the crimson one on the back of his neck. The tattoos on his shoulders and back were inky black, and I wondered how far down they continued after they disappeared into the waist of his trousers, and what else I'd discover if I followed their path.

An ache formed between my thighs, and I bit my lip, part of me wanting to weep that I was doomed to be an unsatisfied wife and the other part wanting to rage that it was so. If the gods truly favored me, then they ought to have delivered an attractive man who knew how to pleasure a woman. Instead I'd first been given to one who treated me as equal parts servant and broodmare, and then one married to another woman—though in fairness, not having to endure Snorri's touch was a mercy.

It is hard to keep one's wits when faced with a woman as beautiful as the sight of shore to a man who has been lost at sea.

Never in my life had anyone said such a thing to me, and I indulged myself by allowing the words to repeat again and again even as I re- membered his touch on my hands. The intensity in his gaze as we'd stared into each other's eyes. The heat and strength of him as he'd held me against the cold.

I wanted to feel all those things again.

It's just lust, I snarled at myself. *Deal with it and then go to sleep.*

Dropping the curtain, I rolled onto my back and reached under the furs, drawing up the skirt of my dress. I slipped a hand inside my un- dergarments, no part of me surprised to find myself already wet. Clos- ing my eyes, I traced a fingertip around the center of my pleasure, imagining what it would feel like to have Bjorn's fingers between my thighs. His hands were so much bigger than mine, strong and calloused from use, but no less deft. So I imagined it was him, not me, stroking my sex. Slipping his fingers inside of me while his other hand cupped my breast.

Biting my lip to silence my moan, I reached down the neckline of my dress, finding my nipples hard and aching, wanting to be touched. Wanting to be sucked into his mouth.

I drifted further into my fantasy, feeling him slide my clothes from my body and settle in the cradle of my thighs, hardness pressing where my fingers currently sought climax. The thought of it nearly tipped me over the edge.

This was not *dealing* with my lust. It was making it worse.

I knew that. Knew fantasizing about Bjorn was only going to make me want him more, but I didn't care.

Because I *wanted*. Wanted so many things, and it felt like I was fated to have none of them.

Release dangled just out of reach, and I plunged my fingers into my wetness, imagining it was his cock. Imagining how he'd fill me, my breathing growing ragged.

I was so close. So very close. My climax began to crest—

And Bjorn stirred.

I jerked my hand out from between my legs, irrationally certain that he'd sensed what I was doing. My face turned molten as I waited for him to leap to my side of the curtain and accuse me of pleasuring myself with his name on my lips.

But instead, Bjorn walked on near-silent feet to the front of the hall, the curtain blowing across my face and then settling as he closed the door behind him, leaving me alone in the hall.

Blowing out a long breath, I waited for him to reenter. Seconds passed. Then minutes, and my unease as to where Ylva and Bjorn had gone grew and grew until I could sit still no longer.

So I climbed to my feet.

Easing the door open a crack, I peered out, fully expecting to find Bjorn leaning against the wall, or at the very least in sight.

But there was no one.

While the hall was warded with runes to protect any inside from those of ill intent, it still didn't feel right that he'd leave me alone and unguarded, especially given that Snorri had instructed him to remain.

What was going on?

My unease deepened, and I opened the door enough to lean my head and shoulders out. In the distance, countless figures moved about between bonfires, but in the area near the hall, no one stirred.

Stay within the wards. Snorri's warning echoed inside my head. I shut the door, then leaned against it, but my pulse didn't slow. Ylva, I suspected, had gone to find her husband, probably because she begrudged her exclusion from his conversation with the other jarls.

But where was Bjorn?

Fear soured my stomach as answers, each worse than the next, cycled through my head.

My life wasn't the only one our enemies sought. King Harald had been more than clear that he'd try to take Bjorn prisoner again. What if he and his soldiers had been waiting outside? What if they'd waited for him to step out to take a piss and then cracked him over the head while he was watering a tree? What if they'd realized they couldn't get past Ylva's wards and decided to cut their losses with one prisoner? What if even now they were dragging him down the southern slopes of the mountain?

You need to stay in the hall, I told myself. *It's warded. Running around Fjalltindr by yourself is an idiot thing to do. Wait for Snorri to return.*

Except that I had no idea when that would be. What if I sat here until morning while Bjorn was marched toward Nordeland?

I needed to get help before it was too late.

My cloak was draped over a bench, so I swiftly donned it as well as one of the antlered masks on the wall, praying that others enjoying the revels still wore theirs so that I might blend in. Then I stepped out into the night.

Moving through the trees, I searched the shadows, wanting to scream Bjorn's name but knowing that to do so would bring unwanted attention. So instead I whispered, "Bjorn? Bjorn?" then out of desperation, "Ylva?"

Nothing.

I needed to find Snorri and the rest of the warriors. Needed to tell them what had happened so they could help in the hunt. But beyond knowing Snorri's intent to meet with other jarls, I had no idea where to find him.

Stepping closer to the revels around the fires, I searched for familiar faces, realizing now why my parents had never brought me to Fjalltindr. Everywhere I looked, men and women staggered around, either drunk or intoxicated on other substances, and those who weren't moving about were coupling in full view. Not only in pairs, but in groups of threes or fours or more, and if I hadn't been in a full-blown panic, I would've gaped.

Such things pleased the gods, who delighted in the carnal. Yet I doubted the revelers were motivated by the gods, instead entirely consumed by their own pleasures. Which was good because it meant they paid no attention to me.

"Where the fuck are you, Snorri?" I whispered, though my heart was screaming, *Where are you, Bjorn?*

The rhythmic beat of drums echoed through the air as I walked, though it did little to drown the moans of pleasure of the revelers as they sought release on the ground or against trees, some wearing masks and some not, all of them strangers. Perhaps Bjorn was among them. Perhaps he'd left the hall in order to find pleasurable pursuits, thinking that I'd have the wisdom to remain behind the wards. My stomach soured, but logic immediately chased away the idea. There was too much at stake for him to take that sort of risk.

Except that he *had* left the hall of his own volition. Which begged the question of why?

The question repeated to the beat of the drums, my stomach twisting even as my chest constricted, every breath a challenge.

I wove through the narrow paths, searching, but not a single familiar face appeared. Shivers stole over me, my arms and legs weak as I eyed the other sleeping halls, but guards stood in the perimeters around them, watching over the jarls and their families within.

What if everyone was dead? "They aren't," I whispered at my terror.

"No one would dare kill them within the confines of Fjalltindr. It's forbidden."

I took a step down a path, then light from the Hall of the Gods caught my eye. Dozens of brilliant torches encircled the structure, and as I watched, a shadow passed in front of them.

Moving closer, I eventually made out the face of Tora. If she was here, then Harald surely was as well, and if he'd taken Bjorn, this would be where he had him. Tora stood with her arms crossed in front of the entrance, expression implacable. Though she was unarmed, and presumably her magic as curtailed as my own by the power of this place, she was still twice my size, which meant I would not get past her by force without warning those inside.

Shit.

I circled the building, wishing the revelers would quit laughing and humping and banging on drums so I could bloody well hear, but knowing my people as I did, they'd be at it until dawn.

The only door was the one guarded by Tora, and there were no windows. Stepping over the stream that flowed beneath the building, I paused, because if the water that flowed around the statues inside could exit, that meant there was an opening. Picking my way upstream, I reached the outcropping on which the hall sat. Water trickled down the rock, making soft tinkling sounds.

Feeling for handholds, I climbed, cursing silently as the antlers on my mask scratched against the wood of the hall's wall. The freezing water numbed my hands, but I barely noticed as I peered through the narrow opening through which the water flowed. Immediately, my eyes went to where Harald stood.

He was speaking but I couldn't make out his words over the tinkle of water and the noise of the revels. Just as I couldn't make out the face of the individual he was speaking to, for the person, or persons, were hidden from view by Loki's statue. I searched the shadows for any sign of Bjorn, Ylva, Snorri, or the rest of our companions, but found nothing. So my eyes drew back to the king.

He was angry, gesticulating and pointing.

Who was he speaking to?

"Did you think there wouldn't be a cost to this?" I caught some of his words during a lull in the drums and leaned forward. ". . . he'll destroy everything you care about if . . . this is the only way you can be certain Snorri won't . . ."

My heart broke into a gallop at Snorri's name, and I silently shrieked at the revelers to be silent as they broke into song.

"A good mother protects her son . . . does what it takes to . . ."

Loud voices from the revels drowned out the rest, but Harald ceased gesticulating, focusing intently on the unseen speaker.

The singing stopped.

"Then that is our plan," Harald said. "He trusts you. Go—" A loud shriek of laughter drowned out the rest of what Harald said before he turned and left the building, leaving whomever he'd been speaking to in the hall alone.

I needed to see who it was.

There wasn't space to climb through the hole and into the hall, so I swiftly climbed back down, scuttling around the side of the building. I crouched in the shadows, waiting to see who'd emerge, but the door remained shut. Unease filled my chest, and I crept up to the door, quietly opening it.

Lanterns still burned inside the hall, illuminating the statues, but nothing stirred. Whoever had been in here with Harald was gone.

"Shit," I snarled, twisting on my heels to scan the shadows, searching for a fleeing figure, but all I saw were people dancing around fires in the distance.

Who was it? Who had been conspiring with Harald?

Was it someone I knew?

A good mother protects her son . . . Unease filled my chest, and I circled the revels, searching. *It couldn't be her. Couldn't be . . .*

Indecision froze me in place. Should I hunt for the spy? Continue my search for Bjorn? Attempt to find Snorri to warn him?

A group of revelers staggered past me, one nearly knocking me over, only to shout, "Join us!"

I ignored him as I righted myself, but when I looked up, it was to see a hooded woman walking toward the hall where I was supposed to be sleeping.

Where Bjorn was supposed to be sleeping.

A building protected only by the wards that *she* had cast, because *she'd* ensured no guards stood watch. And she'd done so in order to meet with Harald, because she was plotting with him to get rid of Bjorn to make way for Leif to inherit.

Ylva. I was sure of it.

My hands balled into fists as I watched her reach for the door, already relishing the shock that would fill her face when she realized neither Bjorn nor I was inside. When she realized her plan hadn't worked.

Ylva's hand closed over the latch, opening the door, but as she moved to cross the threshold it was as though one of the gods themselves had swung a mighty fist, launching her backward. She landed square on her arse, a half dozen paces back from the door.

I almost crowed with delight. Her *own* wards had worked against her, denying entrance to any who desired to harm our party. Denying *her* entrance.

My elation was short-lived, as hands closed on my arms, yanking me back into the trees.

CHAPTER

20

I wrenched free from my attacker, swinging my fist toward the shadowy face, only to pull up short as I recognized Bjorn in the dark.

"What are you doing out here, Freya?" he hissed. "Anyone could take you."

Relief flooded my veins, though it was replaced by irritation. "Where did you go?"

"There was someone I needed to speak to," he said. "When I returned to the hall, you were gone. I've been hunting for you. Where have you been?"

"Looking for you. And spying." Then I blurted out, "Ylva is working with Harald."

He went still. "What are you talking about?"

"I overheard them speaking in the Hall of the Gods," I hissed. "She's conspiring with him to kill you so Snorri will have to name Leif heir."

Silence.

Slowly, Bjorn asked, "You saw *Ylva* speaking to Harald?"

We didn't have time for this. We needed to find Snorri. "I didn't see her, but I heard enough of the conversation. I . . ." My words trailed off, because through the trees, warriors who looked incredibly sober were walking among the revelers, examining the face of everyone they came across.

"I don't know if she convinced him to take you or if he still plans to kill you," Bjorn whispered, then pulled on my arm. "I need to get you to my father and his warriors."

"Where is he?" I hissed, tripping over a root as I followed him at a trot.

"Meeting with other jarls. This way."

I was forced to break into a run to keep up, but then Bjorn slid to a stop. Ahead of us, men carrying torches walked through the trees, searching the shadows. We turned, but behind us there were more men.

"How many warriors does Harald have?" Fear turned my hands to ice because there was nowhere to go. Unarmed as we were, there was no chance this number of men wouldn't be able to subdue us. Then it was only a matter of dragging us outside the borders of Fjalltindr and tossing us off the mountain.

"Too many." Bjorn turned to me. "We'll have to hide in plain sight."

I could feel the hammer of his heart where my hand pressed against his chest, feel the quickening of his breath that betrayed his fear, magnifying my own. "How?"

"Do you trust me?"

More than I should, I thought, but only nodded. "Yes."

"Follow my lead," he said and pulled the hood of his cloak forward. I didn't have so much as a heartbeat to wonder what that might entail before his mouth closed over mine.

For a second, I froze, so astonished that *Bjorn* was kissing me that I couldn't move. Couldn't think. And then instinct took over and my arms slipped around his neck, and I kissed him back.

Bjorn stilled, and I wondered if he'd expected me to slap him rather than respond in kind. Except not only did I understand that this ruse could save our necks, I *wanted* Bjorn to kiss me.

And I didn't want it to stop there.

Bjorn's surprise vanished in an instant, his hands catching me by the hips and lifting me, my legs wrapping around his waist and my shoulders pressing against the tree behind me. His lips found mine again, his breath hot, and his stubbled chin rough against my skin as he consumed me.

There was nothing sweet about it. Nothing tender.

Which meant it was exactly what I wanted. What I needed in this moment where I was getting what I'd dreamed of even as danger walked ever closer.

Though I knew this was meant to be a distraction that would cause the searchers to pass me by, that seemed a distant concern as Bjorn's tongue slipped into my mouth, stroking over mine. He tasted of mead, and with every inhale I scented pine and snow and wind over the fjord. It unleashed something wild in me, and I tightened my legs, drawing him closer to me as my skirts pushed up my thighs.

Pine needles crunched as footsteps came closer, and I drew back, biting at his bottom lip and meeting his gaze. "This isn't enough to dissuade interruption, Bjorn," I said under my breath. "Make it convincing."

"Gods, woman," he growled, then his mouth was on mine again, his tongue teasing my lips open as he let go of my arse with one hand. Reaching up, he caught hold of the laces of my dress, pulling them loose with a sharp jerk.

The footsteps drew closer, and a seed of doubt formed in my heart that this would work. Growing certainty that they wouldn't be fooled into believing us revelers and would demand to see our faces.

My heart hammered a rapid beat as I let go of Bjorn long enough to pull my sleeves down, the fabric of the bodice rubbing over my breasts in a way that made my back arch. My shoulders pressed hard against the tree and the antlers on my mask scratched against the bark in a seductive rhythm as I ground my hips against him. The night air kissed my nipples, though it was his slow exhalation that turned them hard, a moan tearing from my lips as he cupped one breast, his thumb stroking over the tip.

Never in my life had I been kissed like this. Touched like this. And gods, it made me feel things I hadn't believed possible. Things I thought only talk and exaggeration and stories, but the aching need building between my thighs told me that I'd been very wrong. I wanted to peel the clothes from his body and taste every inch of him. Wanted to rid myself of my dress and discover what it would feel like having him buried deep inside me.

This is madness, the last vestiges of logic in me screamed. *You need to run! You need to hide!*

I ignored the warning and dug my heels into the small of Bjorn's back, sliding one foot down to catch the waist of his trousers, pulling them low. Feeling the heat of his naked arse against my ankle as I bit at his lip, relishing how he groaned into my mouth. The front of his trousers remained caught between the tight press of our pelvises, but it did nothing to hide the hard length of his cock. Gods help me, he was as aroused as I was, which meant neither of us were thinking straight. Yet I found I didn't care as I rubbed against him, the fabric dragging against my sensitive flesh, and my body turned hot and liquid as tension rose and rose inside me. I would have this, would have *him.* Would revel in this moment right up to the second I was caught, and *then* I'd fight.

And I'd show these men no mercy for stealing this moment away from me.

"We need to see her face."

I tensed at the demand. But Bjorn snarled, "She's occupied. Now fuck off before I break Fjalltindr's peace."

Hiding my face would only raise suspicions, so instead I trusted that the mask would do its duty and reared back, my shoulders slamming against the tree. "Shut up and fuck me," I gasped loudly. Both warriors gaped at my breasts rather than my masked face, and I silently thanked the predictability of men.

But they didn't leave.

Go away, part of me prayed, but that logical voice was drowned out by the wanton part of me demanding that Bjorn see this performance through. The part of me that needed his cock deep inside me. It was *she* who won. She who rode him like a wild thing, release stalking ever closer.

Yet still the men remained, watching.

Panic twisted with my desire, my heart exploding under the pressure, all of which was drowned by horror as Bjorn pulled back his hood, revealing his face. "You must truly have a death wish."

What was he doing?

I balled my hand into a fist, readying for the men to recognize him and attack, but they only laughed. "I hope she's worth it, Bjorn."

And they moved on.

The shock stilled me. It had worked. They were gone.

But why?

"Why did they just leave?" I whispered, watching their retreating backs. "Harald made a deal with Ylva to kill you. I heard them."

"You're the king-maker, Born-in-Fire. The only life Harald cares about is yours," Bjorn said, and the tone of his voice drew my eyes back to him. He was looking up at me, bands of moonlight crossing his too-handsome face. His expression was strange, almost reverential, and we stared into each other's eyes for a long moment.

Then he gave his head a shake, looking away from me. "You gave a very convincing performance."

Shock radiated through me. He'd thought that I'd been faking my reaction to him? Thought all of *that* was nothing more than an act to put Harald's warriors off my trail?

A hollowness formed in my stomach, and I allowed my legs to slip from his waist, righting the bodice of my dress so that my breasts were once again concealed. I was painfully aware of the slickness between my thighs, my core aching with need that hadn't been satisfied, and never would be.

But that was a familiar disappointment. Nothing compared to the hurt in my heart, because I'd thought . . .

You're an idiot, Freya.

I'd nearly been kidnapped by Skaland's greatest enemy, and my concerns were for my cursed feelings.

Sucking in a deep breath, I said, "Why did that work, Bjorn? Why didn't they demand to see my face?"

His grip on my hips tightened, then he dropped his hands. "Because they know I'm not fool enough to cuckold my own father."

Apparently I was the only one foolish enough to do that.

Shouts and commotion drew my attention back to the hall. Snorri stood before the open door, barking orders.

What I should have felt was relief, but next to him stood Ylva, and the sight of that backstabbing bitch filled me with fury. I wanted to stride across the space between us and knock her on her arse before revealing what she'd done, even if it hadn't worked out in her favor.

A hand closed around my wrist, and I looked up into Bjorn's eyes.

"Don't," he said. "If you make accusations without proof, my father won't believe you."

"She was the one who convinced him to take all the guards. How is that not proof?"

"For which she had good reason. He trusts Ylva, but more than that, he knows of the tension between you two. He'll see your words as an attempt to discredit her out of jealousy."

"I am *not* jealous of her." The words came out from between my teeth. "I want to push her off a cliff."

Instead of being horrified at such a dark truth, Bjorn laughed. "So say all jealous women."

I gave him a flat stare, but he only smirked. "Go. And hold your tongue, for it is to your advantage that those who conspire against you believe you unaware."

He was right, but I still wanted to grind my teeth that Ylva was going to get away with her actions tonight. I needed to be smart, needed to be strategic, but I was so tired. Tired and embarrassed and *unsatisfied.* My eyes pricked with tears even as I cursed myself for caring so much about the wrong things.

Twisting out of Bjorn's grip, I took two steps, then froze as he said in a low voice, "It isn't you who has cause to be jealous, Freya."

A shiver ran through me, though I didn't know why. Ylva was no more jealous of me than I was of her. Not answering, I pulled off the antlered mask, throwing it into the bushes before I walked through the revelers to where Snorri stood, still shouting orders.

His eyes fixed on me, widening. "Where did you go? Why did you leave the protection of the wards?"

"I woke to find myself alone." Hesitating, I added, "I feared the worst for you and went in search." Better he believe *that* than the truth.

Snorri's frown softened even as Ylva scowled. "The hall was warded. You were an idiot to leave."

I bit my tongue and hung my head, and to my surprise, Snorri snapped, "Where were *you*, Ylva? You were no more supposed to leave the wards than she was!"

"Bjorn was with her," she retorted. "The question we should be asking is where is he now?"

Snorri's eyes panned over the revels beyond, then focused on Ylva, his voice frigid. "You didn't answer my question."

He was suspicious, and though it was for the wrong reasons, I waited for Ylva to start squirming.

I should've known better.

The lady of Halsar lifted her chin and glared at her husband. "You wish to know where I was? I was with—"

"She was with me."

At the sound of the voice, everyone turned.

A tall woman approached. She was dressed in a warrior's attire, less the weapons, with a dozen other women at her heels, all dressed similarly. She was perhaps Snorri's age, her silvered hair pulled back in war braids and her bare arms marked with faded scars. Coming to a stop, she hooked her thumbs into her belt. "Jarl Snorri."

His jaw tightened. "Jarl Bodil."

I gaped. I couldn't help it. Bodil was a famous warrior and the only woman living who claimed the title of jarl. But more than that, she was a child of the god Forseti, able to tell truth from lie, no matter who spoke. Which meant if Ylva lied about what she'd been doing, Bodil would know.

Whether she'd share that information might be another matter.

"Ylva met with me to discuss an alliance," Bodil said. "Given what I witnessed tonight, the very gods themselves stepping onto the mortal plane to accept Freya's sacrifice and claim her as their own, I saw merit in her proposition. I will follow the shield maiden into battle against our mutual enemies."

Her words were lost in a drone of noise because this didn't make sense. Ylva had been with Harald, not with Bodil. I'd seen . . .

What had I seen?

The answer to that was *nothing*. But Harald had been talking to someone and what I'd heard of the conversation had been damning; plus I'd seen Ylva unable to cross her own wards into the hall.

You never saw her face. The first kernels of doubt filled my chest that perhaps I'd jumped to a conclusion. Except everything I'd seen, everything I'd heard . . . it pointed to Ylva.

"I accept your allegiance," Snorri finally said, the tone of his voice suggesting that he wished it were coming from anyone but her.

"My allegiance is to the shield maiden, not you."

Snorri's face darkened, but Ylva stepped between them. "She is wed to Snorri, so it amounts to the same." Meeting her husband's eyes, she added, "Bodil has long been a friend to me, so her alliance is one we can count on."

There was nothing Snorri could say, and everyone present knew it. Given he'd said nothing about having convinced any of the other jarls to join him tonight, I doubted he'd been successful. He *needed* an alliance and couldn't afford to be particular about where it came from. The muscles in Snorri's jaw worked back and forth, likely his pride warring with practicality, but he nodded. "Let us drink to first steps down the path the gods have foretold."

Someone retrieved a jug of mead and Snorri lifted it. "To a united Skaland!" he roared, and everyone shouted "Skal!," toasting the alliance as the jug was passed around. When it reached me, I took a mouthful and muttered "Skal," but as I handed it off, the skin over my spine prickled.

Twisting on my heel, I watched Bjorn approach, his expression grim.

"Where were you?" Snorri demanded. "Why did you leave Freya alone?"

"I needed to speak to a seer," Bjorn said. "I was gone only for a short time, but when I returned, Freya was gone. I searched for her, though I see she is quite fine."

"Are you mad?" Ylva snarled. "Why would you risk speaking with another jarl's seer?"

Bjorn shrugged. "Seers always speak the truth for fear of the wrath of the Allfather. I sought guidance."

I glanced to Bodil to see if her magic scented a lie on his lips, but the jarl's face held only curiosity.

Snorri's eyes narrowed. "What did the seer say that was so worth you leaving Freya alone?"

"She told me that an unwatched hearth spits the hottest embers and that an untended hall is formed of the driest kindling."

My pulse quickened even as Ylva's eyes widened. "Halsar."

Bjorn lifted one shoulder. "She offered no clarity."

"We cannot wait until dawn!" Ylva rounded on Snorri. "We must leave now. Send word down the mountain to Ragnar, so that he might ride ahead and avert whatever disaster this seer has foreseen."

"It's a test," Snorri murmured, his eyes distant. "The gods are testing my commitment. Forcing me to choose between that which I have and that which I *might* achieve."

"We left our people undefended," Ylva shrieked. "Every warrior we have is here or at the base of this cursed mountain. The women and children stand alone."

Nausea rolled in my guts as I remembered what Bjorn had told me the night Gnut had attacked: that Snorri valued his warriors over innocents and that he'd sacrifice the latter to ensure the strength of the former. Because it was the warriors who would see him to the crown, not helpless children.

Yet those very warriors shifted uneasily, for it was their friends and families we'd left undefended. Several of them looked on the verge of speaking out, but then Snorri lifted his voice over the crowd. "The gods themselves stepped onto the mortal plane tonight to honor the shield maiden who will unite Skaland beneath one king. One army, which we will wield against our enemies with no mercy. Together, we have the might to defeat our enemy when he steps out of the confines of Fjalltindr, but you'd rather race home for fear of a seer's obscure ramblings?"

It was a struggle not to roll my eyes at his hypocrisy.

Shoulders back, Snorri strode among the warriors. "Don't you see? This is a test! Not only a test of your faith in the shield maiden, but also of your faith in the gods themselves, for she is *their* chosen one."

I felt ill, not wanting to be the reason that these men and women abandoned their families to whatever fate awaited them.

As if hearing my thoughts, Snorri shouted, "The fates of those in Halsar are already woven, whether they live or die in our absence is already known to the gods. But the shield maiden is *unfated* and all our threads are twisted around hers. Let us stand our ground at the base of the Hammar and bring a reckoning to our greatest enemy, King Harald of Nordeland. Let us have vengeance!"

It twisted my head, the idea that all lives were fated except for the few of us who had a drop of god's blood in our veins. That somehow, by standing with one foot in the mortal realm and one in the divine, the rules that bound all, including the gods, did not apply. The idea that my actions could catch and tangle the threads of those around me, forcing them into a different pattern than the Norns had intended. And it made me wonder about the reach I possessed. Could I change the fates of those in Halsar?

"Tell me," Snorri roared, "will you scurry back to those whose fate is already decided, or will you stand in the shield wall with the one favored by the gods? Choose!"

Destroy our enemy or protect our home. I squeezed my hands into fists because the alternative was to squeeze my head. This was all beyond me, the realm of great thinkers, not fishmongers' wives.

Except I was a fishmonger's wife no longer.

I was Freya, child of Hlin and lady of Halsar, and it was the latter that drew words up my throat to my tongue, and then out into the ears of all who listened. "What good is vengeance when all we know and love are dead? What glory will we feel in defeating our enemy if it means no hearth fire for us to return to? The Norns may have woven Halsar's fate, but together we will force them to weave a new pattern, and with the strength of our families and allies, we will turn our eyes north for vengeance!"

Cheers rose from the warriors around us, and my chest tightened at the relief I saw in their eyes. Not only that I had removed the need for them to choose between their honor and their families, but because I had the power to alter what the seer had seen.

I had the power to save Halsar.

Yet not everyone was smiling. Snorri's jaw was tight, his mouth drawn into a straight line. He cared more about defeating Harald than about the lives of those in Halsar, and I'd stolen the opportunity to have his prize. But almost as much as that, I suspected I'd earned his wrath by making a decision at all. People who were controlled did not make choices—choices were made for them.

He eyed his warriors as they lifted their hands and cheered my words, and he said, "Let Harald scuttle home to Nordeland to hide, for every day he evades us we will grow stronger. When the gods will it, we will strike our blow and vengeance will be ours!"

Men and women shouted their agreement, promising blood, and my own grew hot with anticipation of that moment, whenever it should come.

"Ready yourselves," Snorri shouted. "We march, and if the gods are with us, we'll see the bottom of this mountain before dawn."

All became organized chaos, my clothes—still filthy and stinking—once again on my body, along with my chain mail, and then we were walking to the gates of Fjalltindr, the gothar waiting with our weapons.

As we passed over the threshold, Bjorn's axe flared to life, lighting our path downward. I wanted to ask him why he'd left the hall. Why he'd gone to speak to a seer when the threat surrounding us was so great.

And most of all, what we should do about what had happened between us.

That question terrified me, because it was driven by the fact that I cared about what had happened. That I cared far, *far* too much. So instead I asked, "Do you believe we walk toward battle?"

Bjorn was quiet for a long moment, then he said, "My mother once told me that the trouble with foretellings is that you never truly understand them until they come to pass."

I frowned. "Then why did you bother asking the seer about Halsar?"

"And there lies the trouble with seers," he said, stepping away even as Bodil strode up next to me, her maidens arraying around us. "They rarely answer the question you ask."

CHAPTER

21

By the light of torches, we made our way down the southern slope of Hammar. No one spoke, every bit of concentration required not to slip on the treacherous pathway. Yet for all the slightest misstep that might send me tumbling to my death, flickers of memory invaded my mind's eye. The sensation of Bjorn's mouth on mine, our tongues entwined, the taste of him lingering like spice. Of his hands on my body, my legs wrapped around his waist, his hardness rubbing against my sex as I ground against him. Each time my boots skidded on loose rock or I stumbled over a root, I'd snap back to reality, my cheeks flushed and thighs slick with liquid heat, shame in my heart.

Why had I taken it so far?

Oh, it was easy enough to tell myself that we'd done what we needed to do, but that had only been the impetus. The escalation had been all desire, *my* desire, for while Bjorn's body had reacted, that was only because he was a man and men had little control over such things. He was loyal to his father, and I'd shamed that loyalty. Embarrassed myself and him, and each time he reached out to steady me, mortification filled my core.

Yet for all my self-admonitions, it felt like a string stretched between us, my awareness of his proximity never faltering, and I could swear that even if my eyes were closed I might reach out to him with unerring precision. My eyes went to him of their own accord, only force of will driving them back to the ground, and my ears perked up every time I heard his voice.

You're a stupid, lovesick fool, I snarled at myself. *Lives are at stake, yet you lust over muscles and a pretty face. Act like a grown woman, not a girl who's never had a man between her legs.*

It's more than that, my heart pleaded in protest. *It's more than just lust.*

Which was what terrified me the most. Lust, I could satisfy myself. But the emotions burning in my chest? Those were not something that could be sated by deft fingers in a dark room. And certainly not by me.

It was with relief that the village at the base of the mountain appeared in the dawn light, and alongside it multiple camps with picket lines full of horses, all flying different banners. One of which was Snorri's. Those on guard duty must have recognized us, for I'd not trodden another dozen feet before Ragnar approached. "My lord," he said, "we were not expecting you so soon."

"Halsar may be at risk of a raid." Snorri's voice was clipped. "Break camp and ready the horses. We must make haste."

Bodil and her maidens split off to their camp, while our party trudged toward our own. As we drew closer, a familiar figure stepped out of a tent, her dress and cloak marked with travel stains and her face with exhaustion. "I am pleased to see you well, my lord," Steinunn said, then to Ylva, "You as well, my lady." Bjorn she pointedly ignored, but to me she said, "I would have your story, Freya Born-in-Fire." Her voice was cool, expression stony, something in her gaze causing discomfort to twist my stomach.

"She's tired," Bjorn snapped. "While you've been at ease in camp, Freya has barely slept in days."

"On the contrary," the skald snapped back, "I arrived at the camp not an hour past, because that idiot man with the horses left before—" She broke off as Bodil approached, inclining her head. "Jarl Bodil."

The big woman gave her a considering look, then said, "It has been long months since you've graced Brekkur with your presence, Steinunn. I look forward to a performance."

"I will tell the tale of how Freya defeated the draug to reach the summit of the Hammar."

"How do you know that is what happened?" Bjorn asked. "Perhaps the tunnels were empty and we merely climbed to the top."

The look the skald gave him was withering, but before the conversation could devolve further, I said, "It was a great battle, and I will tell you all of it, as I promised."

"Since you've made clear you do not wish to tell me anything, Bjorn," Steinunn said, "perhaps you might retrieve our horses."

Bjorn's eyes narrowed, but Bodil said, "I will stay with Freya, Firehand. This is a story I greatly wish to hear."

"It's fine," I said to him, "I will make no mention of Bjorn Shitshimself."

Bodil coughed on the mouthful of water she'd just drunk, but Bjorn only smirked. "It is to my good fortune that the skalds' magic can only reveal the truth."

I smirked back, trying to ignore the flips my stomach was doing. "If I believe it, is it not the truth?"

"My reputation already cowers, Born-in-Fire," he answered. "I shall flee lest it take more abuse."

Turning on his heel, he strode toward the picket line, and I tore my eyes from his form to find Bodil watching me, and my cheeks warmed. "He did not actually," I swiftly said. "It's just a—"

"Perhaps start from the beginning," the jarl said, then jabbed Steinunn, who was glaring at the ground. "Pay attention, girl, you don't want to get anything wrong on this one."

I spoke until I was so hoarse my throat hurt, telling the story of our journey through the draug-infested tunnels. Of our battles and how my magic protected me so that I might wield Bjorn's axe, and how the gods had intervened in the final moments, when all seemed lost, to drag the remaining creatures down to Helheim. It was fortunate that the moments I did not wish to share were the quiet moments, and no one seemed to notice their omission. Bjorn stubbornly refused to be involved in the telling, riding instead at the rear of the column.

The telling distracted me from thoughts of him, but it also served well to distract those I rode with who feared for their families in Halsar. Yet as the sun faded into night, Ylva insisting that we ride by torchlight, sleep took me. And in the confines of my mind, I was not so similarly spared.

Once again, I stood atop the great hall of Halsar, except this time everything burned. People ran screaming, their clothing aflame, while warriors made of shadow pursued and cut them down, black blood spraying even as their victims fell screaming. And I could do nothing. Could not move from the place where my feet were fixed to the roof of the hall, my body frozen in place. All I could do was scream and scream, for I'd brought this upon all of them.

I jerked upright, only the ropes tying me to the saddle keeping me from falling off the side of my horse.

"You have troubled dreams."

My head snapped to my left where Bodil rode, leading my mare. Though she'd stayed by my side the entire journey, listened to every word of my tale, she had said little about herself. Logically, I knew that I needed to be careful about what I said, for she would discern any untruth and there were secrets I needed to keep, but there was something calming about her presence that made me want to confess my fears.

"I have a troubled life," I finally answered. "Those troubles find their ways into my dreams."

Her head tilted slightly. "You fear for those in Halsar, despite it only recently becoming your home?"

"Yes." Shifting in the saddle, I silently willed those ahead of me to increase their speed so conversation would be impossible. "They were left undefended for my sake."

"That was Snorri's decision, not yours."

Just as it had been his decision to sacrifice the thralls as decoys during the ascent of Fjalltindr, but that hadn't eased my conscience. "I don't want anyone to die because of me, especially not innocent people."

"If that is their fate, that is their fate."

I scowled, though she spoke a truth I'd heard all my life. "I weave my own fate, Bodil, same as you. Same as all children of the gods. If by changing my path I might alter theirs, why shouldn't I try?"

"I did not say you shouldn't." Bodil reined her horse around a bush. "But how are you to know whether the choice you made changed anything?"

"If everyone in Halsar is well, I'll know, because it means what has occurred is different from what the seer foresaw."

"Perhaps." Bodil was quiet for a long moment. "Or perhaps the seer's words did not mean what Ylva believed they meant. Perhaps she spoke of a moment far in the future. Or perhaps"—she gave me a long look—"of a place other than Halsar. Only the gods know for certain."

"Then why ask a seer anything at all if what they tell you is useless?" I exploded. Not out of anger toward her, but out of a growing sense of powerlessness.

"The words the seers speak are given to them by the gods," Bodil answered. "Do you not think it the greatest vanity for a mere mortal to believe he can take divine knowledge and bend it to his purpose?"

My eyes shot to her so fast my neck cracked, for, of a surety, she spoke of Snorri. "Speak plainly, Bodil. I'm too tired for riddles."

The jarl shrugged, her silvered braids falling over her broad shoulders. "The gods love riddles, Freya, and I am as much at their mercy as you. But the question I find myself asking is this: How can a man control your fate when he is not even the master of his own?"

I opened my mouth, then closed it, unable to come up with an answer.

"If you'll excuse me," Bodil said. "I must go speak with Ylva. She is much consumed by fear for her home and Snorri has a man's ability to offer comfort, which is to say none at all."

Likely made worse by her knowing that Snorri had been more interested in taking vengeance against Harald than defending her home. "You know her well?"

Bodil smiled. "Why do you think she came to me for help at Fjalltindr?" Nudging her horse with her heels, she pressed into a canter, calling over her shoulder, "Think about what I said."

I bit the insides of my cheeks, considering her words. Except the answer seemed obvious. Snorri controlled me with threats. His blade hovered over my mother's neck, and above Geir's and Ingrid's, which meant I would do as he asked. While that wasn't as worthy of song as gods and fate, it was every bit as effective.

"Foolishness," I muttered to myself. Likely what Bodil was trying to do was undercut Snorri, which meant I should be wary of her.

"What is?"

For the second time in minutes, I jumped, finding Bjorn next to me, a shiver running over me as his knee bumped against mine with the motion of the trotting horses. "What?"

He took a bite of dried meat, jaw working as he chewed, the breeze sending pieces of his dark hair dancing against his skin. Swallowing, he said, "What is foolishness?"

I blinked, wondering what sort of teasing he was subjecting me to, then realized he'd heard me talking to myself and my skin flushed. "Nothing. I . . . It's nothing, only idle words with Bodil."

"Didn't look idle."

His leg brushed against mine again, the track not really wide enough for two horses abreast, which his mount made clear by flattening his ears to his head and snapping at my own. Yet I didn't urge my mare ahead, instead allowing Bjorn's leg to bump mine again. *Curse you, Freya!* my conscience shouted. *What is wrong with you?*

"Why did you go speak to the seer?" I asked in order to give myself justification for not putting distance between us. That, and the fact no one carrying a torch was near us.

"Because I had questions," he answered softly, ducking under a branch. "Decided to take advantage of the opportunity."

"What did you ask?" My eyes stole to his face, but Bjorn was staring down the trail, expression unreadable.

He took another bite of the dried meat, chewing and remaining silent for so long that I thought he didn't intend to answer. Which of course made me question why he wouldn't. Then he said, "I asked whether the gods would tell me if I walked the path they wished me to. You already know how she responded."

My horse stopped and it took me a moment to realize that I'd tugged on the reins, Bjorn slowing to look at me over his shoulder. Shaking my head sharply, I heeled the mare back into a trot, even less certain than I'd been after my conversation with Bodil. "I don't understand . . ."

Before more could be said, the sound of galloping hooves filled the air. A female sob echoed down the trail and my stomach plummeted. "No."

Digging in my heels, I cut into the trees, moving past the group and back to the path before heeling my horse into a gallop. Dimly, I heard shouts. Heard my name and orders to pause, but I ignored them and pressed onward.

This can't be.

I made the choice to come to Halsar's aid.

I changed fate.

Yet as I broke from the trees and was greeted with an orange glow on the dark horizon, smoke gusting over me on the wind, I knew I'd changed nothing.

Halsar had burned.

I galloped down the road, slowing only once I was at the outskirts of the ruins, the flames already dying down to embers. Nothing remained standing, not the great hall nor any of the homes. Even the docks that I'd once trained upon with Bjorn were destroyed, the pillars they'd rested upon jutting from the water like jagged teeth, blackened wrecks of fishing boats and drakkar floating beyond. And amongst the ruins, there was no mistaking the still forms of those who'd died fighting, trying to defend it all.

Bjorn's horse slowed next to me, but he said nothing, only circled my own mount, eyes taking in the ruins of his home. Then his gaze met mine. "This is not your fault."

I hadn't asked for this. Had done what I could to try to prevent it. But that didn't mean I wasn't the cause.

More horses galloped into the ruined streets, Ylva's wailing piercing my ears. She slid off Snorri's horse, falling to her knees in the mud and ash before the remains of the great hall, face streaked with tears. "Where is my son?" she screamed. "Where is my child?"

All around, warriors were dismounting, their faces filled with grief and fury and fear, some racing through the ruins, shouting the names of those they'd left behind. Left undefended. Cries of anguish filled the air.

Snorri alone seemed unmoved, his jaw rigid as he surveyed the ruins of his stronghold. He opened his mouth, and I tensed, ready and willing to lash out if he told these people this was another *test*. Yet all he said was, "Search for survivors. And answers."

I dismounted, my shoes sinking into the mud, but before I could go further, shouts rang out.

"Oh, thank the gods!" Ylva's cry filled the air as I circled my horse. Beyond, dozens of people walked toward us, mostly women and children, dirty and exhausted and with seemingly nothing but the clothes on their backs. But they were very much alive.

The two groups, warriors and survivors, surged toward each other and my chest hitched as I watched Ylva fling her arms around Leif, whose skin was stained with soot and blood, a scabbed gash marring his forehead. Only Bjorn and I held back as families and friends were reunited, the air filled with tears of joy, but also with cries of grief, for both groups had suffered losses.

Resting his forearms on his saddle, Bjorn watched, and I was struck with the sense that he was not quite one of them. That despite his father being jarl and Bjorn set to inherit the role someday in the future, he stood apart. I wondered if that was by choice or whether it was forced upon him by all those long years he'd spent in Nordeland. Ylva's words to him echoed in my head: *You were gone too long and are more of a Nordelander than a Skalander.*

Snippets of conversation drew my attention. Explanations that scouts had seen the attack coming but not with enough time to evacuate the village. That those who were able fought back so that those who couldn't fight were able to flee into the forest to hide. That all had been lost. But one word, one *name,* I heard repeated over and over.

Gnut.

The other jarl had come to finish the job he'd started the night Bjorn and I set his ships on fire, taking advantage of Snorri's absence to strike a blow that would not be easy to overcome. Not only was every home destroyed, but all the stores and supplies and tools within them were lost to the raiders' fire. Everything would need to be rebuilt and replaced during the months most dedicated to farming and gathering, which meant all would be in a weakened position when winter struck.

I knew this because I'd seen it before. Had lived it.

These people had survived the raid, but that might only mean a prolonged death as they suffered and starved over winter, and my hands balled into fists. Gnut had done this to strike a blow at Snorri, but it would not be Snorri who suffered.

It wasn't fair.

Which was perhaps a childish thing to think, because nothing about life was fair, yet I was so sick of seeing those who were powerless harmed by the actions of those who were supposed to protect them.

Snorri's warriors and the survivors began bringing the fallen to the square before the ruins of the great hall. I moved to help them, but then hesitated. They were all strangers to me, whereas those who tended to them were their friends and family. Although I was Skalander through and through, I was also an outsider in this moment. At least I was until I saw a familiar form supported by two of Snorri's men. "Oh, Liv," I whispered.

Of their own accord, my feet took me to the still form of the healer, her eyes glazed and unseeing, the wound in her chest so catastrophic that I knew her end had been quick. Kneeling in the mud, I closed her lids, whispering my hopes that the gods had met her with open arms and full cups.

Bjorn knelt next to the healer, every muscle in his face tight with grief. And, I realized, anger.

"Why didn't you run?" he asked under his breath. "What the fuck were you thinking, Liv?"

I knew what she was thinking. These were the people whom she had spent nearly every day of her life healing with her gift. She was connected to every single person in Halsar, whether it had been delivering them or their child, mending wounds from accident or battle, or chasing away sickness. She'd known what losing the village would mean, and though she opposed fighting to her core, she'd picked up a weapon to fight for her people. Had earned a place with the gods.

Bodil approached on horseback, her maidens holding back, their watchful eyes on the surrounding forest. Dismounting, she went to Ylva's side. "I'll send word to Brekkur requesting supplies and ships and laborers."

"You have our thanks, my friend," Ylva said, wiping tears from her face. "We will rebuild and—"

"We will not rebuild, for that is what Gnut wants!" Snorri roared, silencing everyone even as Ylva's face filled with dismay. "He fears me! Fears the fate the gods have in store for me! That is why he struck when our backs were turned, attacking women and children, and burning homes—because he believed it would keep us from making war upon him. That he'd be able to hide in his stronghold another season while we toiled to rebuild. Gnut believes he has struck us a grievous blow, but I say he is mistaken!" Snorri paused, then shouted, "I say that he has given us the gift that will see his destruction!"

From the other side of Liv's body, Bjorn made a noise of disgust, but I found myself leaning in Snorri's direction, desperate to learn what silver lining he saw within this catastrophe. I was not alone. All around us, the people of Halsar watched their jarl with hope in their eyes, and for all I prayed that he had answers, it was not lost upon me that it was the consequences of his choices that we needed to be delivered from.

"Long have we known that Halsar was vulnerable!" Snorri leapt onto a pile of debris, his voice projecting across the smoking ruins. "Long have we known that its position was weak, ever a target of raiders from north and south, east and west. Yet it was our home, so we clung to it, allowing habit and sentiment and apathy to weaken us. But no longer." His eyes surveyed his people. "For like a healer excises a rotten bit of flesh, so has Gnut burned away our weakness, leaving behind nothing but strength!"

I felt a fervor growing in the people, a restless energy stirred by Snorri's words. Felt it in myself, and for the first time I saw a spark of why the gods foresaw him as king of Skaland, for he *was* a man whom other men followed on the strength of his words alone. Ylva, however, seemed unmoved, her arms crossed and eyes frosty.

"The gods themselves have seen a united Skaland. Have seen a king. And a king does not live in a muddy fishing village." He paused again for effect. "And neither do a king's people!"

Villagers and warriors alike voiced their agreement, lifting their fists into the air.

"So we will turn our backs on this pile of mud and ash," Snorri shouted. "Will turn our eyes across the mountains and prepare for war. Will prepare to strike our enemy! And I swear to you this: The next roof you sleep beneath will be within the walls of Grindill!"

Roars of approval echoed across the ruins, everyone, including me, shouting for Gnut's death. Shouting for blood. And shouting for vengeance. I allowed myself to be swept away by it, for a path forward was an escape from what had come before. From what surrounded me now.

"We're going to make the bastards bleed for this," I said, turning to Bjorn.

Only to discover that he was gone.

We set up camp near the ruins of Halsar, Snorri sending riders through his territories to call in every man and woman who could fight. Bodil sent for reinforcements from her own lands. Warriors and ships and supplies to feed those who'd lost everything to fire.

"Gnut's scouts will hear of this," she warned. "He will be ready for us."

Snorri only scoffed. "Let his scouts go running back to him. I want Gnut cowering in terror behind his walls, knowing that I'm coming for him. I want his people to have time to understand that their jarl has brought this pain down upon them in his refusal to swear an oath to the rightful king of Skaland. In his refusal to bend to the will of the gods. Mark my words, they will turn on him sure and true."

Despite the arrogance of his words, there was a fervor in them that fueled the fires in the hearts of all who heard. Only a few drowned in sorrow, all others turning their minds and hands to preparation for battle, forging weapons, fletching arrows, and gathering the supplies that would be needed. It was the nature of our people to spit in defiance of adversity, to look forward rather than backward, to fixate on vengeance rather than to grieve for the fallen.

Sitting next to a cookfire, I ate food that someone had prepared, my mind tossing and turning over what my role would be in the battle to come.

Bodil sat across the fire from me, a bowl in her hand. Despite not knowing her for very long, and the difficult questions she'd posed of me, there was no denying that I felt at ease in her presence. She was of an age with my mother, but whereas my mother was endlessly prying into my business so that she might pick apart flaws in my behavior, Bodil's interest seemed motivated by curiosity rather than the desire to uncover my failings.

For a long time, the jarl said nothing, only watched as the others gathered around fires, drinking and singing and dancing, the air thick with energy, like in the moments before a storm. Finally she said, "Snorri believes his words. Believes that this is the fate the gods foresee for him. There is a sort of magic in that." She gestured to the dancers. "A power to make others believe as well."

Finishing my food, I set my bowl down. "Do you believe?"

Bodil considered the question, and it struck me that she rarely spoke without thinking first. Probably a skill I'd do well to learn, though I found it frustrating having to wait for her responses.

"I believe," she finally said, "that we stand on the brink of great change for Skaland, though what that change will be, I cannot say. Only that I hope to be part of it. To influence it for the better, if I can."

An answer that was not an answer, another habit I'd noticed of Bodil. It made me want to dig, to extract something solid and tangible from her, so I asked, "How do you know when someone is telling a mistruth?"

Bodil smiled. "My feet itch."

A flicker of surprise ran through me, first that she had said something forthright, and second that the answer was so . . . mundane. She was the child of Forseti, her ability to discern truth the god's magic, and to have it manifest in such a way made me smile. "I'd say that would be irritating, but I suppose those who know you refrain from deception in your presence."

Pushing a silver braid over her shoulder, Bodil said, "Being wholly honest is harder than you might think, Freya. Nearly everyone is deceiving someone about something, even if it's only themselves. Words uttered might be the truth but the tone or sentiment false, and my gift does not tell me the difference, only that something in the exchange is deception." Taking a mouthful of food, she chewed and swallowed. "In my youth, I suffered tremendous anger because it felt as though everyone was lying to me and that I could trust no one."

Gods, but I understood that feeling. "You must have felt miserable," I said to her, though my eyes drifted from Bodil's face to the other fires, hunting and searching for Bjorn, whom I'd not seen since we'd returned to Halsar. He was the one I trusted above all others, yet he was the one person I had to guard myself against the most.

"It was," Bodil answered. "I found peace only when I learned to tell the difference between mistruths told from empathy, shame, or fear, and those told with malice. Knowledge of that came not from magic but from experience."

"It's amazing that you didn't go mad in the intervening period," I mumbled, then I heard a familiar tread coming up behind me, and I turned.

Bjorn approached, firelight casting shadows across the hard angles of his face in a way that made my stomach flip.

"Bodil." He nodded at the jarl. "Freya."

"Where have you been?" I asked, then instantly cursed myself for doing so, swiftly adding, "Avoiding real work, as usual?"

He sat next to me, sending my heart into a gallop as I inhaled the scent of pine and fjord. "Why? Was there something you needed me to do for you?"

My cheeks instantly reddened, and I prayed he'd only think it the light cast by the fire. "Other than cutting off heads, the list of things that you can do that I can't do better is very short, Bjorn. So to answer your question, no."

Bodil cackled and slapped her hands against her thighs. "She speaks the truth, boy."

Bjorn's smile turned sly. "Maybe so, but the items on that list I do very well indeed."

Memory crashed over me, of his hands on my body and his tongue in my mouth, heat flaming in my core. "So say all men," I muttered.

Bjorn laughed, but Bodil's eyes narrowed on me. "Truer words never spoken."

True words. False sentiment.

Shit.

Knowing I needed to recover the situation, I said, "Besides, napping isn't a skill, so you shouldn't brag about it."

"I beg to differ," he answered. "But the point is moot, given I wasn't exercising said skill. Liv's home and all her supplies were burned in the fire, so Ylva requested those with knowledge search out plants needed to help the injured."

My chest tightened, partially in shame that I'd accused him of sloth and partially because I was reminded of the fallen healer. Liv and all the others had died because their warriors weren't here to defend them. "That was good of you."

Bjorn shrugged, then reached into his pocket and pulled out a jar. "Given my relationship with fire, Liv taught me how to make your salve years ago. It's likely not as good as hers but it should do until another healer can make more."

Of all the things that needed to be done, of all the things Bjorn could've been doing, he'd been making more salve for my hand. A flood of emotion made it abruptly impossible to breathe, but I managed to choke out, "Thank you."

"It's nothing."

It was everything, and my eyes burned, tears threatening. I hoped both of them would think it smoke from the fire.

Bjorn took hold of my right hand. Though I had little sensation in the scars, I could still feel the heat of him, and my breath caught.

"How were you burned?" Bodil asked, and I jerked, realizing how this must look. Extracting my hand from Bjorn's, I took the salve and rubbed it over my scars, more than aware that *this* was something Bjorn excelled at. But if I allowed him, I'd *feel* things that I shouldn't. I knew that while I might be able to hide those feelings from most people, Bodil would sense the deception.

"Born-in-Fire needed a weapon and the closest one to hand was my axe," Bjorn answered the jarl, his voice clipped. "She's a woman who does what needs doing."

"The best kind of woman."

My cheeks heated at being so discussed, and I bent over my hand to put extra vigor into my application of salve so as to seem not to have heard.

Silence hung among the three of us, thick enough to cut with a knife, then Bodil said, "You left in the middle of your father's speech, Bjorn."

He huffed out an irritated breath. "Grindill has never been assailed. That's one of the reasons Gnut can afford to be an unapologetic prick—his position is strong. The only way to take it is by starving those inside, which I suspect is not the glorious victory my father has in mind."

"So you left because you disagree with his strategy?"

Bjorn's knee bumped mine as he shifted, and I leaned away despite feeling drawn to him like iron to a lodestone. "Grindill is a fortress. Towering walls of earth and oak ringed by a moat filled with sharpened stakes. Snorri says he wishes to take it to give his people better lives, yet how many will die in the taking of it?"

I . . . hadn't known that.

Though Snorri had spoken of walls, I'd envisioned a slightly grander version of Halsar. Not a fortress. I wondered how many others who'd lifted their hands in support of Snorri's plan were the same. People who'd never ventured more than half a day from Halsar, the town we intended to capture nothing more than a name to them.

"All great accomplishments come at a price, Bjorn," Bodil answered. "Between Snorri and me, we have many good warriors. We have *you*." She gave him a pointed look. "But most importantly, we have Freya, who is favored not just by Hlin, but all the gods."

Bjorn snorted. "Yes, yes. To make a king out of the one who controls her fate. Yet no mention of how many will die to achieve that end. Perhaps he will be king of no one, all dead beneath the heels of his ambition."

The sourness of his tone surprised me, and I twisted at the waist and looked up at him. "You don't believe your mother's foretelling?"

"I believe it," he muttered. "But that doesn't mean I wish to rush into a battle like this on blind faith."

"Yet you've a reputation across all of Skaland, and Nordeland, as a risk-taker," Bodil said. "For throwing yourself to where the battle is thickest. How is this any different?"

Bjorn's jaw tightened and I watched him intently as he met the woman's gaze. "With respect, Jarl Bodil, just because you can discern the truth does not mean you are entitled to it."

I didn't disagree with him, but at the same time, if his concern was only for the lives of the warriors who'd be part of the battle, why not say so, given that he basically already had? Why get his back up now?

In a sudden rush of motion, Bjorn stood. "Take care of your hand, Freya. You'll need it in the battle to come." He nodded at Bodil. "Good night to you both."

Then he strode away, weaving through the multitude of campfires.

"Apologies for his behavior," I said, turning back to the jarl. "He's . . . he's not had much rest, and Halsar is his home. To see it burned . . ." I gestured outward, unsure whether any of this was the reason for Bjorn's rudeness but needing to say something. "He does not wish people to risk their lives unnecessarily."

Bodil rubbed her chin. "I don't think that's his concern. Or at the very least, his concern is for *one* person, in particular."

I didn't answer. How could I when she knew truth from lie, and the truth was not something I dared to voice.

With my heart in my throat, I waited for her to push the issue. To voice her opinion or demand an answer from me. Yet Bodil only picked up a stick and poked the fire before adding more wood. Only when the flames were roaring high did she ask, "Do you believe this is the right path, Freya?"

"I . . ." Trailing off, I stared into the flames, because this was the first time someone had asked my opinion and I didn't know that I had one. Or rather, I was afraid—given the recent reminder that I was ignorant of many aspects of the situation—that my opinion was wrong. "I think myself not well enough informed for my thoughts to matter."

Bodil leaned back on her hands, and I swore I saw disappointment on her face through the haze of smoke, so I added, "I think Snorri is correct that to rebuild Halsar as it was is folly. Not only is it easy to attack, but it is now the greatest target in Skaland, thanks to my presence. We are vulnerable not only to more attacks by Gnut, but to all who feel like-minded in their resistance to seeing Snorri as king."

"I agree," Bodil said, and I felt a flush of pride. "But would it not be better to merely build somewhere else? To construct his own fortress?"

"Such an endeavor would take years and a fortune of silver," I answered. "And in the meantime, all these people will be at risk in whatever temporary homes we construct for them. Winters will see suffering, for many will have been taken from fields or from the hunt to build."

"Raid. Take what you need."

"We haven't the ships to raid across the seas, and raiding those we wish to swear oaths to Snorri seems not a path best taken. They'll only smile to our faces, then stab us in the back at the soonest opportunity."

Bodil nodded approvingly, and my cheeks warmed because I wasn't used to such a response when I voiced my thoughts. Eager to give her more, I said, "Gnut has earned our retaliation by attacking Halsar twice, and by voicing his defiance to Snorri. Not attacking him makes us look weak. Makes us look as though we will tolerate such behavior, which will cause more to do the same until soon we have attacks coming from all sides. To protect our people, we must take action against him. Not only to discourage others who think to capitalize upon our weakness, but to protect those who've sworn to Snorri already. Prove to everyone that Snorri will lift up high those who follow him and walk with heavy heels over those who seek to bring us low. Warriors must be proud to follow him even as they fear to defy him."

My heart thundered. I'd said what I believed, felt it in my bones, and I'd fight to see such a thing achieved. Yet I waited with anticipation for Bodil's reaction, for now that she'd unleashed my voice, I craved her validation. "Do you agree?"

She tilted her head. "Steinunn will spread word with her songs, and time alone will tell how Skaland reacts to the deeds that have been done. But tell me this, Freya. Bjorn is not wrong in how he speaks of Grindill's defenses. How do you propose we take it?"

I bit the insides of my cheeks, then admitted, "I've never seen this fortress, Bodil. Never fought in more than a skirmish. Until the day that Snorri took me, I had never traveled more than half a day from my village, so I've no business telling anyone how this siege should be fought. But . . ."

She smiled and poked the fire again, sending sparks flying. "But?"

The answer sat on my tongue, yet I had a hard time speaking it because it felt arrogant. The last thing I wanted was to be in possession of an inflated sense of self-worth. The trouble was, the more I spoke, the more I saw how Skaland could be united. Not by battle strategies and victories, though those would play a part, but by *belief*. "I have to be the one to win it."

Swallowing hard, I added, "For Skalanders to agree to follow Snorri, they must believe that the gods wish to see him as king. That this is fate. And for that to happen, I must play my part, else no stories will be told of me."

"Yes, you must play your part," Bodil answered. "And as to the rest, *we* must play our own parts by making you ready. Tomorrow, you will train with me and with my warriors."

Excitement filled me even as my stomach plummeted, because I'd assumed that Snorri would have me resume training with Bjorn. That I wouldn't have a choice and therefore no one would question the time spent with him improving my fighting skills.

As if sensing my thoughts, Bodil said, "Bjorn's skill is unparalleled, but he fights like a man, relying too much on brute strength, never mind that axe of his. You must learn to fight like a woman and the only ones who can teach you that are other women. I will speak to Snorri on it."

"Thank you," I murmured. "You honor me."

Bodil gave a soft snort, then rose to her feet. "Skalanders are not known for their altruism, Freya, and I am no different. I wish to rise on the tide, not sink beneath it, and the best way I can do that is to be at your side. You are a clever, passionate woman with a good heart—a woman worth following."

The mix of honesty and flattery in her answer drew a smile to my face, but it evaporated as the jarl added, "You are right that for Skalanders to follow, they must hear tell of your exploits and conquests. But keep in mind those exploits and conquests must be fitting of a leader, else they are naught more than the fishwife gossip. And the consequences of gossip aren't always for the person being spoken about."

She'd noticed. The reprimand for whatever was going on between me and Bjorn stung all the more after her approval, and I visibly flinched, barely managing a nod.

"Tonight, my maidens and I will celebrate the lives of the fallen," she said. "And I believe Steinunn will sing some of the ballad she has composed to spread word of your battle fame. We would like for you to join us, Freya."

Without waiting for me to respond, she disappeared into the darkness.

Hunched over against the cold, I stared at the fire. Her warning was clear and nothing I didn't already know, but there was something about hearing it from the lips of another that made it more real. Made the consequences more threatening, because Bodil was right: I wouldn't be the one who'd be harmed if Snorri discovered I was lusting after his son. It would be my family. Would be—

"I see she finally gave up prying."

I stiffened as Bjorn sat next to me. "Be wary of what you say to her, Born-in-Fire. The woman hears too much."

"I know." My tongue felt numb, my throat thick, and the sudden urge to cry fell over me.

What would Snorri do to Bjorn if he found out I was enamored with him?

A sickening feeling filled my core, because becoming king was Snorri's obsession and he'd proven that he'd sacrifice everything and anything to see it through. He cared for Bjorn and seemed to truly believe that his son was entwined in my fate, but if the right gossip reached his ears, that could easily change.

I rose to my feet. "Bodil gives good advice," I said. "She's offered me the opportunity to train with her and her maidens, and I have accepted. It will do me well to learn from them."

Bjorn's voice was clipped as he said, "You barely know her."

"Then I suppose I should remedy that."

And lest my traitorous heart betray me, I turned and walked toward the female warriors dancing around a distant fire. "Spare a cup for me?" I asked when I reached them.

Bodil laughed. "Of course. It will be our honor to drink with Freya Born-in-Fire!"

One of her maidens pushed a cup of mead into my hand, and I drank deeply as the women shouted my name. Laughing, I held the cup out for more, then allowed the women to draw me into their dance.

My feet struck the ground to the rhythm of the drums, and I shrieked as someone threw more wood on the fire, sparks and embers flaring up into the night sky. The mead settled into my veins, the world spinning as we circled around the bonfire, women tossing aside heavy clothes as heat flushed our skin. Honoring both the dead and the gods they had joined, singing their names and praising their deeds.

When was the last time I had danced? When was the last time that I'd honored the gods as I should? When was the last time I surrounded myself with women whom I might one day call friends?

Men attempted to approach, drawn by drink and bare skin, but Bodil's maidens chased them off with spears and laughter, the jarl shouting, "This is a place for women, get you gone or face our wrath!"

Grinning, I caught up a spear, joining the fray. Beyond the men encircling us, my eyes locked with Bjorn's, and I lifted my spear, daring him to come closer. But he only shook his head and disappeared into the woods.

Then everyone went still, the rhythm of the drums fading into silence. It took me a heartbeat to understand why, then my eyes found Steinunn, who approached, a small drum hanging from a strap around her shoulders. The skald waited until all had grown still, then began to beat on her drum, the rhythm slow and ominous.

Bodil moved to my elbow, catching my arm as I swayed, my balance all of a sudden unsteady. "Have you heard a skald perform a song about your own exploits before, Freya?"

I shook my head, unnerved at how my heart had adopted the rhythm of Steinunn's drum.

"For those who were not in the tunnels with the draug, this will be a thrilling adventure. Entertainment of the first order," she said. "But for you . . . it will be like being back in the darkness with monsters coming from every side."

My palms turned cold and I took a long drink from my cup, though I knew I'd already had far too much. "All right."

Steinunn's lips parted, and wordless song came forth, riding the rhythm of her drum. I felt her magic cascade over me, the world around me swirling. I blinked, no longer certain what I was looking at, only that it was not the dark ruins of Halsar. It was daylight, the sun strange and watered as though I looked at it through glass, and I swallowed down rising bile as the Hammar appeared before me.

Vaguely I was aware Steinunn was telling the story of approaching the mountain, that our way up the south side was blocked by our enemy, and that this was a test set me by the gods and communicated by the specter. Except it wasn't the skald I heard, but the wind. The clatter of bones hung from trees. The crunch of the horses' hooves. I clenched my teeth as the stink of rot filled my nose, and fear wrapped a band around my chest, tightening to the point I could barely suck in a breath as I watched myself dismount my mare.

I was seeing, I realized, through Steinunn's eyes, feeling what she had felt as we walked to the entrance to the tunnel. Steam rushed out of the blackness, the noise deafening, and I took an involuntary step back even as those around me gasped.

Perspective shifted, and it was through my own eyes that I watched, my breathing rapid as I stepped into the darkness and Bjorn's axe flared to life. Stinking mist swirled around my feet as I eased past dead animals, and I felt everyone near me shift on their feet, feeling my trepidation.

"I don't like this," I mumbled, feeling sick to my stomach as Steinunn sped up time, only flickers of moments filling my eyes as I climbed and climbed. "I don't feel well."

"Steady," Bodil said. "It is just memory. You aren't there."

But all I could see was Bjorn edging through the narrow space, knowing what was coming, knowing that draug would soon be upon us. He cursed as he tripped over the cup, and I looked down as it shot past my feet.

Those aren't my shoes.

I had no chance to think about the unfamiliar red laces on the leather shoes before the roar of the mountain *breathing* struck my ears, the rising drums, the scratch of bony feet against stone. Vertigo and a wave of nausea hit me, and I twisted out of Bodil's grip to fall to my knees.

"Are you well, Freya?" I dimly heard her ask right before I fell sideways, the world going dark.

I awoke to Bodil's face inches from mine. "How do you feel, Freya?
Are you ready to fight?"

"No." I rolled over, burying my face in my cloak. Clouded
memory of vomiting into the dirt came back to me, and I winced, realizing that Bodil and her maidens must have had to drag my drunk self
into the tent. "Is it already dawn?"

"Dawn came and went hours ago," Bodil replied.

"What?" I sat upright, peering through the open flaps of the tent,
which revealed dark gray sky, rain misting down into the mud. "Why
did no one wake me?"

"Because Bjorn has been sitting in front of your tent since he carried
you in here last night," she said. "He threatened to cut the throat of
anyone who disturbed you, saying you needed sleep, or you'd be no
good to anyone." She fished in my cloak pocket and extracted the pot
of salve. "I'm supposed to remind you to put this on your hand."

I grimaced as I took the pot from her, and found myself tucking it
back into my pocket rather than putting it on. "We are to begin training now, then?"

Bodil laughed. "Unless you need another few hours to sleep off
your hangover."

It was already shameful enough that I'd drunk so much mead, then embarrassed myself puking into the dirt and passing out. As though sensing my thoughts, the jarl said, "No one noticed, so enraptured were they in Steinunn's tale."

"But not you?" I drank deeply from a skin of water I found sitting next to my pallet. "I thought you knew Steinunn. Liked her."

Bodil shook her head. "I only met her a year ago. I've never cared much for skald magic, particularly when I know it's being deployed as propaganda, which was why she traveled to Brekkur on Snorri's behalf. I stuffed my ears with wool when she began singing." Straightening, she added, "I'll wait for you outside."

Again, I was struck that while Bodil might have an interest in a united Skaland and in seeing what the gods had in store for us, she was only tolerating Snorri and had little desire to see him as king. Which made me wonder what her endgame could be. Made me wonder if Bodil, like all the other jarls, saw herself as the one who would control my fate, but was clever enough to come at it by a circular approach.

I belted my father's sword and a long-bladed seax to my waist, then donned my cloak and left the tent.

Mist immediately coated my face, and I shivered and stomped my feet as I walked, needing my blood to flow so that it might vanquish both the chill and my headache. Most of Snorri's warriors seemed hard at work fortifying our camp's perimeter with stakes, others forging and fletching weapons, and judging from the absence of women and children, others were out hunting and foraging. Everyone set to a task but me, who'd slept away the morning. So it was shame that drove away the chill, my cheeks burning hot as I followed Bodil through the opening in the stakes and down to the beach.

"Freya!"

My spine stiffened at Bjorn's voice, and I turned to find him walking toward us with an armload of sticks for stakes. Before he could start in with his teasing, I snapped, "I don't need to be coddled. I will rise when everyone else rises, and I will pull my own weight. I don't need you interfering."

Irritation flared in his eyes. "Maybe you should've considered that before drinking yourself sick."

He wasn't wrong. "That's my problem, not yours." Crossing my arms, I glared at him. "If I want your opinion or your assistance, I'll ask." I twisted on my heels and strode down to the ash-streaked beach.

Bodil gave me an approving nod. "Men need to be taught their place." Then a lopsided smile formed on her face. "But the boy did clean vomit off your face after you fell nose-first into it."

My cheeks flamed, and I kicked at a rock because I knew Bjorn didn't deserve harsh words from me. "My head hurts."

Which wasn't a lie, but it also wasn't the reason for my anger. By treating me the way he did, Bjorn was tempting fate in the worst sort of way. Already, Bodil suspected there was something between us, so how long until Ylva did as well?

No matter what sort of trickery Ylva had used to give herself an alibi in Fjalltindr, I knew she'd been conspiring with Harald to get rid of Bjorn. She wouldn't need to resort to such desperate measures if she could prove I'd broken my vow. While my *husband* might not kill his son for the betrayal, he'd most certainly disinherit him in favor of Leif, which was what the bitch wanted.

And Bjorn *knew* that. Knew that Ylva was looking for ways to get rid of him. Yet instead of treating me like his father's wife, he treated me as . . . as his *own*.

My breath caught as the thought registered, visions of every moment that had passed between us flickering through my mind's eye. A flush of warmth filled me, but it was swiftly chased away by icy fear. It was as Bodil had said: Bjorn was a notorious risk-taker. So of course he didn't fear the repercussions of being caught.

But I did.

Feared for him. Feared what Snorri would do to my family. Feared the guilt I'd have to bear as a result.

It was better that I'd said what I said, because maybe it would cause him to keep his distance. Would drive him into the arms of another, so that suspicions would fade. Yet even as *that* thought filled my head, my eyes pricked with tears and my chest tightened so that it hurt to breathe.

Why was I acting this way? Why was I constantly having to remind myself of logic and consequences to the point I wanted to scream at myself?

Why did I keep asking the same questions despite knowing the answers to all of them?

We'd reached the beach, Bodil's maidens rising from where they crouched in the rain. Each of them held a shield, and I stared at the circles of painted wood. *This is your fate, Freya,* I told myself. *This is what the seer foresaw for you. What the gods want from you. Nothing else matters.*

We drilled for hours, Bodil calmly instructing me in how to fight in a shield wall and how to fight against larger opponents in single combat, her maidens gleefully battering me with weapons wrapped with wool. I learned a great deal, but not once did I feel impassioned the way I had when I'd trained with Bjorn. Which was likely for the best, given I rarely made good decisions when my temper was high. Yet I couldn't help but sigh with relief when Bodil called for an end to our practice, her maidens wandering off in search of food and drink.

"That was good fun," Bodil said, sitting on a log with her weapons discarded at her feet.

"For you, maybe." I groaned, muscles protesting as I eased down to the ground. "Every inch of me will be purple tomorrow." Crossing my legs, I examined my hand, which throbbed mercilessly, my scarred palm raw from fighting with a stick all day.

"You're supposed to use the salve." Bodil leaned closer, taking my hand. "The one Bjorn made for you."

Scuffing my shoe in the sand, I remembered all the moments today that I'd felt his eyes on me. I'd refused to meet his gaze, only waited, tense and breathless, until he'd abandoned the beach again. "I don't know why he cares so much."

Bodil was silent for a long moment, but I could feel her scrutiny, weighing and measuring the question before she finally said, "It's because he feels guilty that it was his axe that burned you."

An obvious excuse for his behavior. One that I should've thought of. "Wasn't his fault."

Bodil snorted. "Not having willed something to have occurred doesn't render a person blameless, woman. You know that as well as anyone."

Given that guilt was a near-constant companion these days, I probably knew it better than most.

"The real question we need to discuss," Bodil continued, "is why *you* don't tend to your scars."

My spine stiffened. "What are you talking about? Of course I do."

"I've not seen you voluntarily do it once." The jarl pried my hand free from where I'd shoved it in my pocket, examining the burn scars, her own hands marked with the countless nicks and cuts that came from being a warrior. "The salve takes away the pain and makes your hand limber, but you choose over and over not to use it, despite Bjorn's reminders."

Was that true? I wracked my brain, searching for an instance where I'd done it myself without Bjorn's prodding, but came up empty. "I . . . I'm forgetful."

"I think not." Bodil straightened my fingers, digging her thumbs into the aching tendons. "And while Bjorn has a reputation for having talented hands, I don't think you're the sort to suffer for the sake of gaining attention. I think"—she hesitated—"that you believe you deserve the pain."

It suddenly hurt to breathe, and I squeezed my eyes shut.

"Why, Freya?"

Twin tears squeezed out from under my eyelids, running down my cheeks as the answer lurking deep inside me rose to the surface. "My husband Vragi was a piece of shit," I finally whispered. "He ruined my life and would have done his best to ruin Ingrid and Geir's, but . . ." I tried to swallow but it stuck, making me cough. "I murdered him, Bodil, and he didn't deserve *that*. Didn't deserve an axe in the back of the skull just for being a bastard."

"I disagree," she replied. "Vragi's reputation was known even in Brekkur. I'd bet all the silver in my pocket that cheers went up throughout your village when they heard the news."

I gave a tight shake of my head. "He might have been an arse about it, but no one ever starved. He made sure of that." And in Skaland, that *mattered*. Our world was harsh and cruel, winters taking countless lives as the unprepared or unlucky starved. But not in our village, for we *always* had fish.

Or had.

Now, thanks to my violence, how many would be lost when winter came?

Though that wasn't the reason I neglected my scars. Wasn't the reason I embraced the pain. "I feel guilty for the harm I've caused my village," I choked out. "But I don't feel bad about killing Vragi. I don't feel anything."

"Because he deserved it, Freya. That's why."

I clenched my eyes shut again, scrubbing away the tears. "It's not. With the other people I've killed, it was me or them, so it makes sense that I felt little remorse over their deaths. But Vragi wasn't threatening my life, or even Ingrid's life, only promising misery, and I killed him in cold blood rather than trying to find another solution. If I were anyone other than who I am, Snorri would have punished me as a murderer, but instead I walk free. I should feel terrible guilt, but I don't. So I need to make myself feel hurt another way, to punish myself, because I'm afraid if I don't, I'll do it again."

Bodil exhaled a slow breath, then wrapped her arms around me and pulled me close like a mother would a child. "You don't deserve to hurt. Hlin's blood runs in your veins, so it's your nature to want to protect those you care about. Vragi was a man who destroyed the lives of everyone he touched, and no amount of fish makes up for that. He didn't need to go after this Ingrid you speak of. He could've taken

Snorri's gold and walked away, but he chose to attack you and yours. It's his own bloody fault that he picked a fight with the wrong woman."

There was logic to what Bodil said, yet I remembered the surge of emotion that had filled me when Vragi uttered his intention. Protectiveness, yes. Fear, yes. But above all else, *rage*. And that was not something I could cast at Hlin's feet.

Bodil reached into my pocket to extract the salve. "Put it on."

I rolled the jar between my hands. "I will. But I'd like a few minutes alone to sit, if that's all right."

She hesitated, eyes considering. But she must have heard the truth in my words, for she rose, casting a warning over her shoulder as she departed. "Do not wander, Freya. There are many who seek your death."

Sighing, I opened the jar and smeared some of the salve on my scars, feeling almost instant relief from the stiffness. When I'd finished, I leaned back in the wet sand, turning my face up to the misting sky and closing my eyes. If only there was a way to clear my head. A way to silence the problems warring for my attention. A way to not constantly be *thinking*.

What I needed was not respite from the world but respite from myself. Except short of someone knocking me over the head, there was little chance of that.

"Breathe in," I murmured, attempting one of Bodil's exercises for settling the mind that she'd taught me earlier in the day. "Breathe out."

My heart steadied as I breathed, pushing away every thought that came for me as I hunted stillness.

Breathe.

My mind quieted but the silence was short-lived, for a crackle soon filled my ears.

Along with the stench of charred meat.

Jerking upright, I panned my surroundings and my eyes instantly latched on the source.

Walking down the waterline, embers and ash falling in its wake, was the specter.

I froze, watching the hooded specter walk down the beach, not one of the people working along the shoreline paying it any notice.

Because, like the last time it had appeared, no one could see the specter but *me*.

This time I didn't stop to question why that was, my mind instantly leaping to the fact that this . . . this *thing* might have answers to the endless questions that I faced about my future. And now might be the only opportunity I had to ask it.

Snatching up my sword, I shoved it in its sheath and started down the beach after the cloud of smoke and embers. I didn't run, because running would cause people to notice me. Would cause alarm. Might cause someone to try to stop me.

Or worse, given the specter clearly didn't want to be seen by anyone but me, might make it disappear.

I walked swiftly, smiling and nodding at those I passed so as not to give them any cause for concern, but though the specter's pace appeared a slow plod, I did not draw nearer. Smoke tickled my nose, the stink of burned hair and flesh making my stomach sour. I could taste the ash, feel the tiny burns from the embers as they floated back on a preternatural wind to char the fabric of my clothes.

Yet for all the creature burned, the wind blowing from it was as icy as the depths of winter, and the dichotomy made my skin crawl with the awareness that what walked before me bridged two worlds.

It reached the edge of the beach and moved into the forest. A flicker of trepidation filled me, because the last thing I was supposed to be doing was wandering off alone. Yet I dared not lose sight of the specter to retrieve someone to go with me. So, gritting my teeth, I ventured into the forest.

Other than the hiss and crackle of the flames consuming the specter, there was no sound, as though the creatures of the forest saw what those on the beach had not. Whether it was reverence or fear, I didn't know. My heart ricocheted against my ribs and my palms were slick with sweat, yet I forced myself into a trot. Then a run. Yet no matter how fast I sprinted, branches slapping me in the face and roots threatening to trip me, I couldn't close the distance. "Wait," I called between gasps of breath. "I want to speak to you!"

The specter stopped.

Cursing, I slid on the thick layer of needles and dirt, nearly colliding with the creature. "Please, wise one," I said. "I—"

The specter turned.

I sucked in a breath because the alternative was to scream, for what looked back at me from beneath the hood was the ruin of a face. Flames of orange and red ate at tendons and bone, teeth visible through the blackened holes where cheeks had once been. Whether it was male or female, I couldn't have said, for the only thing that was whole were its eyes. Bloodshot though they were, the green was vivid, capturing me with their gaze.

"I—"

It cut me off with a gesture up the hill, and with my stomach churning with nausea, I moved to look over the lip and into the shallow ravine below. Through the trees, I could see that a small fire burned on a rock in the middle of a stream, the wet wood sending up clouds of white smoke. Curious, I moved to descend the steep slope, but something icy cold pressed down on me.

Heart in my throat, I slowly turned my head to find the specter's hand on my shoulder. Flames danced over blackened bones, only bits of bubbling flesh remaining, and yet for all I could see the fire, it felt like its fingers were made of ice.

The urge to run filled me, but I only dragged in a shuddering breath, allowing the specter to push me to my knees. It knelt next to me, mercifully removing its hand, which it used to gesture downward. "Look."

Just as when it had spoken to me when we'd left Halsar to go to Fjalltindr, the specter's voice rasped painfully, making me want to recoil. To run. Instead, I listened. And looked.

Wings fluttered through the trees, and I saw flickers of a bird in flight. I ignored it, searching for what the specter had brought me to see. Motion caught my eye.

A cloaked figure stood before a tree. Only their back was visible to me, and as I watched, they withdrew a short seax and carved something into the bark. They sheathed the weapon, then turned and walked down the ravine and out of sight.

"Who was that?" I breathed once they were gone, turning to the specter. "Where did—"

But the specter had disappeared.

I hissed out an aggrieved breath, but then started down the slope, knowing that the specter wouldn't have expended the effort to show me this if it wasn't important. I hoped that whatever was on that tree would give me answers.

There were carvings in it. Deep gouges that left parings littered on the moss at its base. Runes drawn in a circle, at the center of which was carved an eye. I traced my finger around the circle, uncertain of the meaning, then touched the eye at the center.

Light exploded in my vision, then Snorri's face appeared. I staggered backward, the vision disappearing the moment I ceased touching the carving.

Runic magic.

I swallowed hard, unease filling me. Tentatively, I reached out to touch the carving again. My eyes flashed bright, then Snorri appeared again, faded and blurred, drifting in and out of focus like I was looking at him through water.

But his words were clear enough.

Heart in my throat, I watched him give his speech about abandoning Halsar and moving on Grindill, his eyes flashing with passion the way they had when I'd witnessed the speech myself. Then the vision faded, and I was left staring at the tree.

Someone who'd witnessed Snorri's speech had left this message. Had revealed our plans.

But who had cause to do such a thing? And who was the message for?

Gnut was the obvious answer, except everyone who'd witnessed Snorri's speech had been from Halsar, which surely meant they would hate the other jarl for what he'd done. Another jarl perhaps? Or . . .

King Harald.

My jaw tightened, pieces of the puzzle falling together. *Ylva.*

She wanted Bjorn out of the way, I knew that for a fact. And though she'd said she was with Bodil the entire time at Fjalltindr, she'd been gone more than long enough to have a conversation with both of them. But the true proof was in the runes themselves.

This was sorcery that few had the nerve to practice, but I'd *seen* Ylva do it. First for the ritual where Hlin had given me my tattoos, and then in Fjalltindr when she'd warded the hall. This was within her power, *and* she had more motive than anyone who'd witnessed Snorri's speech, because she didn't want to abandon Halsar.

"Bitch," I hissed, then spun on my heels, fully intending to drag Snorri himself up to this tree to show him the proof of the conspiracy.

I took one step and ran smack into a solid chest.

Rebounding, I swore and reached for my sword, only to realize a heartbeat before I drew it that the chest belonged to Bjorn.

He crossed his arms. "What are you doing in the woods alone, Freya?"

Not alone. With *him*.

Which was the exact opposite of what I'd been trying to accomplish. If anyone saw us out here together, it would only add fuel to whatever rumors were swirling, and there would be consequences to that. "Why are you following me?"

One dark eyebrow rose. "Because my father has ordered me to keep you alive, and allowing you to wander off alone and get yourself killed runs counter to that."

My cheeks burned. "Fine. It doesn't matter." It was hard to focus, thoughts dancing in and out of my head as I struggled with what to say. "The specter appeared to me. It walked around the beach and led me here."

Bjorn tensed. "The specter?"

"Yes." It was a struggle to meet his gaze. "It brought me up there"—I gestured to the slope—"and it told me to watch. It touched me, and though it was burning, its hand felt like ice."

He shifted uneasily, and I couldn't blame him. "What did you see?"

"That signal fire"—I gestured to the now faintly smoking ashes—"was burning hot. A woman was there."

"A woman? Did you see her face?"

I shook my head. "She was hooded. But she carved the runes on the tree and then disappeared down the ravine." I turned back to the tree to point them out, and my stomach plummeted.

The runes were gone, only a smoldering circle left where they'd once been. "No," I snarled. "This cannot be. They were right here!" Rounding on Bjorn, I said, "I touched the runes and they showed a vision of Snorri giving his speech detailing his plans to abandon Halsar and take Grindill. It was a message."

"I believe you." Stepping around me, Bjorn bent low to examine the char. "There are combinations of runes that can burn themselves away once their magic has been spent. Prudent for anyone leaving a message that they'd rather no one see."

"Fuck!" I kicked a rock hard, sending it spinning into the underbrush as my anger rose.

"Why are you so angry?" Bjorn asked, eyeing me warily.

"Because now he'll never believe it was Ylva!" Picking up another rock, I hurled it at the tree, not caring if I looked childish. "It will be just like Fjalltindr where it is her word against mine that she's conspiring with Harald, and you *know* who Snorri will believe."

"You think this was Ylva's doing? To what end?"

"Obviously it's her." I bent double, trying to master the irrational twist of fury that wanted to send me back to camp in search of blood. "She's a volva. She knows how to use the runes. We know she wants to be rid of you, so that Leif can inherit."

Bjorn was silent.

My chest hollowed, because if he didn't believe me, no one would. "You think I'm lying?"

"I don't think that." His gaze was on the charred remains of the runes; then he glanced skyward, eyes searching the clouds before moving back to me. "But I struggle to believe Ylva would risk her people just for the sake of getting rid of me."

"Mothers will do anything for their sons," I retorted, guilt rising in my chest when Bjorn flinched. "She wants Leif to be king one day and you're in the way of that."

Bjorn looked away, his jaw tight. "Perhaps so. But my father trusts her and will not believe these accusations. Better for us to return to camp and tell him what you saw in the runes. He'll come to his own conclusions based on what we tell him."

We.

My stomach soured, because telling Snorri anything meant revealing that I was alone in the woods with Bjorn. Which would beg the question of *why,* especially since Bodil had told me not to wander. "I'll tell him myself. You didn't see anything, so you need not be involved."

Turning, I picked my way down the creek bed and into the narrow ravine, which I knew would lead me back to the fjord.

"Why are you avoiding me?"

Bjorn's words echoed between the stone walls of the ravine, stopping me in my tracks. "I'm not avoiding you. Why would you think that?"

"Because you've run away from almost every encounter we've had since we left Fjalltindr."

"*You* ran away from our conversation at the fire last night," I pointed out, though it was no defense, given I *was* avoiding him.

Water splashed as he made his way down the stream, not taking the care I had to remain dry, and stopped behind me. Despite fear of discovery making my palms sweat and my stomach churn, being this close to Bjorn was intoxicating. Every inhale filled my nose with pine and the salt of the fjords, and the heat radiating from him made me want to draw closer.

"Bodil thinks that just because she's allied with my father, she's privy to clan business," he said. "So it was her I was escaping, not you. What's your excuse?"

That I want to lose myself in your arms and I'm afraid everyone knows it. I swallowed the lump in my throat. "I've been occupied with my training."

"With Bodil." His voice was flat.

"Yes, with Bodil and her warriors." Why couldn't I look at him? Why couldn't I meet his gaze? "What of it?"

Bjorn opened his mouth, but instead of allowing him to speak, I blurted out, "You made it clear it was not a role you wanted. Denied in no uncertain terms that our destinies were entwined."

"Freya—"

"Even if you felt differently, Bodil is a better teacher." My underarms were dampening, my voice breathy in a way I detested. "You rely on size and strength when you fight, but I'm small and weak and—"

"You aren't weak."

My cheeks flushed. "Well, perhaps not. But I am weaker than most men, which means that I can't fight like a man. I want to learn to fight like a woman."

Silence.

Biting the insides of my cheeks, I waited for Bjorn to speak, the anticipation of what he would say the purest form of misery. I was sweating like a pig, and even if he couldn't see it beneath my cloak, he could probably smell it and all I wanted to do was jump in the deeper current of the stream and allow it to wash me away.

Instead, I forced myself to turn around.

Rather than glowering, Bjorn's expression was thoughtful. As our eyes locked, he gave a nod. "You have the right of it. Bodil will teach you better than a man ever could." But then his head tilted, his eyes narrowing. "Yet that does not explain why you refuse to even look at me."

My heart skipped, then raced, and I swallowed hard. Excuses sat on my tongue like thorns, words that he'd have to accept even if he didn't quite believe them.

But I didn't want to lie. Not to him.

Taking a deep breath to steady myself, I said, "I've been avoiding you because of what happened between us at Fjalltindr."

Bjorn huffed out an aggrieved breath. "We did what we needed to do to keep Harald's men from taking you, Freya. Not even my father would judge."

"Then why did neither of us tell him?"

"Because it wasn't necessary!" Bjorn threw up his hands, looking away. "It didn't mean anything."

I flinched, then tried to cover it by shifting my feet. Wasted effort because Bjorn's eyes narrowed as he said, "What more is there to say?"

Everything.

It would be easier to shrug and say nothing than to admit the truth. Easier to leave the conversation as it stood and walk away, my pride intact.

Except that would be the act of a coward who'd rather lie and pretend than own the truth, and that wasn't who I was. Or rather, that wasn't who I wanted to be.

"It wasn't nothing. Not—" My voice cracked, my chest painfully tight. "Not to me." My eyes burned and though the last thing I wanted to do was cry, I could sooner have stopped my heart from beating than hold my tears in check, hot droplets rolling down my cheeks. "I wanted to do what we did. Wanted you."

Bjorn went still, not even seeming to breathe.

I tried to suck in a breath to calm myself but my whole body shuddered. I was supposed to be a warrior. A leader. The woman who'd unite Skaland beneath the rule of a king. Yet I couldn't get through a conversation without crying like a child. "I know you know this," I said, struggling to speak without my breath catching on every word. "That you're excusing my actions to spare me shame and make things easier for us both. I know I should feel grateful for that, but . . ."

"Freya." His hands cupped my face, thumbs brushing away my tears, but I pushed him away because his touch would shatter what remained of my composure.

"I am married to Snorri." The words came out in a rush of breath, and I squeezed my eyes shut. "He is your father, and while you might not always see eye-to-eye, I know you are loyal to him. Which means my behavior disrespected you both. You were trying to protect me, whereas I . . . I . . ."

Then Bjorn's lips were on mine.

I gasped, my eyes snapping open as my back struck the wall of the ravine. His hands caught my wrists, holding them above my head even as his hips pressed hard against mine, holding me in place. "Bjorn—"

He silenced me, tongue delving into my mouth and stroking over mine, stoking the heat that had already ignited between my thighs. "*I*," he whispered, biting at my jaw, then my throat. "*I, I, I,* Freya. You love that word because you relish taking the blame for everything, whether it is your fault or not."

My eyes shifted left, looking down the ravine, because all it would take was one of the hunters or foragers seeing for us to be doomed. We needed to stop this. But as he ground against me, any thought of leaving evaporated.

"I came up with the plan. I kissed you first." His mouth claimed

mine, sucking and stroking and biting. "I touched your perfect breasts."
He pressed my left wrist against my right, gripping them both easily
with one hand so that he could run the other up my side, his thumb
rubbing over my peaked nipple.

His stubbled cheek brushed against mine, his breath tickling my ear
as he said, "And don't you dare tell me that it was *respect for my father* that
you felt pressed between your thighs that night."

It hadn't been then. And it wasn't now.

No, what I felt was the thick ridge of his hard cock pressing through
his trousers as he lifted me with one arm, putting me back where I'd
been that night in Fjalltindr. Desire throbbed at the apex of my thighs,
and I ground against him, hunting the release I'd been denied before.

Bjorn groaned into my throat and released my wrists. Freed, I
wrapped my arms around his neck, unfastening the tie holding his hair
and then tangling my fingers into its silken lengths.

Why couldn't I resist him? Why was I so cursedly weak?

Bjorn gripped my arse with one hand, holding me in place against
him, his other hand cupping the side of my face. "Not burying my
cock inside you that night almost broke me," he growled. "I wanted
you the moment I first set eyes on you. I wanted you in Fjalltindr. I
want you now, and tomorrow, and all the tomorrows, Freya."

His breath seared my skin as he said my name. As he said the words
that had echoed through my darkest fantasies about my deepest desires.
Not just one time but *every* time.

Gods, but I wanted this. Wanted him.

The crunch of footfalls on the forest floor split the silence and we
both jerked away from each other, Bjorn casting his eyes upward. Neither of us spoke for a long time, then he muttered, "Was just a deer."

But the moment was broken, allowing reason to return. I scrubbed
the tears from my face, then met his gaze, my voice finally steady. "If
we do this once, it will open a door. And it will happen again and again
until we inevitably get caught. Because we *will* get caught. Already
Bodil is suspicious."

Bjorn's jaw tightened, but he didn't argue.

"When Snorri finds out, he'll hurt my family, possibly murder one of them. He'll execute or banish you." I lifted my chin. "But I'm too irreplaceable to kill, which means I'll have to live with the guilt that those I care about most are dead because I couldn't curb my *lust*."

If only it was *just* lust.

Lust I could control, lust I could satiate in other ways, but the feelings growing in my heart? Those sought only one release and they spun wildly out of control.

"Freya . . ." He caught hold of my arms, lips parting as though he would argue, but found himself without an argument.

"Stay away from me, Bjorn," I whispered. "Don't look at me. Don't talk to me. Don't touch me, because you now belong to the ranks of people whose lives depend on my good behavior. And if I fall to temptation, it will be the doom of us all."

Then, because I knew if I remained any longer that I'd crack, I turned on my heel and splashed my way down the stream to the fjord.

"There's a spy in our midst."

My voice was more toneless than I intended, but it felt like if I allowed any emotion loose they'd all explode out of me.

Bodil crossed her arms, clearly angry that I'd wandered, but I ignored her and added, "The specter appeared to me again and brought me to the forest to show me where a message had been left using runic sorcery." I explained everything that had happened, only leaving out Bjorn's appearance.

Snorri had looked ready to strangle me when I appeared, but now his anger vanished. "Did it speak to you?"

"It only told me to *look*," I said, the echo of the specter's strained voice filling my head.

"Where is Steinunn?" Snorri demanded, and when the skald approached, he caught her sleeve and hauled her forward. "This could be another trial. You need to hear what Freya has to say."

The skald pulled free of his grip, then wrapped her cloak more tightly around her body before asking, "What did you see?"

I had to be careful, for everything I said to Steinunn could be revealed in one of her songs, and I had not forgotten Bjorn's belief that she was spying on Snorri's behalf. "The specter. I saw it up close. It was burned nearly down to the bone and speaking seems to cause it pain. Only its eyes were whole. They were"—*human*—"green. The color of leaves."

A shudder ran through Snorri, and Steinunn stepped back in alarm as he dropped into a crouch, his head in his hands. "It's her."

"Who?" I demanded even as Ylva said, "You don't know that."

"There are too many coincidences to be denied." Snorri looked up at Ylva, ignoring my question. "She foretold Freya's coming, and the specter did not appear until Freya's name was born in fire. She appears only to Freya." His throat convulsed as he swallowed. "She burned alive, Ylva. Was only recognizable from the jewelry on her bones."

Realization slapped me in the face even as boots splashed in the mud and Bjorn approached the group, his arms crossed and eyes shadowed. "I see Freya decided to return."

No one spoke. No one even seemed to breathe.

Snorri slowly straightened. "The specter appeared to Freya and led her to proof we have a spy in our midst. I . . . I believe the specter is your mother."

Bjorn didn't so much as blink, only lifted a shoulder and said, "It seems she is loyal to you even beyond the grave, Father."

"Yes." Snorri looked away. "Or else tied to Freya's fate."

Though his face was expressionless, tension simmered in Bjorn's green eyes and my chest tightened in sympathy. If the specter was indeed his mother, it meant that all these long years she'd lingered between worlds, suffering the agony of her death. If there was a way to help her, I didn't know it, which meant she might languish until the end of days. Perhaps even beyond.

"The message was left with sorcery," I blurted out to draw attention away from Bjorn while he came to terms with the revelation. "The spy is someone who knows runic magic. A woman."

Eyes flickered past Snorri and Steinunn to land on Ylva and it was an effort not to crow with delight as discomfort filled her face, but it was Bodil who spoke. "Show us what runes you saw, Freya."

Shrugging, I bent to pick up a stick and then sketched the runes I'd seen into the mud. As I completed the one in the center, I felt a chill pass over my forehead and I jerked away, dropping the stick.

Ylva elbowed me out of the way and knelt, pressing her hand to the eye I'd carved in the dirt.

Sudden panic filled me. Had I unwittingly placed a memory in the rune? If so, which one? What if it was of Bjorn? What if, even now, Ylva was watching him kiss me through my eyes?

"It is as Freya has said." Ylva straightened. "I saw the runes as she did. Simple magic, easily taught to anyone."

I opened my mouth to call her a liar, but the runes in the circle abruptly began to smoke, the dirt charring into a black circle at our feet and proving her point. If I could replicate it, so could anyone else.

"Gather everyone who witnessed Snorri speak," Ylva snapped. "Bodil will question all and use her magic to discover who betrayed us."

"I agree," I said. "Let none be exempt."

Ylva's lips pursed as her eyes met mine, and though it might be foolish, I allowed her to see that I *knew*. And that I wasn't going to let her get away with it.

So it was with great shock that I watched the lady of Halsar turn to Bodil and declare, "The memory was not mine. I did not carve the runes. I did not betray my husband."

Bodil eyed her for a long moment, then nodded. "Ylva speaks the truth."

"Gather everyone," Ylva called out. "Let no stone go unturned until we discover who has betrayed us."

"Enough!" Snorri roared. "Saga did not reveal herself to Freya to help us root out a traitor. She revealed herself to show Freya her path forward."

I blinked, because that was the last thing I'd taken from my exchange with the specter.

"Our plan to attack Grindill is known by our enemies." His hand
drifted to his weapon. "Which means that Gnut will be prepared for us
to come. Will have scouts watching the sea and the passes through the
mountains. That is what Saga revealed to Freya. Not that we have been
betrayed, but that Freya must change the course of fate."

"How?" I demanded, because the alternative was to point out that a
day prior, he'd been certain that Gnut would be cowering behind his
walls out of fear of Snorri's wrath. All talk to win support, it would
seem. "She said nothing of what I should do."

"Because she does not control you." Snorri's eyes burned into me
with utter fanaticism. "I do. And I say we do not go around the mountains, but over them. I say we attack now."

N
o sane person would go over the mountains in a Skaland spring. Not when it was a simple journey through the passes or by water via the fjords. Certainly not when the sky was releasing a deluge of rain and sleet, the temperature plummeting to freezing each night.

Which meant that while Gnut and his warriors might know we were coming, they'd not expect it this soon.

If, that is, we survived long enough to attack, which seemed less likely with each passing minute.

Gasping for breath, I paused on an outcropping and wiped sleet from my face. Every muscle in my body burned from climbing all day, yet I'd all but lost feeling in my hands and feet from the cold. My teeth chattered with such violence the noise would have echoed through the peaks if not for the fact that the howl of the wind drowned out everything but the loudest of shouts.

"You all right?"

I twitched, turning to find Bjorn slightly below me on the slope. The hood of his cloak hung loose down his back and his hands were bare, no part of him touched by the cold. Tyr's fire burned within him at all times, and I curbed the urge to step close to him. Bjorn had honored my request to keep his distance to the extent that Snorri's orders allowed, and I needed to do the same. "I'm fine."

"You look like you're freezing your tits off."

I scoffed, giving him a disgusted glare. "Oh, my poor frozen breasts. If only some generous man would offer to warm them for me."

He shrugged, voice flippant as he said, "Your words, not mine."

I kicked snow at him. "Piss off, Bjorn. I can take care of myself."

Fixing the furred hood of my cloak, I shoved my mittened hands into my armpits, trudging after Bodil up the slope, the older woman resembling a bear beneath her heavy furs.

"That is a foolish way to walk, Born-in-Fire," he said, following me. "If you fall, you won't be able to catch yourself."

"I'm not going to fall." Or rather, the risk of doing so seemed far less than losing my fingers to frostbite.

"Quit being so stubborn and let me warm your hands for you."

Against my backside, I felt a sudden glow of heat and knew that if I turned it would be to find his axe blazing bright. I ground my teeth together, desperately wanting to hold my numb fingers over the burning weapon until they were warm again, but I kept trudging forward, adjusting my shield strap as I glared at Bodil's back. Everyone else was managing, so I would as well.

"Freya—"

Twisting, I snarled under my breath, "I told you to stay away from—"

My feet slid out from under me, a gasp tearing from my lips. Bjorn reached for me, his eyes wide, but my arm was tangled in my cloak.

I bounced painfully off the slope, my fingers clawing for purchase on the icy rock and frozen mud, but they found nothing. My body flipped and I flew through the air, a scream tearing from my lips as I dropped—

And landed hard with a splash.

Water closed over my head, bubbles exploding from my lips as my shield struck rock, the handle digging into my back and driving the air from my lungs.

I thrashed, desperate for breath, then hands grabbed the front of my clothes and jerked me to the surface.

Spluttering, I met Bjorn's panicked gaze. "Don't even say it," I said between coughs, cold piercing down to my very bones. "Don't you dare say it!"

"What is it that you think I planned to say?" He pulled me out of the pool of slush and water that I'd landed in, setting me on my feet.

"That you told me so," I muttered, stealing the words so that he wouldn't have a chance to embarrass me with them.

"That was not what I intended to say."

He pulled off my shield and soaked cloak, casting them aside before wrapping his own cloak around my shoulders, heat encasing me and his scent filling my nose. But not even that was enough to ease the violent trembles wracking my body. "What then?" I demanded, seeing Snorri sliding down the slope toward us, eyes full of panic.

"I was going to point out that you have a habit of getting very wet around me," he said. "I'm starting to wonder whether it's purposeful."

For a heartbeat, my body forgot that it was freezing to death and sent blood rushing to my cheeks. I'd told him to stay away. Told him the reasons why I couldn't be in his presence even though revealing the truth had been humiliating, and now he was making jokes. "Don't flatter yourself!"

He gripped my hands, his skin scalding against mine. "It is you who flatters me."

"I did *not* fall down a mountain to get wet for you, Bjorn!"

"Oh, I know," he grinned. "It's really only a hill with lofty aspirations. That"—he pointed off in the distance at a rocky peak—"is a mountain."

"The only lofty thing I see is your sense of self-worth," I hissed as Snorri shouted, "Is she hurt?"

"She's fine," Bjorn answered. "Only wet and cold. We need to make camp and get a fire going to warm her."

"We cannot lose the hours," Snorri growled, throwing up his hands.

"We need to crest the summit before nightfall or there will be no chance of making it to Grindill to attack tomorrow night. If we delay, we risk word reaching Gnut that our forces have departed, and he'll be prepared for an attack from the mountains. We'll lose the advantage."

"Better the loss of the advantage than the loss of your shield maiden," Bjorn snapped. "She'll do you little good as a frozen corpse."

"This is the gods testing her!" Snorri gave a sharp shake of his head. "She must prove herself again." He started to turn, then fixed Bjorn with a glare. "Hlin set you the task of protecting Freya. Allowing her to fall down the mountain was *your* failure." Without another word, he stalked up the mountain.

Bjorn abruptly pulled me against him, wrapping his arms around me so that my head was pressed against his chest. "It's not a fucking mountain," he muttered and I was too miserable to argue, watching as the rest of the warriors trudged onward until only Bodil remained.

"You truly are favored by the gods, Freya," the jarl said, handing me a skin that smelled of strong drink.

I took a sip, coughing as it burned down my throat, then chased it with another. "Doesn't feel that way."

She lifted one furred shoulder, then gestured to the ledge I'd rolled off, higher than Bjorn was tall. "If you'd landed a few feet to the left or right, you'd have cracked that pretty skull of yours beyond repair, but instead the mountain tossed you into a pool of water just deep enough to cushion your fall."

"It's not a fucking mountain!" Bjorn shouted. "It's only a hill!"

Bodil's eyebrows rose, then she laughed. "Although the truly amazing thing is that Bjorn didn't piss himself when he didn't save you from falling off the"—she smirked—"hill."

She laughed as Bjorn's hands tightened around me, and I didn't understand why he cared so much about semantics to pick a quarrel over them. His heart thudded where my shoulders pressed against his chest, slowing its thunder only as Bodil began pulling off her shirts and he asked, "How many shirts are you wearing, woman?"

"Six," she answered. "And three pairs of trousers. I've little tolerance for the cold."

Taking another mouthful of liquor, I reluctantly pulled away from Bjorn and handed back his fur cloak, wanting to weep as the icy wind sliced my soaked body. Shaking hard, I tried to pull my mail over my head, but it felt like my arms weren't working properly and Bjorn had to intervene, pulling it upward and then dropping it to the ground. "Close your eyes," I said between chattering teeth, then glanced up to ensure he had complied.

His lids were closed, black lashes resting against his cheeks. Yet with unerring precision, he caught hold of the hem of my padded tunic, removing it before moving on to the shirt I wore beneath. The backs of his knuckles brushed against my skin as he lifted it carefully over my head, easing my stiff and unwieldy arms from the garment as the wind clawed at my naked breasts.

I wanted to be back in his arms, to curl into the heat of him and inhale the smell of him. I wanted him to open his eyes and *look* at me. I wanted him to drive away not only the cold crippling my flesh but also the cold consuming my heart. Instead I forced my arms up so that Bodil could lower her shirt over my head, barely feeling the fine wool against my numb skin. She added a thicker wool tunic, then lifted Bjorn's cloak over my shoulders.

"His blood is the temperature of boiling water," she said. "He could walk naked up this mountain and not feel the chill." Reaching out, she lifted the skin of liquor to my lips again. "Drink up, Freya. Will keep your toes from freezing off before we reach the top."

All I could manage was a jerky nod, allowing Bjorn to gather my soaked clothing and mail, leaving me with only my shield to carry as I followed Bodil up the slope. Each step was an act of will, my muscles so stiff that, if not for the pain, they'd have seemed made of wood rather than flesh. Hugging myself, I pressed on, my chest aching, each breath a ragged gasp of cold air.

I stumbled, Bjorn catching my elbows and keeping me from falling.

"Don't you dare carry her," Bodil called over her shoulder. "She needs to keep her blood moving."

Tears leaked onto my cheeks to mix with the sleet, my nose running and forcing me to gasp in air through my mouth, my bottom lip drying, then cracking. I licked at it, tasting blood, then I tripped again.

Bjorn caught me. "I've got you."

He started to lift me into his arms, and I desperately wanted to let him. Instead, I twisted away and fixed my eyes on Bodil's heels. "This is my test, not yours."

Which meant I had to walk on my own feet.

Tomorrow, I'd lead all the warriors in our camp into battle on their *faith* that I was someone worth following. I wanted to *prove* I was worth it. Wanted them to fight at my side not because of signs from the gods but because I was strong and capable. No one would think that if I allowed Bjorn to carry me into camp because I was *cold*.

I clenched my hands into fists, the sleeves of Bodil's tunic mercifully long enough to cover my hands, because my mittens were soaked. And I climbed.

Higher and higher, the sleet lashing my face, the wind attempting to tear Bjorn's cloak from my body. I couldn't feel my toes and I stumbled every few steps, but I brushed Bjorn away whenever he tried to help me.

I could do this.

I would do this.

The sky dimmed, the sun dipping below the horizon, all warmth leached from the air. How much farther could it be? Exposed as we were on the mountainside, the thought of stumbling around in the cold and the dark looking for the rest of the group kindled embers of fear in my chest.

So much could go wrong in the dark.

Then Bodil called out a greeting, responses filtering through the wind into my ears. I lifted my head and saw faint shadows moving in the dark. We'd reached the camp.

But there was no fire.

I staggered to a stop and Bjorn stormed past me. "What is wrong with you," he snarled at a shadow I could only assume was Snorri. "You left us alone on the trail and now you wish to watch her succumb to frostbite? She will fight poorly if deprived of fingers and toes. Light a cursed fire or I will."

"You will do no such thing." Snorri's voice was steady and unmoved, and as I moved closer it was to find him sitting on a rock, furs wrapped around his body. "Gnut has scouts. All it would take is one of them seeing a fire on the mountaintop and our advantage will be lost."

Bjorn's hands balled into fists, and I thought for a heartbeat that he'd strike his father. Yet he only said, "I don't understand why you risk Freya the way you do. You say she is of value, that she will make you a king, and yet you make no effort to protect her, only to prevent others from stealing her."

"The gods protect her." Snorri tilted his head. "You've seen evidence of it time and again, Bjorn, yet still you don't believe: They will not let her fall."

"They let her fall today."

"So she might survive what no one else could," Snorri answered. "Steinunn will sing of her exploits and her stories will move through Skaland like wildfire and people will have no choice but to believe Saga's words. They will come in droves to follow her into battle, and they will swear oaths to me as their king. To interfere with the gods by sheltering Freya would be to deny her that fate, and in doing so, alter my own for the worse."

"So you will throw her to the wolves time and again, certain the gods will spare her life?"

"It is her destiny."

"No matter how much suffering it causes her? She is your *wife*. Don't you care about the pain she's enduring tonight?"

Snorri sat unmoving in the darkness. "I think, my son, that you care enough for both of us."

My stomach dropped and if my hands and feet weren't already frozen, they'd have turned to ice. Despite all my efforts to keep my distance from Bjorn, Snorri sensed what I was so desperate to hide. I clenched my teeth, fear for what consequences would come from this overwhelming my physical discomfort. I forced my frozen hand to my sword beneath the fur cloak even as I saw Bjorn's bare fingers flex.

What would he do if Snorri confronted him? What would I do?

I held my breath, praying I had the strength in me to fight if I needed to. But Snorri only gave a sharp shake of his head. "You don't think like a jarl, Bjorn. You fixate on the hardship you see in front of you and think not for the countless others whose lives depend on this jarldom for protection. If Skaland unites beneath me as its king, it will grow stronger and more prosperous, but this will only happen if Freya continues to please the gods. The gods want you to protect her, but do not let your *softness* jeopardize her destiny."

It took a moment for his words to settle, my heart still pumping at a violent pace as I slowly realized that Snorri hadn't been accusing Bjorn of forbidden sentiment but of *softness.* Which should have been a relief, but instead my temper flared and I snapped, "Might I find the comfort of food and blankets, *husband,* or is it your opinion that the gods would favor a fool who sits naked in the north wind?"

"Do what you will."

Even in the darkness, I felt Snorri's irritation. Knew that he wished I would remain silent. If he wanted that, he'd need to cut out my tongue. "The people of Skaland will unite beneath the rule of the one who controls my fate." I smiled into the darkness, but it was all teeth. "So control it."

The silence was broken only by the vicious howl of the wind, no one speaking. No one even seeming to breathe as they waited to see how their jarl would respond to the challenge.

For it had been one, I realized. Not a slip of my tongue, either, but my heart voicing a question that had been growing from the moment I'd learned the seer's prophecy. Bjorn's mother had not named Snorri as the one who must control my fate, which meant it could be anyone. He controlled me using a farce of a marriage, threats against my family, and oaths bound by magic, and where that had once seemed like more than enough to keep me under his thumb, now . . . now I wondered if the gods might have something else in mind.

As if sensing his power over me slipping, Snorri said, "Save your spirit for the battle to come, Freya, and remind yourself of the cost of failure." Then he jerked his chin to Bjorn. "Get her fed and warmed, but no *fucking* fire."

"If she's without feet come morning, blame yourself," Bjorn answered, motioning for me to follow.

I walked slowly, feeling the impact of each step in my legs rather than my feet, and unease chased away the glow of defiance. The gods had already seen fit to cripple my hand. What was to stop them from taking a few toes with frostbite to further *test* my will, and thus my worthiness? I considered what I might look like by the time Skaland had its king, scarred and bent, parts of me ceasing to function if they weren't lost entirely, and my eyes stung. Like a tool used until its blade dulls and its haft breaks, then left to molder in the corner, having served its purpose.

Visions filled my head. Of myself in the future, having achieved all that was set for me, and now forgotten in the corner of the king's great hall. Old and worn. Surrounded, yet alone. A tear escaped my eye, and I didn't bother wiping it away.

Dimly, I was aware of Bjorn conferring with Bodil. Of one of them taking my hand and leading me behind a piece of canvas that had been stretched between two trees to block the wind. Of my shield being removed before I was lowered to the ground.

The light from the sun had faded entirely, the thick clouds blocking the moon and the stars, casting the world in darkness so that all I could see were the visions in my head.

Stop, I silently pleaded, begging my mind to quit torturing me, but I might as well have spat into the wind for all the good my pleas accomplished. My body was heavy, no longer shivering, as though the effort were too great. Each breath felt like an act of will.

"Freya?"

I heard Bjorn say my name, but he sounded distant, as though a vast canyon separated us, growing wider with every one of my labored heartbeats.

"Freya, are you all right? Freya? Freya, look at me!"

The muscles in my neck didn't want to obey, pain lancing through my body as I turned toward his voice. "I . . ." My mouth was so dry. Too dry to form words.

He cursed, then I felt the heavy cloak pulled from my body. I started to moan a protest as the cold bit into my shoulders, then my body moved and I was enveloped in warmth. Realizing I was wrapped in Bjorn's arms, I tried to pull away but his grip around my waist was implacable. And as he drew the cloak over us, my will to resist disappeared.

"See to her feet," he said, and my legs shifted as Bodil pulled off my frozen boots and leg wrappings, a shocked gasp exiting her lips. "Those are cold!"

From the pressure on my legs, I suspected my feet were in her armpits, but I couldn't feel anything. "My toes . . ."

"Will be fine." Bjorn's breath brushed my ear. "You've god's blood in your veins."

The rapid pound of his heart against my back belied his words, but instead of my fear rising, I drifted, sound and sensation moving in and out of focus. *Is this the end?* I idly wondered. *Not death in battle but freezing to death on the side of a mountain?*

"It's not a fucking mountain, Born-in-Fire."

I smiled, not certain whether Bjorn had actually spoken or if it were my imagination. "Is this the hill you wish to die upon?"

"Not funny." His fingers tightened, and sudden regret filled me. That I'd not had the chance to drown in his touch, to taste him, to feel him inside of me.

"It's a bit funny," I whispered, because the alternative was to weep.

I lost myself to darkness, then. Floating in a warm pool of blackness that beckoned me down and down. Dimly, I heard Bjorn calling my name but I couldn't move my body to swim back up to him. Wasn't sure I wanted to.

Going back meant pain and grief and loneliness. Why should I fight for that?

"This is not your end, daughter," a gentle voice answered. "You must battle on, for them."

"I don't want to," I answered, not sure whether it was a truth or a lie. "I don't want to go back."

"You must," a harsher voice, devoid of patience, snarled. "For *yourself*."

Hands pressed against my back, lifting me through the dark waters. I struggled, trying to escape back down, but I could not slip their grip. Higher they pushed me, pain burning through my body as I drew closer to the surface. "No," I moaned as the burning intensified. "It hurts!"

"That means you are alive," the voices answered in tandem, and I gasped in a breath of air and screamed.

Agony stabbed up my legs, my feet feeling as though they were pressed against Bjorn's axe and my skin was melting away. I screamed wordlessly, struggling to pull away from the fire, but hands gripped my legs, holding them in place.

"Stop," I pleaded between sobs. "You're hurting me!"

"I know it hurts, but the pain is a good thing." Bjorn had me locked against his chest, the roughness of his chin rubbing against my cheek. "It means your feet are warming."

"It's too much heat." Tears and snot ran down my face. "You're burning me! Take them out of the fire!" I shrieked the last because no one was listening and *oh gods* it hurt.

"There's no fire, lass," someone said. "Just Bodil's armpits. Won't harm you but for the stink."

"Says the man who smells like arsehole," Bodil answered, and a dozen voices chuckled. We were surrounded by Halsar's warriors, I realized. It was their hands holding my legs in place, their bodies blocking the wind. Protecting me despite the fact it was supposed to be the other way around.

Sudden, irrational panic filled me that the gods would punish them for this. I was supposed to stand alone, to overcome my trials alone, to *be* alone.

Fear must have given breath to my thoughts, for everyone went silent, the only howl the wind, then an old warrior said, "The gods said nothing of the sort, girl. I was there when Saga spoke her foretelling, and I watched the gods themselves appear during your sacrifice at Fjalltindr. Nothing was said about you doing anything alone."

I clenched my teeth, waiting to hear Snorri's voice telling them that they were wrong, but if he was there, he was silent.

"You've never been alone," Bjorn said, his voice so soft that no one but me would hear over the wind and my weeping. "I will be at your back until I cross the threshold to Valhalla, Born-in-Fire, whether you want me there or not."

My chest tightened, and cloaked by darkness, I allowed myself to turn my face into his chest and give in to the pain. To sob and shriek as sensation burned its way back into my feet and hands, not because it was more than I could bear but because I needed to get the hurt out. Bjorn held me tight, stroking my hair, the certainty that he would not walk away crumbling all the walls I'd built around my heart until exhaustion drove me to sleep.

I woke, the pain of frostbite reminding me instantly where I was, which was fortunate, given I was surrounded by blackness.

And wrapped in someone's arms.

I went rigid, awareness of all the places I was pressed against Bjorn slapping me into instant alertness. His arm cushioned my head, my cheek resting on his thick biceps and his other arm around my middle, gripping my hands in his larger one. My back was against his chest, my arse tight against the hard plane of his stomach, and my feet were caught between his calves. Though every inch of me hurt, I was blissfully warm beneath the thick fur.

Bjorn shifted. "You all right?"

"Yes." My mouth was dry, and I swallowed, trying to clear the rasp. "Thank you."

He didn't answer, and for a moment I thought he'd fallen back asleep. Except there was a tension to him that suggested he was very much awake.

Move, I told myself. *You're warm now—sleep on your own.*

Instead I held my breath, waiting for him to speak . . . to do *something,* though I wasn't certain what.

A loud snort only inches from my face startled me and Bjorn gave a soft laugh. "Bodil snores." I felt his arm straighten under my head, and Bodil muttered a curse and rolled noisily away from us, presumably to escape another shove. Blinking away the crust of tears on my lashes, I saw other furred shapes, barely visible in the darkness. Though that they were visible at all meant dawn was coming.

And with it, the first significant battle of my life.

I blew out a long breath, trepidation rising in my chest. In a few hours, we'd descend to attack Grindill, and so much depended on me. On my magic. If I failed, dozens would die. Men and women who'd risked Snorri's wrath last night to help me would put their lives on the line with total faith that victory was my destiny, and the sudden weight of that burden would have staggered me if I'd been standing.

I, having barely escaped death last night, might die today.

The thought reminded me of the regret that had coursed through me when I'd believed my life was over. A few hours from now I might well be lying bleeding in the dirt and feeling the same regret, and I didn't want that for myself.

I wanted *more.* Even if it was just for a moment, because no matter whether my life ended today or my fears of growing old alone and forgotten came to pass, I could cling to the moment like a candle in the darkest night.

Knowing I was treading on dangerous ground, I shifted backward, molding my body against Bjorn's.

He'll just think you're cold, I told myself, even as the heat pooling in my core hoped he'd think something else.

I held my breath, waiting for him to react, anticipation making my pulse thrum.

"Cold, Freya?" There was not an ounce of concern in Bjorn's voice, only amusement and the edge of something far less innocent than laughter.

It was that something else that made me bold. "No," I breathed, shifting against him. "I'm not cold."

"Hmm." I felt the rumble of the acknowledgment more than I heard it, and I bit my lip, waiting for him to respond to what I'd done. But Bjorn only asked, "Do you need to piss?"

Indignation flooded me. "No!"

"Then why are you wriggling around? It makes it hard to sleep."

Indignation turned to mortification but then I felt the vibration of his silent laughter, and a heartbeat later his thumb began stroking the back of my scarred hand in small circles, stoking the heat in my core higher. "Stop."

His hand stilled. "Stop?"

"Talking." I bit my lip. "Stop asking me questions, was what I meant."

"Ah."

He renewed the small circles, sending a shiver through me even as I realized my demand wasn't fair. Bjorn had every right to be wary of me. I'd blown hot and I'd blown cold, ridden him like a creature possessed by lust, only to shout at him to stay away from me. He should want nothing to do with me, because I was entangled and inconstant, yet he remained at my back. "I might die today."

Bjorn tensed, then he said softly, "Is that why you want me to stop asking questions? Because you fear death?"

The wind howled and Bodil's snoring intensified. It was a miracle that all those around us didn't rouse. Yet no one stirred, which meant I had no excuse not to answer. "I don't fear it," I whispered. "But last night I faced it with regrets, and I don't want to do that again."

Bjorn didn't answer, and if not for the soft strokes of his thumb I might have thought I'd erred in confessing my heart. In truth, I didn't know what I was asking from him, given we were surrounded. Given his father—my husband—must be very nearly in earshot from where we lay tangled in each other's arms. But gods, I *wanted*.

Then Bjorn's hand moved from mine to press between my breasts, over my heart, which skipped at the contact, then sped. "You will not die today, Born-in-Fire, because I will slaughter anyone who comes near you. That is a promise." He was quiet for a long moment, then added, "Knowing that, do you still wish for me to *stop asking questions?*"

I drew in a shaky breath, his words making my skin burn hot and my pulse roar, because he was asking for a greater admission from me than I'd intended to give. It was easy to take risks when one faced death but far more difficult to take them when one faced life, and that was what he promised.

I *wanted*. But above all else, I wanted *him*.

Interweaving my fingers with his, I inhaled and then moved his palm to my breast. I felt a shudder run through him and I shifted my hips lower so my arse pressed not against his stomach, but against the thick ridge of his already hardened cock.

"Freya . . ."

"No more questions, Bjorn."

He was silent for a long, painful moment, then his teeth caught at my earlobe, the sensation sending a jolt of pleasure through me even as it answered my request. I rolled my hips against him, a throbbing pulse forming between my thighs, needing his touch. Instead he curled his hand around my breast, toying with my nipple as it peaked beneath my borrowed tunic.

I bit back a whimper as he pinched it between his thumb and forefinger, my body flushing hot. It cared not for risk, cared only for the satisfaction of the aching desire to be filled by him, and I reached behind me, catching hold of his tunic and pulling it up. The muscles of his stomach were like carved stone beneath my palm, and I dragged my nails down the trail of hair dusting them and into his trousers, closing my hand around him.

He shuddered, teeth biting sharply on my earlobe as if he were trying to muffle a groan, and I very nearly had to clamp a hand over my mouth to do the same. Gods, he was thick, and I ran my palm down his considerable length, smiling as he thrust against my hand, need already dampening his tip.

But before I could stroke him again, he abandoned my breast and caught hold of my wrist, forcing my hand out of his trousers. I bit back a snarl of frustration even as I felt his chest shake with silent laughter. He transferred my wrist to his other hand, binding me in place as his leg slipped over mine.

Putting me, I realized, entirely in his control.

My sex throbbed, already slick, and I clenched my teeth to keep from moaning as he slipped his hand under my tunic, fingers tracing over the muscles of my stomach, along my ribs, down my spine, making me breathless.

I needed more. Needed to be touched, needed to be filled, but my wrists were locked in his grip and all I could do was discreetly squirm, rubbing my thighs together, ever wary of discovery. But then Bjorn moved his leg, pinning my thighs in place, denying me even as he drove my need higher.

His fingers explored my torso, my breasts, and the lengths of my arms, his breath hot where his lips pressed against my neck. I wanted him to kiss me, wanted to taste his tongue in my mouth, but kisses were loud and already my panted breathing felt dangerous.

Lower, I silently pleaded, straining against him, desperation making me see stars. *Touch me. Sink your fingers into me. Finish me.*

As if sensing I was close to breaking, he bit at my throat, then reached down as he moved his leg. Catching hold of the waist of my trousers, he eased them over the curve of my arse. His palm left fire in its wake as he cupped my bottom, then stroked down over the top of my thighs.

Please.

Vaguely I was aware that the sun grew brighter by the second. That dawn would soon be here and we'd be out of time, and by the gods, if he left me unsatisfied, I was going to fucking kill him.

Then his hand slipped between my thighs and over my sex, cupping me, and I sucked in a breath, quivering in anticipation. I tried to move against his hand, needing *more more more* but he held me in place, possessing me even as he denied me. "Please," I breathed. "I need you."

"You have me," he answered, then drew a finger down my sex, parting me. I twisted my face into his bicep to silence my sob of pleasure, feeling his intake of breath as he found me wet and wanting.

He buried his face in my hair, the throb of his heart against my spine seeming to echo the throb of need at the apex of my thighs. Spikes of pleasure jolted through me as he circled my entrance, the icy wind pulling at my hair and creeping under the furs almost welcome, I burned so hot. Yet it was like comparing the light of the stars to the burning glow of the sun as he sank a finger into me, then two, stroking my core, my body climbing higher toward release.

Yet still, I *wanted*.

Wanted him to bury that thick cock inside me, to take me with the strength that currently held me pinned in place. Wanted him to ravish me and consume me and *fuck me* until I shattered. Yet for all Bjorn's fingers were buried in me, the same hand kept me at a distance, his palm holding my backside, thumb digging into the flesh of my arse to keep me from rubbing against him.

A snarl of desperate fury rose in my chest, but it was vanquished as he withdrew his slick fingers from my core and found my clit. I clenched my teeth, tasting blood as I caught the inside of my cheek between them, but I didn't care. Not as his finger circled me, my body soaked and ready and climbing ever higher.

More, I pleaded, unsure of whether I thought or said it, only that I wanted it, and he moved his leg from where it restrained mine, allowing me to spread my thighs wider. He plunged his fingers back inside me, slickening them, then caught that tiny part of me that seemed to contain every want in my body, tugging on it even as his thumb caressed over it.

Release struck me with the force of a cresting wave, my back arching. I would have screamed his name, forsaking us both, but Bjorn's mouth was suddenly on mine. He consumed my cries, tongue stroking mine, teeth catching my lips as wave after wave of pleasure rolled through me.

Only when my release had eased its claim on me, leaving me spent, did his lips abandon mine, going to my ear. And under the cover of the howling wind, he murmured, "You are mine, Born-in-Fire. Even if only the two of us know it."

I was. Gods help me, but I was. And for the first time in my life, it felt like I wanted for nothing.

awn broke as we lay panting in each other's arms, concealed now only by the furs draped over us. I knew I should move away, that there needed to be distance between us before others woke or it brightened enough for the scouts on duty to see clearly, but I didn't want to. In Bjorn's arms, I felt content and safe for the first time in so long, which is why I was still in them when Bodil yawned and sat upright.

"Morning, Freya," she said, giving me a look that told me we'd not been half as discreet as I'd hoped. "Blood running hotter this morning? Fingers and toes still attached?"

"Yes." The word came out as a squeak, for I was intimately aware that for all Bodil was close, Bjorn was closer. "I'm quite recovered."

Bjorn snorted, then sat up, using the motion to pull my trousers up over my naked arse. He then reached under the furs to extract my hands, which he examined in the growing light. My skin was reddened and my fingertips were white and waxy, but I still had sensation. "Can you grip?" he asked, and I was tempted to point out that he knew damn well that I could, but instead I squeezed my fist. "Yes."

"What about her feet?"

All three of us looked up at the sound of Snorri's voice. He picked his way through the rousing warriors surrounding us, furs pulled up around his head so that his face was cast in shadows. I reluctantly extracted one foot, knowing from the pain that my feet had not weathered my ordeal as well as my hands. As I pulled off the two pairs of woolen socks I wore, my stomach sank. My feet were well enough, but my toes were purple, the pain growing the more I stared at them.

"Can you walk?"

I pulled the stockings back on, relieved not to have to look at my toes any longer. Bjorn rose next to me, then reached down to catch me by the arms, lifting me upright. I clenched my teeth as my full weight pressed down, the pain intense but manageable. So I took a step, then another, my balance precarious.

"Freya can't fight in this condition." Bjorn's voice was low, anger simmering beneath the surface. "I hope you are content, Father, for this is your doing."

I bit the insides of my cheeks. Bjorn was trying to protect me, I knew that. But if this truly was a test set for me by the gods, I had to keep going. Even if it wasn't, the people of Halsar were counting on us being victorious. On us winning them homes and walls that would protect them from the long winter.

"I sent for my healer before we left Halsar, but he'll be two days in reaching us," Bodil said, examining my feet. "Yet perhaps worth waiting for."

"I'll be fine," I said. "Eir is more likely to grant favor and heal me if I prove myself in battle, so I will fight and see your healer after."

"You'll risk your life for the sake of a better chance of a god sparing your toes?" Bjorn crossed his arms, glaring at me. "I think your wits froze worse than your feet if you'd make such a decision."

He wasn't wrong, but I didn't see what other choice we had. Timing was everything if we were to be successful in this siege, so this was a risk I was willing to take. "I won't jeopardize the lives of everyone in Halsar to protect myself." Rounding on Snorri, I said, "How long until we reach Grindill?"

Three hours, Snorri had said.

It felt like an eternity.

Sweat ran in rivulets down my back, making me long for the frigid winds of the prior day, but the sky was clear, the morning sun cutting through the boughs of the trees and giving me no respite as it melted away the prior day's snow. Though the tips of my toes were numb, the rest of them throbbed unmercifully with each stride across the wet earth, the full belly of food Bodil had cajoled me into eating threatening to rise.

"You look ready to spill your guts," Bjorn said under his breath from where he walked at my left. "You're going to get yourself killed."

"You said I wouldn't die today," I reminded him. "Besides, once the battle starts, I won't feel the pain."

"The former was said while very little of the blood in my body was servicing the part that does the thinking," he hissed. "As for the latter, who the fuck told you that bullshit?"

"Probably you." I winced as my toe caught against a tree root, pain lancing up my leg. "The source of all bullshit."

Bjorn kicked a rock, sending it flying through the trees and nearly hitting Bodil, who turned around and shot him a glare before disappearing into the distance.

"Everyone is in position," I reminded him. "If we delay for the sake of my toes, we risk discovery. We need this fortress. Not only to house our people come winter, but to protect them when Nordeland tries to attack."

"I'm aware of the stakes." He caught hold of my arm, pulling me to a stop. "You don't attack the strong when you're weak, Freya. You bide your time."

"I am *not* weak." I snapped the words despite the fact it was fear, not anger, that blossomed in my veins. So much depended on me in this fight. So much depended on us *winning* this fight, because retreat would not take us out of reach of winter. Jerking free, I strode forward until I reached Snorri, hoping he'd deter Bjorn from making any more comments to undercut my confidence.

A fool's hope.

"Father," he said, coming up on Snorri's opposite side, "we need to delay. Wait for Bodil's healer and have him see to Freya before we proceed." He hesitated, then added, "Her role is crucial. If she falters, all of us are dead men."

"I'm not a man," I muttered.

"Thank you for clarifying that point," Bjorn retorted. "I hadn't noticed."

"You two quarrel like children!" Casting dark glares at both of us, Snorri gestured with one hand. "Freya, run to those trees."

"What?" I demanded. "Why?"

"If you can run, you can fight. Go."

Not giving myself time to think about it, I broke into a sprint, my shield bouncing on my back. Each step felt like knives slicing my feet but I ignored the pain and pushed for more speed, focusing on finding level ground so that I wouldn't stumble. I could do this. I had to.

Sweat poured down my brow as the trees drew closer, then my eyes moved beyond. To one of Snorri's warriors, who was riffling through the pockets of a man bleeding out on the ground. A hunter, judging from the bow next to him. Sliding to a stop, I demanded, "Who is that?"

"Someone with eyes," the warrior answered, pulling silver rings off the hunter's fingers and shoving them onto his own. The dying man stared at me, mouth opening and shutting, blood trickling down his chin courtesy of the arrow through his throat, then his eyes went dim, body limp.

Dead.

I'd seen more dead men than I could count, victims of raiders who'd come to take from my people. To kill my people. To steal away my people and turn them into thralls. But this was different.

This time *I* was the raider.

My throat burned and I swallowed bile even as I turned to Snorri, ready to tell him that my feet were too injured for me to fight. To buy time to figure out another way to take this fortress than by force. But before I could speak, he said, "The time for retreat is over. Now we fight. Send up the signal."

All around us, the warriors sloughed off the things they would not need, pulling shields from their backs and drawing weapons, the markings on their faces monstrous and terrifying where a heartbeat before they'd been only ashes and paint. Bodil withdrew a pot from her belongings and approached me, removing the lid to reveal blue paint. With her fingers she covered the skin around my eyes, then drew small droplets down my cheeks. "They say Hlin kisses away the tears of those who weep for the fallen," she murmured. "May the world drown in the tears left in the wake of our blades today."

I swallowed and gave a tight nod even as one of the men called, "The decoy forces have signaled. They move to attack."

"As do we," Snorri said. Reaching down, he ran his hand across the blood pooled next to the cooling corpse, then went to Bjorn, dragging his palm across his son's face. "Don't disappoint me."

Bjorn didn't answer, but his axe appeared in his hand, the divine fire burning in a silent inferno as his gaze locked on mine, sending a shiver coursing over me. He looked as dangerous as I'd ever seen him, eyes full of anger, and I turned away.

Because his anger was for me.

We moved down the mountain slope toward the plumes of smoke rising above the fortress. Not the orderly ranks used by the nations in the distant south, but like a pack of wolves moving through the trees on silent feet, teeth and claws formed of steel.

We reached the tree line, and I got my first glimpse of Gnut's fortress, my chest tightening, for Bjorn's description had not done it justice.

Easily three times the size of Halsar, Grindill was flanked to the north by a turbid river, called the Torne. The west side overlooked a cliff, leaving the south and east sides of the fortress approachable. Except it was also surrounded by a deep trench filled with sharpened stakes, passable only over a wooden bridge. But what stole my breath was the circular wall beyond. Steep embankments of earth covered with stakes were topped with towering wooden walls, which must have had a platform behind them, for I could see the heads and shoulders of a handful of archers standing upon them. There was only one entrance on this side, which was shut, more archers peering out of a covered structure built over the thick wooden gate.

Shouts filtered out from the fortress, the decoy force formed primarily of Bodil's maidens having begun their attack on the south gate, and those trapped outside raced toward the east entrance, seeking refuge.

The archers above only shook their heads, their eyes on the tree line where we lurked, expressions grim. I didn't blame them, for they were few in number, which meant the diversion had worked. Gnut's spies had told him that I trained with Bodil's maidens, which meant he believed I was with them and had drawn his forces to meet me at the main gate.

Leaving his arse exposed to the true attack.

"This one," I heard Snorri say, and I turned to find him pointing at an old oak within the sea of pines. Bjorn dropped his shield, taking hold of the haft of his axe with both hands. With a grunt of effort, he swung, and the tree groaned as the blade of fire dug deep into its flesh. Bjorn wrenched it free, muscles straining, then swung again with unerring aim. A drop of sweat cut a line through the blood smeared across his face as he swung a third time.

The oak moaned its death cry as it slowly toppled, gaining speed as it fell to smash into the open field. Those gathered at the base of the wall screamed in panic, some wisely running away from the fortress, though many remained, pleading to be let in.

I squeezed my eyes shut, knowing their fear. Knowing what it felt like to be descended upon with safety just out of reach. *Run,* I willed them as Bjorn cut the tree to a manageable length, others moving to wrap rope around the trunk. As they hoisted the ram off the ground, those on the wall called the alarm. Called for reinforcements.

They'd never make it in time.

Feeling as though I watched myself from afar, I took my place next to the ram, Bjorn ahead of me and Bodil behind. My shield was dead weight in my left hand, kept low until we needed it, my magic hidden until the final moment.

"Ahead," Snorri ordered from where he stood near the front, and those supporting the ram strained with effort as we broke into a slow jog across the field between the forest and the wall. Our feet thundered as we crossed the bridge, and a bead of sweat rolled down the side of my face as I took in the countless sharpened stakes below.

"Shields!" Snorri called as the archers on the wall lifted their weapons, and I lifted my shield, interlocking it with those to either side of me. The air filled with a soft hiss, and a heartbeat later arrows thudded into the shields above our heads. One punched through Bjorn's shield, the tip stopping just shy of his shoulder, and I had to clench my teeth to keep from calling forth my magic to protect him.

"Hold," Snorri shouted as if sensing my thoughts. As though he knew I was on the brink of giving myself away. "Hold!"

Someone near the front of the ram screamed, the tree trunk dipping as those holding it stumbled over the man who'd fallen. My stomach twisted as I stepped over the body.

Don't look down, I ordered myself. *Don't do anything that might make you fall!*

"Hold!" Snorri roared as we drew closer, now near enough that I could see the faces of those manning the walls. Their grim determination and fear as they dipped their arrowheads in pitch and set them aflame.

I clenched my teeth as the fiery brands flew toward us, striking our shields. A piece of burning pitch fell through a gap and landed on my wrist, the leather instantly blackening. I hissed, shaking my arm before it could burn through the thick leather. Others were less fortunate, screams rattling my ears.

"Hold!"

Only another dozen paces.

"Hold!"

Ten.

"Now, Freya!" Snorri shouted, and I screamed Hlin's name.

Magic coursed from my hand, covering first my shield and then Bjorn's, moving ahead and behind me until all were aglow with silver light.

And not a heartbeat too soon.

The ram slammed into the gate with a *boom*. But it was nothing compared to the explosion above us. In my periphery, I saw liquid shoot in all directions as my magic repelled what must have been boiling water, steam clouding the air.

"Back!" Everyone shuffled backward at Snorri's bellow, stumbling over the bodies of two who'd been struck by arrows, and I struggled to keep my footing. Fought to keep my shield in place, for if it separated from the others, they'd lose the protection of my magic.

"Heave!" Snorri roared, and we raced forward again, the ram swinging on the ropes slung between a dozen men. With each pass, warriors fell to arrows, the ground turning to an obstacle-filled slurry. It was chaos. My breath came in desperate pants as I focused on where I stepped, my feet sliding in the muck.

Boom!

The deafening noise of more boiling water exploding off my magic rattled my ears right as the ram struck. I staggered, catching myself against Bjorn, but managed to keep my shield high.

Steam stung my eyes and made me cough as we swung the ram again, the bodies beneath our feet crushed into a pool of blood and mud.

Boom!

On the heels of the explosion came screams, and under Bjorn's arm, I watched one of our warriors spin away from the ram, face brilliant red with burns, his clothing soaked. I panicked, certain my magic had failed, but when I looked up, my shield still blazed bright above our heads.

"It wasn't you," I whispered to myself as we moved back to swing again. "It wasn't your fault."

I could do this.

I would do this.

Then my foot caught on a corpse.

I stumbled, trying to catch my balance, but my toes hadn't the strength to hold my weight.

A shriek tore from my lips as I fell, slamming into Bodil, who caught me against her chest, holding me as I gained my feet. "Arm up, Fr—"

A clap of thunder split the air as I forced my shield back into place, twisting in time to watch Bodil drop, a blackened hole in her shoulder. I screamed, horror and disbelief filling me as she hit the ground.

And Bodil wasn't the only one who fell.

My misstep had ripped my magic from the shields of my comrades, and all around me men were soaked with boiling water, their faces brilliant red from burns. Screaming. Dying.

The ram fell with a crunch, and dimly I heard Snorri shout, "They have a child of Thor! Fall back!"

"Bodil," I howled, seeing that there was still life in her eyes. If I could get her out of this mess, maybe she could be saved. If I could get her to a healer in time, then maybe she might live.

But Bjorn's arm was around my waist, lifting me and tearing me away from her. "She's lost," he shouted. "We have to fall back!"

An arrow whizzed past my face, but I still fought him, reaching for Bodil as she lifted her hand to me. Our fingers brushed, then I was ripped away, an explosion sending Bjorn and me both flying sideways.

I landed hard right as the thunder clapped. Thick steam filled the air, and I couldn't see Bodil. Couldn't find my way back to her. Hands caught hold of me, dragging me over the ground. "Get up," Bjorn screamed in my ear. "Run!"

Blinking away the haze of tears revealed that the gate was an inferno, the bodies and ram having been lit aflame by the lightning. I screamed in wordless fury as Bjorn hauled me toward the trees, my heels bouncing on the torn-up grass, my eyes fixed on the scene.

Which is why I saw the child of Thor.

Standing in the covered structure over the gate stood a hooded figure with arcs of lightning crackling back and forth between their upraised palms.

The one who'd killed Bodil. The one who'd stolen her from me.

Screaming wordlessly, I tore out of Bjorn's grip. Snatching up a fallen shield, I ran, calling forth my magic. My shield burned like a silver sun as the child of Thor lifted their hands.

Dropping to one knee, I raised my shield.

A clap of thunder split the air when the lightning struck my shield, as though Thor himself had stepped out of the sky and into battle. My ears rang. Light seared my eyes, and I knelt frozen in place, blind and deaf, until, slowly, the lights cleared and the ringing eased.

Revealing a hole where the gate had been, an entire part of the wall lying in ruin, the child of Thor gone.

Dumbfounded, I stared at the smoking ruins, charred remains of men resting atop blackened and smoldering wood.

"Attack!" Snorri screamed.

Warriors streamed past me, racing for the breach. Climbing over the remains of our clansmen. Over Bodil.

Never again would I hear her council. Share drinks with her over a fire. Fight by her side.

They'd taken her away from me.

My blood surged and I scrambled to my feet, feeling no pain, only endless, ceaseless rage.

Pulling loose my father's sword, I climbed over the rubble and through the smoke, racing after Snorri and the others between the buildings. Everywhere I looked, people ran screaming, but my eyes glossed over the women with children in their arms, the infirm, the weak, as I hunted for a fight. Hunted for release from the agony burning like acid beneath my rage.

A bearded warrior exploded out of a building, half his face burned away, though he didn't seem to feel it as he raced toward me. His axe slammed against my shield, my magic sending it spinning away.

A wild laugh tore from my lips and I swung my own weapon, cleaving through the leather he wore, his innards spilling out. I spun away, meeting another man's attack and leaving him less his throat as I moved on to the next. And the next.

Until there was no one else to fight.

Blood dripped from my face as I paused, my anger hunting for *more* because it was not satisfied. *Could not* be satisfied.

Only for my eyes to land on Bjorn. He stood a few paces away, covered in blood and gore, shoulders rising and falling as he panted for breath. There were dead men at his feet that didn't fall to my blade, yet I hadn't even known he was there. Hadn't seen anything other than the men and women who'd fought against me, their faces already a blur.

"Do you know how many times you almost died," he hissed. "How many men came at your back while you were lost to bloodlust? How many times I screamed your name and you never heard?"

I bared my teeth, still lost to the rage. I didn't want to find my way out, because once I did, I knew there would be a reckoning. So I twisted away, screaming, "Where is Gnut? Where is your jarl who brought blood and ash upon you rather than swear allegiance to the king of Skaland?"

"Freya!" Bjorn snarled, but I ignored him, moving between the buildings, my voice a strange singsong tone as I crooned, "Come out, Gnut. Where are you?"

Vaguely I was aware others had joined Bjorn. Heard Snorri demanding that I silence myself, but I ignored them all as I hunted.

310 DANIELLE L. JENSEN

Then a familiar man with an axe stepped from between the buildings, a dozen blood-spattered warriors behind him, all of them eyeing me warily.

"There you are, Gnut." I gave him a bloody smirk. "I thought I was going to have to hunt you down among the children."

"You let them be, witch," he hissed, hefting his axe.

"It isn't me they should fear." I stalked closer. "It's you. You, who cared more for your pride than for their safety."

"Says the monster who slaughtered their parents!"

A shudder ran through me, the tip of my blade wavering, but I shoved away the rising guilt. Buried it deep beneath my *rage*. They deserved everything they got for standing against us. For killing Liv and burning Halsar. For taking Bodil from me.

My eyes filled with crimson and smoke, my skull throbbing with such ferocity that I couldn't think. There was only wrath.

Lifting my sword, I screamed wordlessly and charged, needing his blood on my hands.

A flash of flame shot past me.

Gnut's grin faded. The spark of malice in his eyes dimmed as his severed head slid sideways, landing on the ground with a thud a heartbeat before his body collapsed.

Dead.

"Do the rest of you surrender?" Bjorn's voice cut through the silence. "Or do you wish to die to the man?"

The remaining warriors shifted uneasily, then tossed their weapons forward and fell to their knees.

I stared at them, my hands shaking, the magic on my shield pulsing. Gnut had been mine to kill. All these men had been mine to kill, and Bjorn had stolen that away from me.

Whirling around, I stalked toward him. "Why did you steal vengeance from me?"

He snorted in disgust. "You mean, vengeance from them?"

Knocking aside my weapon with a careless swipe of his hand, he caught hold of my shoulders, spinning me to see Snorri's warriors shove a pair of archers out from behind cover. "Gnut was luring you in, Freya. Another few paces and you'd have had a pair of arrows in you, and Gnut would have died with the honor of having put you in the grave."

He twisted me back around, bending so that we were nose-to-nose. "But maybe that was what you wanted?"

"Back off!" I shoved him hard, but I might as well have shoved a stone wall for all the good it did.

"Why?" Bjorn demanded. "So that I won't be close enough to save you the next time you try to get yourself killed?"

"Silence yourselves!" Snorri roared, but I ignored him.

"Gnut deserved to die," I shouted. "All of this is because he refused to bend. Bodil is dead because—"

"Because she willingly went into battle, and in battle, people fall. She knew the risks as well as anyone, Freya. Certainly knew them better than *you*."

I flinched, stepping back from him, my rage faltering beneath the onslaught of sharper emotions. I'd chosen to fight today knowing that I was weak. I'd stumbled. I'd dropped my shield. I'd left Bodil exposed. *I'd* killed her.

My shield slipped from my hand, magic extinguishing as it hit the ground. Bodil was dead because of *me*.

"Bodil was a warrior." Bjorn's voice was quiet, as though his anger had been extinguished alongside mine. "She died with a weapon in hand and will be in Valhalla now."

Except she hadn't.

My breath caught, my chest a riot of pain as I remembered Bodil's blade on the ground, dropped so that she might catch me. And I hadn't stopped to put it in her hand before fleeing. I'd left her to die without it.

Suddenly, I was running. Sprinting through the smoking fortress toward the gate, each step like running over knives, but I embraced the pain. The gate was entirely gone, charred wood littered across the ground as though it had been smashed by a giant fist. But my eyes went beyond, to the smoldering remains of the ram and the unrecognizable figures scattered around it.

The smell of burning flesh and hair filled my nose and I gagged, slowing my pace as I picked through the wreckage.

So many bodies.

So many, and their faces were gone, leaving only size and shape and soot-stained armor to identify them. The wind gusted, sending plumes of smoke rushing sideways, but I caught a flash of silver.

Tears dripping down my face, I moved closer. A long lock of silver hair, spared by some act of the gods from the fire, floated on the breeze from where it was pinned beneath the charred remains. Dropping to my knees, I caught hold of the hair, tangling it around my fingers as it pulled loose. "I'm sorry," I whispered. "This is my fault."

Taking a deep breath, I moved my gaze from her skull, down her arm, to where her skeletal fingers clutched the hilt of her sword. I exhaled a loud whoosh of air, my shoulders slumping in relief. *She is in Valhalla.*

The ground burned my knees, but I didn't move as I wrapped her hair into a coil, then gripped it tight in my fist as I heard him approach.

"Come to say that you told me so?" I asked softly. "If I'd waited for a healer to tend to my feet, Bodil might still be alive."

Exhaling a long breath, Bjorn shook his head. "Or perhaps she would have slipped and fallen to her death as we retreated to find the healer. Perhaps it was her time to die."

I dug my nails into my palms, wanting to scream.

Bjorn crouched next to me, his gaze fixed on Bodil's blackened blade. "To have these thoughts will drive you mad, Freya, for there is no way to know if your choices caused certain outcomes." He was quiet for a moment, then said, "I think most people find comfort in being fated. In knowing that everything has already been set out for them, because . . . because no decision is truly yours but rather something determined by the Norns. Even the gods must take comfort in knowing that their fates are certain, the outcome of the end of days already known. But for whatever reason, those like you, and me, and Bodil are able to alter the weave of our threads, which means we must bear the full burden of every choice we make."

"They say being given the blood of a god is a gift," I whispered. "But it's a curse."

For a long moment, Bjorn was silent; then he said, "You were not yourself today. You—" he broke off, giving his head a sharp shake. "If you keep down this path, Born-in-Fire, if you allow yourself to be controlled by my father, it will destroy you. You need to change your fate."

"You may be right." I rose to my feet and headed back inside the fortress. "The trouble is that each time I try to change the course of fate, everything becomes so much worse."

CHAPTER

28

"Freya?"

A soft voice filtered through the door, but rather than answer, I rolled over in bed and buried my face in the furs. Just as I'd done for the past several days. At first it had been exhaustion that drove me to my bed, but it had grown into a desire to avoid facing what I'd accomplished.

Or rather, how I'd accomplished it.

"Freya? It's Steinunn. I was hoping to speak to you."

Go away, I wanted to scream. *Leave me alone.* Because the last thing I wished to do was recall the taking of Grindill. Bodil falling. Losing myself to the rage.

The silence stretched, and I hoped the skald had given up. Gone away. Then her soft voice said, "King Snorri has ordered me to speak to you before I finish my composition."

King *fucking* Snorri.

I bared my teeth into my pillow, knowing that I had no right to be angry because it had been *me* who allowed him to claim the title.

"Freya," Ylva's voice pierced the walls. "Open the door."

I sighed, because there wasn't a chance that ignoring Ylva would cause her to go away. The lady of Halsar, now the lady of Grindill, I supposed, had arrived not long after the battle was finished, and it was likely only because she'd been busy tending to the wounded and to rebuilding that I'd avoided her scathing tongue.

Crawling to my feet, I flinched as my bare soles pressed against cold wooden floors. Everything in Grindill was made of oak. It should have felt safe and secure, but instead I felt trapped.

Unfastening the latch, I swung the door open. "Sorry," I muttered. "I was sleeping."

Ylva frowned, likely because it was midday, although it might have been my appearance. I hadn't bathed since washing away the blood and gore of battle, nor had I done anything with my hair since braiding it wet, and the lengths were fuzzy and unkempt. My room was filled with dirty bowls and empty cups that the servants left at the door, but which I hadn't allowed anyone in to clear away. If my mother had seen me this way, she'd have smacked me upside the head.

But I didn't care. All I wanted to do was sleep.

"You will answer Steinunn's questions," Ylva snapped. "Else you will answer *mine*."

"Fine." I allowed the skald to step inside, then slammed the door in Ylva's face.

"Your brother has come to stay at Grindill," Steinunn said by way of greeting. "He has brought his wife, Ingrid, with him."

Wife.

I hadn't even known they'd been married. Certainly hadn't been invited to the wedding, not that there had been any time to attend. With the exception of recent days, I'd had not a moment's respite. But it still stung to have been excluded. "Thank you for letting me know."

Steinunn moved into the room, surveying the mess and then perching on the corner of my rumpled bed. Not for the first time, I was struck by how truly lovely she was, her light brown braids in perfect order and rounded cheeks flushed a becoming pink. Her dress was perfectly cut and devoid of stains, the cleavage I deeply envied peeking out above a modest neckline. Though she was older than I was, the only signs of it were faint crow's-feet next to her eyes. Yet despite how lovely she was, I'd never once seen anyone pursue her with romantic intent, man or woman, and I wondered if it was because she dissuaded attention or whether everyone saw just a voice.

I remained standing with my arms crossed. "I thought you were still traveling around singing your song about Fjalltindr." Spreading word and growing my fame, because Snorri believed that was what would bring the jarls to swear oaths to him as their king.

She gave me a faint smile. "Would you like to hear it? You fainted before I'd hardly begun when I sang it in Halsar."

"Not really." I knew I was being unpleasant but couldn't remove the edge from my tongue. "I already lived it."

"I understand," she said. "It takes a certain type of person to want to see themselves in the magic of my songs. Bjorn said he'd rather listen to seagulls fight over a fish than hear anything with him in it."

"Bjorn's an arse," I muttered, though I very much agreed with him. "You've a beautiful voice. Everyone says so."

Steinunn inclined her head. "You are kind to flatter me, Freya."

Given I was acting like a miserable hag, I couldn't help but grimace. "What do you wish to know?"

"I would like to hear you tell your story of the battle."

Turning away, I went to the table covered with dirty bowls and cups, loading them onto a tray. I needed to do something productive because it was the only way to curb the rise of frantic emotion in my chest. "There were others there. Ask them."

"I have. But the song is about you. It's meant to tell all of Skaland that you are a woman to be respected. To be followed. What you share with me will help shape the song so that it better captures your spirit."

So that she could use it to spread my reputation. Which really meant spreading Snorri's reputation, for I served at his pleasure. "There is nothing I can tell you that others wouldn't already have shared."

She frowned. "You're certain?"

Irritation rose in me that she was pressing the issue, and sharp words started up my throat. I gave a swift nod before they could exit, biting my tongue.

Steinunn rose and inclined her head. "I will sing for our people tonight—it would be well for you to be there. Though you should refrain from drinking your weight in mead beforehand."

Cracks formed in my self-control, my temper flowing out. "I know what happened, Steinunn. I didn't take pleasure from being there and I won't take pleasure from seeing it again, so please excuse my absence."

The skald nodded, moving to the door. Yet instead of leaving me to bury myself back into furs and misery, she paused. "I endured a tragedy that cost me nearly everything I held dear, so I understand your grief, as well as the desire to avoid all mention of it. That said, while you will not enjoy my song, I do believe you need to see what all those around you witnessed and why they feel about you as they do."

Without another word, Steinunn left, closing my door behind her.

I stood staring at the planks of wood for a long time, my feet growing so cold they ached. Yet rather than climbing back into my furs, I swiftly washed myself with water that a servant had brought at some point, then donned a clean dress. I removed the ties on my braids, combing my fingers through until my hair hung long and loose down my back.

The door creaked when I opened it and I winced, though I wasn't entirely certain why. Perhaps because I felt uncertain about whether I really wanted to reenter the world, needed my first steps to be taken without notice. Stepping out, I pulled the door shut, and then nearly jumped out of my skin when I noticed a figure from the corner of my eye.

"Bjorn," I stammered, my heart galloping.

"Freya."

Bjorn was leaning against the wall, but at his feet was a neatly rolled pallet and a half-empty water cup. I swallowed hard as the understanding that he'd been outside my door filled me. "Please tell me that you haven't been sleeping out here."

He lifted one shoulder. "My father is concerned for your well-being."

My teeth dug deep into my bottom lip because I knew the concern was less about what others might do and more about what I might do myself. "I'm fine."

His jaw tightened, green eyes boring into mine until I looked away. But not before I noted the dark circles under his eyes, his cheeks scruffier than was his preference, and his clothes rumpled. Whether he'd been here every moment I'd spent hiding in the room, I couldn't say, but he certainly hadn't taken any time to care for himself.

"Steinunn told me that my brother and Ingrid have come to Grindill," I blurted out, needing to end the silence.

Bjorn snorted. "It's true enough. They arrived with Ylva and the others from Halsar."

"Did Snorri order him to come?" Unease filled me, because the only reason Snorri had to bring them here was to have more immediate leverage over me. Was it because I'd challenged his authority during the siege?

"No." He gave a sharp shake of his head, irritation palpable. "Your idiot brother paid a healer to mend his leg, then came to beg he be allowed to have his place back in my father's war band. Which my father has agreed to as reward for the successes you have achieved."

Geir had *chosen* to come to Grindill? Had brought Ingrid of his own volition?

A tide of anger surged through my veins at his utter *fucking* stupidity. "Where is he?"

"Enjoying the fruits of *your* labors, I expect." Bjorn pushed away from the wall. "I'll bring you to him."

He led me into the great hall, and though I'd probably come this way when I'd been given a room after the battle, nothing seemed familiar. My eyes skipped over the riches that Gnut had accumulated over his time as jarl of this place, carved furniture and thick wall hangings, all of it now Snorri's. All of it befitting a king.

"Already Jarl Arme Gormson and Jarl Ivar Rolfson have come to swear oaths," Bjorn said, breaking the silence. "More will follow, especially once Steinunn begins her travels through Skaland, spreading word of your"—he hesitated—"battle fame."

More like infamy.

"Steinunn wishes me to listen to her sing," I said, wondering if Bjorn was one of the people she'd spoken to, whether part of her story was his. "I told her no."

He said nothing, but I felt his eyes on me as we stepped out of the great hall and into the streets of the town.

Little had been done in the way of repairs to the damaged buildings, though a quick glance told me that was because all efforts had been put toward repairing the gaping hole I'd blasted in the wall. Dozens of men and women worked to replace the charred planks of wood, even the children set to helping, small forms racing about on errands. Busy though they were, everyone paused in their tasks to watch Bjorn and me pass, and I felt their wariness as though it were a tangible thing, not one of them meeting my gaze.

Nausea twisted in my guts because this was what I'd been hiding from.

Judgment.

And it didn't feel fair. Ours was a violent people, and what I'd done was no worse than what any of the warriors here had done. Bjorn had likely killed more men than he could count, yet no one was watching him like they half expected him to cut off their heads for looking at him.

"That wall won't rebuild itself," Bjorn shouted. "And I think none wish for there to be a hole in it when our enemies arrive at the gates!"

They all obeyed, but I still felt them watching me from the corners of their eyes, as though unwilling to turn their backs entirely.

"Why are they staring at me like that?" I muttered, though I felt like I was choking on a strange mix of anger and guilt. "They *have* walls because of me. They are *safe* because of me."

"I'm sure they are planning how best to lick your boots later."

Bjorn's tone was clipped, and I jerked my eyes to him. "Why would you say that? I'm not asking them to grovel in gratitude, but I don't see why they hate me."

"They don't hate you, Freya," he answered, stopping before the door of a long house. "They fear you."

Before I could say anything, he pushed open the door, revealing a large common space. Ingrid sat at one of the tables. My friend's eyes widened at the sight of me, face filled with dismay that I half wondered I'd imagined as she swiftly smiled. "Freya!"

Shoving past Bjorn, she hugged me but I swore she felt stiff as a board as she called, "Geir, Freya is here!" before stepping back, smile still plastered on her face.

"Good to see you too, Ingrid," Bjorn said, leaning against the door frame.

Ingrid's smile faltered, but she called out, "Bjorn is with her."

A heartbeat later, Geir appeared from one of the rooms in the back. "Sister!" He caught hold of my hands and pulled me into a hug, squeezing me tight. "My sister the shield maiden! The warrior! The victorious!"

"I see your leg is healed." Extracting myself from his grip, I moved inside, noting that the home was far finer than anything Geir could have paid for himself. Large and full of heavy wooden furniture, it had probably belonged to one of Gnut's warriors killed in battle.

Perhaps one I'd killed.

Shoving away the thought, I waited for Bjorn to shut the door behind him and then said, "Why are you here, Geir? What madness drove you to come to Grindill, and to bring Ingrid with you no less?"

My brother made a face, turning away from me to retrieve a silver cup of wine sitting on the large table. "Jarl Snorri told me I could return to his war band when I could walk. I can walk, so here I am. And Ingrid is my wife—her place is by my side."

Ingrid's eyes shifted back and forth between us. "Freya, the jarl was pleased for us to come. He gifted us a room in this house. Said it was fitting, as we are family now."

Behind me, Bjorn huffed out a laugh and I pressed my fingers to my temples, trying to control my temper. "Of course he wishes you here, Ingrid. You and Geir and my mother are hostages against my good behavior, which means having you close allows him to use you against me on a whim. Whereas before he had the inconvenience of sending someone to Selvegr to mete out punishment." My head was aching. "A home—which is stolen, I might add—is a small price for him to pay to tighten my reins."

Instead of appearing chastised for his stupidity, Geir gave me a look of disgust. "What are you, Freya? A small child who will only behave properly for fear of punishment? You are the wife of the jarl. You are given everything your heart desires. You are living the life you always dreamed of. Yet still you gripe and misbehave. Always I gave you the benefit of the doubt in your complaints about Vragi, but now I wonder if it was not him that was the problem."

Shock lanced through me, and from the corner of my eye, I saw Bjorn tense. I held up my hand because I could fight my own battles. Especially against my brother.

"You are an idiot." The words came out as a snarl between my clenched teeth. "How do you not see the stakes?"

"I earned my place in the jarl's war band before he even knew your name," Geir shot back. "It was because I kept your secret that I lost it at all! I belong here just as much as you do, Freya. More, because I earned my place whereas you are here by virtue of a drop of blood."

Gods, he was *jealous*.

I could see it stewing in his amber eyes, knew it, because once, I'd felt the same emotion. The difference was that I'd chosen to hide everything I was rather than to pursue it. "You bloody fool. You care more for your wounded pride than you do for keeping your wife safe."

"That's not true," he hissed. "I love Ingrid."

"Then you should keep her as far from me as possible!"

People around me risked their fates being tangled by my choices. People around me risked losing everything. People around me risked their threads being cut short.

Geir stepped back and I saw the flash of cruelty in his eyes a heartbeat before he said, "Why, Freya? Is it because what everyone says is true? That you're a mad bitch?"

Before the weight of his words could register, Bjorn was across the room. He caught my brother by the throat and slammed him down on the table, shattering it. Ingrid screamed as they fell to the floor in a flurry of fists, ending with Geir facedown, arm twisted behind his back.

I didn't move. I couldn't move. *Does he really think that about me? That I'm a mad dog, feral and dangerous?*

"I'm going to break both your wrists, you stupid piece of weasel shit," Bjorn snarled. "See how well your wife tolerates your stupidity when she has to wipe your arse for the next month!"

Ingrid screamed at the top of her lungs, and the door exploded inward, three warriors racing to investigate the commotion. They stopped, staring in confusion as Bjorn lifted my brother and slammed him down again, Geir groaning.

"Help him!" Ingrid shrieked. "Stop this!" But the men stood their ground, unwilling to intervene.

"You don't deserve to call her family!" Bjorn shouted. "You don't deserve her loyalty!"

"Freya!" Ingrid grabbed me by the front of my dress, shaking me. "Make him stop! You're supposed to protect us!"

I stared at her. All of what I'd endured, all of what I'd done, had been driven by my desire to protect my family, including her, but that desire was faltering.

"Please," she begged. "Please!"

It's who you are, a voice whispered inside my head even as a darker voice whispered, *What if it isn't?*

It was fear that the second voice was right that snapped me out of my stupor.

"Enough." My throat strangled the word, so it came out no louder than a breath of air. "Enough!"

Bjorn went still, his eyes going to me.

"Let him go," I said. "They've made their beds. Now they can sleep in them and pray that fate doesn't turn those beds to graves."

Then I turned on my heel and walked out.

"Where are you going?" Bjorn demanded, quickly catching me with his long strides.

"I'm done fighting it," I said, stepping around a goat and then over a pair of chickens that clucked their way into my path. "Done asking questions, done trying to change things for the better. It's time to accept the path that was intended for me. The path your mother foresaw for me."

Bjorn caught my arm, pulling me to a stop. "Accept it? What does that mean?"

"It means allowing your father the control he was fated to have." I forced myself to look up to meet Bjorn's eyes. "He's meant to rule, not me, so it's time I swear an oath to him as king."

"Freya—"

I tried to pull out of his grip, but his hand tightened on my wrist, so I rounded on him. "What exactly is it you want me to do, Bjorn?"

"I already told you." He bent down so that we were nose-to-nose. "Change your fate."

He'd said that to me over Bodil's body, but I hadn't really questioned what that meant. "You don't wish for me to unite Skaland?"

"I . . ." He exhaled a long breath, moving closer. Too close, given that we were in view of dozens of prying eyes. "Ask yourself how Ska-land will become united. Then ask what you'll have to become to achieve that end."

"What does it matter?" I demanded, because I didn't want to look into myself to find the answers to those questions.

"It matters to me." His thumb rubbed over the back of my wrist. "You matter to me."

You are mine, Born-in-Fire. Even if only the two of us know it. The echo of what he'd said to me on the mountaintop filled my ears, and I shivered. "What do you want me to do?"

He swallowed hard. "I want you to listen to Steinunn sing tonight."

A platform had been placed in the middle of the square at the center of the fortress, and it seemed every last man, woman, and child in Grindill had come to see Steinunn sing her ballad.

Not that I was surprised.

To hear a child of Bragi sing was more than entertainment; it was a privilege very few would have the opportunity to witness in their lifetimes. Not only were the stories the skalds told with their songs passed down from generation to generation, so too was the experience of hearing the song direct from the skald's lips. Because one didn't just hear, one *saw.*

That was the part I was terrified about, because seeing the tunnels leading to Fjalltindr had been bad. This would be far worse.

"You don't have to do this if you don't want to," Bjorn said from where he stood at my left. "I won't fault you."

"I'll fault me." I squared my shoulders. "I lived it, which means that I can watch it."

I had to. Needed to see what everyone else had seen that had caused this newfound fear of me. Needed to see what Bjorn had seen.

The crowd stirred, parting to allow Snorri and Ylva to escort Steinunn to the dais.

Carrying a simple drum, the skald wore a dress of crimson wool trimmed with fur, and on her head she wore a headpiece designed to look like a raven, midnight feathers cascading down her shoulders and back. Its eyes were formed of polished glass, its claws and beak of silver, and I swore the cursed thing stared me down as she turned to face the crowd.

Snorri and Ylva retreated to chairs set at the rear of the dais, and with no preamble, Steinunn parted her lips and began to beat the drum she held in her hands.

A deep, huffing chant spilled over the crowd. My heart immediately began throbbing in rhythm, anticipation and trepidation filling my chest in equal parts because I felt her power. Felt the magic of her voice drawing me back to the moment we'd flowed down the mountainside toward Grindill, vengeance burning in our hearts.

And then Steinunn began to sing.

The breath I sucked in was ragged, the air not seeming to reach my lungs. For I didn't just hear the story in the lyrics.

I saw it. I tasted it. I *smelled* it.

Not through my own eyes, but through the eyes of all who had been with me, the perspective shifting from person to person, giving me a strange sense of omniscience. Like . . . like I was seeing events as the gods did.

I watched myself, mouth drawn tight and amber eyes bright with fear, my gait stilted and pained. All around me, there were gasps as those in the crowd felt an echo of what each step had been like for me, and I flinched.

But it was nothing compared to the lance of agony that struck me when the vision focused on Bodil's face.

I couldn't do this.

Couldn't watch her die again.

Bjorn's hand closed over mine, squeezing. Holding me steady as my courage wavered.

Born-in-Fire, I reminded myself as I watched him cut down the tree. *You were born in fire, you can do this.*

The vision intensified, Steinunn's song replaced with our labored breaths as we carried the tree. The screams of panic. Snorri's shouted commands.

The impact of the ram against the gate.

The perspective shifted.

Now we looked down from above, and I realized with a start that Steinunn had spoken to the survivors of our attack. That I was now seeing from their eyes.

Feeling their terror.

My breath came in too-rapid pants as the hands belonging to the eyes helped lift a vat of boiling water. They poured it over the wall, crying in despair as it exploded off the magic of my shield.

Despair that was tempered as a tall and hooded figure approached, face hidden, lightning crackling between their palms.

It was coming. My heart was chaos in my chest, hammering against my ribs.

I couldn't do it. Couldn't watch.

Wrenching my hand from Bjorn's grip, I clapped my hands over my ears and squeezed my eyes shut. But I couldn't drown out Steinunn's magic and the vision only grew in intensity. Sobbing, I watched myself trip. Watched Bodil drop her shield to catch me.

Saw that the thin lightning bolt flung by the child of Thor hadn't been intended for her. It had been intended for me.

I hadn't thought it possible for my guilt to cut worse than it already did, but watching the bolt burn through Bodil undid me.

My knees buckled, and it was only because Bjorn caught me that I didn't fall. He held me against his chest, arms wrapped around me even as I watched myself from his eyes as he dragged me away from Bodil. Felt his panic as I wrenched from his grip and then his awe as I used my shield to deflect the lightning into the wall of Grindill.

Saw the moment when he met my gaze.

And didn't recognize the woman he saw.

I stiffened, shock radiating through me at the mask of cold fury on my face, eyes that burned with crimson fire revealed only for a heartbeat before I twisted to race through the shattered wall and into the fortress.

Perspective shifted to those whose home I'd just invaded, and tears dried on my cheeks even as horror filled my stomach as I watched myself slaughter all who crossed my path, my expression wrath incarnate. It didn't matter who they were, whether they crossed blades with me or tried to flee, I cut them all down. Bjorn fought at my heels, killing any who tried to stab me in the back even as he screamed my name. Begged me to stop. Yet I kept going.

Kept killing.

I witnessed the final confrontation with Gnut through the eyes of his men. Coated in blood and gore with my teeth bared, I was more monster than woman, and a shudder of relief ran through me as Bjorn's axe cleaved Gnut's head from his shoulders, and the last stanza of Steinunn's song flowed away on the wind.

Prying my fingers loose from their death grip on Bjorn's shirt, I turned to find the crowd shifting and shaking their heads as the vision cleared from their mind's eye. Ylva hugged her arms around her body, her face a mask of revulsion that didn't fade as she looked to me. Snorri alone seemed unaffected, moving to rest a hand on Steinunn's shoulder as he shouted, "Saga foretold that the shield maiden's name would be born in fire! Foretold that she would unite all of Skaland beneath the one who controlled her fate. And now you have seen what it means to defy the will of the gods!"

The crowd shifted, turning to look at me. Not with respect, but with fear.

"Tomorrow, Steinunn will leave Grindill to spread word of our battle fame. She will travel through Skaland, moving from village to village, and in her wake our people will come in droves to swear oaths to me, their king," Snorri roared, calling their attention back to him. "And those who fight at my side will be sung about for generations to come!"

The crowd cheered, and a heartbeat later drums began to pound. Jugs of mead were passed around as Snorri broke open Gnut's stores to reward those who followed him. I stared blankly at the festivities, horror rooting me in place, because that couldn't have been what I'd done. Wasn't how I remembered it all, because in the moment, it had felt like justice. Like I'd been righting a wrong.

Like I'd been punishing those who'd taken Bodil from me.

Bile burned my throat. Afraid that I'd vomit in front of everyone, I twisted on my heel and muttered, "I need air."

I walked with no destination in mind, knowing only that I needed to be away from the crowd. Needed to be away from all those people who'd stared at me like I was a monster. Who'd follow me not out of respect but fear. Vaguely, I felt Bjorn on my heels, a silent shadow watching over me. My shoes slid as I skidded to a stop and rounded on him. "It's a lie. I don't know if Snorri made her do it or if those who she spoke to lied, but that wasn't how it went. The people I killed . . . they were the enemy. They were attacking me. They . . ." I trailed off as I took in the look on Bjorn's face. The exhaustion. The grief.

"A skald's magic can't depict lies." His voice was low. "No matter what people told Steinunn, the magic of her song reveals only the truth as seen by the gods."

My lip quivered. "Is . . . is that what you saw, then?"

Bjorn's silence was all the answer I needed.

"I don't know how you can stand to look at me," I whispered. Spinning away from him, I took one step before he caught me around the middle and pulled me into a narrow space between buildings.

"I saw you lose yourself." His breath was hot against my face, forehead pressed to mine and hands gripping my hips, holding me in place. "To grief. To the battle."

I wanted to accept his excuses, except that I'd seen how my eyes had burned red, nothing about them human. "What if I didn't lose myself, Bjorn? What if I found myself?"

Lifting my chin to meet his shadowed gaze, I whispered, "Since the moment I learned of your mother's foretelling, I've questioned how my

magic has the power to unite a nation. What if this is it? What if . . .
what if my power is *fear*?"

His fingers tightened on my hips, body pressing against mine. "You
have the power to change your fate, Freya. You can leave. We can leave.
Let me take you away from all of this. Force the Norns to alter our
futures and to Helheim with everything my mother says."

We can leave. A tremor ran through me at what he was offering. Not
just a chance to escape this madness, but to do it with him at my side.
"You'd leave?"

"Yes."

"But . . ." I swallowed hard. "You'd be giving up so much. Your
family. Your people. The chance for vengeance against Harald. The
chance to rule Skaland."

"I don't want to rule," he answered. "I want *you*."

Bjorn's mouth claimed mine then, one hand abandoning my hip to
tangle in my loose hair. I whimpered, allowing him to part my lips, our
tongues entwining. My body's reaction to his touch was swift and fierce
because it was always lurking beneath the surface. Always wanting.

I wrapped my arms around his neck, feeding that need with the feel
of his hair on my skin, of the hard muscles of his shoulders beneath my
nails. Liquid heat throbbed in my core, and I pressed my hips to his,
desperate to drown the terror threatening to consume me. "Prove it."

I felt as much as heard his intake of breath, and I buried my face in
his neck, biting at his throat. "Prove that I'm what you want." I ran my
hand down his chest, down the hard muscles of his stomach, and cupped
his cock. He groaned and I stroked the thick length, liquid heat rushing
to my core. "Claim me."

"Freya, not like this." He caught hold of my wrist, pinning it to the
wall of the building. "Not here."

Frustration flooded me. "Why not?" I demanded, kissing him. Biting him hard enough that I tasted blood, his groan of pain and pleasure
spiking my desire. "Is it because of your father?"

"Freya—"

"Because he's never had me. Never will have me."

Shock broke through the haze of desire, because I'd sworn an oath not to tell anyone of the deal Snorri and I had made. But it was as though someone else held control of my tongue. Someone who'd say anything, do anything, to get what *she* wanted. Panic rose in my chest, but *she* had too much control and shoved it away.

She kissed Bjorn, hard enough that our teeth clicked. "Our marriage is a lie, a farce." *She* raked the nails of my free hand down his back. "We made a deal, Ylva and I. That he'd never touch me and that in exchange, I'd lie to everyone. But the gods know the truth, Bjorn. I am a free woman."

Never had a greater lie been told, but *she* told it anyway.

"Then leave with me." His hand slid up my ribs, cupping my breast. "Right now. Once we're somewhere safe, I'll give you everything you want, Freya. I swear it."

She wanted to say yes. But beneath the want, the *covetousness* that was consuming me, a more familiar voice screamed, *You can't leave them!*

"My family." The protest came between desperate kisses, my hands roving down his body. "Snorri will make them pay if I run."

"Then perhaps they should have treated you better." Bjorn kissed my jaw, my throat. "Geir built his own barrow."

He's right, the new voice whispered to me. *All they ever did was use you.*

But the old voice, the familiar voice, pleaded, *Your protection shouldn't have to be earned.*

"I can't leave." The words croaked out, my throat trying to strangle them and my tongue wanting to twist them into something else.

"Then we can't do this." Bjorn pulled out of my grip, retreating a step so that his back pressed against the building opposite. "I won't do it, Freya. I won't skulk around with you in the shadows, living every day a lie while I watch you be changed by my father's ambition. I'll have all of you or none of you."

Fury boiled up in my chest, the purest form of rage that he'd deny

332 DANIELLE L. JENSEN

me what I wanted. "If you want me free of your father's shadow, perhaps you should find your balls and get rid of him yourself."

Bjorn recoiled.

"Can't stomach it?" I hissed, part of me, buried deep inside, repulsed by the words exiting my lips.

He was silent for a long moment, then said, "Your eyes are red, Freya. Same as they were when you attacked Grindill."

Burning with crimson fire.

Nausea and revulsion drowned my anger, and I staggered a few paces away before dropping to my knees. "I'm sorry." I dug my nails into the dirt.

Bjorn's voice was full of unease as he asked, "What exactly is it that you want me to do?"

Kill Snorri, the new voice hissed. *Challenge him and take everything.* I gave a sharp shake of my head. "That's not what I think. That's not what I want."

"Freya . . . ?"

I could hear his confusion. His concern.

Oh gods, I was arguing with myself.

Geir's voice filled my head, repeating *mad bitch* over and over until I breathed, "There's something wrong with me, Bjorn."

I felt the heat of him as he knelt next to me.

"There's something in me," I whispered, staring blindly into the darkness. "Someone."

"It's Hlin." Bjorn cupped my face with his hands, searching my eyes. The red must have been gone, for he relaxed. "I know how it feels, Freya. I know what it's like when the part of you that is *theirs* takes control. But you can learn to hold them in check."

A quiver ran through my body, because what he spoke of sounded like possession. Like madness. And it didn't entirely make sense. "How can Hlin make me behave this way, Bjorn?" I met his gaze, though it was hard to see in the shadows. "She's the goddess of protection."

"I don't know." His grip on me tightened. "She's a minor god. Only a few stories speak of her, and none tell anything of her nature. I can tell you that with certainty, because many sought to learn everything about her when my mother foretold the power you'd have."

Which meant I was at war with someone I knew nothing about. Who *no one* living had ever met. Except . . .

I sat upright, pulse throbbing. "I need to go speak with my mother."

"My father isn't just going to let you go roaming the country-side," Bjorn said under his breath as he walked with me back to the great hall. "Not with half the jarls in Skaland desiring to capture or kill you, and the other half on their way to Grindill to meet you. You're too valuable to allow out of his sight. He'll only have your mother brought here to give answers."

"No." My voice was flat. "Bad enough that Geir and Ingrid chose to put themselves within reach by coming to Grindill, I won't put my mother at risk as well."

"Then I fail to see a solution." Bjorn ground to a halt, ignoring the way those in the streets gave us wide berth. I had a more difficult time setting aside the fearful looks many of them gave me. "It is a full day's ride to Selvegr and another back. Impossible to do without your absence being noted."

I rubbed at my scarred hand, thinking hard. Then an idea occurred to me. "I need to find Steinunn."

Bjorn's eyes narrowed. "Why?"

"Because her magic might be able to give me the answers I need." Twisting away from him, I went into the great hall. As expected, the skald was there, speaking with Ylva and Snorri, as well as two men I didn't recognize. "Keep your father busy while I talk to her," I muttered under my breath.

"There is my prize," Snorri said at the sight of me. "Freya, this is Jarl Arme Gormson and Jarl Ivar Rolfson, who have sworn allegiance to me as king of Skaland." To the men, he said, "My wife, Freya, and my son, Bjorn."

Both names were familiar to me, as their territories were not distant from Snorri's. I inclined my head respectfully, only for shock to ripple through me as both bowed low. "Shield Maiden," Ivar said, "we were present for Steinunn's performance, which was a privilege to behold. Our enemies will cower in terror when faced with you on the battle-field, of that there is no question. Especially as Steinunn spreads word of your battle fame."

I bit the insides of my cheeks, remembering how not so long ago, battle fame had been my greatest dream. I'd thought that would be my reward for enduring Snorri. But now that I'd tasted real battle, those dreams felt like nightmares. *Were* my nightmares, the parade of people who'd fallen because of me marching through my mind every night.

"As Skaland's strength grows, soon we will turn our eyes to Norde-land," Snorri said. "It is rich with gold and silver from years of their raiding. Past time we took back what is ours."

The men nodded their approval, Arme's gaze shifting to Bjorn. "To see revenge for your mother's murder on the horizon must have your blood blazing, Firehand. A thing worthy of one of Steinunn's songs, when it comes to pass."

Bjorn inclined his head. "I have waited many years for vengeance."

The men grinned. "The next time we see each other, it will be on drakkar as our fleet sails across the strait to put Harald in his place."

"My father believes my destiny is to fight by Freya's side," Bjorn said. "So where she goes, I will go. If it is Nordeland, so much the better."

"My lord," I said to Snorri, interrupting the exchange. "It was to

Steinunn I wished to speak. I . . . I had some thoughts I might share with her to add to her songs."

He gave me an approving nod. "It is well to see you coming to terms with your role."

Nodding, I edged past, leaving Bjorn to make idle chatter with the jarls. I approached Steinunn, who was exchanging words with Ylva. Leif stood at his mother's elbow, the boy giving me a wary look, his hand drifting to the seax sheathed at his waist. I smiled at him, despite knowing that there was little chance of me ever winning his regard, but the furrow in Leif's brow only deepened. Ylva's hands closed on his shoulders, drawing him backward. "Go," she said. "It is past time you were abed."

Bjorn's younger half-brother looked ready to argue, but one glare from his mother sent him hurrying to the rear of the hall. Crossing her arms, Ylva said, "I'm less forgiving of your conduct than Snorri, girl. Sulking in your pillow for days, only to go out and inspire fistfights before storming out of a performance meant to honor you. It's—"

"It wasn't meant to honor me, Ylva, it was to make people fear me," I interrupted. "Which is why I wish to speak to Steinunn."

"My magic speaks the truth," the skald swiftly said. "If the truth is terrifying, there is nothing I can do to change that."

"Unless there is more to the story," I said. "An untold piece that might add needed depth." Turning to Ylva, I said, "Snorri wishes to entice the other jarls to swear oaths to him with tales of battle fame, which is well and good. But the people who are to be ruled by him— they need something different. Something . . . *more*. A king takes an oath of loyalty from his people, but he, in turn, gives an oath to protect them. The people must see that. Must believe it is the truth, which cannot be proven by any way better than a skald's song."

Ylva's eyes narrowed. "What precisely could you add, Freya? All you've proven is your adeptness for killing."

I flinched. "Then perhaps what Steinunn's song needs is not more stories about me, but rather the tales of the goddess whose power I wield."

"There are few tales," Steinunn interjected. "What is known of her is already known to all. To make these songs worthy, they must hold new stories that will entice men to action. There is no one who has seen or spoken directly to the goddess in our lifetime who might provide such."

"Except Freya's mother." Ylva pursed her lips, blue eyes distant, though they swiftly fixed on mine. "Is there a compelling story surrounding your conception, Freya? Because I do not think tales of lust and divine fornication will *inspire* people to think better of you."

"In truth, I don't know," I admitted. "My father forbade anyone in our family to speak of my heritage. But Steinunn could travel to Selvegr and speak to her. Learn whatever my mother knows of Hlin, and then use it to temper her song."

"My song requires no alteration," Steinunn snapped. "Already it has proven its effectiveness. On Snorri's orders, tomorrow I leave to travel across Skaland, performing to all who listen so that they might hear of Freya Born-in-Fire's battle fame. Long have these men desired to make war on Nordeland, and the opportunity to make it happen will be beyond their power to resist."

"Your song makes me appear a monster," I snapped.

Steinunn leaned close. "Perhaps because you are." Rounding on Ylva, she added, "Snorri wishes for me to leave tomorrow. I must rest. Good night to you both."

Turning on her heels, the skald strode from the hall.

My hands curved into fists, and I drew in several shuddering breaths, trying to find calm. The rage that consumed me during the battle, that took hold of me not an hour past with Bjorn, was rising again.

It made me wonder if Steinunn was right. That there was nothing more to add to the song.

"The people fear you," Ylva said softly. "You looked as much a monster as the draug you fought in the tunnels beneath Fjalltindr." Her throat moved as she swallowed. "And I helped bring you down upon them."

"You're fated." My voice was cold. Clipped. "It wasn't your choice; it was made by the Norns who weave your thread."

"I do not think that is what it means to be fated," Ylva answered. "I think it means that the Norns know our threads so well that they see each and every decision we will make." Her eyes locked on mine. "So I am not released from culpability, only predictable in it."

A rush of air exited my lips, my anger flowing away, though I wasn't entirely certain why.

"I love my husband," Ylva said. "But he sees only the glory, not the backs of those he must step upon to achieve it. *I* see the faces belonging to those backs, and I do not like the expressions I saw on them tonight." Her eyes flicked to Snorri, who was laughing and pounding Bjorn on the shoulder. "I do not wish to see him rise to power on a tide of fear. Do not wish for that to be my son's legacy."

I held my breath, waiting for a solution from a woman who, I realized now, was more ally than enemy, for many of our desires were the same.

"Ride in secret to Selvegr tonight," Ylva finally said. "Learn what you can from your mother of the goddess whose magic our fates rest upon, then return with haste. I will tell all that you are seeking guidance from the gods and must not be disturbed, as well as delay Steinunn's departure until you tell her what answers the gods have given you." She hesitated, then added, "Enlist Bjorn to help you. He'll know how to get you in and out of Grindill unseen. Will keep you safe on the journey and ensure you return to us."

Not giving me an opportunity to respond, Ylva announced, "Husband, Freya must seek guidance from the gods. She requires solitude for a night and a day to see what answers the gods will give her." She snapped her fingers. "Bjorn, as Hlin has willed you to watch over Freya on this journey, you shall attend her."

The men all blinked at her, and Ylva crossed her arms. "Well? You would have the gods wait? Snorri, fetch the mushrooms. Bjorn, ensure Freya has all she needs to endure her trial. And you"—she leveled a finger at the two visiting jarls—"should be feasting! We are to celebrate our alliance and our great futures together. Bring in food! Mead! Music!"

Everyone fell to their orders, and I muttered to Bjorn, "Get what we need to ride to Selvegr tonight and meet me in my room."

Snorri approached and handed me a cup filled with ground mushroom. "Drink deeply," he said. "I look forward to learning what the gods wish to show you in your visions."

"As do I." I nodded at him, then rushed to the stairs, climbing to the second level where my room was located. Entering, I set the cup on a table and immediately began gathering what I'd need to ride through the night. My father's sword and a seax. A shield. A cloak with a deep hood to hide my face.

The door opened and shut, and I turned to find Bjorn with a sack of provisions. I said to him, "Ylva desires the same truths as I do. She will hide our absence so that we might seek them out from my mother."

"This is disappointing news," he said. "I had hoped you'd arranged for us to spend a night and a day eating our fill while our minds raced through the clouds on mushroom-induced visions. Not riding through the night to see your mother."

I rolled my eyes, then set the bolt on the door before going to the window, hearing drums take up a rhythm in the hall below. "We'll need horses."

"Already outside the wall," he answered, and when I looked at him askance, Bjorn only winked and said, "I assume you've no trouble taking to the rooftops?"

We rode through the night, following the river down to the coast, then riding the road leading round to the next fjord over, on which Selvegr was located. It was midmorning by the time I trotted my horse up the familiar path to my family's farm, dismounting in front of our home. Chickens pecked in the dirt and two new goats grazed at blades of grass around a fence post. The garden boasted an abundance of spring green, and in the distance the cleared field held a crop already high for this time of year, the earth yielding well.

The door opened, but rather than my mother stepping outside, it was an unfamiliar man. Perhaps Snorri's age, he was stout about the middle, and had a long gray beard decorated with silver rings. He held an axe in one hand with the comfort of one who'd used it as a weapon many times before, and my hand moved to my own weapon on instinct.

"Who are you?" I demanded. "Where is my mother?"

"You must be Freya," he answered, then jerked his chin toward Bjorn. "Good day to you, Bjorn."

"Birger." Bjorn had dismounted as well, leading his horse up to stand next to me. "Snorri has given Freya leave to visit her mother. Is she here or should we seek her out in the village?"

"Kelda's abed," Birger answered. "Unwell, but on the mend."

"Leaving you to play at farming, then?" Bjorn laughed. "You're a bit heavy-handed for collecting chicken eggs."

This was the man Snorri had sent to watch over my mother against my good behavior, which meant he probably was the one who would hurt her if Snorri gave the orders. My hands fisted, but it was my tongue that readied a lashing. For while I'd known someone was here, it was different actually seeing him. Different knowing that he was living inside my mother's house. "What's wrong with her? If you hurt her, you stuffed piece of weasel shit, I'll—"

"Silence that viper tongue of yours, Freya, or I'll scrub it with soap!" My mother appeared from behind Birger, adjusting a fur-trimmed shawl I didn't recognize over her shoulders before stepping out, her cane thudding against the ground. "I had a flux, but it's passed. Mercy that Birger was here to mind the animals, what with you wed off and your brother gone to serve in your husband's war band, Ingrid with him. I've been all alone."

Guilt filled my core, for while I'd considered the danger my mother was in, I'd not considered the practical difficulties caused by my absence.

"So thoughtful of your husband to send someone to care for me," she continued, taking my hand as she looked me over. I did the same, noting the new dress and boots, as well as a thick silver bracelet around her wrist.

"Seems you got what you wanted, love," she finally said. "A true warrior now, just like your brother."

Bjorn snorted and I shot a glare over my shoulder before turning back to my mother. "Are you well enough to walk with me?" The questions I wished to ask were personal, and I didn't need Birger listening over my shoulder.

"Of course, love. Birger, those goats aren't going to milk themselves. And mind you climb the roof sometime today to find that leak, else it will be you sleeping beneath the drips."

Birger's mouth opened and shut as he looked between me and my mother, knowing full well he wasn't supposed to give me the chance to take her and run. "I'll escort them," Bjorn said. "You get to your chores."

"You'll do no such thing, *Firehand*." My mother's voice was frigid. "I've heard no end of things about *you,* and I'll not have you at my back. There's firewood that needs chopping, which you may attend to."

"There are many who seek Freya's death," he answered. "So if you wish me to chop your wood, you'll have to remain close enough for me to dissuade anyone with ill intentions."

My mother scowled, leveling her cane at him. "If you think—"

"It's not up for debate," Bjorn interrupted. "I'm not risking Freya's safety just because you don't care for my reputation."

My mother's scowl deepened and, seeing a fight brewing, I swiftly caught her arm. "We'll stay close."

For a heartbeat, I thought both of them would turn on me, but Bjorn only pulled off his shirt and started toward the woodpile. My mother resisted my tugs on her arm, only conceding when Bjorn's axe appeared in his right hand, slicing through a thick block of wood with one swing.

"I'm sorry I didn't come sooner," I said once we were out of earshot. "I—"

"I know precisely your circumstances, Freya." My mother's jaw was tight. "It's my fault that you are in them."

"How so?" This was the first I'd heard of it, though in truth, my mother had always said little about my heritage and nothing about the events surrounding my conception. I, having no interest in details of intimacy between my parents, had never asked, which I now regretted. "Did you know it was Hlin you invited to your bed?"

My mother was silent for a long time before answering. "It was not Hlin we took into our bed, Freya, but another."

I blinked. "But—"

"It was another," my mother interrupted. "We've never spoken to you of this, but Geir . . . he was a sickly baby. The herb women could do nothing, told us the merciful choice would be to leave him out for the cold and the wolves, but . . . I couldn't do it."

It was the way of our people, I knew that. Had known women who bore sickly babies that were in their arms one day and then gone the next, never spoken of again. But to think that my mother was told to do such a thing to my brother made my blood run cold. "It is well you didn't, Mother, for they were wrong. He grew up strong."

Of body, at least.

"They weren't wrong." My mother's throat moved as she swallowed, and I glanced at Bjorn. He was swiftly working his way through the pile, tattooed skin glistening with sweat, and definitely *not* out of earshot. "What happened?" I asked.

"I prayed to the gods to spare him," my mother whispered. "Prayed to Freyja and Eir and all who'd listen, offering up sacrifices to show my devotion, but he only grew worse, soon too weak to eat." Her hand tightened on my arm. "I believed they had all chosen to ignore my pleas, that this was my son's fate. Night came, and I knew it would be his last, your father holding us both in his arms as we waited for his chest to still. And then a knock sounded at our door."

It was like a story passed down from generation to generation until it barely seemed possible it could have occurred. Tales of the gods stepping amongst mortals to do good or ill, depending on their moods, which were ever fickle. But this wasn't a story—it was my life.

"We opened the door to discover a woman," my mother continued. "She was young and beautiful, with skin white as ivory and hair dark as a moonless night. She said, 'I will spare your son in exchange for a gift in recompense for his loss,' and I knew she was a god come at my behest. That my prayers had been answered."

A shiver passed over me, but I said nothing, entranced by the tale.

"Your father asked what she would have in return, and she answered, 'To lie between you, and what our passions yield shall be the sacrifice that pays for the health of your son. Choose.'"

It was known the gods were voracious in their lusts, and it was an honor to have them in your bed. Yet I could only imagine how my parents had felt, compelled to have sex to save their son even while he lay dying in the same room. It felt wicked and cruel, and . . . and not like the goddess whose magic I possessed.

"Of course, we did her bidding," my mother said, "and it was unlike any night I've had before or since, leaving us both so spent we fell into the deepest slumber. When we awoke, the woman was gone, as was your brother."

I gasped, pressing a hand to my mouth, feeling the horror of the moment despite knowing that my brother was alive and well today.

A tear ran down my mother's face. "I screamed and screamed, certain that it had been Loki who'd come and played us this cruel trick, healing our son to fulfill his word but stealing Geir away to deprive us of what we bargained for, and I cursed myself a fool for not being more careful in my terms. Pounded my fists bloody in the dirt even as your father raged against the gods. Yet we were both silenced as another knock sounded on the door."

I held my breath, my heart a riot in my chest.

"Your father tore the door open, ready to rain fists down upon the trickster, only to find a different woman standing outside, a basket in hand. Inside was a squalling baby boy, and if not for the mole upon his cheek, I'd never have known the fat and healthy child as your brother. But it was him."

"Who was she?" I asked. "How did she appear to you?"

"As a warrior." My mother's eyes were distant. "Dressed in leather and steel, blades at her sides and a shield strapped to her back. She appeared both young and ancient, her hair golden and worn in war braids, with amber eyes that glowed like suns."

My own eyes burned, because I'd have given a great deal to see the goddess's face. Hlin, my divine mother who had shared both her blood and magic with me. "What did she say?"

My mother cleared her throat. "She said, 'You have been played false, and all the tears in the world mean nothing to the one who took your son from you, but they mean something to me. So I will offer you a bargain that is pure: Allow the child about to quicken within you to be my vessel, and I will give you back this boy. But choose swiftly, for the moment to do so will soon have passed.'"

I stared at the ground at my feet, wondering why she'd not ever told me this story, for it was something skalds would write songs about to repeat through the ages.

My mother wiped her eyes. "I was not thinking clearly, wanting only to hold your brother in my arms, but I had sense enough to ask why she wanted my child—wanted you—as her vessel. She said to me, 'If the child is gifted only avarice, her words will be curses, but if gifted altruism, what divine power she might make her own is a fate yet unwoven.'"

I frowned, repeating the words in my head. "What does that mean, Mother?"

"Who can say what the riddles of the gods mean to mortals." She tilted her face skyward, releasing a shuddering breath. "In that moment, I cared nothing but for the return of your brother, so I said, 'Yes.

Yes, you may take my child as your vessel.' She smiled and handed me the basket holding your brother, kissed two tears from my cheeks, then was gone."

In one moment, in one desperate choice made by my mother, I had a drop of god's blood placed where my heart would soon beat, and became one of the unfated, my thread free to weave itself through the tapestry as I willed it.

Or as Snorri willed it.

I frowned but the thought vanished from my head as my mother abruptly clutched at me, holding me against her. "I am so sorry, Freya."

"Why?" I demanded, alarmed to see my mother behave so, for it was not her character. "Beyond keeping this tale from me, you have nothing to be sorry for."

"I chose your brother over you." Her fingers dug into my shoulders. "Cursed you to be used as the jarl's weapon."

Had it been a choice? Ylva's words reverberated in my head, the idea that the Norns did not choose, only implicitly understood what choice a person would make, consuming my thoughts. I held my mother against me, our foreheads touching. "To have your child chosen to hold a goddess's blood is a privilege none would turn down, Mother. There is nothing to forgive."

"I thought it was Freyja," she whispered. "Thought that one day you'd invoke her name and create life where there was none, which is why I named you for her. And thought nothing of it when your father returned from Halsar with word the seer had spoken prophecy of a child of Hlin. Only waited for the day you would come into your power, yet what horror when you did, for it was not life your magic promised but *war*. I cursed you, my love. Forgive me."

It was hard not to flinch at knowing that was how she saw my magic, yet still, I didn't understand why she was pleading the way she was. "There is nothing to forgive. I am content."

She straightened and held me at arm's length, eyes locked on mine. "Don't lie to me, girl."

I twitched. "I'm not."

"If you are so content with your husband and your future, why do you risk it all by climbing into bed with his son?"

Shock radiated through me, and I gaped at her. "Pardon?"

"Don't lie to me, love. I know the look of a man possessive of that which he believes is his, and the Firehand looks at you that way. As you look at him." My mother's nails dug into my arms and she shook me violently. "What madness possesses you, Freya? Your life, and the lives of everyone in this family, hangs in the balance of your favor with Snorri, yet you cuckold him with his own son? You think it will remain secret? That he won't find out? You must end it."

I quivered, my stomach twisted with anger and shame and fear.

"Is satisfying your lusts worth your brother's life?" she demanded, and my gut hollowed. "End it, Freya. Promise me that you will end it, for all our sakes. Swear it on Hlin's name."

A strange dizziness swept over me, but with it came unexpected clarity. I could not fulfill Saga's foretelling and be with Bjorn. I could not protect my family and be with him.

I had to choose.

The air seemed to thrum, and from the corner of my eye I saw Bjorn turn from his task, searching for danger.

But I focused on my mother. On what she'd told me. On all the things she'd asked of me over the course of my life. On what she asked of me now. My anger, always simmering, burst into flame. "Do not make demands of me."

Her mouth dropped open. "Have you lost your mind?"

I shook my head. "No, Mother. For the first time ever, I finally see clearly."

"What do you mean?"

Her eyes were full of confusion, and that only fueled my anger, because how could she not know? "My whole life, all you have ever done is take from me for Geir's gain. Or your own. From your own lips, you've put me last since before I was born."

"Freya—"

"You made me hide my heritage, my magic, who I was," I hissed. "Married me to Vragi because he'd bring wealth and privilege to our family even though you knew how he'd treat me. Offered yourselves up like mindless goats for sacrifice so that Snorri might have leverage to control me, because you *knew* it would be to *your* benefit. And now you ask me to turn away the one person who has put me first, the one person who cares about me, because it risks your selfish hide. Perhaps that is the right choice. But it must be *my* choice, not yours."

The tension in the air seemed to snap like a rope stretched too tight, and my mother took a step back. "Then I expect you'll curse us all."

I huffed out a bitter breath. "You cursed yourself. It would have been easy for you to evade Birger and escape, but all you saw was the benefits Snorri's silver brought to you. Same with Geir, who could easily have run away with Ingrid, but refused to give up his choice place in Snorri's war band. In your selfishness and greed, you stuck your own necks under the axe, yet weep that it is my fault when the blade threatens to descend."

"You dare to call us selfish, you little whore!" She lifted her hand to slap me, but then a much larger one closed over her wrist.

"Apologize." Bjorn's voice was like ice.

"You're the one who should apologize." My mother tried to pull free, but Bjorn's grip only tightened. "You're the one who made her like this. Freya used to be a good and loyal woman."

"She still is. You're just no longer worthy of her loyalty."

"Doesn't matter," I said, needing to be away from her before I lashed out with more than words. "I'm leaving, Mother. It's time you made your own way in the world."

Twisting on my heel, I strode toward my mare, Bjorn at my side.

"Freya!" she shrieked over and over as Bjorn lifted me onto my horse. "Please!"

I didn't look back.

CHAPTER

31

"We need to hurry." I rode at a swift canter down the narrow trail circling the fjord, knowing that for all my bravado, I had a decision to make. "We don't have much time to get back."

Instead of answering, Bjorn drew his gelding to a rough halt, the horse tossing its head in annoyance. "Why return at all? This is your chance to escape. We can head down the coast and find a merchant ship heading south, where we'll be out of reach of all of this."

"So that Snorri can execute my idiot brother and my negligent mother?" I snorted. "As tempting as that is at this particular moment, no."

Reaching out, Bjorn caught hold of my mare's reins, preventing me from heeling her into a trot and away from this conversation. "Freya, there's something I need to tell you."

"If it's your opinions on my family, I don't want to hear it."

"It's not about your family. It's about mine." He dragged his eyes up to meet mine. "My mother's foretelling . . . it wasn't the only one she had about you."

My heart skipped, unease pooling in my stomach as I ceased trying to extract my mare from his hold. "What did she say? And when?"

Why didn't you tell me?

"I . . ." His throat moved as he swallowed. "It was a long time ago, when I was still a boy, but I remember it clearly."

"You seem to remember everything about her very clearly and yet communicate none of it," I snapped. "What did she say?"

Bjorn was silent, and nausea twisted my guts. For what he might say. And the fact that he kept it from me at all.

"She went into these strange trances when she was being told something by Odin," he finally answered. "I was alone with her when she was suddenly seized by one. She told me that the shield maiden would unite Skaland, but that tens of thousands would be left dead in your wake. That you'd walk upon the ground like a plague, pitting friend against friend, brother against brother, and that all would fear you."

His words settled into my core, and I struggled to breathe.

"Whatever she saw terrified her," he continued. "I was young, and it sank into my mind that the shield maiden would be more monster than woman. Even as a grown man, I . . . I had this vision of what you'd be like." He looked away. "It couldn't have been further from the truth. Not a monster, but a beautiful and brave woman who rescues fish and walks through fire to protect others."

My eyes burned and I blinked rapidly to keep tears from forming.

"I didn't tell you, because you weren't what my mother described," Bjorn said. "I was certain that I'd remembered wrong. Or that you'd altered fate and that the future Odin had shown my mother no longer existed, not just the darkness and death, but all of it. Except then the tests began, the gods stepping onto the mortal plane to acknowledge you, and I could not deny that you were destined to lead." He took a deep breath. "I watched you make choices to protect Halsar and it didn't seem possible that you would become a monster who'd bring death and destruction. But after the siege of Grindill . . ."

"You decided that maybe I was a monster after all." I choked out the words, horror strangling me.

Bjorn shook his head. "No. But that Snorri would turn you into one if you allowed him to control your fate. I thought hearing Steinunn's song, seeing yourself like that, would drive you to walk a different path, but you just couldn't escape the need to protect the pieces of shit you call family."

I flinched. "Don't speak about them that way."

"Why not?" he snapped. "Despite all you do, all you've *done* for them, your brother called you a mad bitch. Your mother called you a whore. They aren't worth allowing Snorri to turn you into a monster to make himself king."

He wasn't wrong. But neither was he right.

"I thought when you saw how your mother is living, you'd turn your back on them," he said. "Yet though I watched you realize she profited from your pain, it changed nothing. I watched you listen to her tell you how time and again she's chosen your brother and herself over you, and again, it changed *nothing*. You refuse to change your fate."

"So you thought to do it for me?" My skin flushed with anger. "Because I'm not the only one with a god's blood in my veins, with the power to make the Norns alter their plans. You can do it too."

"I would tear their plans to shreds if it meant sparing you the fate my mother foresaw," he said. "But I want you to choose to leave, Freya. All I've done is given you the opportunity."

Though I wished he'd told me the whole truth sooner, I still found my anger fading. "I want to say yes, Bjorn. What I saw in Steinunn's magic terrifies me. But if I go, I'm condemning my family to die."

"They condemned themselves."

Turning my mare, I walked a short distance away to stand on the cliffs overlooking the sea. Gulls sailed over the whitecaps, a north wind tugging my hair loose from its braid. It would be so easy to ride down to the shore. To find a merchant vessel from one of the lands far south of here and sail away, never looking back. Never even knowing if Snorri followed through on his threats.

Not knowing would be worse. To have the uncertainty of whether those I loved lived or died. Would happiness even be possible, or would the guilt poison whatever life I built?

"Hlin told my mother that if I possessed only avarice, my words would be curses, but if I possessed altruism, what divine power I might make my own was a fate yet unwoven." I hesitated. "I know there is no way to know what she meant by that, but to me, it means that choosing others before myself will be how I achieve a destiny different from what your mother saw." Turning my head to look at him, my breath caught, because I knew that making this choice meant giving him up. "I have to go back. I can't leave knowing that they will die, because that would mean conceding to the avarice that Hlin warned of."

I held my breath, waiting for Bjorn to react. Waiting for anger and condemnation for my choice. Instead, he exhaled softly. "How is it that the part of you that I hate the most is also the reason I love you?"

Love.

Emotion drowned me, threatening to double me over, and I wanted desperately to tell him that I loved him as well. That I loved him more than I'd ever dreamed was possible.

Except what did that even mean, given that I hadn't chosen him? So instead I said, "If you want nothing more to do with me, I'd understand that. I wouldn't fault you."

Even if it breaks my heart.

"You're mine, Born-in-Fire," he answered, reaching out to take my hand. "And I'm yours, even if only the two of us know it."

I clung to his hand, barely able to breathe. Knowing that if I looked at him I'd crack; instead I stared out at the fjord. In time to see a large drakkar with a blue-striped sail appear around the bend. "Bjorn . . ."

"I see it," he answered, lifting his hand to shield his eyes. "Fuck."

Unease filtered into my chest. "What is it?"

Or who?

"Skade." Bjorn spat in the dirt. "We need to go."

Snorri had mentioned the name Skade while we were in Fjalltindr, but I had no idea who she was. "Is she one of Harald's warriors?"

"His hunter. Who he sends to find those who don't wish to be found." His throat moved as he swallowed. "She's a child of Ullr."

My stomach tightened, for I knew Ullr's children had bows with magical arrows that never missed their target. "Who is she hunting?"

Bjorn turned his head to meet my gaze, the muscles in his jaw so tight they strained against his suntanned skin.

"No," I breathed. "That makes no sense. Everyone thinks that I'm in Grindill."

"There is no other reason for her to be here, Freya. We need to go. Get a head start before she finds our trail."

The fear singing in my blood told me that he was right, except there was only one place to dock a drakkar of that size on this fjord. Selvegr. My home.

Ignoring Bjorn's protests, I dug my heels into my horse's sides, urging the mare into a fast canter. Too fast for the narrow trail, but I didn't care. Every man and woman in Selvegr who could fight had been called to join Snorri at Grindill, which meant the village was undefended. Full of women with children, the elderly, and the infirm. Entirely unaware that a drakkar bristling with Harald's warriors sailed toward them.

"Freya!"

I risked a backward glance at Bjorn, his horse on my heels. "I have to warn them!"

"You won't make it in time!"

He was right. As fast as I was riding, the drakkar had a strong wind at its back. But I had to try. Had to do something.

Through the trees, I watched the drakkar lower its sail, the rowers maneuvering it to the single, empty dock. They'd have been spotted by now, and everyone would be racing to find their children. To grab weapons.

To hide.

"Freya! Stop!"

In my periphery, Bjorn's bigger horse gained ground. I urged my mount for more speed but the mare was spent, and as the trail widened, Bjorn moved alongside me. I tried to widen the distance, but he leaned recklessly far off the side of his horse and caught my reins, pulling both mounts up.

Hissing, I leapt off my horse and broke into a run. Boots hammered the ground as he gave chase, easily catching me by the arm. I fought against him, but Bjorn swept my legs out from underneath me, both of us falling hard.

"Quit hissing like an angry cat and look," he snapped, pinning me to the ground. "They aren't attacking!"

"I can't see anything!" I squirmed, trying to get loose, but Bjorn was infinitely stronger than I was, his hips holding mine against the dirt.

"Listen!"

Instinct demanded that I struggle, for my people needed me, but I forced myself to stillness. The only sound was Bjorn's ragged breathing, the wind, and the waters of the fjord lapping against the shores. No clash of steel. No screams.

Easing off me, Bjorn led me on hands and knees to the edge of a ridge overlooking the water, from which I could clearly see Selvegr and Skade's drakkar tied up to its dock. Some of the warriors had exited the drakkar, but most sat idle, waiting.

"That's Skade." Bjorn pointed, and I made out a woman with crimson hair standing and speaking in earnest to a villager, no weapon in sight. "She's looking for you, not a fight."

"Then why does she have a full raiding party of warriors on her drakkar?"

Bjorn didn't answer for a long moment, then said, "That's a good question."

There was an edge to his voice that made my skin prickle, but when I tore my eyes from Skade to look at him, Bjorn's face was unreadable. "A better question is how do they know we are here at all?"

His brow furrowed.

"The *only* person who knew where we were going was Ylva." My guts twisted. "I was a fool to trust her."

Bjorn gave a sharp shake of his head. "It doesn't make sense. When you accused her of leaving the message with the runes, she denied it and Bodil confirmed she was telling the truth."

"What if Bodil was lying?" The thought hollowed out my core because I'd trusted Bodil. Put my faith in her. To discover that she'd lied to me, conspired with Ylva, with Harald . . .

"That doesn't make any sense," Bjorn argued. "What could Bodil have possibly had to gain from such an alliance? And why would Ylva give you up when she's sacrificed so much to achieve my father's destiny?"

"Because she's lost her nerve for it! You saw her face when your father wished to abandon Halsar in favor of ambushing Harald when he left Fjalltindr. Her distress when we returned to find it burned and her *anger* when your father refused to rebuild. Her *fear* when she listened to Steinunn's song. Ylva wants no more of this, and what better way to put an end to it than to give us both over to Harald?"

"You must have hit your head when I knocked you down," Bjorn snapped. "It makes no sense to hand you over to her enemy. A better answer would be poison in both our cups. Ylva is no ally of Harald's."

"Then who? Because we know there is someone in our midst who is a traitor!"

Before Bjorn could answer, a flurry of motion on Selvegr's docks caught our attention. Skade had returned to her drakkar, and my stomach sank as half the warriors climbed out onto the dock, following the man Skade had been speaking to into the village.

And exiting out the other side.

My skin turned to ice as I realized the direction they were walking, where the man was leading them. "My mother."

Bjorn grimaced. "She might just question her, Freya. It's you Harald has sent her to find, else Selvegr and all its people would be dead or dying."

"Are you certain?" I demanded, my pulse roaring. "You clearly know Skade from your time in Nordeland. If my mother won't help her, are you certain that Skade won't kill her out of spite?"

Bjorn stood, pulling me up with him and then drawing me back to the horses. "Do you honestly think your mother won't tell her every-thing she wishes to know?"

I bit my lip, tears threatening. "That's not what I asked."

"Skade's a killer," Bjorn answered. "But she's loyal to Harald and won't go against his orders."

"Bjorn . . ." Tears trickled down my cheeks because I was the reason Skade was here. I was the reason my mother was in danger. "Will Skade hurt her?"

"I don't know." Bjorn kicked a rock. "This . . . I don't know what he intends, only that if we go after them, we'll be giving him exactly what he wants."

I'd told my mother that I was through with her. *It's time you made your own way in the world.*

A lie, because I refused to abandon her.

Catching my horse's reins, I swung onto the mare's back. "Are you coming with me, or do I need to do this alone?"

Bjorn swung into his own saddle. "Where you go, I go, Born-in-Fire. Even if it's to the gates of Valhalla."

I dug in my heels, taking the lead, for I knew this ground by mem-ory. We swung wide of Selvegr so that those left with the drakkar wouldn't catch sight of us, then down the narrow tracks and game trails that would take us to the rear of my mother's farm. We dismounted, leaving the horses and hurrying through the trees, the hunting skills my father had taught me serving well and Bjorn making almost no sound, despite his size.

"Skade does not miss," he said softly. "Her arrow is no more made of wood than my axe is of steel. The only way to kill her is to catch her unaware, but her instincts are second to none."

"But my magic can block her arrow," I said, tightening my grip on my shield. "Just as it blocks your axe and Thor's lightning."

"Her arrow doesn't travel as a mortal's does," Bjorn answered. "Skade might appear to aim at your face but be aiming at your back. Kill her before she shoots or die where you stand."

Reaching the edge of the tree line, we dropped low, keeping behind brush and scrub as we pressed closer to my family home. My mother stood in the field, grazing goats around her. Birger was on the roof, likely repairing the leak my mother had complained about. I opened my mouth to shout a warning when he abruptly stiffened, and I gasped at the sight of a glowing green brand jutting out the back of his head. It disappeared almost immediately, and Birger fell backward, rolling off the roof to land with a heavy thud.

My mother heard the sound and started, eyes searching, but Birger had fallen out of her line of sight. I moved to rise, to defend her, but Bjorn pulled me down a heartbeat before Skade appeared from the trees on the other side of the clearing.

"Who are you?" my mother demanded, pulling out the seax she wore, the short blade glittering. "Birger! Birger!"

"I am known as Skade," she answered, her voice carrying the accent of Nordeland. The same accent as Bjorn's did. "I am King Harald of Nordeland's warlord."

My mother took a step back, but Skade's warriors were encircling the clearing, leaving nowhere to run. I held my breath as two passed only a few paces from the brush behind which we hid. Which meant there was no chance of us getting close enough to attack Skade before she killed one of us.

Sweat poured down my back, my fingers icy cold where they gripped the handle of my shield and the hilt of my sword. *Please,* I prayed to Hlin, *protect her.*

"You are Kelda. The mother of Freya, Erik's daughter, yes? Also known as Freya Born-in-Fire, child of Hlin?"

My mother didn't answer.

"We know it is so," Skade said. "Your clansman brought us to you."

Traitorous bastard, I wanted to scream, but at the same time, I understood why he'd chosen to help her. He'd smelled the danger and chosen to protect himself and his own.

"Has your daughter come to see you?" Skade asked. "It was her intent."

"Why do you want to know?"

"I don't," Skade answered. "King Harald does. So you'd be well to give me the answers he seeks, else meet the fate of Snorri's man." She smirked. "He died with a fist full of thatch, so I think he is not on his way to Valhalla."

Tell her the truth, I willed my mother. *Tell her what she wants to know so that she leaves you alive.*

My mother hesitated, then said, "She came. Left an hour past."

Next to me, Bjorn's hands tightened around a handful of dirt, his knuckles turning white.

Skade didn't answer, only tilted her head.

"On horseback," my mother swiftly added. "The jarl's son, Bjorn, known as the Firehand, was with her."

"Just the two of them?"

"That I saw," my mother answered. "There could have been more waiting elsewhere. She didn't say where she was going, but I expect back to Grindill. If you hurry, you might catch them."

Good, I silently told my mother even as Bjorn seethed next to me. *Clever thinking.*

Skade nodded slowly, then glanced sideways. "The house is searched, yes?"

"There's no one in there," a man's voice called. "And the hoof tracks in the mud tell the same story. Two horses came and went, heading in the direction of the fjord. Do you wish us to take horses from the village and pursue?"

Skade tilted her head, her eyes distant as though what she saw was not what was before her. "No. I think we have the answers we seek." She inclined her head to my mother. "You have been most helpful."

She turned to walk away, her warriors following her. I slumped, breathing a sigh of relief because there could be no better outcome. My mother was safe. Skade did not intend to pursue. And we knew now with certainty that Harald plotted to try to take me again.

But when Skade reached the tree line on the far side of the clearing, she paused, her voice loud and clear as she said, "Only a cowardly bitch betrays her child." A glowing bow of gold appeared in her hand as she turned, along with an arrow, green from fletching to tip. Before I could move, before I could call to Hlin to protect me, so I could protect my mother, the arrow was loosed.

It flew through the air, punching through my mother's heart.

Bjorn clamped a hand over my mouth to silence my scream as she dropped slowly to the ground, the arrow disappearing from her chest.

"Return to the drakkar," Skade ordered, and she and her men disappeared over the rise, footfalls fading and leaving behind only the wind in the trees and my muffled sobs.

"They're gone," Bjorn said, and I pulled from his arms. Abandoning shield and sword, I raced to my mother. My foot caught on a rock, and I tripped, sprawling on the ground. Sobbing, I crawled onward, reaching her.

She was still breathing.

Gasping, I pressed my hands to the wound in her chest, bending over her. My mother's eyes latched onto me. "Freya?"

"I'm here." Blood flowed around my fingers, soaked the front of her new dress, her cane lying next to her in the grass. "I'm so sorry. That this happened. For the things I said."

But the light was fading from her eyes, her chest stilling beneath my hands. "No!" I screamed. "This wasn't supposed to happen!"

Bjorn was behind me then, pulling me into his arms. "I'm sorry, Freya," he said, and I buried my face in his neck, the force of my sobs making my body ache.

"The things I said to her." I sucked in a mouthful of air, trying to get enough breath. "I didn't mean them. I didn't. She died thinking that I didn't love her."

"To nearly her dying breath, she betrayed her own daughter," he said. "She earned her fate."

"Just because she was a coward doesn't mean she deserved to be murdered!" My fingers dug into his arms, hard enough that it would leave marks, but I didn't care. "I brought this fate upon her. I chose to come here. My decisions led to her death. Everything I do, it always means death."

"This is why you need to go," he said, breath warm against my ear. "Not because you are a bringer of death but because those who *are* seek to use you to achieve their ends."

Like Ylva.

"I'm going to kill her," I hissed, my grief turning to rage. "I'm going to fucking kill that traitorous bitch."

"You have no proof it was Ylva."

"My proof is that it could be no one else! Ylva was at Fjalltindr. She witnessed Snorri declaring his intention to take Grindill. Has the skills to use rune magic. Was the *only* one who knew where we were going."

"None of which is proof! If you kill her on speculation and hearsay, my father will punish you," Bjorn retorted. "Regardless of what she did or did not do, killing Ylva changes nothing. What you need to do is run, Freya. To get yourself out of this mess before you lose any more of yourself!"

"And lose the chance to avenge my mother?" I pulled away from him. "Not just on Ylva, but on Skade? On Harald himself? You more than anyone should understand that the need for vengeance is worth *any* sacrifice."

"It's different." He caught hold of my arms again. "I know exactly who came into my mother's cabin that night with murder in his heart. Saw it with my own eyes. And still, I will give it up for your sake."

He's not going to let you go back, my rage whispered. *He's going to deny you your vengeance.*

"Just as I know exactly who knew we were coming here." I stared into his green eyes, and he recoiled at whatever he saw in mine. "It can be no one but Ylva. Why won't you believe me? Why are you protecting her?"

"I'm protecting *you!*" His fingers tightened. "I'm not letting you do this. Not while you're consumed by this . . . this rage. You need to be yourself to make this decision."

"I am myself."

"Your eyes are red again! Your rage is controlling you!"

You're going to have to elude him, the voice whispered. *Be clever.*

"Fine," I said. "Let us see to my mother and when I've calmed down to your satisfaction, I'll prove to you my choice is the same."

There was unease in Bjorn's expression, but he nodded. On my directions, he carried my mother's body inside the home my father had built and put her on the bed where my life's story had begun, then muttered, "I'll retrieve the horses."

I stared at my mother's body. There were things that needed to be said. Words that needed to be spoken from deep in my heart, but my fury refused to allow them to my lips. Everything seemed tinged with red, a pulse throbbing in my temples that whispered only vengeance. My focus sharpened as I heard hooves against the ground when Bjorn returned, and I abandoned the home to go outside.

Taking my mare's reins from him, I said, "Please burn it."

Bjorn didn't answer, only handed the reins of his own horse to me before muttering Tyr's name, his axe blazing bright. My mare recoiled, and I allowed the animal to draw me back several paces, Bjorn's horse following.

You'll need to be quick.

My heart pounded, sweat slicking my palms as I fastened my shield to my saddle and flipped the reins over my horse's head. Bjorn cast a glance at me, and I nodded, waiting until he pressed his axe to the side of the house, the wood instantly blackening.

I flung myself into the saddle and dug in my heels.

Bjorn's gelding snorted as I hauled on its reins, dragging it along with me.

"Freya!"

My anger faltered at Bjorn's shout, but the dark voice whispered, *He'll stop you if given the chance.* The voice was right. I kicked my horse into a gallop, leading his horse away from my family's farm.

I didn't allow myself to look back.

CHAPTER

32

I abandoned Bjorn's mount just past Selvegr, for the gelding kept trying to bite me, and I knew that I had all the head start I needed. Then I rode my mare as hard as my anger rode me.

Visions of how the confrontation would play out repeated through my head. Of the things I'd say to the lady of Halsar. Of the ways I could kill her. Of the curses I might spit upon her when the deed was done.

A part of me, deep down, knew this wasn't right. Knew that I was allowing the darker half of me to have the sort of control that I might one day come to regret, but it was better than the alternative. Better than remembering the last things I'd said to my mother. Better than watching Skade's arrow punch through her chest. Far better than watching the light go out of her eyes and knowing that it was because of me.

The trail reached the end of the fjord, the northern strait stretching out before me, the water steely blue and covered by whitecaps. I searched for signs of Skade's blue-striped sails but saw nothing other than small fishing vessels on the water as I cut down the coast. Waves crashed against the rocky beach, gulls shrieking overhead as they dived and fought over scraps flung onto the rocks by the water.

I made better time than Bjorn and I had in the darkness coming here, but my mare was still laboring hard by the time I reached the inlet into which the river Torne flowed, the town bearing the same name on the northern banks. The gates were open, and I trotted my mare inside, heading toward the stable. "I need to trade for a fresh horse," I said to the man cleaning out a stall.

He eyed my winded animal and, knowing that I didn't have much time before Bjorn caught up to me, I dug a piece of silver out of my pocket and held it up. "Now."

The man moved swiftly to retrieve a tall gelding, and I dismounted, leaving him to swap the tack from one horse to the other. I dimly watched the people of the town going about their business. Women bargaining in the market. Men loitering in front of the mead hall, cups in hand. Children chasing chickens and goats through the muddy streets. This town supplied Grindill, was vitally connected to it, yet if the battle and change of rule had made an impact on this place, I couldn't see it. Life went on, their cares for putting food on the table and shelter over their children's heads, not for which lord claimed what title in the fortress on the hill.

"I'll take that silver," the man said, snapping me from my thoughts, and I handed the coin over before mounting the gelding.

I followed the road that ran parallel to the river at a fast canter, fording the dozens of small streams that fed into it, my eyes on the cliffs in the distance. I could make out the walls of Grindill, the Torne flowing past the fortress to cascade over in a waterfall fifty feet high. Mist exploded from its base, but I drew no closer to it, the road veering south before beginning the steep climb up the hill to the fortress.

The gelding was breathing hard by the time I reached the top of the slope, but I drove him at a gallop toward the gate. The walls were repaired, warriors walking along the tops of them, and I was swiftly noticed.

And recognized.

"It's Freya!" My name repeated from above as my horse's hooves clattered across the bridge over the moat of stakes, the gate swinging open to admit me. I rode into the open yard before drawing up my gelding, my eyes skipping over the curious stares of those nearby, hunting for my prey.

"Have you lost your mind, girl?"

Ylva's voice filled my ears, and my wrath burned wild and hot as I saw her exit the great hall. Flinging myself off my horse, I stalked toward her.

"This was not the plan," she whispered, holding her skirts out of the mud, her breath coming in rapid pants as though she'd run to intercept me the moment she heard I'd returned. "How am I going to explain why you—"

I swung, my right fist connecting hard enough with her cheek that pain ricocheted up my arm. "You traitorous bitch," I snarled as she fell into the mud. "I'm going to fucking kill you!"

Ylva crawled backward even as shouts of alarm echoed around us. "I betrayed nothing," she gasped. "Everyone thinks you are in your rooms!"

"Is that so?" I pulled my sword and pursued her, satisfaction filling me as she recoiled in terror. "Then how is it that Skade knew exactly where to find me?"

Ylva blanched. "What? No . . . no, Freya, I've no notion of how Harald learned this information, but it was not from me. I swear it!"

"Lies," I hissed. "All this time, it has been you who is conspiring with Harald. To get rid of Bjorn. Now to get rid of me, because you haven't the stomach for war that you thought you did. Except neither Bjorn nor I are dead, but my mother is! Because of *you*!"

I lifted my sword. Readying for a down strike that would take her head from her shoulders, only for a wash of heat to warm my face as my blade was struck and wrenched from my grip.

I stumbled, nearly falling, and as I regained my balance it was to see Bjorn astride his exhausted horse just inside the gate. Screaming with wordless fury that he'd deny me my revenge, I snatched up my sword, anger and grief filling me, to find the blade warped from the impact of his axe on the metal. Ruined, but it would serve well enough.

Ylva screamed, but before I could drive the blade into her heart, someone slammed into my side. I toppled into the mud, more hands than I could count pinning me down, shouts filling my ears.

"What is going on?" Snorri roared, and I choked around a mouthful of mud and horse shit, "She's a traitor!"

Hands jerked me upright and I coughed and spat, trying to clear away the foulness.

"You told me Freya was in her rooms seeking guidance from the gods." Snorri leveled a finger at Ylva. "Yet she just came through the gate on horseback."

"She needed to see her mother." Ylva climbed to her feet, aided by Ragnar. "Wanted to learn what she could about Hlin so—"

"She told Harald where we were," I screamed. "And my mother is dead because of it!"

"I did no such thing!"

All I could see was red, because even now she denied it. "Then who, Ylva? We know there is a traitor in our midst. One who was in Fjalltindr. One who betrayed Snorri's plans in Halsar. One who betrayed that I was going to see my mother. You were the *only* one present all three times, the only one with the magic, the only one with the knowledge!"

"It was not me!" Ylva shrieked, only Ragnar's grip on her keeping the woman from attacking me. "Bodil vouched for the truth of my words in Halsar!"

"Then she lied!"

"Enough!" Snorri stepped between us. "I will hear you two in private, not listen to you screech like two fishwives in a market!"

"That's because she is a fishwife!"

I tried to get loose of the men holding me, and when I couldn't, I spat at her.

"Bring them into the great hall," Snorri snapped, then looked to

Bjorn, who still stood at the gate. "You will come as well, as it would seem you are complicit."

Men dragged me through the muddy streets and into the great hall, forcing me down at a bench. Ragnar escorted Ylva in like a queen and helped her to sit at the far end before leaving. Snorri stood between us, while Bjorn sat at another table, face expressionless. Not unexpectedly, it was to him that Snorri turned first. "Explain why you took my shield maiden out of my fortress on some fool's errand, boy."

Bjorn lifted one shoulder. "She wished to see her mother to learn more of Hlin. Ylva agreed that you would not allow such a meeting to occur and facilitated the opportunity for Freya to leave Grindill unaware. We had just left her mother's farm when Skade came with a ship full of men, having been informed that Freya would be there. She killed Freya's mother and then left."

Snorri's jaw worked back and forth, and slowly he turned on Ylva to regard her. A thrill ran through me that he was finally seeing the truth.

Ylva slid off the bench to her knees, shaking her head. "I did not betray you, my love. You know that I am loyal. Through everything, I have been loyal."

Snorri's eyes swung to me. "Justify your accusations."

"In Fjalltindr, when I worried about how long Ylva and Bjorn were gone, I left to try to find help," I said. "I saw Harald speaking with someone in the Hall of the Gods, conspiring to protect her child. Someone Harald believed you trusted, Snorri. Then a hooded woman attempted to enter our hall but was repelled by our wards."

"Why would I be repelled by my own wards?" Ylva snapped. "Besides, I was with Bodil. You know this!"

Snorri ignored her, waving at me to continue.

"In Halsar when the specter led me into the forest, it was a hooded woman who carved the runes into the tree with the vision of your speech."

"It was not me! Bodil vouched for the truth of my words when this little bitch accused me the first time," Ylva shouted.

"Bodil is dead and cannot be asked a second time," Snorri answered, refusing to look at her, his eyes locked on mine.

"Then fetch Steinunn," I said. "Her songs only show the truth."

"She left last night."

Frustration caused my hands to ball into fists. "Ylva was the only one who knew Bjorn and I intended to visit my mother." Tears ran down my cheeks. "She was the only one, and my mother is dead because of her actions. I demand vengeance."

Silence stretched, and I didn't dare speak. Barely dared to breathe.

"I will not condemn you without trial," Snorri finally said, and I saw his hands were fists, trembling as though he were containing violence by a thread. "But know that Freya's accusations are compelling."

Ylva's face crumpled. "My love, you know—"

Her pleas were interrupted by the bellow of a horn, the noise causing me to twitch in alarm. Especially when it sounded again.

A warning.

Seconds later, one of Snorri's warriors exploded through the door. "Nordeland forces have landed in Torne," he gasped out. "Dozens and dozens of ships. They are demanding that we give them the shield maiden."

My stomach dropped, for though we'd known this moment would come, I didn't think anyone believed it would be so soon.

Ylva pressed a hand to her mouth. "We need to flee!"

"Was this your plan?" Snorri screamed at her. "Is your desire to rebuild Halsar so strong you allied yourself with my greatest enemy?"

"I did not betray you," Ylva sobbed. "I swear on the gods, I am loyal. But we must protect our people, Snorri. Our allies have not arrived, so we cannot hope to hold against Harald. We must retreat!"

"I didn't win this fortress with blood just to concede it at the first threat against us!" Snorri snarled, then rounded on the messenger. "Abandon Torne! Draw all the men into the fortress and make ready."

An explosion of thunder split the air, the ground shuddering, and outside, people screamed.

"Tora is with him," Bjorn said. "And most certainly Skade will be as well. Ylva is right—this is not a battle you can win. We need to run."

Snorri struck out, his fist catching Bjorn in the jaw and sending him stumbling back a step. "You think this is how you earn a place in Valhalla, boy? With cowardice? By running in the face of a fight?"

"Recognizing a losing battle is not cowardice," Bjorn spat back, his hands balling into fists. "I think Odin would rather seat men at his table who know how to pick their battles so they might have victory than those who race toward defeat!"

"It was the Allfather himself who saw Freya's greatness!" Snorri screamed. I flinched at his vehemence, his fanaticism, but Bjorn stood his ground as his father shouted, "It was Odin who told your own mother what Freya would allow me to achieve, and yet you fight the fate he saw for her at every turn. You think that I haven't noticed? You think it doesn't weigh upon my mind that my own son allows fear to guide his steps, and not ambition?"

"Fear has nothing to do with it," Bjorn shouted back, and I tensed at the fury in his eyes. At the hatred that boiled beneath it, for I'd never seen that in him before. "It's that I don't believe you control Freya's fate!"

Color drained from Snorri's face, then in a rapid motion he drew his sword and pressed the tip to Bjorn's throat. I yanked out my own weapon, but then froze as a trickle of blood ran down Bjorn's skin, knowing that any action on my part might see him killed.

"Why?" Snorri demanded between his teeth. "Because you think it should be *you* who controls her fate?" Before Bjorn could answer, he added, "You think I'm blind? You think that I don't know lust when I see it? I tolerated you coveting *my wife* because I believed you loyal. But now I see that you care more about ensuring *my wife* remains available for satisfying your lusts than you do about her achieving her destiny."

My hands turned to ice, and from the corner of my eye I saw Ylva clench her teeth and shake her head, this clearly no revelation to her.

We'd fooled no one, and if we survived this battle, it would be to face the consequences of our actions.

Bjorn didn't answer, as he was already moving. In a flash, he'd slammed his father's blade away from his throat, his axe flaring to life as he drove Snorri backward across the room. "Know that you are alive only because I swore an oath not to satisfy *my own desires,*" he snarled. "But do not think that the gods will allow you to go unpunished, and there are fates far worse than death for men like you."

"Empty threats." Snorri spat on the ground. "Either kill me now or get out of my sight, because I'll not name a coward my son."

My heart fractured, because I'd done this. I'd destroyed Bjorn's life, torn him away from his family, and ruined his reputation all because I'd wanted what couldn't be mine. *Kill Snorri and you can have whatever you want,* the dark voice whispered inside my head and my hand tightened on my sword hilt.

I ground my teeth, trying to force myself to draw the blade, to do what Bjorn would not, or could not, but my hand wouldn't obey.

Snorri laughed. "You swore your own oaths, Freya, so it seems both my fate and life are safe from you."

Thunder boomed, closer this time, and Ylva scrubbed away tears even as she snapped, "Enough. There is no time for this. We must prepare to fight Harald or flee while we can."

"I'll not fight for you." The words came out without thought. "I'm leaving, so that there will be no reason for there to be a battle at all. Let you all dedicate yourselves to hunting me down, but know that I will not fight for you, or for anyone else." I looked to Bjorn, and he nodded, reaching for my arm. "We're leaving."

Snorri said nothing, only watched as we left the room.

"We're going to have to ride hard," Bjorn said once we were outside. "We need to get out of Skaland, out of the dominion of our gods to a place where they hold no power."

I started to nod, then drew up short at the sight of my brother on his knees, Ragnar behind him with a knife to his throat.

"Freya!" Geir's eyes widened at the sight of me. "They took her. When you came back, they took Ingrid. I don't know where she is!"

Slowly, I turned around to find Snorri standing with his arms crossed. "The stakes are the same as they've always been, Freya. By all means, walk out that gate with your lover, but the ghosts of your family will haunt you all the rest of your life."

A shudder ran through me. "I *hate* you! How the gods foresee you as king of Skaland is a mystery to me, because you are a monster to whom no one will willingly bend the knee!"

He snorted. "This is Skaland, girl. What does *willingness* matter? Our people rule with steel and fear, and those who swear oaths do so because they know that same strength will be turned upon their enemies. That the *monsters* will keep them safe. For all your power, Freya, you are little more than a girl-child ruled by impulse and emotion. The gods chose me because you need to be controlled. To be wielded like a weapon, not left to sow chaos. But it seems you need more proof of that before you'll see reason."

"Call his bluff," Bjorn said under his breath. "If he kills them, he'll no longer have leverage over you. He won't do it."

Geir and Ingrid chose this, the voice whispered from the depths of my mind. *They've earned this fate. Why sacrifice your own destiny to protect them from it?*

I gave a sharp shake of my head to silence it, even though I knew it was part of me that had whispered the words. Staying would have a price. Leaving would have a price. Indecision wracked my body, threatening to tear me apart, because I didn't know what to do. Didn't see a way forward. So I took a step backward in the direction of the gate.

"Freya," Geir pleaded, his eyes full of panic. "Please! Ingrid . . . she's pregnant!"

I froze.

"I might not deserve your protection," my brother said, tears running down his cheeks, "but the baby does. Please don't abandon your own flesh and blood."

My brother had his failings, but duplicity was not one of them. I had prayed they would be granted children, but as always, the gods gave, then took away in the next breath.

"Freya, if we are to leave, it must be now," Bjorn said. "The Nordelanders are nearly upon us!"

I didn't know what to do, and the weight of all the fates entwined with mine pressed down and down.

Remember who you are.

"I'll stay." The words croaked from my lips. "I'll fight."

"It is your destiny," Snorri said, then shouted, "To the ramparts!"

I stood staring at the mud for a long moment, then lifted my head to meet Bjorn's gaze. "You should go while you can."

Bjorn lifted a hand, his fingers curving around my face as he bent down and kissed me. "Never. I will stay at your side, whether in life or as we walk through the gates of Valhalla. I swear it."

"They're here!" voices shouted from atop the walls, and my stomach clenched because for all I'd agreed to stay and fight, I did not see how we could hope to win.

"To the ramparts! To the ramparts!"

The urgency and fear in the voices of my people sent a jolt through my veins, and I broke into a run, climbing to the battlements. The sight stole the breath from my chest.

Stretched out before the gates and rapidly encircling the fortress were the armies of Nordeland. Warriors in thick leather and mail, all armed to the teeth, shields held at the ready. And before them waited a familiar form.

King Harald, flanked on one side by Skade and the other by Tora, who was battered and bruised, the hair on the left side of her head burned away. A sickening suspicion filled my stomach at the sight of her injuries. Snorri's warriors had never found the body of the child of Thor who'd killed Bodil, and had assumed it had been incinerated in the blast. But Tora's burns suggested an alternative that made my anger rise, and I muttered, "Harald was allied with Gnut."

Snorri cursed and spat over the ramparts, seeming to have made the same connection.

Keeping out of range of Snorri's archers, Harald's eyes locked on mine. He slowly withdrew a length of white fabric from his belt and, with utter fearlessness, approached the deep trenches surrounding the fortress.

"Such a shame to meet again under these circumstances, Freya," he shouted upward, the wind catching and pulling at his golden-brown hair. "But for the sake of my kingdom, I could not stand by and watch you continue down this path. Surrender yourself to me, and you have my word that I'll take my army, get back on our ships, and return to Nordeland."

"And why should I believe that?" I shouted back to him. "You are the one who has brought an army onto our lands, the one who allied with our enemies. You are the one who offers threats!"

"What choice did I have?" His chest rose and fell with a sigh. "I'd hoped to avert the future Saga saw—the future Saga foretold to her own son—in ways other than war, but my wishes have not come to pass. I cannot allow you, under the guidance of *King Snorri,* to bring death to my lands, so here I stand."

"That is not what Saga foretold!" Snorri roared. "Which is why you killed her for it!"

"We both know it wasn't me who brought violence to Saga's door," Harald answered, and next to me Bjorn shifted his weight. "That's a lie you've used to justify your intentions to make war upon Nordeland."

Snorri lunged against the wooden balustrades, seemingly ready to hurl himself off to attack Harald man-to-man. "Liar! You killed Saga and then stole my son!"

I risked a sideways glance at Bjorn, who was the only one who knew with certainty which man was telling the truth and which man was a liar performing for his army, but he was staring forward, hands gripped tight on the balustrade.

"We can stand here shouting accusations at each other all day,"

Harald said, rocking on his heels. "But it changes nothing. From your own lips at Fjalltindr, you intend to use Freya to attack Nordeland, and I cannot allow that to happen. So either give her to me, or we will battle over her here and now, allowing the gods to choose the victor."

"The gods have already foreseen my victory," Snorri shouted, "but if you need proof, you shall have it." He looked sideways, his eyes meeting mine. "Shield wall."

My fingers were numb, and my stomach twisted into knots as I fixed my eyes on Tora, who'd stepped close to Harald's side. Memory of my last battle with her filled my mind's eye. Visions of how bolts of lightning had torn into flesh and earth, rending both asunder. How lightning had exploded through Bodil's chest. Yes, I'd managed to repel a bolt and stopped her, but what were the chances of managing such a feat again?

"Shield wall!" Snorri shouted, then slammed his sword against his shield. "Shield wall!" The warriors around us took up the refrain, hammering their weapons against their shields, the noise growing louder and louder until I could barely hear myself think.

Shield wall.

Sheathing my warped sword, I placed my hands on the balustrade, watching as lightning crackled between Tora's raised palms. "Hlin," I whispered. "Protect us."

Magic surged through me, flowing out of my fingers and onto the wall, spreading left and right with blinding speed until it encircled the fortress with glowing light.

"It's not too late, Freya," Harald shouted. "No one need die today. All it takes is you deciding to change your fate."

I turned my head enough to see behind me. Geir was still on his knees, Ragnar's blade at his throat. And Ingrid . . . the child . . . if I didn't at least try to fight off Harald, I fully believed whoever had her would kill her for spite.

There was no path through this. No choice that wouldn't cause death. "Bjorn . . ." I trailed off because I couldn't ask him what I should do. Couldn't put the burden of this on his shoulders when it was mine to carry. But I could ask for the truth. "Which one of them killed her?"

His throat moved as he swallowed. "Neither of them killed her, Freya."

"But you said you wanted vengeance against the man who harmed her?" I stared at him. "Against Harald?"

With visible effort, he forced himself to meet my gaze. "I do. But neither of them killed her."

A chill ran through me as understanding sank into my bones. Bjorn had a scar on his shoulder from the first time he'd called Tyr's flame—from setting a cabin on fire. Saga had *burned* alive.

"My vengeance is my own, Born-in-Fire," Bjorn said. "Do not base your choices upon it."

I clenched my teeth because that only made this harder. I wanted there to be a right path, for then no matter what happened, I could walk it without regret, yet it seemed a fate that would forever be denied to me.

Murmurs of dismay drew my eyes back to the army before me. Civilians from Torne were shoved forward by Harald's men so that they stood between Tora and the glowing wall of my magic. Some stood frozen, but many raced toward the gate, begging to be let in. Snorri gave a slight shake of his head. "Hold steady."

"This is your last chance to end this peacefully," Harald shouted. "Lower your shield and surrender yourself, Freya. End this before anyone dies."

"It's a trick," Snorri snarled at me. "The moment you lower your guard, he'll take you and then slaughter us all."

"I swear that if you come down, my army will leave these shores, Freya!" Harald walked through the sea of sharpened stakes in the trenches, stopping close enough to touch my magic. Close enough for any of the archers to shoot, but he still held the white fabric, and honor stayed their hands. That, or the fact that the true threat stood out of reach, lightning crackling between her palms. "Come down," he said. "There need not be war today."

I quivered, sweat soaking the hair at my temples, though I felt cold. What was the answer? What was the right path? What should I do? Turning my back on my mother had led to her death. Could I do the same to Geir and Ingrid?

No.

Except if I didn't, all the innocent people screaming to be allowed in the gates, screaming for the protection of my magic, would die by Tora's lightning just as Bodil had. And how many more after that? How long could I keep these walls protected until exhaustion caused me to falter? Because the moment it did, Tora would blast through the walls, and it would be over.

You have to try. It's who you are.

I shook my head sharply, then shouted, "I am a Skalander. I'll die fighting before I concede to Nordeland!"

A roar of cheers rose up from my people, but Harald only gave a disgusted shake of his head.

"If you choose to kill these people, their blood is on your hands," I shouted at his back as he retreated. King Harald didn't respond, only nodded once as he passed Tora, then joined his army, which retreated slightly down the slope.

The child of Thor met my gaze a heartbeat before lightning exploded from her palms. Except it wasn't the people below she aimed her power at, but rather my magic. The lightning struck my shield and rebounded, splintering into a dozen jagged arcs that went in every direction. The crack of thunder split my ears, but it was not enough to deafen me of the screams that filtered upward.

I looked down, seeing dozens of people on their backs many paces away from the wall, where my magic had flung them as it repelled Tora's lightning. They clambered to their feet, racing again to the gate, screaming to be allowed sanctuary.

Tora lifted her palms, and another bolt arced toward my shield, the civilians again flung backward, more violently this time. I howled wordlessly as their bodies were tossed every which way, some landing on stakes in the trenches. The thunder was a short-lived mercy, for the moment it ceased its roll, the screams of agony and fear filled the void.

"Don't touch it," I shrieked at them. "Don't touch the walls! Stay down!"

Some listened and drew away from the walls, while others who either didn't hear or were too terrified to understand again tried to reach the gate.

Lightning flashed, rebounding off my magic, splintering into arcs as it did. To my horror, it struck some of those who'd moved away. They dropped to the ground, smoke rising from their bodies, and I screamed and screamed because there was no escape for them. No way to protect them as bolt after bolt of lightning shattered against my magic, only for its glowing fragments to find victims.

"Stop!" I howled, the stink of charred flesh filling my nose. "Please!"

Tora didn't stop. Only stood out of reach of the desperate attempts of Snorri's archers to take her down, watching impassively as her magic broke against mine.

Bjorn's words echoed in my head. *She told me the shield maiden would unite Skaland, but that tens of thousands would be left dead in your wake. That you'd walk upon the ground like a plague, pitting friend against friend, brother against brother, and that all would fear you.*

Bjorn's mother had been right in her fears. Right to instill them within him, for before me was the future that Odin had shown her. Skalanders, dead and dying because of me. Dead and dying because men of power wanted to possess me. To use me. And there was no path I could take to stop it.

Except for one.

A bolt of Tora's lightning struck, and the second it did, I withdrew my magic from the wall. From the corner of my vision, I saw Bjorn reaching for me, but for once I was quicker than he was.

Slinging my body over the edge of the wall, I jumped.

The ground raced up to meet me, my heels slamming into the embankment hard enough to rattle my spine. Then I was rolling. I ground my teeth as I somersaulted into the trench, slamming against corpses and stakes as I fell. My body screamed with pain, but I ignored it and scrambled to my feet.

"Freya!"

Bjorn's shout filled my ears, but I didn't look back. Only clambered to my feet and ran.

Tora's face was filled with shock, and she cast a backward glance at Harald. "Catch her," he shouted.

The taller woman broke into a sprint, but I had a head start.

You can do this, I told myself, my eyes fixed on where the river poured over the cliff, the thunder of the falls growing louder with each pounding step I took. *You can end this.*

Tears poured down my cheeks, fear constricting my chest. *If they don't have something to fight over, they'll stop. No one else has to die.*

"Freya!"

Bjorn's voice. He was chasing me, trying to stop me. But I couldn't let him.

Forgive me.

I reached the river, a stitch forming in my side as I sprinted down the bank. The waterfall loomed ahead, rocks slick from the mist.

Saga had seen a future, but I was unfated. I could change the course of my destiny and, in doing so, change the fates of so many others. Could save them from falling beneath axe and sword.

"Be brave," I whispered, my hand going to the hilt of my sword, hoping that my sacrifice would earn me a place in Valhalla as I gathered myself to leap, knowing that the rocks at the base of the falls would make it quick.

The specter appeared in front of me.

I skidded to a stop as it held up its hand, embers and smoke drifting from it. Then fingers latched onto my wrist, yanking me away from the edge.

I shrieked, certain that it was Tora. Certain that I'd failed; but the chest I was dragged against was Bjorn's. "Where you go, I go," he said, hauling me back upstream. "And I'm not letting you go to Valhalla without me at your side."

"It's the only way," I pleaded, trying to get out of his grip. "I need to change my fate. I need to save my people."

"And you will." His axe appeared in his hand as he pulled me farther upstream, his eyes on Tora, who kept pace with us, her expression wary. Beyond, Harald and his men raced closer even as Snorri's warriors poured out of the gates, a battle soon to be upon us.

My efforts would be for nothing.

"How do you think this will work, Bjorn?" Tora shouted. "You think you'll just escape with her? Every king and jarl within a thousand miles will be hunting for you. It will never end. *Never.*"

"Then let us end it here and now, with weapons in hand," Bjorn said, and taking two quick steps, he heaved his axe.

Tora's eyes widened as the flaming weapon flipped end-over-end. She had no shield. Nothing to block it. Nothing but magic.

Lightning crackled from her hands, arcing toward the axe.

Only for the weapon to disappear right as Bjorn caught hold of my waist and pulled me backward. I caught a glimpse of the lightning striking the ground where we'd stood, dirt and rock exploding in all directions with a clap of thunder before water closed over my head.

I kicked my way to the surface, the rapids whipping me this way and that. Waves splashed me in the face as I gasped in a breath, searching for Bjorn, panic filling my veins when I didn't see him. "Bjorn!"

What if he'd hit his head?

What if he'd been dragged under?

"Bjorn!" I screamed his name, but my voice was drowned out by thunder. For a heartbeat, I thought it was Tora attacking us from the bank with her lightning, but then I realized.

The falls.

Sucking in a breath, I dropped under the surface, searching. It was all froth and bubbles, my fingers finding nothing as I reached around me. Kicking back up, I drew in another breath, ready to try again.

But hands caught hold of my shoulders.

I gasped, twisting my head. Only to find Bjorn behind me. His hair was plastered to his face by water, but otherwise he seemed unhurt.

"We need to get to the bank!" I screamed. "We'll die if we go over the falls!"

"Deep breath, Born-in-Fire." His grin was wild. "And trust Hlin to protect you."

"What?" I shrieked, realizing that he was kicking us to the center of the river. Realizing he intended for us to go over.

And then we dropped.

CHAPTER

33

My stomach rushed to my throat, my eyes going down, down, down to the deadly froth of water and rocks. A scream rose but as it tore from my lips, it was Hlin's name that came forth.

Magic flooded from my fingertips, first covering Bjorn and then my own body with silver light. A heartbeat later, we struck.

Even with Hlin's protection, the impact drove the air from my lungs. And there was nothing to fill them as we rose up, then were slammed down into the riverbed again, the water holding us in its perpetual churn. Spinning us around and around until I didn't know which way was up. My elbows struck rock but instead of the water dragging me upward in its inescapable cycle, Bjorn tightened his grip on me, pulling me along the riverbed.

I needed to breathe.

Desperate, I fought his hold. I needed to reach the surface. Needed a mouthful of air even if it meant the falls dragging me back under a second later.

Bjorn pinned my arms to my ribs, dragging me along the river floor. My eyes dimmed, the pain in my chest demanding *air air air.*

Then I was surging upward.

Bjorn lifted me above the surface, and I gasped in a precious mouthful as the river tore us downstream and around a bend.

"Get to the bank!" Bjorn shouted. "Swim, Freya!"

Kicking hard, I kept my eyes on the edge of the river, fighting my way through the current. Rocks banged against my legs, bruising and scraping my flesh. I ignored the pain and swam. Finally, coughing and spluttering, I dragged myself onto the bank of the river, every inch of me aching. Only when I was able to breathe again did I round on Bjorn, who was on his hands and knees hacking up half the river. "Have you lost your mind?"

He rolled onto his back, staring at the sky, strands of his dark hair plastered against his face. "Says the woman who tried to throw herself off a cliff."

My stomach tightened. "I was trying to stop the battle. I was trying to take away their reason to fight."

"I know what you were trying to do," he answered. "And it is done."

Bjorn turned his head to meet my stare. "Everyone saw Tora's lightning fling us into the water, Freya. Watched us go over a waterfall too high for anyone to survive. They think we're dead." A strained grin worked its way onto his face. "But we're not."

No, we were not.

Bjorn caught hold of my arms, pulling me on top of him. The heat of his body was welcome after the freezing river, but I forced myself to focus as he said, "*Everyone* believes we're dead, Freya, and no one fights to possess the dead. We can leave Skaland without consequence, because Snorri won't punish Geir or Ingrid for you falling in battle. No one will come hunting for us. We can choose where we go and what we do, and no one, not even the gods, can stop us, because we are the unfated. We make our own destiny. Together."

Together.

My heart skipped, then sped, because this was a future I'd never allowed myself to imagine.

A life with Bjorn, nothing standing between us and no one controlling us. We could live without others trying to use us to further their own ends. Bjorn smiled, and lifting a hand, he tucked a sodden braid behind my ear. "You will have everything I have the power to give, Freya. I swear it."

Twin tears dripped down my cheeks, splashing against his chest. "But what about avenging your mother?"

What about avenging mine?

A flicker of pain crossed through his eyes, and Bjorn squeezed them shut. But as he reopened them, he said, "No oath is worth your life. No amount of vengeance is worth your happiness. I'll let the past burn to ash, Freya, because you are my present. My future. My destiny." He lifted his other hand to cup my face. "I love you."

And I loved him.

Loved him in a way that defied reason, words not enough to convey the emotion that burned in my heart. A sob tore from my lips and I buried my face in his neck, inhaling him. Drinking him in because he was mine. And we'd never be parted.

"We need to go." His fingers tangled in my hair. "They'll break off fighting to search the riverbanks, and there can be no sign we ever escaped the churn of the falls."

Wiping at my face, I climbed to my feet. Bjorn kept a grip on my hand as he kicked water onto the mud to hide the marks left by our bodies, then led me downstream, our feet splashing in the shallow water. Only once did I look back, my stomach flipping at the sight of the enormous falls, mist rising from the base. He'd willingly taken that plunge, trusted my magic would save us, believed we were strong enough to survive it.

All to save me.

Of their own accord, my eyes focused beyond the falls to the smoke rising above the clifftops. But no lightning flickered, no thunder boomed.

"Harald came for *you,* not to take Grindill," Bjorn said. "He'll abandon the fight to search for us."

"Are you certain?"

"Yes. Don't forget that I know him well."

Tension receded from my shoulders. It was over. It was done.

"This way," he said, gesturing up a narrow stream that flowed into the river. "We'll be there before nightfall."

"Where?" I asked, relishing the feel of my hand in his. Never wanting to let him go.

Bjorn only smiled. "You'll see."

We walked upstream for hours, the water growing progressively warmer until what flowed over my feet was the temperature of a bath. We spoke little, Bjorn casting the occasional glance skyward where the sun crawled toward dusk. We passed the ruins of a burned-out cabin, the blackened wood being slowly consumed by time and moss. "That was the home where I lived with my mother," he said. "I haven't been here since the night it burned."

I bit my lip, then asked, "What happened?"

He stopped in his tracks, staring at the ruins in silence for long enough that I thought he might not tell me. Then Bjorn said, "We lived here alone. As far away from people as she could have it."

"Why?" I asked, my pulse thrumming with anticipation, because Bjorn never spoke of his mother.

"Knowing the future is a burden," he answered, "for it is often full of pain and heartache and loss. Being around people is what causes"—he winced—"caused her gift to show her the future, so she avoided it when possible. Which meant it was just her and me most days."

"Your father didn't visit?"

Bjorn's jaw tightened. "Only when he wished answers from her. My existence was the source of a great deal of conflict between Ylva and him, so he never brought me to Halsar."

I hesitated, then asked, "Did they not suspect you had god's blood?"

"My mother knew." He swallowed. "She forbade me to speak Tyr's name. One of my earliest memories is of her telling me that to do so would set me on the path to losing those I loved to fire and ash." He shook his head. "She painted these visions in my head of people screaming, people dying, and everything was always burning."

It was hard to hear that. Not only because she'd been right, but in the attempt to change the fate she'd foreseen for him, Saga had filled her child's head with nightmares that I suspected remained even now.

"I was asleep one night," he continued. "My mother shook me awake and told me to hide, pushing me under some blankets in a chest. Moments later, I heard a man's voice. Heard him making demands of her. Heard her refusing. Then she screamed." His throat bobbed as he swallowed hard. "I knew he was hurting her, and though I was afraid, I got out of the chest. I don't remember saying Tyr's name, but I must have because a burning axe was suddenly in my hand. I panicked and dropped it, and within seconds the cabin was ablaze. My mother was screaming and struggling with the man, the air so thick with smoke I could barely breathe. Could barely see. And there was no way out."

My palms slickened with sweat, and I stared at the burned ruins with new horror.

"Out of desperation, I picked up the axe again to try to help her, but the roof collapsed and a beam struck me. The last thing I remember is my mother screaming, and then when I woke again, it was to find myself in Nordeland."

As the prisoner of his mother's murderer. "I'm so sorry, Bjorn."

He gave an abrupt roll of his shoulders, then motioned up the stream. "We should keep moving."

As the light faded, we reached the source of the warm water. The black mouth of a cave yawned before us, the stream flowing over and through a roughly constructed dam of rocks.

Bjorn led me out onto the banks, ducking into the cave opening before muttering Tyr's name, his axe flaring to life in his free hand and illuminating the darkness. A gasp pulled from my lips as a large steaming pool was revealed, almost the entirety of the cave flooded. Against one wall was a pile of supplies, as well as char marks on the stone floor in the shape of an axe.

"You've been here before?" I bent down to touch the water, which was blissfully hot.

"When I want time alone, I come to this cavern. My mother brought me here often when I was a child, because I was always filthy." He gestured to the dam. "She built this."

Not for the first time, I was struck at how vividly he remembered his mother despite her having died when he was a boy. Like her every word had imprinted on his soul.

And he was abandoning his quest to avenge her. Was leaving with me what he truly wanted? Or was he only leaving to save my life?

"Bjorn . . ." I trailed off, afraid to ask, because what I so desperately wanted was within my grasp and I didn't want to ruin it by making him question himself. Except I knew that the questions would come, and it was better now than later. "I don't want you to regret making this choice."

Didn't want him to regret choosing me.

"Freya . . ."

I went to the water's edge, watching the steam eddy and swirl without really seeing it. Instead, visions of our future filled my head, and in them I saw Bjorn growing bitter and angry at having been denied his destiny, endless arguments and nights spent with our backs turned, cold empty space between us. My eyes stung, the grief that rose in my chest as real as if my visions were reality.

The scuff of boot on rock and the swirl of steam told me that he'd come up behind me. His arms wrapped around my waist, pulling me against his chest, his chin brushing my temple. "There is no future where I would regret choosing you."

I sucked in a ragged breath, but it felt like no air reached my lungs, my heart a riot in my chest as my emotions warred within it.

"I wish I'd realized it sooner." His breath caught and he swallowed hard, his struggle to say what he wanted to say making me want to hear it all the more. "For nearly all my life, revenge for what was done to my mother was all that mattered to me. It consumed my every waking breath and I refused to allow anything else to matter. Then the most fierce and beautiful woman I've ever laid eyes on hit me in the face with a fish and proceeded to wind her way into my heart. To make me want a life ruled by something deeper than hate."

My mouth curved into a smile, but my heart ached to hear him put voice to what I'd always sensed: the discontent simmering beneath quips and quick smiles, the tension in him that never seemed to ease.

He turned me in his arms, one hand rising to tangle in my mess of braids. "I used to dream only of fire and ash," he whispered, running a thumb over my cheek as I lifted my face to meet his gaze. "Now when I close my eyes, all I see is your face."

Tears drenched my cheeks because hearing those words was *my* dream. Was what my mind had created in the dark hours where I'd allowed it to drift into fantasies that I thought the gods and fate and circumstance would never let me have. It had always been him.

"I love you, Bjorn," I whispered. "And the only future I wish for is the one with you by my side."

He let out a shaky breath, tension seeping out of him in a rush, then his mouth was on mine.

I gasped, catching hold of his neck so that I didn't fall backward, but he'd already taken hold of me. Lifting me even as he kissed me, tongue tasting mine and sending bolts of pleasure down to my already throbbing core. I wrapped my legs around his waist, rubbing myself against him, a moan escaping me as his arm tightened around my hips, dragging me closer.

But not close enough.

I wanted to feel his skin against mine, yet we both still wore sodden clothing and mail. "Off," I said between kisses, straightening my legs to slide down his body. "I want it all off."

And lest he miss my meaning, I caught hold of my mail and lifted it over my head, tossing it aside, the tunic and undershirt I wore beneath swiftly following, baring my peaked breasts.

Bjorn growled, his eyes dark as he dropped to his knees, catching the tip of one of my breasts in his mouth. I moaned as he sucked it deep, teeth nipping to the point I couldn't tell whether it was pleasure or pain, only that my thighs were slick with the need for more.

Not just more of his hands and mouth on me, but mine on him. I wanted to taste that taut tattooed skin, to dig my nails into the hard curve of his muscles, to stroke my palm over his thick cock.

So I pushed him back, stepping down into the pool, the heat of the water stinging my skin as I backed deeper. "It's hot," I murmured, reaching down to remove one shoe and then the other, tossing them past Bjorn even as I held him in place with my gaze.

As I took a step deeper, the water rose to just above my hip bones. I unlaced my trousers, pulled them off, and sent them flying onto the bank with a wet slap. Then I leaned backward and pushed with my toes, sending myself floating to the far side of the pool, feeling his eyes on my body. Feeling his desire, the sensation making my sex throb almost painfully with the need to be touched. To be filled. Resting my elbows on a ledge at the far end of the pool, I said, "Coming in?"

Bjorn didn't answer, and backlit as he was by the burning flame of his axe, I couldn't see his face. But my answer came as he pulled off his mail, tossing it aside, shirt and boots following. He was all hard lines and thick muscle, shoulders broad and waist tapered, and I held my breath as he slowly unbuckled his belt, anticipation making me clench my thighs together.

He caught his thumbs in the waist of his soaked trousers, dragging them down. My breath caught—

And his axe extinguished, plunging the cave into darkness.

"You arsehole," I snarled, hearing both Bjorn's dark laugh and the splash of water as he entered the pool, ripples moving ahead of him to brush my breasts. "I'm starting to question whether you have something to hide. Or rather, a *lack* of something."

"We both know *that* isn't the case, Born-in-Fire." His chuckle was closer this time. "Besides, they say anticipation makes all pleasures sweeter."

"The gods spare me from the ego that comes with a big—" I gasped as his hands caught my waist, pulling me close, the part in question pressing against my stomach.

His teeth caught at my earlobe. "You were saying . . ."

As though I could remember words as his tongue trailed up the rim of my ear, his cock rubbing against my sex as the current pushed against us. I tilted my head, whimpering as he licked my throat and bit just above my pulse, his fingertips trailing down the inside of my arm with featherlight touches that made me see sparks in the darkness.

But I wanted to see more.

Capturing Bjorn's lips, I kissed him hard, then bit at his bottom lip until he groaned before pulling back to whisper, "Hlin."

Magic flowed into me, and I pushed it out of the fingers of my left hand. The silver light illuminated Bjorn's skin as I traced a finger down the hard muscles of his shoulders, resting my cheek against his collarbone as my eyes followed the light. Drinking in the swell of his biceps, the carved shadows between the muscles of his forearm, and the broad expanse of his palm as he flattened his hand against mine before interlocking our fingers.

I smiled, extinguishing the magic, only to relight it on my other hand. Brushing my lips over his and curving my palm over the roughness of his cheek. Wrapping a stray lock of his black hair around my glowing fingers, painting him in silver light. He didn't like to cede control, I knew that. Yet I could also see the rapid throb of his pulse in his neck, hear the low groan that tore from his lips as I trailed my fingers down his throat to his chest, feel his cock growing harder still where it rubbed between my thighs.

"Why wouldn't you ever let me touch you?" I murmured, leaning back to trace my glowing fingertip over the intricate tattoo of runes on his chest. "Didn't you want me to?"

He made a strangled noise. "Gods, woman. It was for the exact opposite reason to that." His fingers tightened, digging into the curve of my arse. "Touching you had me on the verge of breaking. Having your hands on me would have snapped my control entirely. And . . ." He drew in a breath. "I didn't want to take from you, not knowing if I could return it in equal measure."

So many of those in my life were content to take and take from me, leaving me a barren well. Bjorn alone had taken nothing, asked for nothing, but given me so much. Around him I felt so full, so alive, and I burned with the need to give all of myself to him. To hold nothing back, not my heart, not my soul, and most definitely not my body. I traced the tattooed lines down his stomach to where my pelvis pressed against him. "And now?"

"All of me is yours, Freya." His head was tilted back, eyes closed, the light from my magic casting shadows over the chiseled lines of his face. His beauty was as otherworldly as I'd ever seen it, as though it had been Baldur, the loveliest of all gods, who'd gifted him blood rather than the god of war. "It may not be equal measure to your value, but it's all I have."

"It's all I want." All I could ever dream of.

I caught hold of his face, kissing him fiercely, needing him to feel my words as much as he heard them. Then, loosening my legs' grip around his waist, I reached between us and took hold of him. Bjorn groaned my name as I stroked him root to tip, and heat that had nothing to do with the hot springs surged in my core. The side of my hand brushed my slick sex as I pumped his length, and I leaned back, pressing into it even as I felt my climax rise.

"I want you in me," I breathed, but Bjorn caught hold of my wrists, his voice a growl as he said, "I think first I must prove my worth, love."

In that moment I might have sworn that nothing could stoke my need higher than the way he'd said *love,* but then Bjorn carried me deeper into the cavern, laying me down on a slope of rock worn smooth by water running from another chamber above. It was nearly hot enough to burn, running in rivulets of fire over my throat and breasts, between my legs, but I barely felt it as Bjorn parted my legs wide, exposing me.

A breath, held too long within my lungs, shuddered free as I gazed at him, large and strong as a god between my thighs, waiting for him to push into me. Waiting for him to claim me as his.

Instead he consumed me.

Bowing his broad shoulders, he bent, rough cheek brushing against the inside of my thigh and making me gasp. He only spread me wider, lowering his head, tongue parting my sex. My back bowed, my legs wrapping around his neck and my hands finding the lip of the basin behind me as I held on.

"I've wanted to taste you for so long," he growled, licking me again. A sob tore from my lips, because the gods strike me down, nothing had ever felt this good. "Do you have any idea the madness it drove me to, sliding my fingers into you that night and feeling how *fucking* wet you were but not being able to have you on my tongue?"

As though to remind me of that night, he let go of my right knee and slid a finger into me, curving it to stroke my core. "Show me what you wanted to do to me," I gasped, rocking my hips against his fingers, driving my pleasure higher. "Please."

He said nothing, only closed his mouth over my clit, tongue circling it with small little swipes. I bucked beneath him like some wild thing possessed, crying out his name as he sucked on me, fingers slick with my wetness as his caresses found a rhythm, stroking me harder. Higher.

I was so close. So close that I wanted to scream. Wanted to beg for more. Wanted—

Bjorn slipped a third finger into me, and my body shattered, release washing over me in a fiery flood that made me cry out, the muscles of my legs contracting, binding him to me. The waves kept coming, like a storm unleashed against a shore, leaving me gasping and spent.

This was how it was supposed to feel. What I'd always dreamed it would be like. Not to be used as a means to an end, but to be worshipped as a woman beloved. To *matter to my lover*.

Bjorn unhooked my legs from his neck, moving them around his waist so that the water once again poured over me. "You're so beautiful, Freya," he whispered. "Like a goddess."

I opened my eyes, blinking at the brilliance all around me.

Magic poured from my hands where they gripped the edge of the pool above me. It clung to the water as it swirled down, painting my body with rivulets of silver light, spilling over the curve of my hips to fall into the pool below where it spiraled away on the current.

Bjorn bent over me, kissing my lips with such reverence that my heart broke and re-formed. Gods, but I loved him. Wanted him. Couldn't imagine ever being parted from him, the very thought of it sending a slice of panic through me. I wrapped my arms around his neck, my magic spilling over his skin as I tangled my fingers in his hair, my tongue in his mouth. He tasted of salt, every breath I took filled with the scent of him.

"I want you in me," I whispered, pressing myself against him, a whimper pulling from my lips as his thick tip entered me. "I want all of you."

"Not yet," he murmured, lips tracing fire down my throat even as he slipped a hand between my legs, holding my hips down against the rock, thumb stroking the throbbing knot of my clit. "I want you wet and ready when I take you."

I moaned as he stroked me, his other hand on my breast, teasing my nipple and sending sparks of pleasure through my body. My breath came in rapid pants, my back arching off the rock, and my muscles clenching around his tip, which teased the inside of me with the promise of more. "I'm no maid," I hissed, the need to be filled surpassing my need for breath, wild and desperate. "I'm ready."

"Not ready enough." His teeth caught the curve of my shoulder and marked me, claiming me as I cried out. "I want you hot and wet and so desperate for my cock in you that you beg for it, Freya."

All featherlight touch was gone, his thumb rubbing me hard, throbbing pulses spiking down my legs with each stroke. Another climax was rising, my breath rapid pants, the *need* so intense it bordered on pain. I opened my mouth to scream, *Please.*

But he already knew what I needed. He always did.

Bjorn's arm slid under my back, lifting me off the rock and dragging my hips forward as he thrust into me.

A sob wrenched from my lips as he buried himself deep. So long and thick it seemed impossible I could contain him, but my body took him in like the first breath of air after too long under water.

"Gods, you feel good," he groaned, withdrawing and thrusting into me again, the sensation driving me to the brink. "And you are *mine*."

I was his.

Every part of me for all of eternity. I clung to his neck as he drove into me again and again, with each stroke the base of him rubbing against the spot his thumb had abandoned. My nails clawed his skin, my heels digging into the hard muscle of his arse as I pulled him into me, my climax teetering on the brink.

Bjorn kissed me, our teeth knocking together with the force of it, his tongue chasing over mine as he plunged into me, breath hot and rapid. Then his hands gripped my hips, nearly pulling me off the rock as he drove deep.

Release surged over me like a storm. Like a tempest that would tear the world apart, my body shuddering as it drowned me in pleasure, dragging me back under each time I broke the surface. Never had I felt anything like it, the sensation washing away sight even as it drowned me in color, my ears filling with the sound of my name on Bjorn's lips as he climaxed, spilling into me in a flood hotter than the waters we swam in.

He buried his face in my neck, rocking against me, leaving me boneless and spent. "I love you," I breathed, allowing my magic to dissipate, leaving us wrapped in darkness. "You are all I want."

Bjorn shuddered, fingers tightening around me. "I'll kill anyone who tries to take you from me."

I shouldn't like it, the violence, but it was men wishing violence upon me who would try to tear us apart, so I relished his words. Relaxed into the protective embrace of them as he lifted me down into the water, holding me close in the darkness.

"How long can we stay here?" I asked, beads of condensed water and sweat running down my cheeks as I nuzzled his throat. Part of me hoped he'd say forever because I never wanted to leave. Never wanted to step outside to face the world, despite the knowledge it was a different world we'd walk toward.

"We should leave in the morning." He traced his finger over the curve of my hip. "I want to get you out of Skaland."

"South?" I murmured. "Where it's warm?"

"Not too far south or I'll overheat." He carried me down the length of the pool. "I need to feel the bite of winter for at least part of the year."

I drowsed against him, thinking of summer lands. Imagining building a home. Having a child. Raising animals and tilling the land. My mind stalled on the last as I tried to imagine Bjorn farming, the vision refusing to manifest. Refusing to give me anything other than images of him running into battle, blazing axe in hand.

It's only because you've never seen that side of him, I told myself. *Not that it doesn't exist.*

Bjorn carried me out of the water, a cool night breeze blowing into the chamber and chilling my skin. I shivered as he set me down, the rock cold beneath my bare feet. Still naked, Bjorn left the cave, returning with an armload of branches. Using his usual haphazard method, he dumped the wood on top of his axe and waited for it to light. "Here. It's a bit soggy, but edible," he said, handing me some dried meat that had been in his belt pouch, then retrieved my sword and both our mail shirts, which were probably already setting to rust.

"Throw them away." I rested on my elbow as I watched him work, drinking in the sight of his naked body. "I never want to wear armor again," I added, full well knowing that wearing it had once been my dream.

Bjorn lifted his face, firelight glinting off his eyes. "We aren't out of Skaland yet, love. And no matter where we go, there will be dangers we'll need to protect against. Besides, this mail is worth a small fortune and—" He broke off, giving his head a shake. "You don't have to wear it, Freya. I'll pack it away."

I knew what he'd been about to say. That wealth would no longer be ours for the taking. He was used to being the son of the jarl. To raiding every season to fill his pockets with gold and silver. Neither of which would be possibilities where we planned to go. Which meant that, in many ways, it would be a harder life.

Unease chilled my stomach and I tried to push away the many challenges that would face us in the days to come, the euphoria of finally being together fraying around the edges. I was used to a simple life on the farm, so it would be easy for me to give up the weapons and the fighting, to turn my back on power. Much less easy for him, because he'd been a warrior all his life.

Was that why he didn't want to give up the armor? Because he couldn't imagine life as something other than a warrior? *Ask him,* I told myself. *Better to know now than later.*

My tongue felt numb and my throat tight as I finally managed to say, "What do you think it will be like?"

He lifted his shoulder in a shrug, then moved to hang up the oiled mail away from the steaming pool. "We'll want to keep to the wilds until we're far enough away that no one will recognize us. Even then, we'll want to keep our magic hidden until we're out of Skaland and across the sea. They have different gods and magic than ours, and rumors about strangers travel far."

"I meant," I swallowed hard, "afterward."

He had my sword in hand, warped blade half out of the scabbard, but he paused, then sheathed it. "Wherever we end up, whatever we do, all that matters is that I am by your side, Freya."

I bit the insides of my cheeks because that was no answer to my question, and I instantaneously began to fret that he was withholding his true thoughts because he knew they were different from mine.

The corner of Bjorn's mouth quirked in a half smile, and setting aside my sword, he rose in a smooth motion, circling the fire. Dropping to his knees, he pressed me onto my back, pulling down my damp cloak to expose my breasts. My nipples instantly peaked and it had nothing to do with the cool air and everything to do with the hungry way his eyes roved over my body.

"You want to know how I see our future?" he murmured, stubble rough against my sensitive skin as he kissed his way from my throat to my navel. "I want to see this body beneath me every night and"—he gave me a dark smile, breath teasing my sex—"every morning. I want to see your face when I make you come each and every time."

"Bjorn . . ." I wanted him to be serious, needed him to be, but desire burned hot between my legs as his tongue caressed me, made me forget what I'd asked in the first place.

But rather than bringing me to climax, he moved to lie down at my side, pulling me backward so that he was curled around me. "I see you asleep in my arms in the home I've built for you," he said, breath tickling my ear. "I see you full on game that I've hunted for you, baking bread from grain that I've grown in our fields after you teach me how, because I don't know the first fucking thing about growing plants."

I laughed, but he wasn't finished.

"I see you fat with our child in your belly." He kissed my neck. "See you laughing as you run with her in the snow." His hand curved over my thigh, slipping between my legs. "I see you growing older, silver hair, face marked from smiles rather than worry, more beautiful with every passing day."

I closed my eyes, drunk on his words, on his touch. "What of Valhalla?"

"I shall earn my place killing the little fucks who come chasing after my daughters, who will certainly inherit their mother's beauty." He kissed me. "Though if they inherit her sharp tongue, I won't have to."

"Are you sure?" I breathed the words into his mouth between kisses. "Are you sure you want to give up this life?"

"There is no life without you, Freya. So yes, I'm certain."

I moaned softly as he slipped a finger inside of me, felt his chest heave as he found my wetness, my desire. Thought began to drift as my blood pulsed faster through my veins, his cock hard against my backside as he pleasured me. He'd told me what I needed to know—that he wanted the future I dreamed of for us, and all that was left was for me to trust that he'd never lie to me.

And I did trust him.

More than anyone. Everyone else lied and manipulated and used me to achieve their ends or to protect themselves, leaving me cold and alone, but never Bjorn. He was ever and always the rock at my back. My love. My life.

Twisting in his arms, I straddled him, my knees pressed against the furs as his hands stroked my thighs. Firelight illuminated half his face, the other half shadowed, but all of it so painfully beautiful I thought I might weep. "I love you," I whispered, leaning forward to kiss him. "I trust you."

And I wanted him.

The need to be filled throbbed deep in my sex. I rubbed against him, slickening his length, smiling as he groaned my name.

Lifting my hips, I reached between us to take hold of him, stroking his tip against me as he caught hold of my breast. He rolled my nipple between his thumb and index finger, dragging a gasp from my lips as pleasure spiked through me, but then I took hold of his hand and pulled it back to my hip.

Giving him a dark smile, I eased his tip inside me, a thrill running through my veins as his eyes closed, a growl escaping his parted lips. "Gods, woman," he gasped as I moved up and down, the pleasure on his face doing almost as much to stoke my own desire as the sensation of his cock inside me. "What did I do to deserve this torment?"

"I think you know," I purred, remembering well how he'd teased me with his fingers. How he'd made me beg for release. "Say *please*."

"Please," he groaned. "I need you."

I should've drawn it out. Teased and pleasured him until he broke. But I was through denying myself, so I thrust down, taking him as deep as I could.

A sob ripped from my lips as Bjorn's back arched, his fingers digging into my hips hard enough to bruise as I lifted myself and thrust down again. And again, my release climbed its way to the surface. My fingers locked around his wrists as I rode him, feeling his eyes on my bouncing breasts, my wet braids slapping my back.

Bjorn moved a hand, his thumb brushing the apex of my sex, but I pulled his hand back to my hip, wanting control.

"Freya," he gasped even as he obliged me. "You're going to break me. I can't—"

I gave a dark laugh because he needed to see that I was his match. That we would be all each other ever needed. That there would never be anyone else.

Reaching behind me, I slipped my hands between his thighs to cup him, stroking and pulling, sweat running in beads down my spine. His teeth were clenched, and I knew he was fighting it, that he didn't want to concede.

But I would have my way.

So I thrust harder, riding him, my own release on the brink as my name roared from his lips. "Freya!"

His hips thrust up to meet me and I felt the hot flood inside me as he pulsed, the sensation of it tipping me over the edge. Release hammered into me, and I howled his name, my voice echoing through the cave as I ground against him, taking every drop of pleasure from this moment as could be had before collapsing against him.

Our chests heaved, his heart hammering like a drum against my ear as he pressed a hand to my back to hold me against him.

"Every time I think I have your measure, you surprise me," he murmured. "I hope that never changes."

I smiled, too breathless for words as he eased me onto the ground, curling around me and pulling my cloak over us before pressing a hand to my stomach and murmuring, "Sleep. Dawn will come soon enough."

The embers of the fire glowed brilliant reds and oranges, sizzling each time a drop of moisture fell into them, the crackle and hiss lulling me. Wrapped in the arms of the man I loved, I slipped into sleep.

CHAPTER

34

I woke to dawn light peeking in through the branches Bjorn had used to cover the entrance to the cave, my ears filled with the sounds of trickling water, birdsong, and Bjorn breathing in my ear, still asleep.

A giddy smile grew on my face, the purest form of happiness expanding my chest, and if not for the press of my bladder, I'd have allowed myself to drift back to sleep. Sighing, I gently lifted the heavy arm wrapped around my middle, the fact that he didn't so much as twitch speaking to the depth of his sleep.

Outside, dawn had already come and gone, the sun above the horizon and the summer air warm. Nothing stirred but the faint breeze in the trees, though I heard the chatter of squirrels as they shouted at me for breaking the peace of the morning. Taking care of my needs, I slipped back inside the cave to find Bjorn still sleeping, eyelashes black where they pressed against suntanned skin, his hair a tangled mess.

As was my own.

Frowning at the chaos that was my braids, I stepped into the pool and found a rock to sit on while I unraveled them, careful to set the ribbons on the bank lest they slip downstream and betray that I'd not died in the falls.

No one could ever know we were still alive.

A sharp pain struck me in the chest as I thought of the news that I'd fallen being delivered to my brother and Ingrid. For all their failings, I knew they loved me, so learning that I was with the gods would hurt.

Though possibly for the wrong reasons.

With me dead, Snorri's bitterness might cause him to exclude my brother from his war band. But Geir and Ingrid would be alive, able to go in whatever direction they saw fit.

Yet I couldn't help but wonder if they'd mourn my death. Or resent it.

My chest tightened, and I tried to force the thoughts from my head as I unraveled the last of my braids, my hair floating long and loose in the water. But what Bjorn and I were leaving behind refused to relinquish its hold so easily, and my mind turned to thoughts of my people. How had they fared after the battle? Did they still follow Snorri? Or, after my death, had they all gone their separate directions?

It's not your problem, I told myself sternly. *They don't need you.*

Yet guilt still bit at my core, because I *was* abandoning them for selfish reasons. How would it feel if word traveled across long miles that Harald hadn't abandoned the battle with my death. How would it feel if we learned that Harald now ruled our people? Would I be able to bear it, or would the fact I'd left them to that fate burrow its way into our happiness, growing like a cancer until guilt consumed me?

"They don't deserve you."

I twitched as Bjorn's voice filled my ears, ripples brushing against my skin as he waded down into the water and pulled me against him. "What do you mean?"

"I know the look you get when you're feeling guilty," he said, kissing my throat. "I also know that everyone you feel guilty about leaving behind used you like a thrall, caring nothing for your happiness. If your absence causes hardship, it is their own fault for not treating you as you deserved."

"They're your people, too," I said, for while I agreed with his words, it was not as simple as that. "They relied on you to protect them and now you're gone. Doesn't that bother you?"

"They lived happily without me for many years." He kissed my lips. "They'll do so again, for they will no longer be a threat to Nordeland."

Not for the first time, I sensed that Bjorn didn't consider himself Skalander at all, the time he'd spent in Nordeland refusing to let him go. But my growing sense that he was glad Skaland was no longer a threat to Nordeland was new.

The thought troubled me, and I pulled myself from his grip. "We should go soon."

I felt his frown as I stepped out of the pool, but neither of us spoke as I pulled on my clothes, which smelled strongly of smoke from drying near the fire. I was painfully aware of Bjorn's eyes on me with every motion I made.

Did he care? Did it matter to him what happened to those we left behind? I knew that his relationship with Snorri was strained, made worse by Ylva, but what of his brother? His friends?

What friends?

I bit my lip, thinking back through our time together, remembering his interactions with the other warriors. With the other people in Halsar. Cursory, at best. Like either they or he kept one another at a distance.

Liv, he was friends with Liv. There'd been grief on his face when the healer died, far more than a stranger warranted. The reminder eased the tension in my chest, though in truth I didn't entirely understand why these thoughts were eating me up. "Will you miss your brother?"

Bjorn paused in pulling on his trousers, then tugged them the rest of the way over his arse. "Of course I will. But with me gone, Leif will become Snorri's heir. He'll be jarl one day, and in truth, the people will be better for it."

"Why do you think that?"

Bjorn's eyes narrowed and he was silent for a long moment before saying, "Because he's one of them in a way I never will be."

My stomach roiled with unease, but I kept silent.

Exhaling a long breath, Bjorn sat on the floor. "I spent too many years in Nordeland, and that left a mark. In the way I do things. In the way I speak. In the way I think. Whereas Leif is Skalander through and through, and that makes the people like him better. Ylva was right to want him to lead the clan."

I needed to know. "Are you a Skalander?"

He tensed slightly, then shook his head. "Soon neither of us will be, Freya, so I fail to see why this matters."

"Because you don't seem to care, and I want to understand why that is." Accusations were going to spill forth, my temper hot, though it shouldn't be.

Why was I so agitated? So angry?

"It's complicated!" Bjorn rose to his feet. "My past is complicated, Freya. Nothing is simple, but what *I* don't understand is why you feel you must dig into it now."

"Because I want to know the truth about the man I'm abandoning everything for," I exploded. "Especially given that you've all but admitted there are important things you haven't told me about yourself."

"Freya." He reached for me, but I took a step back. "I love you. All I want is to be with you somewhere you are safe. To build a life together *away* from my past."

Dread pooled in my chest, because if it was nothing, he wouldn't be this cagey. He'd tell me if for no other reason than to calm me down. "I want those things, too." My voice was breathy and strange, my head pulsing with tension. "But . . . but I can't go until I know everything. If you won't give me the truth, then I'm going back."

All the color drained from his face. "You can't go back."

"Yes, I can." I felt like I couldn't breathe, because how had everything devolved so quickly? How had I gone from absolute certainty in him to . . . to this? "I can tell them I escaped the falls. No one ever has to know."

"You don't understand. If you go, he'll—" He reached for my arm but I leapt backward, nearly sprawling as my feet caught on a rock.

"He'll what?" I demanded. "What will Snorri do?"

"It's complicated." There was sweat beading on his brow. "Freya, I'll explain everything, I swear it. But we need to leave. We need to run."

"I'm not going anywhere." Twisting on my heel, I strode out of the cave, my eyes burning. But I made it only a few steps before sliding to a stop, terror filling my chest as I found myself face-to-face with King Harald of Nordeland.

"Good morning, Freya." Harald smiled, tucking a lock of golden-brown hair behind his ear. "It fills my heart with joy to see you hale and healthy after such a terrifying plunge. I confess, we feared the worst when Tora knocked you into the river. But I should've known better than to doubt Bjorn."

To doubt Bjorn.

His words sank into my heart, freezing me in place even as I heard Bjorn step out of the cave behind me. Felt him take in the sight of Harald with his warriors standing casually behind him, Bjorn's voice tense as he asked, "Why are you here?"

A question I was deeply afraid he already knew the answer to.

"We feared you might have been injured, so rather than allowing you to bring her to us, we came in search." Harald took a step closer. "While I understand your actions, they were too risky by far. You might have both been killed."

A dull drone of noise filled my head and nausea twisted in my stomach, thoughts rising and falling away like twisting snakes. But all of them whispered words of betrayal.

"How did you find us?" Bjorn demanded, and I wanted to scream at him to stop it. To quit pretending, because every word twisted the knife in my heart deeper.

"Your mother's cabin was the logical choice." Harald frowned, his gray eyes shifting between the two of us. "You keep changing the plans we agreed to, Bjorn. Plans we've worked on together for most of your life. After Fjalltindr, I was convinced by your belief that it was better to take Freya from Snorri, and even your desire to convince her to choose the path herself, but"—he gave a slight shake of his head—"judging from Freya's shock, it seems she knows nothing of your plans. What's going on, Bjorn?"

My knees shook as I turned to face Bjorn, my chest hollow, my heart numb. "I would ask you the same question."

"It's complicated."

"There is nothing complicated about it!" I hissed. "Either he's lying or you are. Answer me now!"

"I wanted to tell you—"

"Answer the fucking question," I shrieked. "Or if it's *too complicated,* answer me this: Are you a Skalander or a Nordelander?"

Everyone was silent, the only sound the wind blowing through the trees.

"Nordelander."

I'd known it was coming, but still I flinched because the admission made it true. "You're the traitor. Time and again, you watched me accuse Ylva, knowing full well she was innocent. That it was you! It wasn't Ylva speaking to Harald that night in Fjalltindr, it was *you.*" I pressed my hands to my temples because that meant all that had happened that night between Bjorn and me had been . . . manipulation?

"I didn't speak to him that night. I spoke to—"

"If it makes the deception any easier to stomach, Freya," Harald interrupted, "it was because of Bjorn that plans to kill you for the sake of protecting Nordeland changed. You're alive because Bjorn believed your fate could be something different from a woman leaving bodies in her wake. Though after yesterday's battle . . ."

"Shut up!" I screamed, because it was Bjorn who needed to explain himself. Bjorn who needed to justify all his *lies.*

"I wanted to tell you the truth." Bjorn moved to stand between me and Harald, and Skade stepped out from the group of warriors to eye him warily, bow in hand. "But I couldn't risk you reacting poorly—not when the fate of Nordeland hung in the balance. I needed to get you away so that you'd have time to understand."

"Bullshit." I moved back, needing space from him. My skin crawled, and a glance over my shoulder revealed Tora standing behind me, burns livid up close. It wasn't just Harald with whom Bjorn was allied, it was Bodil's murderer. And my mother's murderer. "You knew I'd never accept your lies, and you wanted to ensure I couldn't get back once you confessed you were delivering me to my enemy."

"If all I cared about was taking you, I would have done so a long time ago." Flickers of flame appeared and disappeared in Bjorn's hand, betraying his agitation. Then he twisted toward Harald, "Father, I need to speak to Freya alone and—"

"He is *not* your father, Snorri is!" The words exploded from my lips, my hands fisting as fury rose to fill the void in my chest, tears spilling down my cheeks.

"That piece of shit is not my father!" Bjorn snarled, his axe flaring, only to disappear again. "I hate him!"

"You hate Snorri?" I stared at him, not understanding how this could be happening. How he could be saying these things. "Harald kept you a prisoner. A thrall to his whim until Snorri rescued you. What madness is this that you name him Father? He murdered your mother!"

Harald held up placating hands. "I'm afraid there is a great deal you don't know, Freya. And what you do know is mostly Snorri's lies."

"Do not speak!" I screamed, birds bursting from the branches of nearby trees. "Bjorn must answer for himself!"

"Freya, please listen." Bjorn scrubbed his hands over his head. "I had to be certain I could trust you before revealing the truth."

"Trust me?" It felt like my blood was boiling, my vision filling with red, all the world falling away except for the two of us and my rage. "I have *never* lied to you. But it appears that every fucking thing you've said to me has been a deception."

"No." He closed the distance between us. "I love you, Freya. Everything I told you last night was true. I wasn't going to bring you to Nordeland."

Harald huffed out a breath, shaking his head. "Does your word mean nothing, Bjorn? You swore an oath to me to protect Nordeland, but more than that, you swore an oath to your mother that you'd deliver vengeance. Yet it seems your word means nothing in the face of your *lust* for this woman."

I flinched, struck with visions of what had happened between us last night. How I'd given myself to him so utterly and completely while every word he'd whispered was a lie. *Oh gods.*

"I have fulfilled my oaths!" Bjorn shouted. "I swore to destroy him. Swore to bring him low. Swore to rip the crown from his grasp by taking the shield maiden, all of which is done. And she didn't need to come to Nordeland to keep it safe, she just needed to be away from *him.*"

Again, I was rendered nameless. Just a tool, just a weapon to be wielded by all the men around me. But I'd had enough.

"Freya—" Bjorn reached for me.

"Don't you touch me!" I skittered backward, nearly colliding with Tora.

Harald raked his hands back through his hair. "Is this betrayal motivated by the belief that I'd have separated you from her? Gods, Bjorn, when have I ever denied you anything? If you'd only told me that you cared for Freya, I'd have let you keep her. She'd have been queen of Nordeland at your side when you inherited one day."

Keep me? I stiffened, though neither of them seemed to notice.

"On what conditions, Father?" Bjorn retorted. "I know you. There is no chance you'd have been able to resist using her to further your ambitions. All I desire is to take her away to a place where she can make her own fate."

"I would not have *used* her." Harald gave Bjorn a look of disgust. "What you fail to see, my son, is that if you'd given Freya the truth, she might have chosen to serve Nordeland. If she is half the woman you claim, then she'd have surely joined our cause, if only given the opportunity. But instead you denied her the chance to do great things so as not to risk your ability to use her to satisfy your own ends."

Use her, use her, use her.

The words repeated in my skull, growing louder with each saying until it felt like a giant screamed inside my head. Everyone had used me. Everyone—but Bjorn had been different. Had been the one who'd put me first. The one who'd cared.

Except it turned out that he'd used me worst of all.

"I curse you!" I screamed, and it felt like the world trembled, tilting beneath my feet. "I curse all of you never to see Valhalla. I curse all of you to Helheim. May Hel take all of you into her keeping!"

Then the ground surely did tremble, rumbling and bouncing, everyone struggling to keep their balance.

"Freya!" Bjorn stumbled toward me, but before he made it two steps, great blackened roots exploded from the earth, wrapping around his legs.

And not just him.

All around me, roots exploded from the earth to grasp the legs and arms of Harald's warriors, men and women screaming as they hacked at them with axe and sword, but the weapons just passed through the roots as if they weren't there.

Bjorn's axe appeared in his hand, and he too slashed at the roots, flames severing them, but more burst from the ground, trying to drag him down.

Panic overwhelmed my rage, and I lost my footing as a concussive blast of thunder sent me staggering. Tora's lightning exploded the roots attacking her, only for more to appear. Skade was screaming and shooting her magical arrows into root after root.

The other Nordelanders had no such defenses.

On my knees, I watched in horror as the black roots wrapped around the other warriors, digging into their flesh, the screams unlike anything I'd ever heard as they were dragged to the ground.

Then, as one, the roots vanished into the earth.

Leaving only silence.

On my knees, I stared in horror at the dozens of bodies lying on the ground, chests still and eyes glazed. Dead.

"Freya?"

I swallowed my bile, eyes going to Bjorn, who still stood alive, as did Harald, Tora, and Skade.

No one moved.

Harald stepped down from the rock on which he perched, moving toward me. "That was what they meant by 'child of two bloods.' Not god and mortal, but of two gods." He drew in a ragged breath, gray eyes filled with delight. "She's Hel's daughter. The first of her kind."

I wasn't. I couldn't be. "No."

"Yes." Harald grinned. "You cursed all before you to your mother's domain and she took them. All dead. All denied Valhalla because of your power."

A whimper exited my lips and I crawled backward from him, my eyes skipping from corpse to corpse. All dead. All cursed. By my temper.

By me.

"That is why you are so special, Freya," he said. "That is why even the gods themselves recognized your power. The power to unite Skaland, yes. But also the power to destroy all who stand against you."

I gagged, recoiling from his fervor, climbing to my feet.

"No!" Bjorn stepped between us, axe blazing bright. "She's not a weapon."

"Her fate is inked in her blood," Harald said, giving a wry shake of his head. "It's carved in her bones. This power is Freya's destiny."

"Freya, run!" Bjorn lifted his weapon. "Run!"

I twisted on my heels, sprinting into the forest, branches lashing at my face, roots tripping my feet.

Hel's daughter.

I clenched my fists, pushing myself for more speed as though I might outrun the truth of what I was.

But it was the one thing I could never escape.

My foot caught on a rock and I went sprawling, rolling and tumbling down a slope to stop with a sickening crunch against a boulder.

"Get up," I hissed, pushing myself onto hands and knees, but my arm buckled, a sob ripping from my lips. "Keep going."

"Easy, Freya."

A familiar voice filled my ears and I lifted my face to find Steinunn bending next to me. "I need help," I gasped. "Bjorn . . . he's allied with Harald. They're here."

Steinunn smiled. "I know, Freya," she said, her voice no longer that of a Skalander but bearing a Nordelander's accent. "I know everything." Then she lifted a bowl and blew the smoke rising from it into my face.

Panic hit me as I understood, but I was already spinning down and down. As I hit the ground, my eyes fixed on the red leather laces on her shoes.

Then all that remained was darkness.

CHAPTER

36

y bed was moving beneath me, rising and falling as though I'd had too much to drink, the sensation sending a wave of nausea through me. "Bjorn," I mumbled, trying to reach out to him.

Except I couldn't move my arms, rough rope binding my wrists together.

My eyes snapped open and daylight stabbed into them like daggers. At first, all I could see was white, but as I wildly blinked, my vision cleared to reveal the hull of a drakkar, booted legs all around me. Memory flooded my mind, of Harald and his men arriving at the cavern. Of the truth of Bjorn's allegiances being revealed. Of corpses on the ground all around me, dead by my curse.

Of Steinunn, blowing smoke into my face as she revealed her true allegiance.

"Good to see you're finally awake, Freya." Harald's voice filled my ears, and I rolled over, looking up to meet his pale gray gaze. "Where am I?"

"On a drakkar," he answered with a faint smile, mocking me with the obvious. Then he lifted one shoulder. "We are in the strait on our way back to Nordeland."

"Let me go," I snarled, struggling to sit up. But my head still spun from the motion of the drakkar and the effects of whatever Steinunn had drugged me with. The skald herself sat at the far end of the boat, cloak wrapped tightly around her, eyes fixed on the sea.

"I think we both know that freeing you is not possible," Harald answered. "You'd only allow your anger at Bjorn to send you running back to Snorri armed with your newly discovered magic, and he, in turn, would use you against me, whether you willed it or no. He's already proven exceptionally capable of forcing your hand."

"I don't need Snorri to curse you," I hissed. "I need only my own tongue."

Harald eyed me for a long moment, expression considered rather than alarmed. "True," he finally said. "Except I don't think that you will. I saw the look on your face when you murdered my warriors. When you cursed their souls to Helheim when their rightful end is in Valhalla. You might well put a knife between my ribs, but cursing me means embracing a side of yourself that I think . . . *terrifies* you. As it is, I'd ask you to remember that I'm the only one who has never lied to you."

My skin crawled as if a thousand spiders danced across my flesh, his words breathing new life into the horror I'd felt over what I'd done. Not the killing, although that was bad enough, but cursing souls for eternity. Men and women who'd raised no arms against me—had only been following the orders of their king. Worst of all, it hadn't even been them to whom my fury had been directed.

It was Bjorn.

My heart stuttered at the thought of him, and I managed to right myself, eyes skipping over the figures in the drakkar until they landed on his familiar form. He sat on one of the benches, elbows resting on his knees, shoulders slumped.

"Traitor," I screamed, lunging. "I'm going to fucking cut out your heart!"

That my wrists were bound made no difference to me as I tried to crawl over benches to reach him. All that mattered was making him feel the same hurt as I felt. Making him understand the pain of his betrayal.

But then my body was jerked back, my chin slamming against a bench.

Spitting blood, I twisted to find Tora behind me, fingers locked on my belt. "Silence your tongue, Hel's daughter, or I shall cut it out of your mouth."

"Back off, Tora!" Bjorn snarled, reaching for me, only to draw up short as Skade leveled an arrow at his face.

My eyes skipped around the drakkar, which contained no warriors who were not children of the gods. The only others present were thralls working the oars.

In an instant, I understood why: Hel's curse wouldn't work on those with magic. The roots had attacked Tora, Skade, and Bjorn, but they'd been able to repel them with magic.

But why was Harald alive?

Digging deep into my memory, I replayed the moment, feeling the thrum of power in me again as I watched the roots explode from the ground. Yet none had gone near the king of Nordeland.

Why that was, I couldn't begin to explain.

"Calm yourself, Bjorn," Harald said, making pacifying gestures. "I swore to you that Freya would not be harmed. When have I ever gone back on my word to you?"

Some of the tension in Bjorn's face eased, and I wanted to spit with fury, hating the relationship between them.

"That it's happening this way is because of your choices," Harald said. "She's angry at *you,* which makes her a threat to Nordeland, but rather than killing her as others have suggested, I intend to give her a chance to see reason."

"You mean, you wish to have time to convince her to fight for you."

"Of course I wish this." Harald shrugged. "Freya is tremendously powerful and could defend my people in a way no other living being is capable of. But I will not *make* her do anything she does not wish to do." His eyes flicked to me. "On my honor, I swear it is so. In Norde-land, you will be your own woman, Freya."

"As Bjorn was his own man?" My voice was flat. "I'll be your pris-oner, Harald, and I'm not a child to have my mind twisted until I name you Father."

His eyes darkened, the first real display of emotion I'd seen from him, but it was gone in an instant. "Bjorn has *never* been a prisoner a day in his life. Ask him yourself."

There was a part of me that wanted to ask. That wanted to give Bjorn the chance to tell me his truth. Yet every instinct within me screamed warning. This man had murdered Saga, stolen Bjorn away, and while he clearly hadn't been treated as a prisoner or thrall during this time, what manner of poison had been poured into his ears that would cause him to believe Harald was anything other than his enemy?

Lies upon lies upon lies was what my gut told me, and what's more, it whispered that all Harald's platitudes about me being safe were more lies still. I'd seen the delight in his eyes when Hel's magic revealed itself. He intended to use me, I knew it. Use me to increase his power, to expand his dominion, and innocent Skalanders would die beneath Nordelander blades.

I wouldn't let that happen.

I would do whatever it took to keep them all safe.

Taking a deep breath, I lunged to my feet, seeing the shore in the distance as I leapt. *I could make it.*

Cold seawater closed over my head, fear filling my heart even as I kicked my legs, driving as far away from the drakkar as I could before surfacing. Gasping for breath, I tipped my head to check for the shore, then flipped on my back, propelling myself in that direction.

My torso sank, a wave rolling over my face, forcing me to tread water upright. Fear filled my chest, but the drakkar was dropping sail and running out the oars. If I didn't get back to shore, they'd catch me.

Sucking in a breath, I flipped onto my back again, ignoring how the water washed over my face as I kicked toward the beach.

Faster.

My legs churned, but it wasn't long until I needed to take a breath.

I treaded water, sucking in breath after breath as I tried to work my wrists free of their bindings. My legs were already exhausted, for whatever Steinunn had drugged me with still sapped my strength.

Maybe it's for the best, my conscience whispered to me as I slipped under the water. *Maybe it's better that no one with your powers walks the earth.*

But I didn't want to die. I wanted to live.

I broke the surface and sucked in a breath, then slipped under again. *Kick,* I screamed at myself. *Kick harder.*

Another breath, the waves seeming to sense my need, pulling me toward shore.

I would make it. I was going to make it.

Then hands closed around my waist, hauling me upward.

"Is getting away from me worth getting yourself killed?" Bjorn shouted, his hair plastered against the side of his cheek. "Is getting away from me worth crawling back to Snorri so he can use you to achieve his ends?"

"Yes," I gasped, kicking at him, then trying to wedge my knees between us to force him away, but he only spun me in the water so that my back was to him. "You're a fucking liar!"

"I'm sorry!" He struggled to keep us both afloat because I'd stopped kicking, intent on dragging us both under to drown if that's what it took. "But you of all people should understand going to any length to protect family!"

"Snorri is your family," I screamed, choking as a wave splashed me. "Leif is your family! Skaland is family! I don't care what poison Harald whispered in your ears, he stole you from them!"

"No!" His grip tightened. "He saved me from them!"

"It's all lies." My eyes burned, because the drakkar was close. I'd lost my chance to escape. "He murdered your mother!"

"He didn't!" Bjorn turned me to face him, eyes bright. "It was

Snorri who tried to kill my mother. Who tried to kill both of us, because Ylva convinced him it was necessary so that Leif might inherit. But my mother escaped the fire and fled with me to Nordeland, where Harald protected us. Freya, my mother is alive!"

Shock rippled through me. "But the specter. Saga is the specter."

"More of Snorri's manipulation. It was my mother I spoke to in Fjalltindr, my mother whom I convinced that you could change your fate, and who subsequently convinced Harald of the same. She's alive and well back in Nordeland." He pulled me closer, the heat of him seeping into my body despite the chill of the sea. "Let me take you to her, Freya. Listen to what she has to say before you cast judgment. She will have the answers you seek."

I didn't want to go. Didn't want to hear an explanation. Wanted to hold on to my anger and rage at what he'd done.

"Please." He said the word between his teeth, jaw clenched. "I know I have no right to ask it from you, but please do this last thing for me. I need you to understand."

"I'll never understand," I spat.

Yet neither did I struggle when hands reached down and dragged me into the ship, saying not a word as the sails were lifted, Skaland slowly disappearing in our wake. I only stared forward as the coast of Nordeland appeared, rocky and harsh and gray.

A place where I'd find answers, yes.

But also where I'd begin to control my own fate.

ACKNOWLEDGMENTS

Like so many of my novels, *A Fate Inked in Blood* lived in my head for *years* before I opened my laptop to begin writing, so my fierce shield maiden already feels like an old friend. I experienced a great deal of catharsis writing Freya's story for many reasons, but not the least is that I was again writing for myself, with no deadlines or expectations to hamper my creative process. It was an incredibly enjoyable novel to write, and my enthusiasm only grew when it found its home with Del Rey.

As always, I'm indebted to my family for their endless support of my writing career, despite the demands it puts on everyone. I would not be able to create without the love you give me, and I am so grateful to have all of you in my life.

So many thanks to my incredible agent, Tamar Rydzinski, who championed this novel from the first read and found it a worthy home! Thank you for everything you do! To the team at Context Literary Agency, as well as my foreign agencies, thank you for all the work you do behind the scenes getting my novels into readers' hands around the world.

Team Del Rey and Del Rey UK, I will forever be grateful for the passion and enthusiasm you have for Freya and Bjorn, but a special thanks to my editor, Sarah Peed, who stayed up all night reading the manuscript and called the next morning with the best words an author on submission can hear. Working with you has been a delight every step of the way, and I'm looking forward to round two!

So many thanks to my amazing friend and assistant, Amy, who was the captain of #teamfreyorn from day one. My readers owe you a debt of gratitude for Bjorn's BVD energy, because you encouraged me to level him up every step of the way. Freya thanks you, and so do I!

Elise Kova, you are both a friend and an inspiration, and my days would be darker without your messages and support. Melissa Frain, you are a gift from the gods—thank you so much for your help with early drafts! To the ladies of NOFFA, I feel fortunate to know all of you, and our conversations take so much of the stress out of this crazy job we all do.

As always, my biggest thanks go to my readers, especially those who have been with me for over a decade. It is because of you that I've been given so many incredible opportunities, and I hope you are as delighted in the reading of *A Fate Inked in Blood* as I was in the writing.

ABOUT THE AUTHOR

DANIELLE L. JENSEN is the *USA Today* bestselling author of the Bridge Kingdom, Dark Shores, and Malediction series, as well as the Saga of the Unfated. Her novels are published internationally in fifteen languages. She lives in Calgary, Alberta, with her family and guinea pigs.

ABOUT THE TYPE

This book was set in Bembo, a typeface based on an old-style Roman face that was used for Cardinal Pietro Bembo's tract *De Aetna* in 1495. Bembo was cut by Francesco Griffo (1450–1518) in the early sixteenth century for Italian Renaissance printer and publisher Aldus Manutius (1449–1515). The Lanston Monotype Company of Philadelphia brought the well-proportioned letterforms of Bembo to the United States in the 1930s.

/